Lizzie Jordan's Secret Life

'A tremendous, high-spirited farce ... Anyone who's filled in the dreaded UCCA, bought the striped scarf and endured Freshers' Week will need their ribs strapped to relieve the pain from giggling ... Very funny, hugely feel-good, and the perfect antidote for anyone who worries that the only career ladder they've achieved is a run in their tights' Fiona Walker

Chris Manby is also the author of **Deep Heat**:

'A shagadelic giggle with a good twist in its tale' *Ms London*

'Cross your legs, boys: in the best tradition of Kathy Lette, this is girl power at its most painfully funny' Helen Lederer

and **Flatmates**:

'If you've ever shared a flat, been to a bad party or fallen in love with the wrong man, you'll find this book spot on' *Company*

'A funny first novel ... that's more realistic than *Friends*, cleaner than *The Young Ones* and not as frightening as *Shallow Grave*' *Daily Mail*

Also by Chris Manby

Deep Heat
Second Prize
Flatmates

About the author

Now in her late twenties, Chris Manby grew up in Gloucester and published her first short story in *Just Seventeen* at the age of fourteen. She now lives in London and writes full-time.

Lizzie Jordan's Secret Life

Chris Manby

CORONET BOOKS
Hodder & Stoughton

First published in Great Britain in 2000 by Hodder and Stoughton
First published in paperback in 2000 by Hodder and Stoughton
A division of Hodder Headline
A Coronet Paperback

10 9 8 7 6 5 4 3 2 1

Manby, Chris
     Lizzie Jordan's secret life
     I. Title
     823.9 ' 14[F]

ISBN 0 340 76918 1

Typeset by Palimpsest Book Production Limited,
Polmont, Stirlingshire
Printed and bound in Great Britain by
Omnia Books Limited, Glasgow

Hodder and Stoughton
A division of Hodder Headline
338 Euston Road
London NW1 3BH

Author's Note

16 December 1999

Dear reader,

Please excuse me while I do a quick Gwyneth Paltrow
. . . This book is dedicated to the people who supported
me in so many different ways during my very own *annus
horribilis*. Sometimes I feel quite giddy when I think about
how lucky I am to have such a special and steadfast circle
of family and friends. Here goes . . .

To Mum, Dad, Kate and Lee with thanks for their constant
love and support. To Ryan 'cake for questions' Law. To
Jane and Ian Wright for putting up with the world's worst
bridesmaid. To Jane Brown for pretending we had a great
time in Ibiza. To Peter Hamilton and Kate Fell (you know
you've got room for a marquee, so use it!). To Mark
Love and Jacqui Saunders for the 'love cupboard' and
their love. To Geraldine and Dylan Gray for making my
birthday so special. To Mike Elms and Trudy Kelleher
for letting me live with them. To Alex Lay for listening.
To Vicki Fisher and Pam Rutherford for the girls–only
moans. To Jools Simner (that draw was rigged!). To Tom
Callaghan (if I was ten years older . . .). To Malcolm
Alsop, Philip Allard and Lisa Webb for putting up with

my erratic appearances and typing. To Jessica Adams for the hopeful horoscopes (draw more boxer shorts!). To Fiona Walker, Brit-Lit Queen for Groucho gossip and being such a professional in Glasgow!!! To Helen Lederer for restoring my faith in the possibility of true love. To Julie Wright and Jon Stroud for having faith in *Deep Heat*. To Nick Rhodes for the best advice. To Steve Barnham for having the misfortune to be in when Nick wasn't!!! To Bill Sillery for making me feel fanciable at 8.30a.m. on the Fulham Road. To Dr Anna Trigell for being perpetually sunny. To Sian Kelley for giving me the opportunity to have a near-death experience in front of sixty fourteen-year-old boys. To Mike Gayle and Zelda West Meads for the Borders gigs. To Rachel Huggard, ditto plus the dissections!!! To Elaine Noone and Claire Edgar. To Graham Joyce. To Solomon for being wise! To Nick Davies for the vitriol! To Roz Chissick for her endless patience. To Ant and the team at Gillon Aitken Associates for showing me the money. To David Garnett for keeping me on my toes. To Ian Percival for being the best best man. To Nikki Jones. To Nick 'Bombshell' Cornwell and Toby Stone. To Jo Medcroft and Helena Roberts.

To the Americans! To Chris Hobbs and Marty 'Bea-vil' Beal. And to Jenn Matherly, a truly special friend. To the real Brian – Brian Rabin – though of course this book isn't about you . . . And to Collin Madden – my all-time favourite Yank. It isn't about you either, my dear!!!!

Finally, I owe a huge debt of gratitude to everyone at Hodder and Stoughton for their tremendous efforts on my behalf. Especially to Kate Lyall Grant, an editor of great vision (obviously) and a valued friend, who not only corrects my punctuation but has also variously found me a place to live, a clutch of great party invitations and even the occasional hot date. For author care beyond the call of duty (rivalled only by Jon 'discreet' Wood's attention to my coat on *that night*), this book is dedicated in particular to her.

Couldn't have done it without you . . .

Love,
Chris Manby

CHAPTER ONE

Brian.

Hardly the kind of name you'd give a romantic hero, is it? But he was mine.

Brian Coren.

Quite tall. Quite dark. Quite handsome. Brad Pitt had nothing to worry about. But somehow Brian Coren stole my heart.

I met him during my second year at university. I was reading English Literature at Oxford. I wasn't sure how I'd managed to get on to the course in the first place but it might have been because the college I was accepted by – St Judith's – had a quota of poor people to fill. For pretty much the whole of my first term, I was totally overwhelmed by it all. The hard work. The tradition. All that cutlery.

Meanwhile, Brian Coren had been studying economics at some small but exclusive college in a pretty part of New York State. In his senior year, he was sent over to the UK on an exchange programme to increase his understanding of the London Stock Exchange amongst other things. His mother at least hoped that a year at Oxford might give him a certain *'je ne sais* what' that would set him apart from his less well-travelled peers when he returned.

I can still remember the very first time I saw him as clearly as if it were only an hour ago. It was the beginning of the autumn term, still just about sunny and warm enough to sit on the Mediterranean-style mezzanine outside the experimental psychology block for a quick fag between tutorials. I was sitting on a step with my best friends at the time: Bicycle Bill, who was always on his bicycle, and Miserable Mary, a gothic psychology student who was always looking miserable, in case you hadn't guessed.

We were comparing boring summer vacations. Mine in a lens-grinding factory that reminded me of the outer circles of hell. Bill's on a fruit farm somewhere in the West Country and Mary's on the cheese counter at some West London deli. None of us could ever afford to go travelling in the breaks. Well, we probably could have done if we'd really wanted to. But I didn't fancy doing the backpack and diarrhoea thing, so I pretended that travelling was for the idle rich and that I was underprivileged rather than plain chicken.

'Shame God didn't invent the volume control before he invented Americans,' Miserable Mary said suddenly, jerking her head in the direction of two guys and a girl who looked unusually smart for students. The trio were veritably *bouncing* towards the psychology block (which was the only department that served pecan pie for elevenses) in their shiny new leather shoes. *Polished* leather shoes. The girl tossed her glossy brown hair as if she were auditioning for a shampoo ad and the guys punched each other jovially in a jock mock fight. Even without hearing their voices, it was clear that they weren't locals. They stood out like three gaudy tropical parrots in the midst of the flock of hungover pigeons that were the British students in their uniformly 'alternative' grey and black rags.

'Jesus, it's the Brady Bunch,' hissed Mary, as the Americans briefly broke into song.

'More like the Osmonds, I say,' said Bill, adjusting his crotch. Bill was a geography student with a fine line in cycling shorts with reinforced gussets. 'I've got one of them in the room next door to me in halls this year. Americans – I swear they don't even know how to breathe quietly,' he sighed. Just loud enough so that the Brady Bunch who had now drawn up beside us went suddenly silent and stared.

Mary, Bill and I studied the grimy paving stones until we thought they might have passed us. But I looked up first and that is when he caught my eye. Brian Coren caught my eye and smiled right at me for the very first time.

'Hi,' he said.

'Bloody Americans,' muttered Bill, totally missing the greeting.

'Yeah,' said Mary. 'So full of themselves. Get back to Disneyland.'

'Nice to meet you too,' said Brian.

You can imagine how embarrassed I was when I next saw the Americans. It was later on in the same day, in fact, and I was sitting on another step. This time I was outside the college dining hall, waiting for Mary and Bill to return from their lectures.

I rarely bothered with going to my own lectures unless I was in love with the lecturer. In such circumstances I would suddenly be fired with enthusiasm for my subject, which was great until I started to think that the lecturer in question might have noticed my crush and then I wouldn't be able to go to his lectures any more because I was too embarrassed. It was a really vicious circle and as a result, in my first year, I had only been to half my Middle English lectures (Dr Law looked a bit like Indiana Jones, I thought), three lectures on Hardy (Dr Sillery could have been Rupert Everett's twin) and a single symposium on Sylvia Plath (Dr Trigell looked like Gerard Depardieu. That crush didn't last long).

Anyway, college dinner was at seven sharp, but the queue outside the dining block usually began to gather from half-past six onwards. It wasn't that the canteen food was so fantastic, you understand. It was simply that if you got to the dining hall the minute the vile stuff was served, you had a much better chance of getting your hands on a packet of cream crackers and a Dairylea triangle instead of a dubious gelatinous pudding. The crackers were hermetically sealed in clear plastic wrappers and hence the theory was that the college chef couldn't possibly have rendered them inedible with his idiosyncratic gastronomic touch. Five days out of six, however, I seemed to get a packet of crackers that had gone very stale.

'Is this the right place for dinner?' Brian asked. In a whisper, I noticed right away.

'Sorry?' I muttered.

'I said,' he said, even more quietly than before, and having to lean up close to my ear to say it, 'is this the right place for dinner?'

'Yes,' I said, as confidently as I could. He was obviously taking the piss about the volume control crack that Mary had made earlier, so I spoke up extra clearly and slowly – as if I were speaking to somebody French. 'You have to queue up here,' I told him. 'It's an English thing,' I added with a smirk. 'A queue.'

'A queue? Really? So many things to learn,' sighed Brian, taking up a position on the steps beside me while his happy shiny friends perused the club notice boards and signed up for all those things that English students rarely bother with, such as counselling rotas and netball.

Ignoring my new companion, I tried to read the book I hadn't opened since I'd picked it up in Blackwells, Oxford's cavernous book superstore. I could spend days in Blackwells – reading the self-help manuals mostly – but this book was *Far From the Madding Crowd*. One of that term's set texts in fact. I hated it when we had to do actual novels instead of plays and poems. So much more to read. Too much like hard work, which rather defeated the point of having chosen English as a degree in the first place.

'You're reading Thomas Hardy,' Brian observed observantly.

'Yes. Well, I would be if I could concentrate,' I said testily, starting the first sentence of the preface again.

'He's one of my favourite authors actually,' Brian persisted. 'Have you read *Tess*?'

'I've seen the film,' I told him.

'Pretty good adaptation of the book, don't you think?'

I really had no idea. I hadn't actually *read the book* back then. Didn't even know it wasn't just called *Tess* at the time. But I nodded anyway.

'I like the girl in it,' said Brian. 'My name's Brian Coren, by the way.'

'Bw-yan,' I said automatically. I couldn't help myself doing a quick impression of Michael Palin's Roman emperor. We had watched Monty Python's *Life of Brian* at least twice a week in the first year (the Junior Common Room video cupboard had only two films – the other one was *Die Hard*). I clapped my hand to my mouth when I realised what I was saying.

Brian laughed in a pained sort of way. 'Monty Py-thon, right? That film has been the bane of my life. *My life of Bw-yan*,' he added lamely.

'I'm sorry,' I snorted into a tissue. I always had a

cold in those days. 'It's sort of automatic. An in-joke around college.'

'I see. So, what's yours?'

'Uh?'

'Your name?' he asked patiently.

'Oh! Elizabeth Jordan.' I stuffed the tissue back into my pocket and extended my hand automatically.

'Pleased to meet you. Is that Elizabeth after the Queen of England?' he asked, shaking my hand rather stiffly.

'No,' I laughed at the thought. 'My parents aren't exactly royalists. I was named after Liz Taylor, I think.'

'The film star? Wow. You know, I think I can see that,' he nodded. 'You have similar eyes.'

'To Liz Taylor?' I breathed. Didn't she have the most beautiful eyes in the world? 'Do you really think so?' I asked eagerly.

'Well, you both have two,' said Brian, putting a pin in my bubble. But he did it with a smile. A really nice smile that told me that perhaps he was just trying out a bit of English sarcasm out.

'I also have my own teeth,' I added to let him know I hadn't taken offence.

'Hey, here come your friends,' said Brian then, making as if to get up from the step. 'I'd better go. I think they took quite a dislike to me early on and I wouldn't want to get you into trouble for talking to the enemy.'

Bill and Mary were indeed mooching along the corridor towards us. Bill was wearing his prized *Tour de*

France cycling ensemble (which the rest of us suspected hadn't been washed since it crossed the finish line on a British contender's back and Bill won it in a raffle at the university cycle club) and Mary looked as though she had just lost her pet dog to a ravenous crocodile (which actually meant she was in a relatively good mood for Mary). When they spotted me, Mary turned to Bill and whispered something that was doubtless fairly poisonous. She frequently lamented the fact that we never met any new people, but her tendency to hate almost everyone on sight hardly helped our cause. Some of the most socially confident people in college would hide in shady doorways when Mary came into the quad.

'Has someone in your friend's family died?' Brian asked me. 'Only she looks really miserable all the time.'

'She's a gothic,' I explained. 'It's part of her look.'

'Really. Some friends of mine had to dress up like that to be extras on *Interview with a Vampire*. Scary. Well, I guess I'll see you around, Miss Elizabeth Jordan. Better get back to Disneyland.'

'No,' I insisted. Hearing the Disneyland crack again made my cheeks flame automatically. But suddenly I didn't want him to go. Suddenly I wanted to prove that we weren't the biggest xenophobic dorks in the United Kingdom before every foreign student in the university started to avoid us. I wasn't sure why it was so important at that moment but perhaps I had an inkling even then that if I talked to Brian for a bit longer, I might actually discover something interesting. 'Stay and meet them properly,' I begged him. 'I'm sure they're sorry things got off to such a bad start too. Their barks are far worse than their bites, I promise.'

'Well, as long as his bite isn't as bad as his snore,' said Brian, cocking his head towards Bill. 'I've got the room next to him. You know, he should really think about having his adenoids out.'

'Made a new friend?' purred Mary, looking down on us through false lashes that looked like big black spiders stuck to her lids with thick glue.

'Bill and Mary, this is Brian.'

'Bw-yan!' they chorused automatically. Mary even smiled at him. Sort of.

'Er, we've already been through that,' I said.

'*He's not the Messiah – he's a very naughty boy!*' said Bill, in a high-pitched impression of Terry Jones playing Brian's ugly mother. 'That film is so funny.' He slapped his lycra-ed thigh at the thought.

'Actually,' said Brian very seriously. 'Where I come from, *The Life of Brian* is considered blasphemous and I don't find it very funny at all.'

Two mouths dropped open.

'Wow. Are you from Utah or something?' Mary asked in awe.

'Nah! I'm from New Jersey originally. Though I live in New York now. And I'm Jewish. So I don't really give a shit. We don't believe he was the Messiah anyway.'

'What? Brian?' asked Bill.

'Jesus,' I corrected before Bill started to explain to Brian that it was 'only a film'. 'But enough about that. We need to get in there.' I jerked my head towards the dining-room door. The queue had started to move and we had somehow managed to lose our coveted place at the head of it.

'Shit!' said Mary. 'I only wanted cream crackers and now they'll all have gone. I don't believe it. I'm going to starve to death.' She could never resist the opportunity for a spot of hyperbole and right then she sounded like a shipwreck survivor who had just discovered that the last of the weevil-studded biscuits has fallen overboard. 'What is it supposed to be tonight anyway?' she added, just a little more calmly.

Bill sniffed the air floating out from the kitchen like a wolf scenting its prey. 'Mmm, I'd say we're having celery soup to start, followed by a delicious celery *en croûte* with boiled celery as an accompaniment. And for dessert, puréed celery with custard.'

Brian looked faintly disgusted.

'Why so much celery?' he asked.

It was just another in-joke. The college chef had a thing about celery. Either that, or a very cheap supply of the stuff. He put celery into almost everything, including, it was rumoured, the tutti-frutti ice-cream. Mary didn't mind, because she was a firm believer in the theory that eating celery burns off more calories than it contains. But I was heartily sick of the stuff. Besides, have you ever heard of anyone serving up boiled celery instead of proper vegetables like potatoes or carrots? Where are the vitamins when it's been simmered for four days? That's what my mother wanted to know whenever she visited.

Anyway, Mary was reading the menu pinned up by the college door. 'Well, it's actually meant to be egg mayonnaise on lettuce followed by spaghetti bolognese with treacle sponge for afters. Great,' she snorted. 'I can't eat any of that. Eggs bring me out in a rash and spaghetti bolognese has got tomatoes in it.'

'Not at this college,' Bill reminded her.

'I'll give it a try,' said Brian bravely.

But instead he was quickly introduced to the joys of the kebab van which parked outside the college gates every night. For the first year, I had thought of the kebab van man as a saviour; the only thing standing between me and malnutrition. However, when he put his prices up three times in one term at well over the rate of inflation I began to wonder whether the chef was making college food deliberately bad and taking a cut of the kebab van's earnings.

'Any pork in this?' Brian asked, as he took his cold pitta bread filled with slivers of dubious brown meat analogue and those twisty green pickled chillies that you find all the way up and down the High Street in Oxford on a Sunday morning.

'I don't think there's actually any meat of any description in it at all,' said Mary. She was supposed to be a vegetarian, but she made an exception for kebabs. Brian took a cautious bite of the brown matter and spat it out again instantaneously.

'What *is* this stuff?' he asked us.

'Welcome to Oxford,' said Mary.

His initiation was done.

After that, Brian quickly became a regular fixture in our college lives. He zoomed up in Mary's estimation when he revealed that the two corn-fed kids we had seen him with on that first day, and hated at first sight, were simply the people he had travelled over with on the plane, not people he particularly liked hanging out with. He didn't play baseball, or basketball, or live all year just to watch the Superbowl. Though he wore proper lace-up shoes and not disgraceful tattered workmen's boots like the rest of us, it turned out that he didn't have terrible taste in anything but his preppy clothes (all chosen by his mother – he had too many things to think about apart from changing his image, he claimed, and Mary said she actually respected him for that).

He also had several albums of dirge-like goth music unavailable in the UK that Mary borrowed at once and couldn't be persuaded to return for almost three terms. He connected with Bill over long nights of Led Zeppelin and the revelation that his parents, like Bill's (or so Bill constantly claimed), had been at the original Woodstock.

But Brian didn't have to listen to the right music or wear the right clothes to impress me. I just adored his sense of humour. It was so – well, so English actually. Mostly sarcastic and ever so slightly sick. I loved to hear crazy stories about his New York childhood. Before I met Brian, I had harboured no inclination to visit America whatsoever. All Disney and obesity, as far as I was concerned. But listening to his stories, I quickly realised that there were so many other things that I would be missing out on if I never crossed the pond.

I screamed with laughter at his impressions of bolshie *Noo Yoik* taxi drivers ordering *quaffee*. I listened with due reverence when he told me about his experiences as a fresh-faced waiter in a Manhattan Pizza Hut frequented by the Mob.

And when I couldn't stop gazing at his big brown eyes while he told me about the time his grandmother had taken her apricot toy poodle, *Spencer Tracey the Second*, to the orthodontist to fix its overbite, I knew that I was falling in love.

CHAPTER TWO

T he thunderbolt really hit one day about a month after we first met.

We were hanging about in the undergraduate students' common room, Bill, Brian, Mary and I, drinking the vile coffee that we were each obliged to pay three pounds a term into a kitty for. The common room was always chock-full at about eleven o'clock in the morning with people trying to get their money's worth of the stuff without gagging.

'There's a performance of *Antony and Cleopatra* on tomorrow night, in the crypt at St Edmund Hall,' said Brian suddenly. We had been lamenting the fact that we never really got any culture (without admitting that we never really tried). 'Do you think it will be any good?' he asked.

Mary snorted into her cup. 'Why don't you ask Liz?' she said.

'Have you been to see it already?' asked Brian.

I blushed hard and stared into my coffee. What had Mary done to me?

'Actually, I'm going to be in it,' I had to admit. 'So I

don't know whether I'm qualified to say whether it'll be good or not,' I waffled. 'I mean, it's probably not, if they let me on to the stage.'

'Lizzie, this is brilliant,' said Brian excitedly. 'How come you didn't tell us?' He turned to Bill and Mary. 'Isn't this great? Our friend Liz is an actress. We're definitely going to have to go now.'

'Uh-uh,' said Mary, shaking her head smugly.

'She won't actually let us go and see her act,' Bill explained before he added in a squeaky approximation of my voice, 'She says that it makes her shy and then she fumbles her words.'

It did. Knowing that people I knew were in the audience made me fumble my words.

'Liz, I didn't even know you did act,' said Brian in surprise. 'And here you were agreeing with us that you didn't do anything cultural. Now I discover you're doing Shakespeare on the quiet!'

I shrugged.

'Who are you playing?' he asked me.

'She's probably just a spear carrier,' said Mary quite dismissively.

'I'm playing Cleopatra actually,' I corrected.

'Wow,' Brian almost clapped his hands. 'That's a major part. Wait, that's like *the* major part in this play. You're the leading lady and you didn't tell us?'

'Isn't Cleopatra supposed to be all beautiful and dusky?' said Mary, examining her nails like a cat considering unsheathing its claws on the family budgie. 'She didn't have freckles, for a start.'

'I will be wearing make-up,' I reminded her. 'And I haven't got freckles anyway. What are you talking about?'

'Must be a blackhead then.'

'Stop teasing her, Mary,' Brian interrupted. 'I'll bet Liz is perfect for the part.'

'I don't know about that,' I said. Truthfully.

'She's so embarrassed that she practises her lines in the shower,' said Mary. 'So that no one can hear her over the sound of the water.'

'I do not,' I protested. Though in actual fact I had, after Graham the mathematics student in the room next door to me complained that my constant talking to myself while learning my lines was interfering with his ability to concentrate on logarithms. He also got the student dean to break into my bedroom after I practised the bit with the asp a little too loudly. I took it as a compliment at first. My death scene must have been hyper-realistic to warrant such concern. But the dean soon burst that bubble when he warned me that any repeat performance would result not in applause but in a hefty fine.

'I still can't believe I didn't know this was going on. Why hide your talents from your friends?' asked Brian.

'Because I'm not sure that I actually have a talent,' I explained. 'Anyway, I'm not hiding anything. I just don't want to bore you all with my thesping. It's a private thing.'

'But you're doing a play,' Brian reminded me. 'That's not very private.'

'I was press-ganged into it,' I lied. 'And it's a set text. It saves me having to do too much revision if I learn the part to play it.'

'You must want to do it a little bit,' he persisted.

I shrugged again. But oh, I *had* wanted to play Cleopatra. Until Mary let loose the fact. I was actually really excited to have wangled such a great part. But I still wasn't convinced that I entirely deserved it and I didn't want to get a reaction to my acting ability from people I would have to see on a daily basis afterwards. That meant Mary, Bill and Brian. What if they hated my performance? What if they couldn't even look me in the eye afterwards because I was so bad? I would never be able to act again if I had to face my biggest critics over breakfast every day.

Until Mary forced me to admit my part in the play prematurely, I had made a bargain with myself that I would wait for at least five good reviews before I invited my mates along to watch me. Five *good* reviews. It sounded reasonable but the likelihood of that happening was actually pretty slim. Not least because I knew only four student critics would bother to see the play.

'I'd really like to see you on stage,' said Brian, trying to be all persuasive.

'We want to too,' chorused Mary and Bill in irritating harmony. 'If you let Brian see the play, we've got to see it as well. It's only fair.'

'Well, you definitely can't,' I said, all exasperated. 'Do you want me to go wrong? Please don't come. You're not really interested. I'd die of embarrassment.'

'Don't hide your light under a bushel,' said Brian jewishly.

'I'm not. I just want to hide it from you guys. At least for the moment. Look, I know what it would be like. Mary and Bill would make faces at me all the way through. I let them watch me act once before. I was playing the nurse in *Romeo and Juliet* and nearly choked to death trying not to laugh when Bill mooned at me from the back of the hall in the final act. Luckily it looked as though my shoulders were shaking with grief and the snobby git from *Isis* was impressed. But how can I expect to be taken seriously when I'm corpsing through the sad parts?'

'I won't do it again,' promised Bill but I never took Bill's word for anything; not since he made a New Year's resolution to change out of his cycling shorts as soon as he returned from the gym each day so that no one had to look at his finely tuned musculature unless they specifically asked to. He had made that resolution last until, oh, at least the fifteenth of January.

'I wish I could believe you. Does anyone want another coffee?' I asked, desperate to move the conversation on to another topic. Anything other than me. Luckily Brian stepped to my rescue.

'I'll fetch them,' he said. 'But only if you let us

all come and watch you do the nurse thing tomorrow night.'

'No way!' I shrieked. 'I've told you why I can't.'

'I was only joking,' Brian said, backing off with his
hands in a gesture of surrender. 'If you really don't
want us to be there, we won't be. Wouldn't want to
disturb your creative genius.'

'Aw,' Mary moaned. 'I really wanted to watch you
pulling that funny face you pull when you're being
all serious again.'

'Don't pick on her, Mary,' warned Brian.

I sighed in relief.

But I won't pretend that I wasn't ever so slightly
disappointed when the time came for the play to
begin the next night and I couldn't see any of them
in the audience. I'd met Bill in the dining room earlier
that evening and he told me that they were going for
a curry straight after dinner (I've already explained
to you about college dinners as a slimming aid).
But I thought that was just a cunning bluff. I still
fully expected to see all three of them sitting at the
back of the hall with their programmes across their
grinning faces in a pathetic attempt at disguise. But
they weren't. At least not as far as I could see, because
before I could finish checking the audience really
thoroughly from the safety of behind the curtains,
the spotlights came on and I couldn't see a thing
except the stage in front of me.

There were hundreds of theatrical groups at the university. I had signed up for most of them during Freshers' Week but ended up with the minute *Crypt Company* because they were the only group who actually let me finish my audition piece. All the other groups had cut me short in my portrayal of *Twelfth Night*'s plucky Viola arriving shipwrecked in Illyria, and suggested that I might like to help out behind the scenes instead. Perhaps I could operate the curtains? Did I know how to sew a tunic? The members of the Crypt Company were altogether more sympathetic to my acting ambitions. Most of them were on Prozac, which probably helped.

I had wanted to tread the boards from a very early age. I think the bug bit when my brother Colin and I were taken to see a West End production of *Annie* as a special Christmas treat back in 1981. Colin had hated the musical about a plucky orphan. Too much singing and far too many girls as far as he was concerned. But I had been entranced and spent the next six months belting out all the songs at the top of my voice in the hope that someone influential would hear me singing in the street and drag me off to stage school. It didn't happen of course. That kind of thing doesn't happen in Solihull. But my mother did enrol me in a local church-based amateur dramatic group, who were putting on their own production of my beloved *Annie*. I auditioned my heart out, but the title role went to the church warden's daughter (she couldn't sing a note but she had the right hair). Reluctantly I took up the part of one of the other orphanage girls but feigned tonsillitis on the opening night and never actually performed.

After that, puberty struck and the thought of having too many people looking at me while I tried to hide my spotty forehead behind a ridiculously long fringe kept me firmly backstage. I acted as stage manager for my school house in three house drama competitions in a row. Nobody thought to ask me whether I would like to be on stage because I must have seemed so contented pulling the curtain strings; but I found myself watching the leading ladies and thinking that I could do better. I learned all their lines and performed them in front of my bedroom mirror just in case both star and understudy should fall ill. One day, I told myself, I would no longer be so shy.

By the time I got to university, I hadn't entirely got over my shyness but I forced myself to audition for the theatre groups because I had read an article in *Cosmo*, or some worthy tome like that, about confronting your biggest fears. Get back on to the horse, they said. The irony was, I don't think that the idea of an audience in itself bothered me. What bothered me was the opinion of my peers – specifically the people I knew. I wouldn't have minded if Sir Dickie Attenborough saw my Cleo and thought my performance was rubbish. At school, it had been the thought of my classmates thinking I was rubbish that had scuppered my acting career. Now it was the thought of my closest college friends thinking the same.

I had acted my heart out in front of the Crypt Company because I didn't know any of them and they all looked as ordinary and uninspiring as me. They practically begged me to join them, assuming that I must have been inundated with offers from every theatre group going. In fact, only one other group had recalled me to audition again – for the part of a spear carrier in *Julius Caesar*. The Crypt Company offered me the part of Juliet's nurse in *Romeo and Juliet*, and so I took the option of being a big fish in a small pond instead.

Rod, the company's floppy-haired, fringe-flicking director, had decided that we would do *Antony and Cleopatra* after his insistence on producing a disastrous Catalan play about the secret language of sentence structure (at least I think that's what it was about) over the summer had earned damning reviews from every university publication and the subsequent lack of interest had almost wiped out the company's finances.

We needed to do a crowd pleaser and *Antony and Cleopatra* was pretty much guaranteed to draw the crowds with its tale of love and death in equal measure. I thought we had chosen the right play this time, but I wasn't convinced that we had chosen the right venue. Though the crypt at St Edmund Hall was great for all the interior scenes (and had given the company its name), there wasn't enough room for a really impressive crowd and scene changes were a nightmare in the confined space and crepuscular darkness. I forgot to mention that the Crypt Company was so small that we frequently doubled up on parts and even the most important actors had to shift scenery as well. It was particularly difficult for me since my costume had a large amount of padding at the front and on the backside that seemed to get bigger with every performance. I knew that I wasn't exactly womanly in my natural state, while Cleopatra was already a mother by the time she met her man, but I was beginning to wonder whether I was playing the Queen of Egypt or one of the Teletubbies.

Phylidda, who would be playing my handmaiden Charmian, was in charge of the costumes. It was a bit of a step down for her to be playing my maid, since when we'd played *Romeo and Juliet*, she had been Juliet to my nurse. I had auditioned for Juliet too and think I might have got the part if Phylidda's boyfriend hadn't been chosen to play Romeo. When it was announced that Greg was playing the romantic hero, I knew that my chances of swooning across the balcony were over. If Phylidda didn't get Juliet, everyone suspected she would walk; and with her would go the extremely valuable lighting equipment that she had bought with an interest-free loan from her terrifyingly rich step-daddy.

'Don't forget to put your warts on,' said Phylidda as I was applying my make-up that first night.

'I'm not sure Cleopatra would actually have had warts,' I ventured.

'Oh, but they all did,' she assured me. 'Have you

any idea what kind of nasties you can get bitten by in the desert? And what about that plague of boils they had?'

'Was that in Cleopatra's time?' I asked.

'Probably.'

'I still don't see why we have to have them. They're a bit distracting.'

'Rod wants this to be the most realistic production of *Antony and Cleopatra* ever seen at the university,' she explained patiently. 'The warts were his suggestion.'

'Fine.' I was dubious about that but I stuck one right on the end of my nose to keep her happy and was momentarily doubly relieved that my friends wouldn't be in the audience that night.

'Aren't you having warts too?' I asked her as she sketched thick black lines around her eyes, transforming herself from Home Counties to houri in a stroke. 'If Cleopatra had warts, her handmaiden would definitely have had them too.'

'I've got one,' said Phylidda, showing me a minute bump on her chin. 'Now sit perfectly still while I do your eye make-up.'

I closed my eyes and tilted my head backwards.

'Sit still,' reminded Phylidda as she drew nearer, holding the eye-liner pencil like a dagger. 'If you move I'll have your eye out.'

'I'm not moving,' I promised.

'No, you are moving, Lizzie,' she said, before she poked me right in the eye.

'Ow!' I sat up very suddenly clapping my hands to my face. 'You've stabbed me!'

'I told you not to move, didn't I? Does it hurt?' she asked. Her voice was strangely excited. 'Do you want me to call Rod and tell him that you won't be performing tonight?'

'I want you to check that I'm not going blind first!'

'Open your eye!' Phylidda wrenched my eyelids apart. 'Can you see?'

'No. You've got your thumb in it now.'

'God, I'm sorry,' she said, not moving her thumb at all. 'Oh, Lizzie, this is terrible. Your first night playing Cleopatra and now you won't be able to go on.'

'I will go on,' I insisted, batting her hands away blindly. My vision was terribly blurred. Though she had stabbed me in the left eye, they were both filled with tears and seemed to be stinging equally badly. 'What does my bloody eye look like?' I begged her.

'Oh, it's awful, Lizzie. Really, really awful. I don't know what to say to you.'

'Just pass me the mirror.'

'I don't think you ought to look.'

'Pass me the mirror!'

The bell rang to warn the audience that it was time for them to take their seats. I had less than two minutes after the curtain went up to be on stage looking serenely foxy and in control, and there I was with my mascara streaming down my face like an oil spill at Niagara Falls.

'That's the bell for the audience,' shrieked Phylidda, as if I hadn't heard. 'Oh, god, Lizzie. What can we do? I'm going to have to go on as Cleopatra, aren't I? You can do Charmian. The fringe on my wig is longer than yours and you won't need to concentrate so hard if you've got fewer lines.'

'What's going on?'

It was Rod, come to see why we weren't at the pre-performance meditation circle he always insisted on. 'We're doing the mantra.'

'Lizzie's had a terrible accident,' Phylidda explained. 'I'm going to have to go on as Cleopatra instead. It's so awful.'

But it wasn't so awful for her. It suddenly came to me that Phylidda might have stabbed me deliberately so that she could go on in my place. After all, her boyfriend Greg was playing Antony and we all knew that Phylidda didn't entirely believe in Greg's ability to 'act' a love scene.

'I can go on,' I insisted to Rod. Through my blurred vision I saw Phylidda's face take on a look of deep disapproval.

'You're not well enough, Lizzie,' she said quietly.

'I am well enough. I can see perfectly well out of my right eye and I'm sure the left one will be fine by the time we get to the second act.'

'Tell her she's not well enough, Rodney,' said Phylidda, only just managing to keep the edge of hysteria out of her voice. 'What if a delayed reaction makes her forget her lines? What if she falls over or something?'

'Then you can take over,' I told her. 'But I am going on. Have you got any idea how hard it has been for me to get this far? Make me an eyepatch.'

Realising that she wasn't going to keep me off the stage that night, Phylidda set to her task grudgingly. I had intended that she make a discreet little patch that could be hidden beneath the long beaded fringe of my Egyptian-style wig, but when the curtain was finally raised on the first night of my Cleopatra, it was a Cleopatra with a great wad of cotton wool stuck against her eye with sellotape. At least it detracted attention from the warts.

I just tried to forget that I looked like I'd done ten rounds with Frank Bruno. In fact, I felt that the sting in my eye helped me to focus and be extra fiery when I needed to be. Not that the performance went without hitch from then on. Antony nearly met an early death when one of the heavy spotlights came loose from the rig and fell crashing to the floor right next to his feet as he spoke with Caesar. Between scenes it became clear that Charmian suspected Antony of having a fling with a fresher at their college and the poor boy took on a harassed look that must have made the audience wonder why he was bothering with women at all.

I managed to raise a few gasps and murmurs.

I hoped it was my acting and not the eyepatch or the wart on my nose which dropped off on to Charmian's lap while she sat at my feet and listened to me dribbling on about Antony. When we broke off for an interval after the scene, Phylidda returned the detached wart to me with such disgust in her expression you might have thought it was a real one.

'This totally detracted from one of my best lines,' she snarled.

'I won't put it on again then,' I told her.

'No, you must. For continuity's sake. But try putting it on your cheek this time.'

'Won't people find it funny that I have a migrating wart?'

'I'm the wardrobe mistress.'

'I think it suits you,' said Greg, Phylidda's feckless Antony. 'Physical defects can be strangely cute on the right girl.'

'Do you think so?' I asked.

'Of course he doesn't,' Phylidda snapped.

'Is there any money to split tonight?' Greg asked to change the subject.

'No. In fact, you all owe me three pounds apiece for the hire of the venue.'

'What?' said Greg. 'I bet this never happened to Laurence Olivier.'

'I bet Laurence Olivier never fluffed his lines because he was too busy hamming it up for the girl in the front row,' Phylidda snapped.

'What girl in the front row?' Greg asked innocently.

'You know very well who I mean. Her with the nipples from Pembroke.'

'Eh?' said Greg.

'Either she's very pleased to see you or it's very cold in here. Can't she afford to buy a bra, for heaven's sake?'

'It is actually very cold in here,' I said, in an attempt to save Greg's bacon. 'My nipples feel like bloody thimbles.'

That was a mistake. Greg instantly fixed his eyes on my chest. Phylidda fixed her death rays on my remaining healthy eye.

'I can't believe you let her come here on my opening night,' she continued, spinning Greg around and marching him away from my chest. 'How can I lose myself in the lyrical glory of Shakespeare when *she's* sitting in the front row reminding me of what you've been up to while I've been revising for my finals.'

'Don't you think we ought to be ringing the bell for the second act?' I suggested. I'd had enough of being caught in the crossfire and in any case I wanted to get to the curry house for a last poppadom. In between arbitrating for their argument, I'd taken a quick peek out into the audience again to see if anyone I knew had sneaked in. No one. I knew I should be relieved, what with the warty make-up and all, but for some reason I wasn't. So they really hadn't bothered to turn up. Why did I feel so let down?

'I just might kill myself for real in the final scene,' Phylidda sobbed dramatically.

'Phylidda, don't be so ridiculous!' begged Greg.

I made a mental note to make extra sure that the basket full of snakes that would be instrumental in Cleopatra's end contained only rubber ones (it wasn't an entirely stupid notion – Phylidda was studying zoology and I knew she had access to poisonous lizards at least). I was in charge of the props.

Thankfully the play ended without a real suicide. After Caesar had spoken his final word on the dignity of the Egyptian queen and her Roman lover, those members of the cast who had not died in the snake frenzy all bowed their heads, as if to signify that everyone should remain silent until Rod, who was playing the great Roman emperor, looked up and gave the signal for rapturous applause (not that I expected that with so few people in the audience) and my sudden return from death to take a curtain call. Usually the audience understood and waited until the resonance of the final phrase had completely died away before they began to applaud our efforts . . . but not tonight. The carefully measured period of silence was smashed by much clapping of hands and cat-calling from the previously empty back row.

'Bravo! Encore! Three cheers for the one-eyed Queen of Egypt.'

A single red rose came whizzing over my head where I still lay pretending to be dead. That flower was followed by another and another until there must have been – oh, at least half a dozen roses on my body. I sat up and squinted out into the audience. We hadn't even gathered to take our curtain call yet. Many of the cast were still off-stage. This was unprecedented behaviour from a usually sedate-to-the-point-of-comatose Shakespeare-loving crowd.

'Well, they're nothing to do with me,' said Phylidda, struggling to her feet, as suddenly a pair of y-fronts joined the flowers on the stage, followed by a wolf whistle so loud I'm sure I nearly lost both ear-drums. Unfortunately I had already guessed that the rowdy element could only be something to do with me.

I slowly picked up the stray pants and turned them over in my hands. Purple y-fronts. I knew of only one person in the world who could possibly bring himself to wear purple y-fronts except as a dare. More specifically, white y-fronts that had been dyed deep purple in the college washing machine and given everyone else in college lilac-coloured clothes for about a month afterwards.

It was Bill.

Now that the spotlights were off I could see him clearly at the back of the hall, sticking his fingers into his mouth for another raucous whistle. To one side of him Mary was clapping relatively sedately. And to the other side, Brian held the last of the bunch of long-stemmed red roses he had been throwing with such an impressive aim. Now they ran to the stage, as if we actors were a rock band and they were planning to mob us. Phylidda turned to me with raised eyebrows. 'I'll make a note of that three pounds you owe me,' she said. She was the club treasurer as well as the wardrobe girl. Then she left without saying goodbye.

'That was so fantastic,' Brian said, grabbing my hand and kissing it extravagantly. 'You were wonderful, marvellous, you were all the superlatives a man could possibly think of if only he was doing an English degree and not economics.'

'You were pretty good,' said Bill.

'Yeah, not bad,' said Mary. 'Particularly liked the migrating warts. And what on earth happened to your eye?'

'Phylidda. Eye-liner.'

'Nasty. I thought she might have given you a punch because you were too realistic when you kissed Antony.'

'Way too realistic. I know I was jealous,' said Brian, causing me to flush to the bone marrow. 'You were sooo hot, Queen Cleo.' I certainly was right then. I covered my reddening cheeks with my straight black wig.

'But, but I didn't see you in the audience,' I stuttered.

'Ah-ha!' said Bill. 'That was Brian's idea. We ducked down behind the seats in front of us as soon as you first came on and stayed there until the end of your first scene so that you wouldn't see us and think we'd come to make you muck up your lines.'

'You really were brilliant,' said Brian incredulously.

'Yeah. Shall we go for that curry now?' Mary interrupted. She was either very hungry or getting sick of having to congratulate me on my performance. Whatever her motives, it seemed like a great idea. I couldn't take much more flattery and I was dying to take off that terrible wig.

'I didn't think you'd come tonight,' I told Brian as we headed for Tandoori Nights, Oxford's best, and cheapest, curry emporium.

'Did you really think I'd miss it,' he said. 'A chance to see such a good friend tread the boards? You were triumphant, Lizzie.'

'I can't believe you managed to keep Bill and Mary in check,' I added gratefully.

'They knew I'd be mad at them if they didn't behave on your big night. You know, I really admire people who spend their free time learning how to act like that,' he told me. 'You were even better than Liz Taylor in the movie. You're a very special, very talented and endlessly surprising girl, Lizzie Jordan.'

'You don't really mean that,' I stuttered.

'You know I really do,' he said.

'Oh.'

He looked me straight in one eye and the patch.

Special, talented and endlessly surprising?

No one had ever said anything like that to me before and I'm afraid I had to punch him. Only in the arm . . . And only very lightly. But I did have to punch him just the same. Didn't Brian realise that the

English way to pay a compliment was with sarcasm or a joke? I felt hot all over for the rest of the walk to the restaurant and was bright fuschia even before I tasted my first mouthful of the chef's legendary chicken tikka makhani. In fact, I was much less embarrassed when Bill pointed out that I had forgotten to take my warts off.

Special, talented and endlessly surprising.

Brian Coren might just as well have told me that he loved me.

CHAPTER THREE

'**D**o you think he has a girlfriend waiting for him back in America?' Mary asked the next day as we pushed a trolley around Tesco's in search of marked-down food only just past its sell-by date to supplement our diet of cream cheese and crackers.

'He's never talked about one if he has,' I told her.

'That's true. I bet he gets overlooked in favour of all those big football-playing jocks, anyway,' she said. 'American women have no taste in men whatsoever. Just look at all those big-haired girls throwing themselves at Bill Clinton.'

'That's more about power and book deals than physical attraction,' I reminded her. 'There's something inherently attractive about shagging the most powerful man in the world however gross he is in physical terms.'

'Mmmm. I wonder what he looks like without his clothes on,' Mary mused.

'Bill Clinton? Not overly fat, but not too toned. Flabby round the midriff? Better with a tan, I should imagine.'

'Not him, stupid. I meant Brian,' said Mary impatiently.

'Brian? What? *Our* Brian? Oh, I don't know,' I laughed nervously. 'I can't say I've ever really thought about it.'

'You liar.'

'I am not lying. He's a friend of ours!' I protested. 'Not just some piece of boy-meat to drool about while we're walking round the supermarket.'

'So? Are you telling me you've never imagined Bicycle Bill without his clothes on either?' Mary asked, pointing at me menacingly with a green banana.

'Too right I haven't,' I shuddered, holding my hands up. 'That all-in-one lycra bodysuit he wears to go training in hardly leaves much room for imagining anyway. But I try very hard not to. In fact, I like to try and imagine what Bill would look like with a proper pair of trousers on. Nice thick ones made of tweed with a proper fly for modesty and a crease right down the front of each leg. And a shirt that buttons all the way up to his neck so that you can't see that nasty bit of chest hair that looks like it could just reach out and entangle you while you're not looking.'

'Ugh. You've noticed that clump of hair too?' Mary whispered. 'I hate it. But sometimes I just can't take my eyes off it.'

'I know exactly what you mean. It's like not being able to stop yourself looking at a hedgehog that's been killed on the road with its guts spilled all over the place, isn't it?' I elaborated unnecessarily. 'And you do know that he's got hair like that on his back as well?'

'How do you know?' Mary shrieked. 'I would have to scream if I saw that. When did you see that? You didn't actually *sleep* with him without telling me, did you? Did you? Liz, I can't believe you . . .'

'No!' I protested loudly. 'There's a perfectly innocent reason. It was in the summer. He was sunbathing out by the cricket pitch. He put his shirt on again before you came out to join us.'

'Well, thank god for that. I might have fainted if I'd seen him semi-naked. What a nightmare. Do you think Brian has chest hair too?' she asked to change the subject.

'I swear I've never really thought about it,' I lied again.

'He's bound to. The hair on his head is so thick and dark. He looks like he needs to shave at least twice a day. Then there's the fact that he's Jewish of course,' said Mary, raising her eyebrows meaningfully.

'What do you mean by that? Are Jewish men generally more hairy?'

'No! I mean. You know,' she looked groin-wards. 'I mean, he's not going to be a cavalier, is he? *Comprendez?*'

'No? What do you mean?' I asked in exasperation as I threw a canister of UHT squirty cream into our trolley. Well, I didn't know what I hoped to do with it either, but it was only just out of date and had been reduced by sixty pence.

'I mean, he's a roundhead, dumbo. No hood to pull up.' She mimed putting a hood on, which left me none the wiser.

'Eh?'

'I mean, he's circumcised, of course,' she whispered.

'Oh, right,' I said slowly. She had left me behind with the chest hair.

'Don't tell me you've never thought about that either!' she said, giving me a shove in the arm. 'Have you ever seen one? One that's been done? How far do they cut it off to, do you think?'

'I don't know.' But my mind's eye was suddenly unavoidably full of truncated little penises with bandages wrapped around their ends like so many wounded soldiers. 'They don't actually make *it* any shorter when they do it, do they?' I asked.

'Not sure,' said Mary. 'It's only the foreskin that goes, I think. But is it the whole foreskin, d'you reckon? Or just a bit?'

'Wouldn't be much point taking just half of it off,' I suggested. 'I suppose they must chop it right back to the shaft.'

We had reached the refrigerated cabinets. A man choosing thinly sliced luncheon meat suddenly changed his mind about what he wanted for his supper.

'Well, it's about cleanliness, apparently,' Mary told me, as she picked out an anaemic-looking sausage and began to use it as a teaching aid. 'That's why it started. Historically. Stops a chap from getting any infections under the hood.'

'But doesn't it make the whole thing more vulnerable not to have the hood there in the first place?' I countered. We loved an intellectual argument, Mary and me.

'Obviously not,' Mary said firmly. 'And that's not the only advantage apparently. Jemima from my neurophysiology class says that they're much better for blow jobs. For a start, it doesn't take so bloody long, because an exposed tip is that much more sensitive to oral stimulation. And secondly . . .'

'Because you don't have to make the guy a bacon sandwich afterwards?' I quipped, examining a packet of streaky.

'Nice one,' Mary cackled. 'But it's really because you don't have to worry about crusty rim cheese.'

'Ugh!'

We looked at each other and grimaced. I knew exactly what she meant. Sadly, most girls would.

Mary put the sausage back sharpish. And not just because she'd remembered that she was supposed to be a vegetarian for the very highest moral reasons.

'Oh no, I've just had the worst possible thought,' she said then, going all pale and wobbly. She grasped my arm to hold herself up as she said to me in a horrified whisper, 'What if you had to give Bill a blow job? What if you had to give him a blow job or your entire family would be shot dead by fanatical religious terrorists at dawn?'

'Don't!' I pleaded.

'Can you even imagine it?'

'I'm trying my hardest not to.'

'You've got to, Liz. I can't bear the burden on my own. Imagine it. You'd have to peel him out of that funny-coloured jock strap that's always hanging from the back of his bedroom door for a start. Imagine he's just done a twelve-mile jog and then been rowing on the river for a couple of hours and . . . and . . .' She gagged. She actually gagged at the thought of it!

'Come on, Liz. Let's get out of here,' she said, dragging me towards the exit.

'But what about our shopping?' I asked her.

'I can't even think about it now. I think I'm going to hurl.'

Since we only had one can of squirty cream and three green bananas as it was, we abandoned our trolley by the chiller cabinets and fled to the safety of the street and fresh air.

'Are you OK?' I asked Mary, who was doubled over by the bus stop with a horrible mixture of nausea and hysterics by the time I caught up with her.

'I'll be fine in a minute,' she promised, straightening up but unable to stop guffawing. 'You know what, I think I've just invented a new diet. It's called the *Blow Job Diet*. You get all the protein you need by swallowing when you give blow jobs to the guys you really fancy and stave off hunger pangs by imagining having to give a blow job to someone who never washes his knob.'

'Nice theory, Dr Bagshot, but what about the fibre?'

'Oh, you get that from chewing the pillows while

Leonardo di Caprio is performing cunnilingus beneath the duvet.'

'Ugh, please,' I laughed. 'That's practically lesbianism. It has to be a man who can grow facial hair at least.'

'Mmm. Perhaps you're right,' she mused. 'OK. How about this? You can take your pick of gorgeous men. Just imagine your very own heart-throb. The beauty of this diet is that it can be tailored to suit the individual.' She sounded as if she were writing the blurb for the back of the book already.

'Well, I'm going for Brad Pitt,' I told her. 'Little bit of stubble, but not too much.'

We started the walk back to college, stopping off *en route* at the chip shop since our food shopping expedition had failed so miserably. 'Brian could grow a good beard,' said Mary thoughtfully, as she speared the fattest chip in the bag with her wooden chip fork and popped it between her cherry-red lips. 'You know, Jemima said that she quite fancied him but I told her that she couldn't have him because he's strictly ours.'

'Platonically ours,' I reminded her.

'Yes, of course only platonically. It would ruin things, wouldn't it, if one of us had to have him any other way?'

'Absolutely ruin things.'

'Absolutely. So all bets on Brian Coren are off unless one of us falls totally head over heels in love with someone else outside our gang entirely, in which case the other one can have a go with Brian. Agreed?'

She held out her hand to shake on it.

'I suppose. As if he would want either of us anyway,' I sighed.

'Speak for yourself, Ms Low Self-esteem,' said Mary.

CHAPTER FOUR

A s you can imagine, when we saw Brian that evening I could think of little else but the conversation that Mary and I had shared in the frozen food aisles of Tesco and the deal that had been made in the chip shop.

I wondered if, as he sat there drinking Guinness and pretending that he really liked it, Brian had any idea at all how much we girls actually fancied him – unlike Bill, who, by the way he always sat with his legs wide open to accentuate his not inconsiderable lycra-sheathed manhood, clearly thought every girl in college fancied him when in reality we would rather have licked dog hair off a dirty carpet than have to kiss him on the lips. Especially since Bill was in the middle of telling us all, rather proudly, how many fillings he had. There were seven in his top teeth, he explained, and just six in the bottom. I could tell that Brian was trying not to wince when Bill invited him to inspect the mercury in his mouth.

'Yes, you probably could pick up radio signals with that,' Brian told him seriously.

Brian, of course, had zero fillings. His teeth were movie-star straight and whiter than Tippex. As were the teeth of just about everyone in America, from the president to parking attendants – at least the ones I had seen on TV. When he had finished cooing over Bill's extensive bridgework, Brian turned to me and said, 'You know, you have very nice teeth for an English girl, Liz.' I immediately stopped grinning and looked at my hands. For a start, I wasn't sure it was a compliment and secondly, because I could sense Mary's envious stare boring into the top of my head as she kept her chipped front tooth (the result of a particularly raucous Freshers' Week drinks party, followed by kissing the pavement) firmly hidden.

'So,' said Bill, slamming his empty glass down on the table to regain our full attention now that everyone had finished looking into his mouth. 'Are we going to the Two Items of Clothing party at the Union tonight or what? You get free drinks if one of your items is a hat,' he added, as if that was an incentive to strip off in the middle of winter.

Two Items of Clothing parties were Bill's idea of a dream night out. He often said he would like to shake the hand of the man (and it just had to be a man) who first thought of the idea. The principle was simple. You could get into the party only if you were wearing two items of clothing, or less. For Bill it was heaven. Lots of half-frozen girls wearing nothing but skimpy bikinis while he got to maintain his dignity (almost) by wearing his all-in-one lycra bodysuit with hefty gusset reinforcement (bought for rowing in, you understand) and a fedora he had picked up on a field trip to Spain.

'I'm game,' said Brian, surprisingly. 'Look what I bought today.' Then he pulled up his perfectly respectable t-shirt to reveal something that appeared to have been sprayed on underneath. An electric-blue lycra body-suit. 'I got this for rowing in, you understand,' he assured me. He had just been chosen for the college's second rowing team and had been getting up at six a.m. to go training every morning. The nutter. That wouldn't last long. 'You get too much drag if you wear something baggy,' he explained. Bill nodded vigorously in agreement.

'Way too much drag.'

I looked to see what Mary thought of the idea but her eyes were firmly fixed on Brian's pectoral muscles. His not unimpressive pectoral muscles. I had never noticed quite how well-defined he was before. Though, let's face it – I had never seen him in a jumped-up leotard before either.

'It's pretty cold out there,' I tried. 'It is November.'

'So wear your biggest knickers and a fur coat,' said Brian wickedly.

'Come on, Liz,' Mary pleaded suddenly. 'It'll be a laugh.'

I looked at her in absolute horror. A 'laugh'? Mary Bagshot had never before referred to Two Items of Clothing parties as a 'laugh', preferring instead to refer to them as 'pathetic juvenile enterprises' and 'just an excuse for disgusting perverts like Bill to wear their bloody sweaty lycra in public while they ogle semi-naked girls'. Now she was asking whether shoes counted as items of clothing at all. Apparently they didn't.

'You don't have to come, Liz,' Brian told me with a shrug. 'But it would be so much nicer if you did. You can wear your jumper and your jeans. That's two things. You'll be quite warm. I've just got to go to one of these crazy Bacchanalian parties before I go home to America. They simply don't happen in the States in case someone cries sexual harassment.'

'Oh, I don't consider myself to have had a good night unless I've managed to get some of that,' said Mary irresponsibly. And coquettishly, to boot. She really needed slapping with a frying pan that night.

'I don't know if I'm on for it,' I muttered. I had hitherto thought that the whole idea was disgraceful, childish and unnecessarily harrowing for would-be party-goers who didn't tan well. I had managed to get thus far in my university career without ever going to one and didn't feel as though I had particularly missed out. I couldn't believe that Mary wasn't backing me up now. She was usually so humourless about these things. She was a girl who once thought Andrea Dworkin wore too much make-up. What was wrong with her now?

'Oh, come on. Don't be such a party pooper,' Mary teased me with a pinch. 'You can wear your elasticated sta-prest slacks and a woolly jumper when you're fifty.

Might as well make the most of your youthful body now before you get fat and frumpy.'

That swung it. The twin spectres of 'fat' and 'frumpy' reminding me that I ought to be having a good time while I could still wear a tubi-grip as a boob tube if I wanted to rather than strictly as support for knees overburdened by carrying around a ton and a half of cellulite.

'I can't strip off. I haven't shaved my armpits for nearly a fortnight,' I groaned.

'We'll wait for you,' said Mary, sensing that I'd given in.

So, we ended up going to the Two Items of Clothing party after all and thankfully the two rugby team boys organising the event were already too drunk to bother checking how many items we really had on once they had stamped our hands with the smiley face stamp that said we had paid to get in. I was actually wearing three items. I mean, have you ever tried to wear jeans without the protection of a nice cotton gusset between you and the rivets? To escape from the misery of nasty chafing, I was happy to risk being caught bending the rules and losing my entrance fee.

Mary wore a *risqué* lycra dress (a dress that I thought she had thrown out after reading Naomi Wolf's *The Beauty Myth*) and Brian's baseball cap, grabbing me every two minutes to have me reassure her that no one could see up her skirt. Fact was, no one could really see anything of anybody anyway, since the room the party was being held in was so dark you couldn't even be sure whether the pert g-strung buttocks in front of you were male or female.

Brian and I fought our way to the bar, evading the graze of naked limbs which made me feel as though I were in some kind of virtual reality anonymous pleasure palace straight out of a seventies film. Bill was in his element however. And strangely, so was Mary. When Brian and I returned with the drinks in those flimsy plastic glasses, Mary was resting one slender hand on Bill's hairy shoulder and sliding her naked thigh up and down his silky lycra-ed leg as they grooved to the theme tune from *Shaft*. About three minutes later, they were snogging like two fourteen-year-olds who have just had their train-track braces taken off.

'Yuk!'

'Now that is a surprise,' said Brian, as we edged away to give them some privacy. Well, as much privacy as they seemed to want in a room that was so full I expected the walls to give way at any moment. Brian was surprised that Mary was tongue-wrestling Bill and he hadn't even heard our supermarket conversation about knob-cheese!

'Mmm, I certainly didn't think they fancied each other that much,' I told him. 'In fact, to hear them talk you'd have thought they found each other repulsive.'

'Yes,' Brian agreed. 'But isn't that always the way? People who are deeply, uncontrollably attracted to each other often try to protect themselves from the possibility of disappointment and rejection by pretending that they hate each other's guts in public. They were obviously just crazy about each other all along. You know, I think I'd be willing to lay money on a long and very passionate affair starting tonight.'

'Nah, this is just an aberration,' I said confidently, though by now Mary had been examining Bill's fillings for three whole songs.

'Perhaps you've been too close to them to see it happening,' mused Brian. 'I've never said anything about this before, but I had a gut feeling from the very first time I met Bill and Mary that they might get together one day. She's always touching him. Haven't you noticed that? Just little touches. But they're clearly signals of possession.'

'Do you really think so?' I said, screwing up my nose doubtfully. But when I came to think of it, Mary *was* always touching Bill. Though she had pretty successfully passed off those little signals of possession as hearty thumps of exasperation for as long as I'd known her.

'Yep. They're absolutely nuts about each other,' Brian concluded.

'And how do you know all this stuff?' I asked him.

'You can learn a lot from listening to your big sisters. These days I reckon I can spot just about any embryonic relationship forming at least two weeks before the people involved actually know it's happening.'

We had been walking as we talked and found ourselves outside the party now, passing through the peeling lobby of the students' Union that smelled permanently of spilled beer and sick.

'At least two weeks before it happens, eh?' I mused. 'I wish I had a gift like that. It might come in very useful.'

'Well,' said Brian, slipping his arm around my shoulders in what I assumed was a friendly manner. 'It's not actually that useful to me. You see, this gift I have for spotting fatal attraction is a bit like being able to tell people's fortunes. Clairvoyants can't actually use their fortune-telling powers to predict the future for themselves, you know.'

'I didn't know that,' I admitted.

'Well, it's true. You can't use the gift for yourself. Only for the good of others. That's the law of the universe. I felt sure that the moment Bill actually plucked up the courage to make his move, he would be pleasantly surprised to find his feelings reciprocated. But when it comes to me . . .' he raised his shoulders dismissively. 'When I decide that I've met someone I really like and want to get it on with them, I can watch them all I want to and still have no clue whatsoever whether they feel the same way about me in return.'

We sat down on a low wall outside the Union to ponder the mysteries of the world. And then had to move when we discovered that a couple who had clearly just met at the Two Items of Clothing Party were getting to know each other rather better on the grass right behind us. No wonder we students were so resented by the local taxpayers.

'I find myself falling madly in lust and have no idea at all whether my advances will be reciprocated or rebuffed,' Brian continued to a soundtrack of the courting couple's enthusiastic sighs and grunts. Suddenly, he turned to face me, his heavy arm still around my shoulders, keeping me nice and warm.

'That's a bit of a bummer,' I said with a nervous giggle.

'Isn't it just?'

'Mmm,' I mumbled. 'It really is. A bummer.'

I was burbling. Another giggle. Almost hysterical this time. Brian was looking at me in a very funny way. Was he moving in on me, I asked myself? Surely not. It just wasn't possible. I mean, I was *me*. Lizzie Jordan. He couldn't possibly fancy me, could he? I had bigger spots than tits in those days. It simply wasn't an option. I held my breath in anticipation of the moment when he would tell me that he really fancied Jemima from Mary's neurophysiology class and ask my advice to help him sort the matter out.

'I suppose that the only thing I can do is be brave and throw myself into this scary thing head first,' he murmured. 'Will she or won't she? I'm really not sure. But I'm beginning to think she just might.'

He was so close to me now that his face had gone out of focus and I had to close my eyes to stop them from crossing. But before I could open them again, I felt the soft brush of his lips upon mine. Ohmigod! He was kissing me. It *was* me. He had been talking about me!

'Bri-urghh!'

He wasn't stopping.

Chiming bells and crashing waves! A heavenly choir struck up a quick chorus between my ears. A herd of wildebeest stampeded frantically through my stomach, annihilating the butterflies that usually lived there as they went.

The arm that had been draped so casually around my shoulders moved down towards my waist as Brian pulled me on to his shiny lycra-ed lap. As I relaxed, I let his tongue slip inside my mouth. Brian's hand slid smoothly up the back of my jumper and pressed against my chilly flesh. I searched for a way into his body-suit but couldn't find one, so I had to wait until we were back in my room before I found out whether he had a hairy back or not. Mercifully, he didn't.

I don't know how we even got back to college that night. We kissed all the way and I didn't notice the route we took. But we ended up in my room somehow and despite it being just a little cramped for the two of us in my single bed with its lethal mattress (the broken springs were forever getting me in the kidneys), Brian and I were dead to the world when Mary hammered on the door at eight the next morning.

'Liz,' she shouted. 'Lizzie. Open the door, quickly. I've done a terrible thing. A really, really terrible thing! I feel awful!'

'Then go to confession!' shouted Brian, before I could put my hand over his mouth.

There was a moment of horrible, loaded silence as I imagined my visitor registering the strange man's voice coming from inside my room.

'Have you got someone in there?' asked Mary at top volume. I pictured her with her eye to the keyhole now. Only thank goodness there wasn't a keyhole in my door because we had some kind of new fangled magnetic key system in the halls that was forever going wrong. 'Who have you got in there, Liz? Are you with a man? It's not Brian, is it?'

'The very same,' Brian obliged, not sensing, as I had, that it was that time of the day when he should just shut up, climb out through the window and wait on the little concrete balcony outside until summoned back in; so that I could open the door to Mary and pretend that no one had been in the bed with me all along. So much for his psychological insights into people's real feelings for each other.

'Let me in!' Mary demanded. She sounded half-hysterical now. 'Let me in there at once, Lizzie Jordan.'

'We've got to put our clothes on first,' Brian told her, digging me in even deeper. I was already racing around the room picking up random bras, pants and socks and flinging them on in no particular order. At one point I found myself wearing two pairs of knickers. Brian only had his ridiculous lycra cat-suit to get into, so he was dressed in half the time and opened the door to Mary while I still had only one leg in my jeans.

'Morning, Mary.'

'I don't believe it!' she shrieked, catching me *in flagrante*. 'I really don't believe it. How could you?'

Then she disappeared down the hall without waiting for any kind of explanation at all.

'What's wrong with her?' asked Brian.

Mary avoided me for the rest of the day. And it turned out, as I had sort of guessed, she was avoiding Bill as well. So much for Brian's theory about hidden passions running deep. As far as Mary was concerned, when that long-suppressed passion for Bicycle Bill finally broke through the surface of her chilly disdain like an oil drill hitting paydirt, someone should have stuck a finger in the hole before too much spilled over. She later told me she had screamed when she saw the hair on Bill's back despite the fact that I had warned her more than once what she would find if she ever got him out of his lycra.

'And all the time you were getting off with Brian,' she said accusingly, when I finally caught up with her in the queue for the kebab van. 'You made MPL with Brian Coren after what you said to me in the chip shop.'

MPL. Mad passionate love. It had been pretty much like that. I blushed at the very thought of it.

'But . . .' I tried to explain Brian's theory to her, that he had told me that she and Bill had been burning to get together and find out that theirs was true love.

Wasn't there a part of the bargain we had made in the chippy that excused my behaviour if she found true love first?

'True love? With Bill? Oh, for goodness' sake, Liz. I was pissed,' she spat. 'You would have tried to stop me. If you were really my friend.'

'I didn't realise,' I said all meekly. 'And I swear I didn't know that Brian was going to make a move on me either until he actually did it. I tried to stop him. Well, I didn't try to stop him,' I admitted. 'But I swear I didn't start it.'

'Oh, forget it,' she said eventually. 'Brian obviously wanted you. He's wanted you all along. And it's not even about that anyway,' she added hurriedly. 'I'm not jealous of *you* getting off with Brian, Lizzie. I'm just confused about Bill and a bit pissed off that our happy little gang has to be broken up now. Everything is ruined.'

'What? Why should it be broken up? We can still all hang out together. You, me, Bill and Brian. We can all still be friends.'

'Not now that Bill has seen my bottom, we can't. The balance has shifted, Lizzie.'

And so it had. Though I didn't really notice it then.

In fact, later that night, we were all in the bar together again, exactly as we had been twenty-four hours earlier, before the life-shattering events of the *Two Items of Clothing Night*, as it later came to be known. Mary was sitting next to Bill and I was sitting next to Brian. The only real difference I could see was that when Jim the one-eyed barman called time, Brian walked me back to my room and stayed there all night making mad, passionate love.

Until I met Brian, I'd never really known what the fuss was about when it came to sex. My experience of this great international pastime had been limited to a single-figured number of inexpert drunken fumbles. Even in the long-term (i.e. three-month long) relationship I had had the year before Brian's arrival at Oxford, with a rather *naice* boy called James, it seemed that we always had to be completely pissed before we could have sex. And it had to be with the lights out (not at my insistence). And I was categorically *not* allowed to look at him while he did it *to* me as I lay completely still without touching him unless *he* asked me to. I later discovered on the college grapevine that this was a trait peculiar to boys who had been to his internationally renowned public school.

Anyway, with experiences such as that behind me, it was hardly surprising that I was one of the few people who agreed with miserable old Boy George and Morrissey that a cup of tea was probably better than a night's worth of horizontal aerobics. Brian changed all that. He turned me on by pressing buttons I had previously suspected were broken. His obvious adoration of my body eventually even managed to strip away all the shyness I carried about with my cellulite.

I had never imagined that having sex could make me feel so sexy even when I wasn't actually in bed with my new transatlantic lover. I wondered if other people could sense the Ready-Brek glow I felt lingering about me hours after a night in Brian's hunky arms. Could other people see the difference in my walk as I stepped out of the lecture hall? (I'm talking about a newly confident wiggle in my step, not a waddle brought on by friction, by the way.)

The only pity about the whole thing was that I felt I couldn't tell Mary all about it. Before the whole Bill/Brian Two Items of Clothing Night debacle, there hadn't been anything Mary and I didn't talk about. Her secrets were mine and mine were hers. We spoke about our love lives in no-holds-barred detail. The people, the positions, the *smells*. Honestly, we were disgusting. Now, however, I sensed that it wouldn't exactly be appreciated if I burst into Mary's room full of tales about my wonderful new love life. Hers wasn't exactly steaming at that point.

After the Bill episode, which had her swearing that she would join a convent straight after graduating, Mary set her heart on a post-graduate student called Ralph who had five ear-rings in each ear, a sapphire nose stud and a tattoo of a dolphin on his backside (according to the rumour). Ralph had been assigned to be Mary's supervisor while she undertook the cruel and unusual experiments that formed part of her psychology dissertation.

The idea was that Ralph, being young and funky, would stimulate her interest in the subject she had chosen (the acquisition of spider phobias in children – she told me with a yawn) but in fact the quality of her work went rapidly downhill as she spent fruitless hours in the psychology library pondering whether this post-grad with his pierced tongue also had a Prince Albert (Mary had a thing about foreskins). I never did get to the bottom of whether she actually wanted him to have a barbell through the end of his penis or not. And it didn't seem as though Mary would be finding out anytime soon either – all her attempts to find herself locked in a lab with him overnight had failed – hence, I didn't want to incur her wrath by appearing to crow that my love life was going swimmingly.

But we did all hang out together. Bill, Brian, Mary and I. And though it was never quite as jolly and easy as it had been before now that Bill's every *double entendre* was inevitably taken personally by Mary, it was almost as good. Besides, I wasn't too worried, because things between Brian and me were much better than before, of course. I felt guilty about breaking the pact I had made with Mary in the chip shop, but hoped that she would understand. She said she did, after the 'one-night thing' I had with Brian had lasted for over three months.

'I'm over it,' she said. 'Back then, I thought it would be quite nice to get off with Brian myself, but seeing how soft and soppy he is over you, I realise I would have found his overly affectionate nature quite cloying actually.'

OK, so it wasn't exactly complimentary, but I took it as my green card to keep hanging in there.

CHAPTER FIVE

W e had a wonderful winter and spring term together, Brian and I, but as summer approached, the quiet evenings we had once enjoyed – sometimes just sitting in each other's company reading out of boring text-books – began to be tinged with melancholy.

At the end of the spring term, I had tried to remain disinterested as Brian typed out his amazingly impressive curriculum vitae on my computer and sent letters to companies in America asking them for work experience during the long vacation. I persuaded him to apply to companies in London too, so that we could at least have a slim chance of spending the whole summer together. And he did. But it was an American company which eventually offered him the most interesting internship, not to mention a free flight back home to take up the position.

Six weeks before Brian left for the States, I found a flight number and departure time scribbled on a pad by his bedside and suddenly knew the exact moment when he would be flying away from me. Of course, his return to America didn't necessarily mean that I wouldn't ever see him again, but it did mean the end of 'us' as I had come to think of us. I knew that much. I wasn't stupid. Brian and I had had a conversation about that aspect of things very early on. About how hard it could be to keep long-distance relationships going, especially when the people involved were still so young and had so much to be getting on with back in their respective countries. Back when we had had that conversation, however, I didn't really expect our dalliance to last long enough for the question finally to come up for real.

A week before he had to go home to the United States, Brian and I hired a car and drove out of Oxford for the day. We took pictures of each other outside Blenheim Palace. Brian assured me that one day he would be back to buy the place. We had lunch in an oak-beamed tea-room. Brian bought a little model of a thatched cottage for his mother – 'She's nuts about English stuff,' he said – and discovered later that it had not only been made of china but in China as well. We did a whirlwind tour of Cotswold villages. As whirlwind as you can get when you're stuck in a Renault Clio behind a Massey Ferguson and a flock of sheep.

And we ended the day at the Rollright Stones. Bill, Mary and I had discovered this little-known stone circle in our first year. Mary had seen the circle marked on a map and thought we should have a spiritual picnic there one Sunday afternoon. We packed peanut butter and banana sandwiches and set off from college in Bill's battered Mini. With Mary navigating we were quickly lost. Bill said it didn't matter since he could navigate using the power of the local ley lines.

'I can feel the stones,' he assured us. 'I'll just go with my instincts and we'll be there in no time.'

We ended up going twenty miles in the exact opposite direction.

Brian and I arrived at the Rollright Stones for our own adventure just as the sun was setting. We walked around them reverently at first – we'd got into a bit of a coach-tour mentality that day – while I told him the legend of the Stones, that it was impossible to count them. We counted round three times and came up with three different numbers. I told him about the Rollright Stones expedition I had taken with Bill and Mary. The thunderstorm that broke when we finally found them. We took it as a sign from the heavens and got drenched instead of staying in the car.

'I can feel the spirit of the stones washing all the negativity out of me,' Mary had said at the time.

A busload of Japanese tourists took pictures of us driving back to Oxford in our sodden underwear.

'Sounds like a pretty special trip,' Brian said.

I couldn't begin to tell him how much more special it felt to be there alone with him that afternoon. We tried to count the stones one more time. Then Brian and I chose the comfiest-looking rock and settled down against it to watch the sun slip away behind the hills. Brian took my hand and brought it to his lips for a kiss.

'You will always be special to me,' he murmured.

That almost made me cry right away. Suddenly the sun seemed to be setting on something more than a Tuesday in the middle of June.

'I love you,' I told him. It seemed like the only thing to say.

'I know,' said Brian. He didn't say he loved me back but I took his reply as a 'ditto' and squeezed his hand hard. 'But you know how hard it would be for us to keep this going once I'm back in the States,' he continued. 'And I do have to go back to the States.'

There was silence for a beat.

'You could still change your mind and work in London, couldn't you?' I tried. 'There are big banks in London too. American banks even. I bet the one you're going to work for has a branch here somewhere. Can't they arrange a transfer? It would save them the cost of a flight.'

'London isn't New York, Liz. That's where my family is. And you know I love my family. I've missed them while I've been here.'

'I love my family too, but I would go to New York like a shot. If someone asked me,' I hinted.

'We have to finish our degrees,' he said, conspicuously missing the opportunity to make that invitation.

'Do you think,' I asked him then, 'if we had met after finishing our degrees. If we were both, say, twenty-five or thirty now instead of just twenty-one

. . . Do you think that we might have made a proper go of it?'

'We have made a proper go of it,' he told me firmly. 'I will remember this special year I've shared with you for the rest of my life.' His fingers tightened around mine.

I tried to smile, but my eyes were stinging with the effort of holding back the tears. It seemed so unfair, yet oddly incredibly romantic at the same time. Forces beyond our control were tearing us apart. We said nothing while the sun finally sank from view, then we got to our feet, still holding hands, and walked in silence to the car.

When we went to bed that night I felt like Shakespeare's Juliet, who only has until dawn with her Romeo, and knows that the love to be squeezed into that short spell of darkness has to last a lifetime. Even though Brian and I actually had another week until we said goodbye for good, that sunset was our final act.

On the day that Brian finally left for America, I didn't go with him to the airport. He asked if I would but I'm afraid I can't stand goodbyes at the best of times. There's something about waving someone off too extravagantly at a train station or an airport that seems to tempt the gods to prevent them from ever coming back again. And I wanted Brian to come back. I wanted it more than anything in the world. I would have given the rest of my life for another year in his company.

For at least twenty-four hours after I closed my door on the unhappy sight of his retreating back and slumped, sad shoulders, I expected to hear a knock and find him standing in the hallway with a bunch of flowers, desperate to tell me that he realised he loved me after all and simply could not go away again. Not ever. How on earth could he have pretended that he could?

But there was no knock. Not until Mary dropped by at six o'clock to ask why no one had seen me for over a day and to find out whether I wanted to go to the kebab van with her. She was leaving for home next morning and said she couldn't wait to go back to London this time. The post-graduate with the tongue-ring had rebuffed her advances at an end of term party and she wanted to get out of his way. Bill had already left for the holidays. He would be cycling in the Himalayas this time. No more fruit-farming for him.

I had made vague plans to stay behind for a while and catch up with some coursework in the library (I'd done bugger all real work that year – too busy snogging), but suddenly being alone in college didn't seem such a great idea. Far from being free from distractions, with my friends all gone home to their families, I knew it was more likely that instead of working I would only be able to sit in the library and gaze into space while I remembered being in the exact same place a week before, or a fortnight before, scribbling silly soppy notes to push beneath Brian's nose while he pretended to be immersed in some dry text on economics; fondling his knee under the cover of a table; secret trysts in the library toilets. I knew it would be too much to be surrounded by all those memories. I would have to get away too.

I shrugged on my jacket and followed Mary down to the dining hall without even bothering to brush my hair. I knew I looked a real state and I didn't feel like saying much, but Mary hardly seemed to notice. She was too busy chatting about the plans she had for the holidays, which included a serious diet that would miraculously turn her into a supermodel and make the foolish post-graduate rue the day he had ever refused to kiss her with his nasty pierced tongue.

'Next year is going to be great,' she said, uncharacteristically positively for Mary. 'You know, I'm thinking of getting my belly-button pierced as soon as I get back to London.'

'Next year there won't be any Brian,' I murmured. It was the first thing I had said for about half an hour.

'Yes, well,' she said dryly. 'It's a shame he had to go home, but life does go on, Lizzie. Perhaps next year you won't neglect your other friends as much as you have done.'

'I'm sorry if you think I've neglected you,' I said, feeling rather surprised.

'That's OK,' she said softly. I wondered whether she thought she had been just a bit harsh. She put her arm around my shoulders and gave me a half-hearted hug. 'I know what it's like to be in love.'

I nodded, thinking that perhaps she was slightly over-estimating the strength of her feelings for Ralph the post-grad, but grateful for her empathy all the same.

CHAPTER SIX

I spent the summer working at the same lens-grinding factory where I had spent my summer holiday a year before. Apart from the itinerant holiday workers – other unfortunate students like myself who couldn't afford to flee the country till September – the staff at Greville's Lenses was largely unchanged. In fact, everything at Greville's Lenses was unchanged. Irene the tea lady even remembered how I liked my coffee.

'Had a good year at university, have you?' she asked. 'Don't look like you've learned all that much to me.'

She said that every time I saw her. Twice a day. Every day. But oh, I told my melancholy self as I mooned about the office, if only she knew how much I *had* learned since I last carried a clipboard around that stinking, screaming factory. I was a totally different person now. I was no longer content to while away my precious free time ticking off numbers on a clipboard in a factory where the windows had been white-washed to stop the inmates from staring out at the real world and getting ideas above their station. In fact, I had never been content to do it, but now it was even worse than before.

I spent my days in a kind of trance, trying to block out the reality of my grand vacation in hell. When the factory bell rang to signify that it was time to down tools at five o'clock, I tried not to think of Brian in New York, five hours behind me, perhaps just going out for lunch with his high-flying boss. When I staggered home from the stinking pub where I went drinking each night with punk-haired Paula, who was working at the factory to fund her degree in religion and dance studies, I tried doubly hard not to think of Brian just setting out for a night on the town with new friends I had a dreadful feeling I would never meet. Our lives were worlds apart now. Literally and figuratively.

The following September, Mary, Bill and I returned to college as finalists. Our tutors gave us all the pre-dictable lectures about how much harder we were going to have to work in this last year for those all-important exams that would help map out the rest of our lives. The job-seekers 'milk round' had started. My pigeon-hole was already stuffed full of leaflets from accountancy firms eager to sign up the best graduates in return for a pitiful starting salary and a free ballpoint pen. We finalists were given bigger rooms in the halls of residence to spread our numerous books about in. New freshers wandered around the quad making friends and swapping A-level results.

'We're the dinosaurs now,' commented Mary, as we watched two freshers get excited about the prospect of another college dinner (they'd learn – even if it did take a bout of e-coli). *Dinosaurs*. It was what we had called the third years when we were new in town. Bill even looked like a dinosaur now. He had spent his summer cycling up and down mountains and came back tanned like a mummified corpse and with his lower intestine infested by a strange worm that meant he could eat his body weight in chocolate and still not get fat. Mary was spittingly jealous (she had decided to put off having her belly-button pierced until she lost half a stone, though perhaps it was more to do with the fact that Ralph the post-grad had suffered a nervous breakdown over the long vacation and ended up joining a buddhist monastery).

There were new Americans in college too. Another batch of economics students from the very college Brian had attended wandered round the ancient halls I had grown so used to and said things like 'How quaint,' when they banged their heads on a low oak beam. I couldn't help but be interested in them. I even looked one out on my hallway and asked her if she needed any help settling in. Her name was Megan Sanderson. She was from New York too. She had a comfortingly familiar accent and an orthodontically enhanced smile a mile wide. But had she any news of Brian Coren? No, she didn't think she knew him. 'It's a big place, New York,' she laughed. I didn't bother with her much after that and she quickly found friends of her own.

When he first went back home, Brian had written at least twice a week and I wrote twice a week back. Which one of us tailed off first, I'm not quite sure. But three weeks into the new term I realised that I hadn't written to Brian at all that week. I'd been busy. Meeting a new man.

Phil was everything that Brian hadn't been. English. Tall (Brian was only just taller than me). And as blond as Brian was dark. Phil played on the college rugby team. Brian was only interested in indoor sports. Bearing all this in mind, you can probably understand why, when I met Phil, it seemed like a good idea to get off with him to help exorcise the painful memory of the love of my life (so far). And Mary was seeing his best mate, so it meant that we could go out on foursome dates. I would now admit that Bill and Mary had drifted apart since the two items of clothing incident. Bill now chose to hang out with a bunch of guys from his department who were intent on hacking their way into the Pentagon before they finished their degrees.

Ironically, I got together with Phil at another 'Two Items of Clothing party'. He was wearing lycra cycling shorts and a ready-tied bow-tie with red polka dots. I was wearing a fleecy all-in-one sleep-suit that I had brought to college that term just in case such an event should arise, and a bobble hat – so I was getting free drinks. The whole affair might not have happened at all if Phil and I hadn't both been getting free drinks. I knew I hardly looked alluring in my overgrown baby-gro with a bunny on the pocket. And he wasn't looking all that hot either, having thrown up six pints into a wastepaper basket shortly before I arrived. But Mary's advice was ringing in my ears. I needed to move on from Brian and she had convinced me that there is no better cure for a broken heart than getting your talons into a fresh one. So I cornered Phil as he emerged from the gents and thus began a very sorry period in the history of my love life.

He was sweet. He was generous. But if he ever picked up a newspaper at all, it was only to read the sport and the cartoons, and our intellectual discussions were strictly of the 'If a polar bear and an African lion met on neutral ground, which one would win the fight?' variety. Not at all surprisingly, I still felt as though something was missing from my life. Brian had obviously left a hole that was not going to be filled with just any old warm-blooded body.

Which makes it all the more peculiar that when Phil finally pulled the plug on our dalliance two terms later I reacted quite so strongly. Seven days of solid weeping, followed by a fortnight when I would only get out of bed to limp down to the canteen for some cream crackers, and another long month or so of trying to corner Phil whenever he came into college for a rugby match, or dinner, or to pick up some returned coursework.

Phil told everyone that I was a psycho, although I suspect that he was secretly quite delighted by my over-emotional reaction to his departure. My friends couldn't understand it.

'He's an ape,' said Mary. Again and again and again. She was getting rather fed up of finding me sobbing on her doorstep night after night, waiting to ask her if John, her boyfriend, had told her anything that Phil, my ex-boyfriend, might have said about me.

'He said he's thinking of getting you sectioned,' she said, one night.

'That must mean he cares about me,' I translated. 'If he's so concerned about my mental health that he wants to have me taken into hospital against my will.'

'I think he's more concerned that your continuous weeping presence outside his room isn't doing much for his pulling power,' said Mary dryly. 'You know, Liz. I just can't understand what's going on in your head. All the time that you were actually with him, you did nothing but complain about what a neanderthal he is. You used to nod off when he talked to you, for heaven's sake. And don't you remember telling me that he thought foreplay was something to do with golf?'

'He's really sensitive,' I assured her. 'He said he could tell that I was the kind of girl who liked clitoral stimulation.'

'All girls like clitoral stimulation,' sighed Mary. 'But did he ever try it? Look, all the time you were together, you wanted something different. But now he's chucked you, you've gone all *Fatal Attraction* on him.'

'I would never hurt an animal,' I retorted, thinking of the rabbit.

'So what is it then? What's wrong with you these days?'

'I think I must have loved him.'

'Rubbish. You were much happier with Brian, but you didn't cry this much when he left.'

At the time, the implication of Mary's words went in one ear and out the other. But now, looking back, I can see that I made an utter tit of myself when Phil chucked me, not because Phil chucked me, but because the experience had opened up the scar left by Brian's return to the States. I wasn't mourning Phil, I was mourning the loss of Brian. I think I was also far happier to be in romantic misery than having to think about my finals, which were the bane of all our lives at the time.

Needless to say, I did no revision – in fact, the night before my first exam, I could be found, not cramming for my Middle English paper with the other finalists in the library as I should have been, but sitting on the windowsill outside Phil's fourth-floor room, threatening to jump out on to the High Street if he didn't get back together with me. I failed most of the papers I took but, miraculously, so did almost everyone else on my course (it must have been a very bad year), and so I actually managed to limp away from college with a mediocre 2:2. A Desmond, as Bill frequently quipped.

'Desmond Tutu?' he nudged me. 'Tu-tu? Geddit?'

I got it all right.

The last time I saw Phil was when we went to fetch our results. All that heartache he had caused me (or so I thought at the time) and he got a bloody 2:1.

Next time I heard from Brian, he too had completed his degree (first class, *naturellement*) and had taken up a pretty junior (so he modestly said) position with a Japanese bank in New York City. Meanwhile, I went straight back to Solihull and spent six months living at home and getting under my parents' feet while I 'found myself' and decided what I really wanted to do with my life. Or rather, what anyone would let me do with a mediocre 2:2 in English Literature. Teach, perhaps? suggested my sarcastic tutor.

Perhaps I should have taken his advice, but I couldn't motivate myself to fill out a single application form. Every night before I went to sleep I would promise myself that the next day I would set to job hunting in earnest. And every morning I would hit the snooze button for an extra half hour every half hour until eleven o'clock, getting up just in time to catch *Richard and Judy* on daytime TV, getting dressed just before Mum and Dad came home from work.

At Christmas, Brian wrote to tell me that he had already been promoted to a more senior position at the bank and given a hefty raise. My parents warned me that if I didn't get myself a job (any job at all) in the New Year I might be needing the cardboard boxes that my Christmas presents had come in.

In January, Brian wrote to tell me about his sparkling new warehouse apartment in New York's trendy Soho district. I, having finally worn out my welcome at home, packed my green army surplus rucksack and moved into a filthy squat in the somewhat less trendy East End of London, where nobody really cared whether I got a job or not, as long as I rolled a good joint. I was still getting up at eleven o'clock, still watching *Richard and Judy*, but never getting dressed at all some days.

Occasionally I would get a phone call from an old college pal. A half hour of torture filled with their high-flying news and promises that one day we would 'do lunch'. It seemed that everyone but me was going into accountancy. I told myself that they were selling out. Meanwhile I was blazing a trail for individuality. I told myself that I was actually exercising my creativity by making up jobs I was supposed to have applied for on the form I had to fill in fortnightly to qualify for my Job Seeker's Allowance.

A year after graduating, Brian was in charge of six people in his office. I was typing letters and doing the filing for seven different people (six of whom were considerably younger and probably thicker than me) as a temp at an East End packaging factory. On good days I managed to spend up to an hour on loo breaks. I don't know whether this had something to do with why my colleagues never asked me to go to the pub with them.

Two years later, Brian was responsible for a staff of fourteen and spent his working week jetting between smart city offices in New York and Los Angeles. I had at least moved out of the squat (didn't have much choice. My squatmates and I came home from a club one cold winter's night to discover that the squat's owner had made a bonfire out of all our belongings on the front lawn); though the flat I now legitimately paid rent on would have given the squat a good run for its money in the squalor stakes, and my new flatmates – Dizzy Seema and Fat Joe (he introduced himself as that, can you believe it – though he may have meant 'phat' as in 'cool' rather than tubby) – seemed to be quite the weirdest people I had ever met.

But at least I was no longer doing the typing for seven people in packaging either – they had the temp agency replace me with a bubbly Australian because they *didn't like my attitude*. (I think it might have been my constant depressive monologues about the best way to kill oneself with implements found about the average office that finally helped them make the decision to *downshift* me.) I tried to seem grateful when the temp agency offered me one more chance and sent me on a two-week assignment at Corbett and Daughter Estate Agency. I tried to feel lucky when I found myself on a rolling contract there when Harriet Corbett's stinky lap-dog took a tail-wagging, leg-humping liking to me. I can think of no other reason at all for my successful sideways (and slightly downwards wage-wise) move into property management.

Not that I said any of this in my letters to Brian. I confined comments on my miserable new life of data input and cold baked beans straight from the tin to: 'I'm well. I'm working hard. I've just moved into a new flat.' He didn't have to know that my new room was the size of an airing cupboard and that the plumbing in the bathroom never worked so we had to fill the bath from a kettle. Or more specifically, from a big saucepan of water that had to be boiled on the hob since none of the plug points in the kitchen worked either so we couldn't actually use the kettle.

Every time Brian wrote back he begged me to go into more detail about my life in London. He said he knew that I must be up to something interesting. I started to confine my correspondence to postcards that allowed me just enough space to write (in massive handwriting): 'Too busy to write. Sorry. Will call soon. I promise.' Except that I never called. I hoped Brian would imagine that my high-flying new job was taking up too much of my time to allow me to write long letters to old friends, without taking offence and stopping his much-appreciated letters to me.

'Sounds like you've come a long way,' he wrote in one particularly lovely letter – four pages chock-full of amazing events and funny anecdotes about his life in response to my half a postcard of fact-free drivel.

Oh yeah, I'd come a long, long way since we were both fresh-faced students at college. Unfortunately, I'd been travelling in quite the wrong direction.

CHAPTER SEVEN

Yep. My London life. What a bloody whirl.

Dear Reader,

You will no doubt be relieved to know that, after many months of fruitless searching, I have finally found the perfect handbag. What a relief! My little sac of joy arrived just in time for top designer (and close personal friend) Sebastian Heron's birthday party at Marco Pierre White's new eaterie, The Taj Mahal. I had been sick with worry about what I might wear for such a momentous occasion, but with the bag in hand, my conundrum was solved. The bag is a perfect little strapless number in the softest pink leather from Hermes. I popped into Alexander McQueen's and had him whip up a cat-suit to match.

The party was a gas, as you can probably imagine, though the new Chanel lipstick I had been on a waiting list for since February was all but kissed off by the time I got to the birthday boy. As usual, Sebastian's guest list read like a Who's Who of the media world. I got stuck in the corner with the younger one from Oasis (him of the mono-brow), who asked me if I thought I could get his lovely wife a job like mine (he's feeling the pinch since big brother went solo). But it's not all fun, fun, fun, I had to tell him. In fact, I had to leave the fabulous party early to fly to Mauritius at the crack of dawn to report on a new hotel for this very paper.

Anyway, I was in such a hurry to get to the airport without breaking any traffic bye-laws that I forgot to pack my suncream and had to spend my first day in the shade while the lovely receptionist sent to Paris for my favourite brand. I was most upset to lose out on a whole day's sunbathing but decided that I would just have to make do with being pale and mysterious. Almost as good. At least Jack Nicholson seemed to think so when he took me to dinner that very night . . .

I put down my newspaper and picked up my sandwiches.

No Jack Nicholson for me that day. Just tuna mayonnaise. Again. Even though it was my birthday.

As I bit into the thin white sliced and a blob of tuna mayo landed on the newspaper, right on the smirking picture of Arabella Gilbert that accompanied her nauseating column in *The Daily*, I wondered why I tortured myself by reading it. Every time I picked up the glossy supplement she wrote for, I had the sort of shaky feeling of anticipation that a drug addict must get before a fix. I knew I didn't 'need' to read her column. I knew that for at least an hour after I had read her column I would be overcome by feelings of social inadequacy and bottomless depression. But I just couldn't seem to help myself.

I could hardly believe that Arabella Gilbert and I lived in the same city. The places she went to – the most fashionable new restaurants, the private drinking clubs that charged more than a month's worth of my skimpy wages for membership – I didn't even know where they were. While Arabella Gilbert had a fistful of golden credit cards, I wasn't even in credit on my Sainsburys' Reward points.

I was about to sink into a serious blue mood when the telephone rang. I cursed the caller through a mouthful of mayo. I was on my own in the office. My boss, Mad Harriet, the once-gorgeous sixties debutante now gone to seed, was getting her hair done in preparation for a clandestine meeting with her married lover, Bunny. Rupert, the 'property valuer' and the only other employee at Corbett and Daughter Estate Agents but me, had taken the opportunity to go and browse through classic car showrooms with his imaginary bonus (and anything else he could reach through his trouser pockets) in hand. So it was I who had to abandon lunch and answer the phone. As usual. I hoped it was a wrong number and not someone who actually wanted to buy a house because that might entail paperwork and I didn't want to have to do paperwork – not on a Friday afternoon. But I needn't have worried. It was just Seema, my flatmate, who had been off sick all week from her job at the video shop with the kind of cystitis you deserve after a particularly dirty weekend with a Marine.

'Do I look like I'm your secretary?' she asked me irritably, without bothering with such niceties as 'hello' or 'happy birthday'. She had still been in bed when I'd left the house that morning, although she had left a suitably rude birthday card propped up against the toaster for me to find over breakfast.

'Eh?'

'I said, do I look like I'm your secretary, Lizzie Jordan? Some idiot just called here for you and when I said that you weren't in, he asked if I was your blinkin' secretary. Honestly. The bloody cheek of it.'

I was just as surprised as she was. 'Did he say who he was?'

'I didn't ask him, did I? But he had an American accent if that means anything to you. East coast, I think, though I can't really be sure. All sound the same to me. Anyway, if you've been going round telling people that I'm your secretary, Elizabeth Jordan . . .' She went on.

But I was already on another planet. An American planet. The caller had an American accent. I only really knew one American, so, unless I had been unexpectedly invited to appear on *The Jerry Springer Show* to talk about why I couldn't hold down a relationship a job my drink, I had a pretty good idea who had called.

'And you can get a pint of milk on the way home,' Seema continued. 'Fat Joe finished the last of it this morning but he says he's having one of his attacks and can't go out to get another one. I certainly can't go out either. I've got to be within three feet of a loo at all times. I'm still in agony, in case you're interested.'

I wasn't.

'Did he say he'd call back?'

'What?' Seema snapped.

'The American? Did he say he'd call back or leave a message for me or anything?' I asked in hope.

'I don't know. I had to hang up on him to run to the bathroom. But I'm sure he'll call back if it was really important. I didn't know you knew any exotic foreigners anyway,' she added with just the faintest spark of interest in her voice.

'Just the one,' I told her.

'Yeah. Well, don't forget to get the milk on your way home. Semi-skimmed. And a carton of cranberry juice if you can afford it.'

She hung up.

I replaced the receiver slowly and pushed my chair away from my desk. I knew one exotic foreigner. It was Brian. Brian had called.

I felt suddenly very hot. A blush crept over my body as though he had just walked into the room. I pushed away the remains of my tuna mayo sandwich. All thoughts of lunch left me as my stomach contracted in a peculiar mix of anticipation and apprehension.

Brian never called. But he had called. Good news or bad news? What did he want?

That evening, back in Balham, I was on tenterhooks as I waited for *the call*.

Brian would call back. I knew he would. And every time Fat Joe or Seema went anywhere near the telephone I would plead to know for how long they expected to talk. When Seema's mother phoned, I almost told her that her beloved only daughter wasn't in, in order to free up the phone for my far more important call. But I didn't, and they seemed to talk for ever just to punish me for my impatience. I paced the room, rolling my eyes in desperation every time Seema tried and failed to cut short the conversation with her mama.

'Why don't you just phone him?' Seema asked me reasonably, when she had finally managed to convince her mother that: a) she was eating properly, and b) yes, she was wrapped up warm against the bitter August weather – Seema's mother wore two buttoned-up cardigans over her sari at all times.

'Because I'm already way over my overdraft limit this month,' I told her. 'I can't afford to go making long-distance calls to America and I can't call him and hang up after ten seconds, can I? What would that look like? We haven't actually spoken to each other in years. Just letters and e-mails. We'll have loads to talk about. If he calls me, we can talk all night long and I won't have to worry about the cost.'

'But we've only just had a phone bill,' Seema reminded me. 'It's three months until the next one comes. You might have had a windfall by then. I say you should call him. He might want you to jet out to the States, all expenses paid, for a surprise birthday present but if he doesn't hear from you tonight, the invitation's off.'

'He might do, mightn't he?' I said stupidly. It was my birthday. So I picked up the phone and started to dial the massively long number that would put me straight through to him in his Wall Street office. It was picked up at the other end by an answering service. I put the phone down straight away. No point wasting money to talk to a machine.

'Oh, you should have left a message,' Seema sighed. 'So that he's reminded to call you back. I love it when I get a machine instead of the person I'm trying to get hold of. It means that you've done your bit but they then have to pay to call you back.'

'Good point,' I said. I dialled again. I held my breath as the connection was made. The phone was picked up. This time, by Brian.

'Brian Coren.'

I said nothing. I was still waiting for the beep.

'Hello? This is Brian Coren. Who's calling?'

'Oh,' I suddenly realised that my call had been picked up. 'Oh, Brian. I didn't expect to get you. I was calling to talk to your machine.'

'Is that Liz?' he asked excitedly. 'Lizzie Jordan? Is it really you?'

'Er. Yes. It's me. It's Liz. You called me this morning?'

'Oh, Liz. It's so good to hear your voice again,' he said. 'It's been so long. I'd forgotten how English you sound.'

'Oh, everybody speaks like this over here,' I joked. 'Was there something you wanted, Brian?'

'Sorry?'

'When you called today. Did you want something?'

'To wish you a Happy Birthday of course, my darling.'

'Thanks for remembering. Is that all?'

'And to touch base,' he said defensively. 'You sound flustered, Liz. Do you have to get off the phone to go someplace in a hurry? I don't want to keep you talking if you do. I know how busy you must be with your thriving property business and all.'

I could hardly tell him that I didn't think I could afford to pay the resulting phone bill.

'Er, no. No. It's just that you usually e-mail me when you've got something to say.'

'Yeah. But don't you think that's just a bit impersonal sometimes?'

Sure it was impersonal. But it was charged at local rate, I said to myself.

'And I wanted to wish you a Happy Birthday *personally*. How are you?' Brian continued jovially. 'Working hard?'

'Oh, yes. Much too hard. You know how it is.'

'I certainly do. Lots of new projects?'

'Oh yes. Lots of new projects on the go. But how about you, Brian?' I didn't want to have to make up one of those new projects so I quickly changed the focus.

'Well,' he exhaled slowly. 'For the first time in my career, I actually seem to have things pretty much under control here at the bank. I've been going home before midnight lately,' he laughed. 'Can you believe it? I'm practically taking half days as far as my workmates are concerned.'

'You always worked too hard.'

'Yeah, like you. But that's what my physician said too. She said I ought to take a holiday and shake my muscles out a bit or I'll be an old man before my time.'

'Wouldn't want that,' I told him.

'No. Definitely not. So I'm going to.'

'Going to what?'

'Take a holiday, dufus. Next week. Just like my physician suggested.'

'That's nice. Where are you going?' I asked naively. 'Somewhere sunny? Nice and hot?'

'Well, I was rather hoping,' he began. 'You know how it is, Liz . . . You get so wrapped up in your work that you don't have time to meet nice people you could go to nice places with. I don't want to go somewhere exotic but just end up spending the whole week on my own, catching up on my reading, so I was hoping that perhaps I might be welcome in London.'

I must have been quiet for too long.

'Are you still there, Liz? Lizzie?' he called. 'Has the line gone dead or something?'

'Of course I'm still here,' I squeaked.

'Oh, good. Look, it'd just be for three days or so. I may have to go to Zurich for business anyway, so I thought I'd leave the States a little bit early and drop by to see you *en route* to Switzerland.'

'Uh!' I squeaked.

'I guess you're probably pretty tied up with work, and this is very short notice, so I'd stay at a hotel, of course. Perhaps you could recommend somewhere nice that's not too far from your place so we can meet up in the evenings.'

'What?'

'A hotel? Can you suggest a nice hotel where I could stay? My budget's pretty flexible. I can charge it to the firm.'

I don't know where my common sense went right then, but I said, 'Hotel? You don't have to stay in a hotel, Brian. You should come and stay with me.'

'No, Liz. I couldn't possibly. You don't want to have to worry about me,' he assured me. 'I'll stay in a nice hotel and as long as we get to go out to dinner together a couple of times, I'll be more than happy.'

'No, Brian, I insist. I couldn't possibly let you stay in a hotel if you're coming all the way to England to see me.'

'Liz, don't put yourself out. Really. It's such short notice. I didn't even expect you to be around for the whole of my visit. And I don't want to be any bother.'

'You wouldn't be a bother, Brian.'

'I like staying in hotels,' he said.

'I really couldn't forgive myself if you did.'

There was a short pause before he said, 'OK then.'

Then there was another short pause while the words filtered through to my stupid dumb-ass brain. OK then?

Well, he wasn't supposed to say that, was he?!! I was going to let him suggest a hotel just one more time for appearances' sake before I agreed that it was a great idea and packed him off to the Metropolitan.

'What?' I said.

'OK then. It's fixed. I'll stay with you, if you really insist that you can't be without me,' he laughed. 'Next week? Friday afternoon through Tuesday? Just e-mail me the directions and I'll find my own way there when I get to the airport.'

'No!' I cried.

'No?' he asked.

'I mean, no. Don't find your own way here. I'll meet you at the airport. My place is quite tricky to find. It's in a mews, you know.'

Seema gave me a very odd look when she overheard that.

'Well, if you're sure I won't be interrupting your busy schedule. In that case I'll e-mail you my flight details instead. Liz,' he said softly. 'It's been way too long since we were last together. You know I really can't wait to see you again.'

'Same here,' I murmured.

'It'll be great fun, won't it?'

'Brilliant,' I said, with about as much enthusiasm as I reserved for emptying the wastepaper bins at work. 'I'll see you next Friday then.'

'Looking forward to it. Bye.' He put the phone down, leaving me staring at the receiver wondering what on earth I had done.

'Did I just hear you inviting someone to stay here?' Seema asked, all excited. 'The American guy who called this morning? I must say I liked the sound of his voice. Is he rich and hunky as well as gorgeous-sounding?'

'Oh, yes,' I sighed. 'He's all that and more.'

'Yippee. We could use some fresh blood around here. Unless you've got first dibs on him, of course. But you haven't, have you, Liz? I mean, you haven't even mentioned him before. He's not an old squeeze of yours, is he?'

'I don't think there's any possibility of action on that front any more,' I said disconsolately.

'So, I'm in with a chance, am I?'

'Seema, you're man-mad,' I exclaimed in exaspera-tion. 'But he's not staying here, in any case.'

'But you just said . . .' Seema began.

'Forget what I just said to him. Look at this place,' I exploded. 'Haven't you guys heard of a vacuum cleaner?' I picked up a cushion and shook out a snowstorm of cheese and onion crisp crumbs. At least I thought I could smell cheese and onion. It may just have been the aroma of Fat Joe's feet that seemed to linger constantly around the place. 'And I found half a lamb chop in the sink this morning.'

'You know I don't eat lamb,' Seema said defensively.

'So? You could have moved it before I had to. You have been at home all day, haven't you?'

'Studying!' she protested.

'Yeah, *studying*,' I sneered. 'I was a student once myself, remember. Do you realise there are things growing in the fridge that might hold the key to a cure for cancer? You could grow bloody potatoes in the ring around the bath. And as for the toilet – don't even get me started on that disgusting article. I would rather go to that little cubicle thingy outside Safeway than use our own loo. Didn't you know we had a loo brush?'

'We don't. Not any more. Joe used it to try to unblock the drain last October and somehow lost it in the process.'

'Well? Didn't anyone think to buy another one?' I walked around the room, picking up stray items of clothing (largely of the intimate variety) and a handful of fast-food wrappers. A pair of dirty tights was inextricably entwined with the wrapper from a year-old pepperami.

'I did mean to throw those away,' said Seema, hot-cheeked with embarrassment, snatching both tights and pepperami packet from my hand.

I found three single socks that didn't have mates to go home to. A pair of men's trainers that were so rank and rancid they curled up at the toes like Ali Baba's slippers. I found two CDs beneath the sofa that I had thought were gone for ever after a particularly ugly birthday party. Both CDs had been used as coasters. One for coffee. One for red wine. When I shifted the sofa to see if I could find that tenner I had lost about the same time, I found an even bigger red wine stain on the cream/dust-grey carpet.

'Did you know about this?' I shouted at my flatmate. 'How on earth can we shift this stain now? It's dried in. We're never going to get our deposit back!'

Seema ran behind me, running one of the spare socks along the book shelves in lieu of a duster, retrieving knickers from a plant pot, and diligently emptying an over-flowing ashtray into a wastepaper bin before remembering that the wastepaper bin was always empty because some careless smoker had burned a big hole through its raffia bottom with an improperly extinguished cigarette a couple of weekends before.

Struggling with a pint glass that actually seemed to be glued to the mantelpiece, I found a white towel covered in a huge blood-red stain draped along the useless radiator. 'What is this?' I asked, picking it up by a corner.

'It's just henna,' explained Seema quickly. 'I'm sure it will wash out. This isn't *your* towel, is it?' she added cautiously, snatching the offending item from my hands.

'No, thank god. But Brian definitely can't stay here,' I groaned, sinking on to the sofa and feeling the pointy end of a discarded biro jab right in the base of my spine. 'Absolutely no way on earth.'

'It'll be OK,' said Seema, cheerfully. 'Look, this place is much better already with all those empty glasses gone.' She made an expansive arm gesture as though she had just transformed the house into something from *Homes and Gardens* with the flick of a filthy old sock. 'We've got a whole week before he comes here. We can go out right now and buy some Jif, if you like. And dusters. We'll have a house meeting to divide up chores just as soon as Fat Joe thinks he's able to come out of his bedroom again and by the time your mate turns up, this place will be as good as any Hilton. Well, as good as the Bangkok Hilton in any case.'

'No, Seema!' I told her. 'You don't understand. Brian couldn't stay here even if we cleaned the place from now until Christmas. He can't stay here because whichever way you look at it this house is a filthy three bedroom terrace in Balham. And as far as Brian is concerned, I live in a gorgeous penthouse that overlooks Hyde Park.'

The truth was out.

I've already told you that I had become brief to the point of dishonesty in my letters to my old boyfriend. Problem was, since the advent of e-mail, I no longer had an excuse for the once a year postcard that just said ambiguously that everything was 'fine'.

It was Fat Joe who introduced me to the World Wide Web, back in the days when I was still making an effort to get to know my new flatmates and sometimes ventured into his pit of a room to take him a cup of tea. He was only too pleased to take time off from making a tape recording of the sounds he had downloaded from the Jubilee Extension Line website to set me up my very own e-mail address. He showed me how to track people down over the Net. And I quickly tracked down Brian.

Since then Brian and I had become e-mail pals, corresponding almost every day on the information superhighway (when I could get into Joe's bedroom – fortunately he was quite regular in his habits and I usually got fifteen minutes after his first cup of coffee of the day). And with so much cyberspace to fill each day I had quickly progressed from little lies of omission to those old-fashioned big black lies that your mother always warned would land you in strife.

Well, what could I do when Brian e-mailed me to say that he had just had lunch at a table next to Madonna's at New York's most fashionable new eaterie? E-mail him back with a list of the sandwich fillings to be avoided at Greasy Fred's Café in Battersea? No, I'm afraid I had to e-mail him with the revelation that I had once worked out next to Madonna at my exclusive women-only gym in Covent Garden. And it all went pretty much pear-shaped from there.

When Brian e-mailed me to say that he was going to the Hamptons for a weekend with a minor Kennedy, I told him that I was just about to jet off to the south of France to stay with a besotted Arab princeling I'd met in the posh folks' nightclub Annabelle's. When Brian regaled me with tales of a crazy shopping spree at Ralph Lauren, I'm afraid I sent an e-mail straight back saying that Dolce and Gabbana were designing something exclusive for my twenty-sixth birthday party which was to be held in the ballroom at the Grosvenor House Hotel.

But it was when he e-mailed me with details of his latest swanky address that I made my biggest mistake . . .

As far as Brian was concerned, I had moved out of the pit in Balham as soon as we gave up pen and paper for electronic mail. These days I had my very own gorgeous apartment overlooking Hyde Park, bought with the proceeds from a multi-million-pound property deal I had clinched all by myself as a senior partner at Corbett and Daughter Estates – which was of course one of the biggest commercial property companies in England rather than a one-room operation with three vaguely human staff and an incontinent Cavalier King Charles Spaniel on the team.

My e-mails were littered with the names of the in-places to be and the right people to be there with. In my secret cyber-life, I was forever picking up a little sparkling something from Tiffany or Cartier to treat myself for working so hard and to set off that exclusive dress from Donna Karan when I went out to meet movie-star clients who would trust only me to find them that special London *pied à terre*.

My friends were artists, writers, models and princes. Not a penniless business student with a part-time job at Blockbuster (Seema) and a wannabe computer hacker who never came out of his bedroom (Fat Joe). As far as Brian was concerned, I entertained megastars of the stage and screen nightly with recipes I had created myself under the supervision of Michelin-starred chefs and never, ever ate cold alphabetti spaghetti straight from a rusty tin in the company of no one but a flickering black and white television screen.

It had all seemed so harmless. In fact, it was almost good fun. Sometimes I just lifted my stories straight from Arabella Gilbert's *Daily* column with no real editing at all. I never imagined for a moment that one day I would have to prove that all the rubbish I had written over the course of three years on-line was true. Brian was such a dedicated workaholic. He never took any time off, probably didn't even go to the loo during working hours if he could possibly help it. There was no danger that he would suddenly decide to drop by and see me in London on a whim. Oh no.

'Oh no. Oh no. Oh no,' I wailed into the filthy sleeve of my threadbare towelling dressing-gown.

'What are you going to do?' asked Seema, when I had finished my tale of woe.

'I really do not have a clue,' I admitted most unhappily.

'Oh, dear,' she said. 'Oh dear.'

We sat down side by side on the sofa and gazed at the fireplace as if we might see the answer to my dilemma in the orange flickering of the singed electric bars that always smelled as if they were about to burst into real flame.

'What did you want to go and tell him all those silly lies for anyway?' she asked me suddenly.

'Why do you think? He's out there living the high life in New York City while my status in London is about one up from a one-legged pigeon in Trafalgar Square. No. Make that one down. At least those pigeons are a protected species now. I had to tell Brian all those lies because I didn't want him to know how badly I've failed since leaving college.'

Seema put an arm around my shoulders. Sometimes, when she wasn't borrowing my favourite Estée Lauder body lotion without asking or washing her netball socks with my Stergene, she was really quite incredibly sweet.

'Why on earth do you think you've failed?' she asked me seriously.

'Why do you think?' I replied. I waved my arm around the shabby, sorry room we were sitting in in almost the same manner she had used moments earlier in her attempt to convince me that the house was quite fab underneath the baked-on filth.

'Well,' she began in her most positive, junior counsellor voice. 'I live in the same house as you – your real house – and I don't think that I'm a failure because of it. Taking a bit longer than I hoped to move up to that gold card status, sure, but not a failure. Not by any means. You're only twenty-seven, Liz. Cut yourself some slack. You've got a good job, haven't you?'

'Huh! I'm a secretary at an estate agency. I'm not even on a permanent contract. I type labels for a living, for god's sake. I did a degree in English Literature, you know.'

'So? I'm doing a *master's* degree in business and I work at Blockbuster,' she reminded me quite gently.

'Well, my social life is rubbish,' I tried again.

'But you've got some great friends,' she said, not showing if any offence had been taken. 'We could go out together more often if you want to. We could go clubbing tonight. Do some dancing. Drink some cocktails.'

'I can't afford to go out.'

'Look, Liz,' Seema almost lost her patience because, skint as I was, I nearly always had more money than she did. 'Stop beating yourself up. I think you're doing really well, OK? Why should you have a penthouse by now anyway?'

'Brian does.'

'Have you seen it?'

'No.'

'Exactly. For all you know he could be living in a New Jersey trailer park, surviving off the immoral earnings of his two little sisters.' That raised a faint smile to my lips. But only a very faint one.

'His sisters are both older than him,' I corrected her mercilessly.

'OK. His two *big* sisters. All I'm saying is that you shouldn't worry so much about impressing him. Everyone exaggerates on e-mail from time to time. I wasted two weeks giving it my all over the internet for someone who claimed to be Bill Gates's brother but he turned out to be a data inputter for *Dalton's Weekly*. Fat Joe is upstairs right now, probably telling some schoolgirl who's supposed to be downloading facts for her homework that he's a six-foot-four Adonis with a torso like Michelangelo's *David*.'

'I know. I know . . . But Brian doesn't need to lie. Believe me, if Brian says he's done something amazing, then he most certainly has.'

'Is he really such a paragon of virtue that he's never added a few inches or dropped a couple of years?'

'Oh, Seema,' I sighed. 'He really is. He's probably the most scrupulously honest person I've ever met. He even admitted to smelling his own farts when we played "truth or dare" in the college bar, for heaven's sake.'

'That is honest,' Seema had to agree. 'In which case, perhaps you should just come clean, Liz. I'm sure he'll think the whole thing is incredibly funny and even be mightily relieved that you won't expect him to go dutch on Cristal champagne at the Mirabelle every night while he's here on his visit.'

'No,' I shook my head solemnly. 'If it was anyone else I would come clean straight away. Honestly I would. But not Brian. I just can't do it. You don't know him, Seema. He'd be mortally wounded if he knew that I had lied to him and in such a big way. He's American, remember. They've got a different moral code out there. Some of them still abide by the Ten Commandments. I could hardly pass the whole thing off as a grand exercise in irony. He'd think I'd gone completely bonkers.'

'Well, that's me clean out of suggestions then,' said Seema, as she shifted to pull a soft cream cracker from beneath the cushion she was sitting on. 'I'm afraid I don't think I can magic a penthouse out of thin air. You really are a complete tit, Liz.'

Didn't I know it. We gazed at the electric fire for a bit longer. Me, contemplating the only honourable way out of the situation – which seemed at that moment to be hari-kiri with a kitchen knife (if only all our cutlery wasn't so blunt). Seema contemplating I knew not what. Until she came up with this gem. 'I know, why don't you say that you had a terrible fire at the penthouse and have had to move in here with me – your secretary, if you like – on a temporary basis until the cleaning up and repair works are finished. Perfect, don't you think?'

Yes, it did seem perfect. For about ten seconds, until Fat Joe waddled into the sitting room looking like a giant maggot, wearing, as usual, his arctic fox print combat gear beneath his duvet (which never sported a cover over its faint yellow stains). He squashed himself into the sofa between us, not taking his eyes off the readers' letters at the back of the latest edition of *What Hi-fi?* he was carrying, until he spotted the stale cream cracker that Seema had just retrieved with the intention of binning it and crammed it into his mouth.

'Anything interesting in that?' asked Seema conversationally, pointing towards the mag.

'Well, this stupid bloke here has written in to say that he can't find a measurable difference between the Audiolab and equivalent F3-branded products,' Joe spluttered, spraying crumbs all over the carpet. 'What a moron. Ha!'

'Ha, indeed!' said Seema.

We very rarely expected to actually understand something Fat Joe said.

'Anyone mind if I put the television on?' Joe asked then, simultaneously letting out the most resonant fart you can possibly imagine. Seema and I shook our heads, but I knew at that instant that the penthouse fire plan was out of the question too. Brian couldn't possibly stay in our dump of a house while the human slug was in residence. He would be repulsed. I knew I generally was.

Seema and I popped out from our sofa corners and headed for the kitchen to continue our conflab. 'I can't have Brian here while Fat Joe is,' I told her.

'I see your point. We'll have to ask him to move out for a while.'

'Seema, you know as well as I do that even coming downstairs is a major breakthrough for Fat Joe these days. There's no way we're going to be able to make him take an enforced vacation without armed assistance.'

Seema frowned. 'Oh, this is so unfair. I really wanted to meet your American friend. He sounds so nice . . . and rich.'

I plopped three pyramid tea-bags into three chipped and dubiously stained mugs. 'If anyone gets first dibs on him, it's me,' I reminded her. 'You're getting an arranged marriage.'

'But you've already got a boyfriend,' she whined. 'You can't have two.'

And just at that moment the boyfriend shouted from the sitting room. 'Better make that four cups of tea if you're doing a brew, Lizzie.'

Richard had arrived.

CHAPTER EIGHT

Richard. My boyfriend. I'd completely forgotten that he was supposed to be coming round to deliver my birthday present that evening. When I heard him call out from the sitting room, my stomach lurched as if I had been caught betraying him by my need to impress Brian. Fact was, I suppose I already had betrayed Richard. Never mind telling Brian that I had a great flat, what I hadn't told him was that I really did have a reasonably great boyfriend.

A week earlier I had been happy to refer to Richard as my 'new boyfriend'. We had been seeing each other for about seven months. Well, it was seven months since we had first locked tongues in the back of a taxi anyway and he'd been round to our house almost every night since then so I had simply assumed that we were seeing each other properly by now. When you're in your mid-twenties, you can't really ask 'Are we going out, then?' as you would have done aged twelve, however much you itch to do so.

I met Richard at an infamous backpackers' bar in central London, the kind of place where homesick

Aussies and Kiwis, who are almost too drunk to see, gather together to recite old beer adverts wholesale in lieu of chat-up lines. I wouldn't have been there at all but it was Seema's birthday and she was determined that she would start her twenty-second year on earth with a casual shag – especially as her parents had announced in a postscript at the bottom of their birthday card to her that if Seema didn't find herself a suitable husband by her twenty-third birthday, they would be finding one for her.

Anyway, we had been drinking tequila since six o'clock in the evening, had eaten nothing but a bowlful of stale pistachio nuts between us, and were well on our way to a couple of spectacular alcohol-induced blackouts when we stumbled into Richard and his gang.

I say stumbled, because that is literally what we did. Seema and I were standing at the top of a short flight of stairs, arms locked around each other to help us stay steady. Seema leaned too far forward while attempting to adjust the straps on her ankle-breaker silver platform sandals. She still had her other arm around my waist and when she went over, so did I. Arse over tit, as my father used to say (though not in front of my mother). Talk about making an entrance. Thank god there were only four steps between the top of the flight and the humiliating landing with my skirt up round my waist and most of Richard's pint on my head.

I quickly offered to buy him a new pint but he

said that he would buy me a drink instead, for being the first woman ever to throw herself at his feet. After that, it would have been churlish not to snog him. Plus, he and his flatmate Paul (who was using all the exact same lines on Seema at the time, I later discovered) lived in Balham too and it seemed sensible to share a taxi back home when the bar closed. Not to mention cheap, as Seema and I had both run out of money by that point.

Richard leapt on me in the taxi, which was quite embarrassing as I was sitting on the jump seat with my back to the driver at the time and Richard some-how ended up on his knees on the floor between me and the proper seat. Luckily Paul and Seema were too busy with their own bout of tongue-wrestling to see Richard tumble. The taxi driver tutted loudly and turned up the Talk Radio show he was listening to in an attempt to drown out the sucking noises. Taxi drivers – they can be a right pain in the backside, can't they? But I can't say that I envy them doing the Saturday night shift. All spew and strangers snogging. What a job!

Paul and Richard never made it back to their own flat that night. In the morning, Seema and I bumped into each other on the way to the bathroom, both hoping to have a chance to clean our teeth and prettify ourselves before our respective catches woke up.

'What do you think?' Seema asked in a whisper, as she struggled with the love knots in her gorgeous long black hair. 'Is it breakfast in bed, or an urgent early morning appointment with the chiropodist?'

An urgent early morning appointment with the chiropodist was a great excuse to use when you needed to get someone out of your way after a big mistake of a night. Firstly, because it meant that the unwelcome visitor had to leave right away and secondly, because the thought of a young girl having her corns done seemed to prevent any further telephone calls from unwanted admirers pretty damn effectively in most cases.

I was having breakfast in bed. Two days later, Richard asked me to ask Seema how her corns were on behalf of Paul. She hadn't returned his phonecalls. But I was ready for love. I was ready to hitch up with someone I could spend my Sunday afternoons with, drifting around London's parks and galleries, gazing into his eyes; making all those poor single suckers deeply aware of how empty their Marks and Spencer's ready-meals-for-one existence was, just as all those smug couples had been doing to me for the past four years on and off . . .

And Richard fitted the description of the man who would help me do my bit to annoy all those irritating people who had told me how much they envied the freedom of my single life when they were cuddled up on life's sofa with a complementary bod. He was passably handsome – well, he had all the requisite features that go to make up what we refer to as a human face – and his trousers were just about long

enough for his skinny legs. He occasionally wore a
shirt that didn't have a number on the back and
he also had a full-time job (very important that –
upon arriving in London with dreams of becoming
the next Marianne Faithfull, I had gone through a
period of exclusively dating musicians and painters.
I discovered that creative 'artistes' are all very well
until you have to get up to go to work on a Monday
morning, leaving him lying there in bed, and return
on Monday evening to find him exactly where you left
him. Creative thinking – my arse! It's just plain rude).
No, I wanted a man who had to leave the house before
I did. And Richard did, to go to his job in the City.

OK, so he was an accountant and not some super-
rich bonds trader who drank Bollinger like I drank
Perrier, but there comes a point in every girl's life
when she realises that there is a point to comfy
knickers and stops hankering after a pop star for a
mate. My mother had informed me only the weekend
before, seven days before the watershed that was to
be my twenty-seventh birthday, that that big knicker
time had come for Lizzie Jordan.

'Weren't we supposed to be going out tonight?' said
Richard now observing me standing by the kitchen
door in my dad's old pyjamas and a dressing-gown
that was getting as thin as a cobweb around the
elbows.

I looked down at my slippered feet. In the excitement of Brian's impending visit, I had completely
forgotten that I had agreed to go out for a pint and

a pub quiz that night and got ready for bed straight after my bath.

'Don't you want to celebrate your birthday?'

'What's to celebrate?' interrupted Seema gleefully. 'Lizzie's nearly thirty now.'

'I am not,' I protested. 'I'm still in my mid-twenties.'

'Mid-twenties?' Seema snorted. 'Not at twenty-seven, you're not. Mid-twenties is from twenty-four to twenty-six only. Any older than that and you're officially into your pre-thirties.' She poked out her tongue to underline the insult.

'So we're not going out because you've gone all middle-aged on me? Never mind,' said Richard, settling himself into the one and only armchair so that Seema and I had to squish back in beside Fat Joe. 'I haven't got any money on me anyway. You haven't got any beer in the house have you, by any chance?'

'I'll just go and have a look,' I said, secretly relieved to have an excuse not to sit next to the farting bag of soft upholstery that was my flatmate. 'We've probably only got that French crap we brought back from the booze cruise to Calais.'

'That's fine,' said Richard. 'And I suppose it's a bit cheeky of me to ask if you could whip me up something on toast while you're out there? Cheese or beans. I don't mind which. I did mean to go food shopping myself on my way back from work but the cashpoint sucked up my card again.'

'I thought your wages went through last Friday,' I said in surprise.

'They did. But I was so overdrawn anyway that by the time I took out a tenner for my football subs on Saturday morning I was already up to my limit again. I'll just tighten my belt this month and have it sorted by the end of next. Promise.'

Seema shot me a doubtful look when she heard that. Humanitarian organisations the third world over were campaigning to put an end to her horrendous overdraft at the National Westminster but she still wouldn't consider dating anyone with a matching one.

'Hope your card got eaten *after* you bought Lizzie's birthday present,' she said, arching one imperious eyebrow meaningfully.

Richard shuffled uncomfortably. 'Actually, Lizzie, I was going to talk to you about that. I had an idea of what I wanted to buy you but I decided that it might be a better idea if you chose your present yourself and I just paid for it. That way you'll definitely get something you want. What do you think?'

Seema rolled her eyes in disapproval. 'How romantic is that?' she sneered. 'You'd better be prepared for some serious damage to your plastic, Richard.'

'I'll be kind to you,' I reassured him.

That was the difference between me and Seema. If one of her suitors foolishly offered to take her shopping on his plastic, he would find himself remortgaging his flat before she had finished emptying the racks at Joseph. If anyone offered to take me shopping, on the other hand, I would come back with a one-sleeved jacket that had been left over in the sale, muttering that it was exactly what I wanted and that making another sleeve would be no trouble at all. I told myself that my approach marked me out as the nicer person but Seema told me that I needed to sort out my attitude. 'Your approach may not be greedy,' she conceded. 'But it is insulting in another way. Men like to feel that they can provide for their woman. By refusing to take their cash, you're effectively castrating them.'

What a nice idea.

Seema was a perfect example of the Zoe Ball backlash. She didn't want to be one of the lads. She wanted the right to wear pink tulle and feathers and flutter her eyelashes and when she did gifts fell into her lap left, right and centre. Whereas me, I did all the other traditional girly things – like cooking the beans on toast, doing the ironing – and yet still refused to take advantage when any man wanted to stretch his economic muscle in my direction. She was right. I was a mug.

'There's a sale on at Top Shop, Lizzie,' was Seema's parting shot as she went to inspect her reflection for the second time that hour.

'Have you seen this letter?' Joe asked Richard when Seema was safely out of the way. 'Some nutter here has written in to say that he doesn't know the difference between Audiolab and an F3-branded equivalent!'

'You're joking,' said Richard, taking the magazine off him to read the apparent heresy for himself.

* * *

Ho hum.

My relationship with Richard had been on a kind of fast forward since we met. We'd been through the attraction and lust bit on the first night. Now we were already into that period when I was starting to wonder whether someone who couldn't stay out of the red for a whole week could really provide for the gorgeous girl and boy children I had always imagined myself having. With a rich man.

Nevertheless, I pulled a couple of slices of Mighty White out of the bread bin, scraped off the Fortnum and Mason green mould which was already encroaching on the corners, and went to put them under the grill. The grill-pan was, of course, opaque white with a thick smelly layer of bacon fat. If I had been making toast for myself, this is the point when I would have exploded with fury, scrubbed at the pan with a brillo pad until my hands bled, and called a house meeting to insist that whoever used the grill covered it with silver foil first, so that the fat could be removed quickly and easily to leave a shining clean pan for the house pseudo-vegetarian (I wouldn't eat anything with a *cute* face) to use straight afterwards. But I was making toast for Richard and I figured that he would actually appreciate the flavour a bit of old bacon fat might impart.

I shoved the bread under the grill and leaned back against the sink to wait for it to toast. This wasn't how my life was meant to be, I thought. It was my twenty-seventh birthday! I had planned to be living an instant coffee ad lifestyle by now – all swanky Nicole Farhi separates and polished blond-wood floors. Instead I was making mouldy bread into toast for a skint accountant – did other people *really* trust him to look after their money? I wondered – who was showing disturbingly nerdy tendencies, in a kitchen that would have been closed down by the World Health Organisation if they found it being used in a third world country. Far from wearing head to toe Nicole Farhi, I wished I was wearing wellington boots instead of slippers to protect me from the scum on the floor.

Mould crept along the bottom of the walls like an alien creature waiting to reach out and grab my ankles. A miniature archaeology team were searching for artefacts in the rock-solid remains of a disastrous lemon daal that Seema had cooked to impress her brother (needless to say he hadn't been impressed and reported to his parents that they were going to have trouble getting Seema off their hands). Hell, we didn't even have a toaster. Everybody in the civilised world owns a toaster, I told myself. I bet the lovely Arabella Gilbert had one of those great big Dualit toasters in her interior-designed bachelorette flat. I bet Brian had one too. One of those shining bright silver industrial ones that can even do tea-cakes and crumpets without burning them. I dreamed of unburnt tea-cakes . . . I started to dream of Brian.

At which point the bacon fat that had been left to accumulate in the grill-pan burst into flames and what was meant to be toast quickly became ashes.

'Shit!' I shrieked, pulling the flaming pan out from beneath the grill and waving at it ineffectually with a spoon.

Seema, Richard and Fat Joe instantly appeared at the kitchen door to shout instructions with varying degrees of usefulness.

'Get the fire extinguisher!' cried Seema.

'It's bloody empty,' I reminded her. 'You used it to make snow at last year's Christmas party!'

'Put a damp cloth on it,' said Richard.

'That's what you do for chips, stupid,' Fat Joe replied.

'It's not the chips specifically, dumbo,' Richard informed him. 'It's what you're supposed to do for burning fat.' He strode manfully across to the sink, doused a tea-cloth in water and flung it over the pan which I was still holding like the lemon that I was. There was a damp sounding sizzle and the room filled with noxious, choking smoke. Richard gently prised the pan from my hand and put it down on top of the hob with the damp cloth still draped across it. Then he put his arm around my shoulders and looked at me expectantly while he waited for me to either burst into tears or call him a hero. I did neither.

'Jesus!' cursed Seema. 'Can't you even make toast without nearly causing a fatal disaster, Liz?'

'This wouldn't have happened if someone' – I

looked daggers at Fat Joe, the big bacon eater in our house – 'would clean out the grill pan after his Saturday morning fry-up occasionally. There was nearly half an inch of bacon fat in the bottom of that pan.'

'Then why didn't you clean it before you tried to set fire to the flat?' Seema asked.

'Because,' I snarled dramatically, shaking Richard's arm from my shoulder. 'Because I couldn't be bothered. Because I'm fed up of this life of drudgery. I'm fed up of the constant round of clearing up the mess after you lot like I'm your bleeding mother. The dirt. The dust. The grease. It's hideous. Have either of you looked at the kitchen ceiling lately?'

We all gazed ceiling-wards to where little yellow stalactites of grease had been forming over the two years that we had been in residence and deep-fat frying on a daily basis.

'Urgh. That is disgusting,' Seema breathed.

'Well, why doesn't somebody do something about it!' I screamed. 'I don't want to have to live like this any more! I was meant for better things than this!' Then I flounced out of the kitchen and headed for my room with Richard in hot pursuit.

'PMT?' he asked cautiously as I sobbed into my pillow.

'No!' I roared. 'No, I do not have pre-menstrual tension. God, you're so predictable.'

'Sorry I asked,' he said, backing away. 'But "predictable"? That's a bit of a harsh thing to say about me after only seven months together, isn't it?'

He rolled me over to face him. 'Are you depressed because it's your birthday, Liz? Is that it? Is it because of what Seema said? Twenty-seven isn't that old, you know.'

'I know it's not that old!' I snapped. 'I'm not depressed because it's my birthday.'

'Did you have a bad day at work?'

'No, not particularly. But I have been having a bad life for the last five years. What am I doing here, Richard? Why do I live in a horrible place like this stinking house with two insane flatmates who never lift a finger to help me?'

'I think it's rather nice here,' he replied, admiring my peeling wallpaper. And I suppose that compared to his own place it was quite nice. I mean, at least we had an *indoor* toilet. So did Richard's flat, actually. But it had been sealed off for three years and the landlord refused to get it fixed unless the tenants made up the shortfall for a phone bill which had been run up by three South African backpackers before Richard and his friend even moved into the place.

'Why don't I live somewhere glamorous like New York? Like Manhattan?' I asked him with a sniffle.

'Why would you want to live somewhere like that?' he replied. 'You get lots of rats in New York. Even in the poshest parts of Manhattan, so they tell me. Running in and out of everywhere. Eating your furniture. Biting the babies.'

'You get rats in Balham too,' I interrupted. 'I saw one run out from behind the dustbins last week.

It was this big.' I indicated the size of a small terrier.

'OK, so you get rats in New York and Balham but at least you can walk down the High Road in Balham without getting caught in the gun cross-fire of some gang fight,' Richard tried again. 'At least Balham's safer than Harlem.'

'What? Didn't you hear about that chap who got an air-gun pellet shot into his thigh outside McDonalds?' I asked Richard. 'He only went in for a milkshake. He may never dance again.' I was determined not to be persuaded that there was anything great about living in south London at all.

'You really are in a bad mood, aren't you?' he said observantly. 'Do you fancy going for a walk to cheer up?'

'What? In the dark? Where to?'

'Well, I was hoping you might be able to lend me a pound to go to the chip shop, actually. I'm still really hungry. I was sort of desperate for that toast.'

'Oh, come on then,' I groaned, pulling on my jeans over my pyjama bottoms. Anything to get out of the flat, which still smelled like an explosion in a chip factory. In the sitting room, Seema and Joe were watching the television again with handkerchiefs held over their mouths to stop themselves from choking on the smoke which lingered in a thick layer just below the ceiling. A quick glance into the kitchen revealed that nobody had bothered to move the grill-pan yet.

Outside, the drizzle that had coated London all day had at least started to peter out.

'Do you still want me to come and meet your parents on Sunday?' Richard asked as we headed back from the chippy.

Yet another date I had forgotten about. I was due to go home for my monthly appraisal with the parents – not to mention to pick up my birthday present, which would probably be a kettle or an iron – and had, before the Brian saga took over my waking thoughts, gone to great lengths to persuade Richard that he should come too. Since I had made no progress whatsoever on the 'getting a better job' front and my hair was still not entirely its natural colour after a brush with Seema's home-brewed henna, I had hoped that the appearance of a new and, to all intents and purposes, professional boyfriend would at least keep Mum off my back for a couple of hours.

'I've bought a new jacket, especially,' he said, going to great pains to be sweet.

'Well, if you really want to come,' I told him.

'Of course I do. It'll be very interesting to see where you get your temper from.'

'I do not have a temper,' I snapped, as I stabbed at his arm with my chip fork. 'But you had better not show me up all the same. I hope you know how to eat using proper cutlery. I've only ever seen you use a plastic chip fork or chop sticks.'

'I can use a spoon perfectly well,' he retorted. 'Hey, listen, I was thinking, since next weekend will be our seven-month anniversary . . .'

I groaned.

'And since I haven't yet got you a present for your birthday, what do you say to going away for a really dirty weekend to celebrate getting this far?'

'What about your overdraft?' I asked practically.

'I could put the weekend on my credit card instead. If it's still working, that is,' he added. 'We could go to Brighton. Or Bristol. Or Bath. Wherever *you* want to go, Liz. It's your choice. It's your birthday. Let me treat you.'

'Oh, Richard. I'm sorry. But I couldn't go even if you could afford it. I'm busy next weekend.'

'Not washing your armpit hair again?' he joked.

'Actually I've got a friend coming to stay.'

'Great. Has she got a boyfriend? Paul's been a real pain in the proverbial since your heartless mate Seema dumped him after a single night of passion. Perhaps we could set him up with this new girl. Go on a double date. It could save him from going into a decline. He thinks his balls might be atrophying from under-use.'

'Er, Richard,' I stopped him. 'This friend of mine is a guy.'

'Oh. Well, a double date might not be such a good idea then. Old boyfriend?' he asked cautiously.

'A boy who is an old friend, yes,' I admitted that much. 'From America.'

'Oh. Well, I'm sure he's a very nice bloke,' said Richard, sounding utterly unconvinced.

'Oh, he is. Very nice.' I must have looked a bit wistful then because Richard's expression went all odd. He cleared his throat.

'I guess I'll just stay out of your way next weekend then.' We had reached the gate to my flat. I could tell that Richard was waiting to be asked to come in. It would be nice, I thought, to have someone to cuddle up to on my first night as a pre-thirty something. I was feeling pretty wretched. I pulled him in through the gate with me. 'Come on.'

'Actually, I think I might just go back to my place tonight, if that's OK with you,' he surprised me. 'Got to get up early in the morning. Five a side practice. Big match against the boys from Coopers next Wednesday night.'

'Oh.'

'What time do you need me to be ready on Sunday morning?' he asked.

'Ten-ish. I'll pick you up.'

'Yeah.' He kissed me on the cheek. 'See you Sunday morning then.'

I was peeved for about ten seconds. No girl likes to feel as though her charms have been rebuffed, especially on her birthday, and even if she was only using them half-heartedly. But then I found myself feeling strangely relieved. I went upstairs – careful not to look into the kitchen as I passed in case no one had cleared up; I would leave that disappointment for the morning. Once safely behind the locked door of my room, I delved under my bed for the box full of my dearest treasures.

It was just an old shoe-box but its contents were more precious to me than any amount of gold-plated tat from Tiffany. A daffodil pressed between two yellowed leaves from a note-pad. A scrap of paper on which someone – Brian – had scrawled 'see you at lunch time' (it was the first note he ever pinned to the little cork notice board on my college room door – two weeks before he kissed me). Half a dozen longer notes from Brian, finished with love and kisses. A little Valentine's card with a heart-carrying teddy bear on the front – signed on the inside (Americans do that – seemed strange at the time but now I'm glad). A button from his favourite blue shirt, which I found on the floor of my college room after he had gone back to New York. A handful of photographs taken over nine glorious months together.

I pulled out my favourite. It was a photograph of me and Brian at the end of term ball that also marked the end of his all too short stay in England. I was wearing a red velvet dress that had cost me almost half my student grant for that year. My thin hair was pinned up on top of my head in an extravagant style that I had never before or since managed to achieve. Brian was in a smart black tux. He had even bought me a corsage to pin to my dress. None of the girls with an English date that night had a corsage. I had a white lily flecked with red that matched my oufit perfectly – Brian had asked Mary to tell him what I was going to wear.

The corsage had dropped off when we were dancing to the act the ball committee had hired for the night – some ska band that had been big when we were kids and inspired lots of pushing and shoving on the dancefloor. It had been trampled underfoot and by the time I realised it was missing. I could only retrieve the piece of pink ribbon which still lay at the bottom of my box of treasures.

Now I lay down on my bed and just looked at that photograph of the ball for hours. Brian had been so gorgeous. His bright white smile seemed to light up his perfect brown face. Looking at that photograph, I could almost remember how he smelled that night. Davidoff Cool Water – that was his aftershave.

At the bottom of the box I also found a slightly battered tape. It was a tape of tunes that Brian had compiled for me. A tape of tunes that had special relevance to us at the time. There was 'Love Cats' by the Cure, which had been playing at the Two Items of Clothing party while we shared our first kiss just outside the Union. 'Everywhere' by Fleetwood Mac – that had been playing as we first made love. (Fleetwood Mac's greatest hits was one of only two CDs I had.) And finally, a scratchy version of 'Let's Call the Whole Thing Off' sung by a long-dead musical star.

I slipped the tape into the tape deck of my tatty old stereo and spooled it forward to the old song about the fatal differences between lovers from the US and the UK sung by a man with a plum in his mouth. I hadn't played the tape for quite a while and goose pimples peppered my spine as the first piano chords sounded.

> 'You say po-tay-to and I say po-ta-to,
> You say to-may-to and I say to-ma-to . . .'

It was *our* song. Absolutely relevant to Brian and me. Brian would burst into the tune spontaneously whenever I picked him up on the way he said 'erb' instead of 'herb' or mistook a pavement for a sidewalk. By the time the singer got to the bit about breaking hearts I couldn't hold back a nostalgic tear.

It hardly seemed possible that I hadn't actually seen Brian in the flesh for almost six years. He was still so much part of my life in that I thought of him so often. Nothing had happened in those six years that could compare with the happy times we spent together. No one had eclipsed him in my memory.

I wondered if he would have changed. Would his smooth black hair still be so thick and wavy or would the stress of his high-flying job have made it drop out in handfuls? Would he still have a stomach you could iron your shirts on, or would he have spread a bit, as the rest of us definitely had since we were students surviving on kebabs and crackers? Would his eyes still crinkle up at the corners while he tried hard not to laugh? Would he still smell the way he used to – good enough to eat? I went to sleep with the photograph next to me on the pillow. When I woke up, it was all creased.

CHAPTER NINE

A nd sleeping on my picture of Brian had certainly not solved the problem that he posed by proposing to visit me in my Balham hell-hole.

The grill-pan stood on the kitchen table, still covered by the damp tea-towel that was now brown with singe marks. The sink was piled high with mugs, plates, cutlery and part of a dismantled bicycle. The sock that Seema had been using as a duster still hung listlessly from the end of the mantelpiece as though she was expecting an early Christmas. And all through the house, not a creature was stirring that might have had any intention of doing any housework.

I made myself some sort-of-toast by singeing the mould off the edges of a piece of bread using flames from one of the gas rings on the hob and had a cup of tea without milk. There wasn't even an empty carton in the fridge that morning. I knew that Fat Joe had taken to hoarding milk in his room in case Armageddon came during the night but I didn't feel strong enough to go and look for the missing pint right then. If Fat Joe's feet could stink out the sitting room within five seconds of his walking in, then you can imagine how bad his bedroom was. Saddam Hussein had spent millions on research, trying to perfect a gas so bad that it could kill a man, when just one waft from the doorway of Joe's room would have done the trick on a whole army. Even with gas masks.

Anyway, having finished my 'toast' – that is, having thrown it into the bottomless wastepaper basket after just one bite, I pondered the reality of making the house fit for Brian in less than a week since, having slept on the problem, it seemed that Seema's plan to claim that my penthouse had been destroyed in a fire was the only real option open to me other than simply telling him not to come at all. Glancing about me, I could see a great many things that could be improved instantly by banishment to a dustbin bag. I had heard about incredible carpet cleaning hoovers that could be hired for £50 a day. I had heard about incredible cleaners who could be hired for £50 a day, more to the point. But I didn't really have £50 to spare. I would have to do it myself.

I ventured back into the kitchen and, careful not to disturb the mountain of washing up which certainly wasn't doing itself, I had a search through the cupboard beneath the sink for cleaning materials.

Well, I didn't find any Jif, but I did find my cream Armani-lookalike jacket. The one which Seema said must have been stolen from the washing line, after she borrowed it and, she claimed, diligently washed it for me afterwards. Now I discovered a story which I thought might have been closer to the truth. The jacket had a big hole on its front. A hole which corresponded pretty much exactly with the shape of our iron. Seema may have been good enough to wash the jacket but she had still been cack-handed enough to burn a bloody great hole through it. Thinking back, I could even remember the day she must have hidden it in the cupboard beneath the sink. I had come home from work one evening to find Seema standing awkwardly against the sink, explaining away the faint haze of smoke which hung in the air as the result of an afternoon spent baking bhajis. She told me that Fat Joe had eaten the results of course.

But angry though I was, that had been a long time ago. Well, over a year. And I knew that even if I wanted to wear the jacket again now, I wouldn't have been able to since I had recently been porking out on a diet of KitKats, the only thing that could get me through a day at Corbett and Daughter's without crying. I stuffed the jacket into a dustbin bag and resolved to keep the revelation of its discovery for a later date, when I needed to guilt-trip Seema into doing something really awful.

When I emerged from the cupboard again with a rusty pan scourer and a bottle of cream cleaner that had already haemmorhaged most of its contents into a sticky white puddle on the cupboard floor, I wondered whether that moment to make Seema do something really awful might not have come slightly sooner than I hoped.

Pushing the crockery piled high on the draining board into a sink full of luke-warm, but not soapy (we had run out of washing-up liquid, naturally) water, I poured a little of the cream cleaner on to the scratched aluminium and started to scrub. And scrub. But the hardwater scum showed no signs of wanting to give. Perhaps if I just rinsed the draining board down, I thought. If I knew that it was clean, a little bit of wear and tear wouldn't be too horrifying when Brian arrived.

I pulled the plug out of the sink, intending to drain away the brown water which had been sitting in there for about a week. But it didn't drain away. I started to unload the crockery again, in an attempt to find out what was causing the blockage. Soon I had taken out everything I could feel in the water that I couldn't actually see my hands in. Gingerly, I felt my way towards the plug hole where I had once found a fish's head with staring dead white eyes.

This time, I pulled out a mouse.

I screamed until everyone in the house was awake. It wasn't that it was a mouse, you understand. I'm not one of those girls who has to stand on a chair and wait to be rescued at the first sight of a worm-like tail disappearing under the skirting board. I had even kept mice as a child. Perhaps that was why I was so upset at having to pull a dead one out of the sink. It must have drowned while trying to reach some tasty morsel floating in the dishwater, poor thing. Perhaps it had become trapped beneath one of my own dirty plates. The thought would surely haunt me for the rest of my life.

It certainly put me off cleaning anything else that day. All I needed right then was a swift drink as soon as the pubs opened. Luckily, there was someone who would oblige. Miserable Mary was meeting me in town for lunch. She was always game for a swift gin and tonic whatever the time of day. And she was going to pay. Birthday treat. She'd promised.

Though we had been like two peas in a pod while at college, these days I hardly saw my old best friend, despite the fact that we lived less than four miles apart. But that's four miles across the river Thames and, as anyone who has ever lived in London knows, you can't guarantee that you'll get anywhere – from Clapham South to Clapham North even (just two tube stops apart) – in less than an hour by public transport. (Not that Mary ever took public transport these days.) If you're talking about taking a trip from low-rent Balham (so far south it's been nicknamed the Gateway to France) to lovely trendy Belsize Park in the north, you might as well be talking about flying to New York for the night. It's that easy.

So, my relationship with Mary, like the relationship I had been having with Brian, had become confined to hasty e-mail messages two or three times a week. Though Mary genuinely didn't have time to write anything more interesting than 'How are you? Sorry

I haven't e-mailed you in ages.' Because, while my life had been on a strictly downward trajectory ever since we threw our mortar boards into the air in graduation glee, Mary's life had gone into interstellar orbit. Honestly, if I hadn't seen her five times a year or so in the five years since that last day and thus had some idea of the processes which had been in motion since college ended, I wouldn't have believed that the new look Miserable Mary, who was always putting me on hold to take a far more important call, could possibly have been made of the same genetic material as the one who refused to come out of her bedroom for a week when that chap from the Manic Street Preachers went missing near the Severn Bridge.

Her hair wasn't even dyed black any more. Her mother, who turned out to be a PR guru with a massive firm that did public relations for anyone who was anybody from soft drinks manufacturers to Arabian arms dealers (Mary had kept that very quiet during the college years), managed to persuade Mary to both fix her broken tooth and go back to her natural hair colour (honey blonde) before her first job interview and Mary's hair had been getting lighter ever since. When I popped my head around the door of the Mezzo café, I wasn't sure whether I was seeing my old pal Mary or some breakfast TV presenter sitting at her usual table, such was the telegenic sheen on her coiffured golden waves. She was wearing a cream trouser suit over a chocolate silk vest with expensive chocolate leather accessories to match. She looked as though she had been dressed by Thorntons – in the nicest possible way. It was a real champagne truffle of an outfit. I, on the other hand, looked distinctly inedible in my paint-flecked jeans and a jumper I had retrieved from the laundry basket. I wasn't even sure it was my jumper, to be honest.

'Well, we won't be going anywhere nice for lunch, obviously,' she said when she saw me. 'Get yourself a coffee or something, darling. I've just got to make a few more calls before I can give you my full and undivided attention.' She pushed a fiver across the table to pay for my coffee and spent the next quarter of an hour persuading the editor of the *Daily Mail* or some other worthy rag that another arms crisis in Iraq wasn't the kind of story he needed on his front page on a Monday morning.

'Dahling,' she told him in her most flirtatious voice (the one that hadn't worked on the pierced post-grad). 'You run that story all the time. It's just such a depressing way to start the week. People will be topping themselves all over the home counties. How about this instead? A little bird told me that if Anthea Turner's new boyfriend doesn't have an engagement ring on her finger by the end of next week, she's going to join a convent of Carmelite nuns. I can get you the pictures. Now don't you think that deserves a front page headline?' Amazingly, he did.

Mary had moved sideways from her first job in fashion PR into artist management (or *artiste* management, as she liked to call it) and had quickly risen to the top of her chosen career. Her father had bankrolled Mary's very own talent agency when it became clear that she had her own talent for schmoozing celebrities, but that wasn't something she liked to talk about. Now, anyone who was anyone had her business card in their wallet for media emergencies. She was on first-name terms with everyone from mega heavyweight foreign correspondents, whose idea of travelling light was to pack just one bullet-proof vest, to the Spice Girls' toddling children who never went anywhere without a gross of Gucci nappies.

'So how's it going with you?' she finally asked, when she had finished regaling me with the story of a glamour model she had just taken on. (Mary had got her promising new client a date with a gay MP who wasn't New Labour enough to exit the closet. They went to a sushi bar and the model drank the finger bowl, etcetera. The MP took a sip himself to save her from embarrassment.) 'Did you have a lovely birthday?' Mary sighed.

I shrugged.

'Get any decent presents?'

'Definitely not.'

'Well, I hope you like this one,' she said, pushing a package across the table towards me. I fell upon the blue-wrapped parcel eagerly. At least there was some hope that Mary would have got me something I wanted. And she had. The box inside the paper was also pale blue and stamped with the legend 'Tiffany and Co.' The second best phrase in the English language after 'will you marry me' from the mouth of Joseph Fiennes.

'Don't get too excited,' Mary warned me. 'It's only a key-ring.'

It was still the best present I had had all year. And it was engraved with my initials. How thoughtful. 'Thanks,' I said, remembering the cheapo Body Shop bubble bath I had given Mary on her own birthday. 'I wish I could get you something half as good.'

'Perhaps you will one day. You could find me a nice little flat for a start and waive your commission.'

'Nobody ever puts their nice little flats through Corbett and Daughter Estate Agents,' I reminded her. 'Though having said that, there's somewhere in Eaton Place that might come up if Harriet's aunt doesn't pull through from the heart attack she had last week.'

'Eaton Place?' Mary sneered. 'Horribly dark round there unless you're on the top floor.'

'I wouldn't say no.' It was one of the best addresses in Belgravia. Possibly in the whole of London.

'I don't suppose you would,' she said, a little meanly. 'How are your flatmates?'

'One still fat and annoying, one just annoying.'

'Honestly, Lizzie,' Mary laughed. 'You should get yourself out of there before some of their unique charm rubs off on you.'

'I can't afford to move,' I reminded her. The landlord is putting the rent up again at the end of the month and there's still no sign of the new hot-water tank he promised us. I've looked at our contract, but all it really says is that he can throw us out pretty much whenever he wants to with about three minutes notice.' I could see Mary's eyes starting to glaze over as she listened to my tale of domestic terror.

'Love life?' she asked, quickly moving on to something she might be able to relate to.

'Still that Richard chap I told you about in my e-mail,' I said.

'What?' she raised her eyebrows in amusement. 'That's been . . .'

'Seven months.'

'Is he the one?' she asked me conspiratorially. 'Do you think it's MPL?'

'He's an accountant,' I replied.

'Oh. Well, don't get too attached then,' she sighed.

'I'm not,' I only half-lied. 'How's your love life?'

'Didn't you see the picture in *Hello!* last week, darling? It was only a small one admittedly, on the party pages at the back, but at least it was in colour this time. Mitchell and I went to a bash for Ivana Trump's fiftieth. Again,' she added wickedly.

'I didn't know you knew Ivana Trump,' I told her.

'I don't really. Well, perhaps well enough to say "hello" if I see her in San Lorenzo. But I owed her agent a massive favour and he was terrified that Ivana's birthday party would be a media washout. I just had to turn up with Mitchell for half an hour and get him to smile for some photos. It won't have done his career any harm to be in *Hello!* again either. It was a two-way thing.'

'I see. How's his new album going?'

'In the studio from dusk till dawn. Sleeps all day. Works all night. It's been like having a relationship with a bloody vampire.'

Not only was Mary doing meteorically well in her career, in case you hadn't guessed she had managed to bag herself a pretty impressive trophy boyfriend into the bargain.

Mitchell – he only had one name (like the name the 'Artist who was formerly known as' was once known by, if you know what I mean) – was the only surviving member of a boy band called Teenage Crush who had been the big thing of 1999. They had split to pursue solo projects at the height of their popularity, but so far Mitchell was the only one of the foursome who had managed to scale the charts alone – albeit with a number of offensively inoffensive cover versions. Anyway, Mitchell had always been considered to be the handsome one of the band with his movie-star looks and action man body, though he was also rumoured to be slightly soft between the ears (I mean, thick, of course. Not just soppy about animals). But I guessed that Mary must have had a change of heart since she announced that she could never go to bed with anyone who didn't stimulate her mind as well as her clitoris (that was during the pierced post-grad crush). Whatever, I was impressed that Mary was shagging her most fanciable client however appalling his GCSE results had been.

'Is he doing any of his own material on this album?'

I asked, relishing the fact that almost everyone in the café was suddenly ear-wigging on our conversation. *Mitchell* was a name everyone knew right then – darling of every publication from *Tatler* to *Take A Break*. But Mary merely rolled her eyes extravagantly at the idea of Mitchell's songwriting.

'Good god, no. He can't afford to retire yet. Though I foolishly let him spend the first week of this latest session in the studio making a demo tape of his own stuff, just to placate him. You've never heard anything like it, Liz, and thankfully no one else ever will. It was so dark. And absolutely rubbish. All bleeding hearts and unattainable love, with a dash of satanism and vampires thrown in for luck. *Très* Ozzy Osbourne.'

'What?'

'That is exactly what I said when I heard it. Anyway, bollocks to that, I told him. We're in the business of making money, not mistakes. So he's going to do a load of new stuff by the talented one from BoyZone, a couple of old Burt Bacharach classics with some Madonna samples and a version of Slade's 'Come on Feel the Noize' instead. I've promised him that I might let him put one of his own tracks on as a bonus track that you only get to hear if you leave your CD in the player for two hours after the last proper track has finished.'

'That doesn't sound like a very good idea to me,' I told her. 'If it's as full of satanic imagery as you say it is, before you know it you'll have people claiming that Mitchell is trying to subliminally subvert the fresh-faced youths who buy his records. Angry parents will be storming the desks at HMV demanding blood. And refunds.'

I had a pretty good idea which demand frightened her more.

'Mmm, I suppose you might be right,' she admitted. 'Though fresh-faced is hardly how I'd describe some of the fourteen-year-old trollops who were throwing themselves at him when he did a signing at Tower Records the other week. Honestly, Liz, you've never heard such language. If anyone was corrupted it was me, by them. One of them asked me for a light for her spliff for heaven's sake! They know no morality, the kids of today. Sex, drugs and rock and roll? These kids were *bored* of that old crap before they got to senior school. Oh, listen to me,' she snorted. 'I sound like I'm ready to retire to Nappy Valley.'

Nappy Valley was the nickname we'd given to the houses around Clapham Common where *naice* people went to have babies once a year or so until their husbands found temptation in au pairs or the gay cottaging hot-spot near the cricket pitches (made very public by the poor one-time Minister for Wales).

'I can't imagine you in Clapham,' I told her. 'Or Mitchell for that matter.'

'I think he'd rather like to be near the Common,' Mary said, her mouth turning down at the corners as if she had just tasted something nasty.

'You're not thinking of tying the knot, are you?' I asked excitedly.

'Get real, Liz. If Mitchell gets married at the moment his record sales will go like that.' She pointed her thumb downwards into the sugar bowl. 'A huge part of his appeal for the hormonal hordes of screaming girlies is the perpetual perception of availability. They need to be able to imagine that they could have him. Remember how Take That weren't even allowed to have girlfriends in case it upset the fans? It was written into their contracts.'

'Then how come Mitchell's allowed to be seen cavorting with you in the illustrious pages of *Hello!*? Aren't you spoiling his aura of availability simply by being around him at all?'

She shook her head. 'There's a balance to be struck,' Mary explained. 'Between having Mitchell appear available and not having him appear to be afraid of women.'

'Oh. So it's not about *true love* then?' I probed.

'Of course it's about love,' Mary retorted tetchily. 'But he's still my client as well as my lover and I can't start picking fabric for the bridesmaids' dresses yet. His career must come before my feelings right now.'

'What a shame.'

'It's my pension too,' she said flatly. 'When he earns, I earn. Besides, you know I don't really believe in marriage and all that *happily ever after* crap. Not after some of the things I've seen.'

'How are your parents?' I asked automatically. I'd never actually met Mary's parents. Well, I'd seen her mother from a distance once, sitting outside the college gates in her silver convertible Mercedes, tapping her manicured fingers on the leather-covered steering wheel while she waited for Mary to bring her trunk down at the end of term. But I knew enough about them to realise that if anyone had put Mary off the idea of marriage it was the two people who had brought her up.

'Dad's having another affair,' she sighed, confirming my suspicions. 'Honestly, Liz, he thinks we don't know about it. Stupid fool. It's bloody obvious. As soon as he gets besotted with some new tart he goes on another crash diet and picks up the gym membership again, then Mum dyes her hair a shade or two lighter and goes hunting for a casual shag of her own in Browns. They're as bad as each other. I don't know why they don't just cut their losses and get a divorce. Well, I do know. They're both too frightened that the other one would end up with all the money and the house in Palma. How are your parents, anyway?'

'Same as ever. Still together. They don't need to get a divorce now that Dad's got a new shed to hide in when Mum's on the war path,' I joked.

'You're so lucky to have parents like yours,' Mary murmured, looking into her coffee as though she expected the froth to start forming words. Mary was always telling me how wonderful my parents were, but then she had only met my mother *after* the menopause (five long years spent waiting for Armageddon to strike every time someone dropped biscuit crumbs on the carpet had rather coloured my own view of Mum).

'Anyway, am I ever going to get to meet this wonderful man of yours before his star drops out of the ascendant and you're finally allowed to marry him or dump him?' I asked her then to get back into more cheerful waters.

'Of course you'll get to meet him,' Mary promised. 'But you know how difficult it is. I mean, you and I hardly ever get to see each other as it is because of my crazy work schedule. Factoring Mitchell into the equation would make it practically impossible to arrange a night out with all the appearances he has to do.'

'Then perhaps I could meet you both at an appearance,' I suggested excitedly. 'In the VIP room at some swanky nightclub. I'd like that. I've always wanted to be a VIP.'

'Yeah. I'll see what I can do,' she said distantly. But she didn't seem keen. Perhaps she was just fed up of people asking to meet him all the time. I was sure I wouldn't have minded having a celebrity boyfriend myself, but I imagine that it must make you feel quite inadequate if you're not also a big celeb yourself. I mean, you'd get to go to loads of sparkling media parties full of superstars, sure; but no one would actually care whether *you* turned up or not. In fact, most people would probably prefer your other half to turn up alone.

'You'll never guess who phoned me yesterday,' I

said, to break the silence that had fallen since I dared to ask to meet Mitchell.

'Bill?' she guessed, not even looking up from her coffee. 'I spoke to him last Friday. He said he was going to call you. He's comign through Heathrow *en route* from Chile to Nepal next weekend.'

'No. He didn't call.' And I was slightly offended that he hadn't. I only got the occasional postcard from him since we'd gone our separate ways after college but he and Mary always seemed to be in touch by phone.

'Oh. I don't know then,' Mary continued guessing. 'Andrew?'

'Andrew? Who's Andrew?' I asked. I didn't know anyone called Andrew. 'No, Brian called.'

She looked at me blankly for a moment.

'Brian Coren? You must remember Brian?' I said incredulously. 'Brian from America. Our second year? Cute arse. Big smile. The one true love of my life?'

For a moment, Mary's jaw dropped and we were suddenly six years back in time, sitting on the steps outside the experimental psychology block, cringing with embarrassment that the Brady Bunch had heard us bitching. 'Not Brian Coren from New York?' she breathed.

'The very same. He called me last night to say that he's coming to visit.'

'Oh my god.' Mary put down her cappuccino and ran an elegant hand through her perfect hair. I noticed she had given up biting her fingernails (or had some very expensive falsies). 'When's he coming?' she asked.

'End of the week. Friday afternoon, can you believe?'

'Oh my double god, Liz. That's a bit short notice, isn't it?'

'You're telling me. He says he's just got to snatch some time off work while he can.'

'I can appreciate that,' she muttered. 'I haven't had a proper holiday in three years. Where's he staying? Somewhere central?'

'Well, I actually said he could stay with me.'

'What? In Balham? You are joking, Liz,' she exclaimed with a grimace.

'If only. He said he would be happy to stay in a hotel, but I said I wouldn't hear of it. Then he said that he really didn't mind staying in a hotel because it is such short notice but I insisted that I couldn't live with myself if I let him. I told him that I wouldn't even consider it. I had to be his host. He insisted one more time that he'd be happy to stay somewhere else, then I insisted one more time that he shouldn't and this time I won.'

'You idiot!' said Mary. 'You can't possibly have Brian to stay at *Fleapit Towers*.'

'Fleapit Towers? What are you saying? It's not that bad.'

'You think so? Look, I didn't want to have to say this to you, Lizzie, but you remember that night I crashed at your place after . . . you know, that incident . . .'

When she was dumped by Mr Rich, Handsome and Eligible Mark Four, she meant (I think he was the psychotic heir to some supermarket chain – never actually met him) and turned up on my doorstep at three in the morning wearing nothing but her pyjamas and looking as though she should be sectioned. I remembered it well. We were up until four on a work-night drinking neat gin with vodka chasers. It was the first and only time Mary had visited my house in Balham. All our other meetings had taken place in far more salubrious Soho. Only severe desperation could have brought Mary south of the river these days.

'Well, when I woke up the next morning after sleeping on your sofa, I swear I had little red bites all over my legs. Flea bites,' she added in a half-whisper. But not so much of a whisper that everyone in the café didn't turn round to see who was the unclean one with an infestation in the house.

'You did not,' I said indignantly.

'I'm afraid I did. I looked like someone had been at me with a pin cushion. But I'm not blaming you, Liz. I didn't even want to have to tell you about the incident. I'm sure it's not your fault. I mean, you've never even really liked cats, have you? Must have been left over from a moggy that belonged to the previous tenants or something – fleas can live in the carpet for years if they're not treated straight away. All I'm saying is, you can't risk that happening to Brian, can you? You know what Americans are like about hygiene.'

'I know,' I said miserably. I remembered with a sinking heart Brian's vitriolic views on the subject of English plumbing. He couldn't understand the logic of sitting in a bath without having showered first. He was the type of man who wore clean underpants every day and washed his bedclothes at least once a week. He wouldn't be overly impressed to find himself boarding with Fat Joe, who thought that changing his skanky underpants might weaken his spirit, or something sick like that.

'Even though I don't believe you about the fleas,' I continued. 'I know I can't have Brian staying with me in Balham. Particularly as . . .' Then I spilled out the whole sorry tale about the mendacious e-mails from cycling next to Ginger Spice to partying with Arabella Gilbert.

'Oh my god,' breathed Mary when I had finished. She was approximating a shocked expression but I could tell that she was really just struggling not to laugh. 'Oh my god! You told him you live in a flat that overlooks Hyde Park? Well, perhaps if you took a step-ladder up on to your flat roof and a pair of really good binoculars you might be able to see Tooting Common. But Hyde Park? That's hilarious, Liz.'

'I wish I could agree with you.'

'It's the funniest thing I've heard in a fortnight. Whatever possessed you?'

'I wanted him to think I was making a success of things,' I sighed, looking down into my coffee.

Mary pursed her lips disapprovingly.

'Oh Lizzie. You should never, ever tell lies,' she said, still biting back a snigger. 'Unless you really think you can pull them off.'

'Well, I did, didn't I?' I snapped back. 'Whoever told a lie they didn't think they could pull off, for heaven's sake?'

'Keep your hair on. I was only offering some friendly advice.'

'Right. The kind of friendly advice I could have got from my mother, thanks all the same. Mary,' I said weakly. 'I was rather hoping that you might be able to help me in a slightly more practical way.'

She smiled at that. 'I'll do anything I can, darling. Of course I will. You know that.'

'Like, could I stay at your flat while Brian is in town?'

A slow grin spread across her face.

'Please. Pretty please. I'd pay you whatever the going rate is,' I begged, though I was taking the big smile on her face to mean that she was already considering the idea in a positive way.

'You don't have to pay me, Liz,' she said magnanimously as she patted my hand. 'You're my best friend. Of course I'd be happy to help you. And of course you can stay at my flat for just as long as you need. I'll be delighted to have you both. When I was in your position,' she said, as though she were fifty years my senior instead of a couple of months, 'I couldn't wait to live on my own and get out of the whole washing-up rota thing, but now that I have my own luxury flat with a dishwasher to worry about that for me, I actually get quite lonely from time to time. You must call Brian and tell him that I can't wait to play hostess. I'll even throw a party for you both if you want me to. We could hire a room at one of my clubs. Soho House or Groucho? Just let me know who needs inviting. Wouldn't it be great if Bill could be in town too? I think he's flying in on Monday. Perhaps they'll overlap . . .'

I gritted my teeth to tell her, 'Actually, I was also hoping that you might make yourself scarce for the duration.'

'What?' She looked at me uncomprehendingly.

'Please, Mary. It's only for four days. Two of those are over the weekend. You could stay with Mitchell, couldn't you? In that fantastic luxury bachelor pad he was photographed in for *Hello!*,' I added with an appealing smile.

'For god's sake, Liz, he doesn't actually own that flat,' said Mary sharply. 'Besides, I never stay at Mitchell's.'

'Why not?'

'Because . . . because I just don't ever stay there, OK. We like to maintain our own space. Keep our own identities. I don't want him living in my pocket and he doesn't want me hanging round him all the time either.'

'Yeah, but sometimes you must stay round there for a night or two. At weekends.'

'Liz, I can't stay with Mitchell next weekend,' she said firmly. 'Just forget that.'

'Well, you must have a health farm or something you'd like to go to. What about Champneys? You're always saying how much you like it at Champneys.

All those lovely masseurs. Perhaps they've still got that Czech one who asked if he could marry you.' (He was after a visa.) 'I'll pay for you to spend the four days there. How about that?'

'Why do you want me out of my own bloody flat so badly?' she snapped.

'Because . . . because I need to pretend that your flat is mine, Mary. You know I do.'

'Why?' she whined.

'Why?' I echoed sarcastically. Hadn't she been listening? 'Because I don't want to have to tell Brian the truth about my e-mails, that's why. He's only coming to England for four days. After that I probably won't see him again for another six years by which time even I might just have a place of my own. Please, Mary. I just can't stand the thought of having to tell him the truth next week. He'll think so badly of me. We're only going to have four days together as it is. I don't want to have to spend half my time with him making up for the fact that I've been telling him a whopping big pile of lies about my life for the past three years.'

'You should have thought of that before you decided to audition for a job on *Jackanory*,' she said disdainfully. 'I know you've always had pretensions to being an actress, Liz, but this really is ridiculous. You've been a total idiot.'

'Mary, I know that. And I know that I'm asking a great deal of you. But this visit means so much to me . . .'

'So it seems. You're not planning to pick up where

you left off, are you?' she asked. 'Six years ago?' she added with a little snort.

'I suppose so. I mean, yes. I am.' I hoped the idea that I was pursuing true love might soften her into agreeing to help me on my terms.

'Well, I think you're expecting a bit much there,' she said instead.

'Perhaps I am. But you'll help me out. Won't you?'

She straightened her mouth into a firm, thin line before she told me, 'No. No, I bloody won't. I have to be in London for the whole of next weekend. I'm afraid I can't mess up my plans just because you've got yourself into another ridiculous situation. I thought I was being bloody generous offering you both a decent, flea-free place to stay at all, considering the amount of work I've got going on at the moment. When one really deals with celebrities, as opposed to pretending that you've jogged on the treadmill next to Ginger Spice at the Sanctuary, one doesn't have time to engage in elaborate and downright pathetic charades for people who aren't decent enough to accept their rotten lot in life and admit to it.'

She took a triumphant sip of her cappuccino and waited for my reaction.

The cow. She had the answer to my problems at her fingertips and she would not let me have it.

'Mary?' I said pleadingly.

'Absolutely not,' she smiled. 'If you don't want to stay in my flat with me in it simultaneously, you can forget the whole thing.'

Double cow. She had been my best friend all through college. I was the person she turned to when an attempt to dye her facial hair a lighter colour gave her a bright red rash of a moustache. I was the person she turned to when she went through a very nasty case of haemorrhoids and thought that she was dying of something undiagnosable. Once I had known more about her than anyone in the world. I wondered if I should remind her of all those little things we'd shared in the years that we had known one another. The good times and the bad. But no. She'd changed. She'd probably deny that most of them had even happened.

'Shall we get some lunch now?' she asked to close the discussion. 'I know a lovely Italian place just around the corner where they might let you in looking like that. I'm not drinking today though. Empty calories. I need to shift some weight for the start of the party season. You know I got my first Christmas party invitation yesterday?'

'Well, I'm not eating anyway,' I told her frostily. 'I've got to go to the supermarket and pick up some flea powder for my stinking flat, haven't I?' Then I left.

Well, I walked out of that café with my head held quite high, all things considered. But I was no nearer to finding a solution to the Brian problem and I had fallen out with one of my best friends to boot. Why wouldn't she help me? When had Mary been hit with the bitch stick? I had a sudden, awful vision of her sitting at the aluminium table in the café, ultra-powerful lap-top in front of her, tapping out an e-mail to Brian which she would send via the modem on her mobile phone. As far as I knew, she didn't have Brian's e-mail address, but I was sure it wouldn't be difficult for her to track him down and spew out the whole story before I got to him.

And I'd forgotten to pick up my one and only decent birthday present before making my dramatic exit.

On the way to the tube I thought of ways to get my revenge on Mary. If we had still been at college, I could have written something terrible about her on the back of a toilet cubicle door, or forged her spidery handwriting and left a note in the college geek's pigeon-hole saying that she really, really fancied him but was too shy to ask for a date. As it was, I couldn't think of anything I could do that would inflict a suitable amount of psychological pain on her right then, without me winding up in prison as a consequence.

Meandering through Soho towards the nearest underground station, I passed gay couples (in both senses of the word), sitting together outside chi-chi cafés, enjoying the late summer sunshine and each other's company. Everyone seemed to be laughing brightly at private jokes. Touching each other secretly beneath the tables. Kissing openly over their cappuccinos. Everyone was happy. Everyone had someone special. Everyone was in love. If she wasn't already getting hold of Brian, Mary was probably calling Mitchell, arranging a hot date for that evening. Whispering sweet nothings to him over the Nokia. Funny nicknames. Stupid jokes.

Was it so much to ask to be like these happy shiny people? All I wanted was someone I could feel passionate for, who felt the same way about me. Yes, I know I was supposed to be seeing Richard. I should have been feeling passionate about him but the fact was, I imagined that Richard, like me, would feel an outsider if he walked past these ultra-trendy people now. He was just an accountant after all. He thought that the height of individuality was wearing odd cartoon character socks to the office. A Bart Simpson tie when he felt particularly daring. He probably had ambitions to own a Ford Sierra Cosworth and spend his Saturday afternoons cleaning it rather than canoodling outside a café anyway.

But I wanted to be a part of a 'scene'. The kind of scene that they write about in the colour supplements to all the Sunday papers. I wanted to be able to walk into a café and order a latte without feeling as though the girl behind the counter thought I was being pretentious. I knew that Brian could order a latte without wincing. I knew that Brian was part of a glamorous scene somewhere. With someone ordinary like Richard I would always be just a registry office ceremony away from the purgatory of suburbia and I would never reach my true potential. With Brian, I could be my wacky individual creative self. I did have a wacky self somewhere, I was sure. I could feel it sometimes, when I'd had a couple of bacardis.

A girl with bright yellow hair clipped up into fifty or so tiny spiky bunches, suddenly stepped out of a domination gear shop doorway and straight on to my foot in her gravity-defying patent stilettos. She didn't even say 'sorry'. I did, however. I said 'sorry' to someone who had just stepped on me! As I watched her stagger down the footpath in her pink mini-skirt and stripy tights, greeting other funky people outside every café she passed, I bristled with frustration and wondered if she had even seen me standing there in my army regulation jumper and jeans.

'I'm easily as good as you are underneath all that slap,' I said in an imaginary conversation with the confident girl. 'I could be working for some Soho television company. I could be making the coffee in a recording studio, 'cos I bet that's all you're doing even with your high heels and your hair. I'm cultured. I'm educated. I could be anything I want to be. I'm just working as a secretary at Corbett's and wearing these crappy clothes while I decide what I really want to do. And when I do find out, then you'll notice me. I could be a famous actress one day. Then everyone will recognise me. No one would dare step on my feet in the street again without saying sorry to me.'

But before I could catch up with her, or grow the courage to say such a thing to her face, she had slipped inside the doorway to a members-only club. *Soho House*, said the plaque on the door. It was one of the trendy media clubs that I had read about in the *Evening Standard*, or Arabella Gilbert's society column, and written about in my stupid lying e-mails to Brian. I think I had described myself sitting inside on a red banquette, listening to the brothers from Oasis have an impromptu jamming session with the kooky lead singer from The Cardigans. Looking up at the windows, I was reminded with heart-stopping misery that I had no idea what the furniture in that club looked like at all, or whether the Gallagher boys were even members.

'I could be a member too,' I said half out loud. 'If I really wanted to be.'

'Cheer up, love,' said a man lurking in the shadows. When he stepped forward I saw that he was one of the many people who slept rough in Soho doorways. His hair was matted into a single squidgy dreadlock on one side. My guess was that it wasn't a fashion statement. If he had been an animal, Rolf Harris might have picked him up and taken him back to the dog's home for a good bath and some loving grooming.

'You can have some of this if you like. You waiting for a giro too?' He thrust a can of Special Brew into my hand. I thrust it quickly back into his grimy fingers. Once upon a time, I might have been touched by a gesture of such generosity, but right then I was simply mortified that he might have seen me as a kindred spirit. Someone he had something in common with. Another of life's failures. A bottom-feeder in life's big fishtank. A piece of the base metal beneath London's thin layer of gilt. He thought that I was one of them. One of the losers. It must have been because I was talking to myself so passionately.

'Spare any change?' he asked me then.

And, indignity of all indignities, when I reached into my pocket to oblige, I discovered that I couldn't spare any at all. I had just enough money to get the tube home.

When I got home, the burnt grill-pan was still sitting on the kitchen table. My flatmates were nowhere to be seen. But an envelope had arrived for me. Inside was my copy of the college magazine. *The St Judith's Chronicle*. I had no idea why I still subscribed, since it served only to depress me in much the same way as Arabella Gilbert's glittering social column.

But that day I tore the envelope open eagerly, wanting to make a full-blown tragedy out of my miserable morning. I read the news of other alumni. Ryan Fisher had set up his own internet café company. Anna Simner had written a book. Jemima Shad-Chequebook, the college's most renowned slapper was engaged to be married to one of the directors of the vast bank she had gone to work for as a trader (a nice early retirement for her, I thought). Name after name that I recognised. All doing something exciting with their lives. All starting companies, or getting promotions, getting married or moving abroad. One of my Freshers' Week flings had already married and was father to a six-month-old daughter. Even Janie Spright, the college girl-geek, had started to publish her own alternative style magazine and was hoping to be able to float it on the stock exchange within a year. I remembered with a wry smile a conversation I had once had with Mary about whether the thick-rimmed glasses Janie wore in the library were a fashion statement or a necessity. I thought they were merely for her myopia but Mary had obviously been right. Again.

At the bottom of the column, another list asked 'Where are they now?'; and there I found my own name, right next to a request to write in with an update on my achievements and my whereabouts. Everyone was simply *dying* to hear how I was getting on . . .

'Where am I now?' I asked myself. Twenty-seven years old. No career to speak of – I didn't even have a permanent job, although Harriet was constantly promising me a proper contract when her solicitor cousin came out of the clinic. Where was I? Reading the college magazine on a springless sofa surrounded by the pathetic detritus of a life gone horribly wrong. That's where I was.

'Feeling better?' Seema trilled when she came in loaded down with library books and shopping bags.

I couldn't even bring myself to moan in disagreement.

'Look at this,' she pulled a green bottle out of one of the plastic bags. 'Californian Chardonnay is on special offer at Habib's. Probably full of anti-freeze. Do you think it will be nice?'

It was only just past two but I helped her drink three bottles to be sure.

CHAPTER TEN

Having drunk so much on an empty stomach, I fell into such a deep sleep that I could only be woken the next morning by the rather horrible sensation of Richard knocking on my forehead with his knuckles.

'Wake up! Wake up!' I heard him say through the mists of a hangover to rival the one I got after the end of the last Millennium. 'It's half-past eleven. We've got to be at your mother's in half an hour.'

'What? What!!!'

I sat up and banged my head on the angle-poise spotlight which I had taped to my bed-head for perfect in-bed reading. Great idea that had been.

'She's already called to see if you've left yet,' said Seema, who was standing in the doorway. 'I told her you left at ten. Even then she said that she couldn't see how you could possibly make it to Solihull before she burned the beef.'

'Oh, bollocks,' I shouted.

I jumped out of bed and began to pull on socks and shoes. Then I had to take my shoes off again to put my jeans on. 'Are you wearing that?' I asked Richard as I sniffed my *Pulp in concert* t-shirt to see if I could get away with it. He was wearing a smart Mandarin collared shirt and a pair of fairly reasonably well-pressed trousers. 'Where's your tie?'

'I wear a tie all week. Isn't this smart enough for you?'

'Not really. No. Seema, do you think Fat Joe has got a tie?'

'He's got one,' she told me. 'But I think he's been using it to hold his trousers up since he broke his belt.'

'Phone my mum,' I instructed my flatmate as I hopped into my shoes. 'Phone my mum and tell her you've just seen me outside the house trying to change the wheel on my car. Oh, and make sure you tell her Richard's helping or she'll only want to know why.'

A minute later, Seema returned. 'She wants to know why Richard hasn't got a car you could use instead of your old Fiesta.'

'Oh, just tell her I'm on my way. But not to put the Yorkshire puddings in yet.'

'Too late,' said Seema. 'She's already done that. She says everything is going to be ruined because of your selfishness. She said that she doesn't suppose I'd give *my* mother such a runaround. Certainly not, I told her. If I did, I'd have been sent to live with my aunty in Mumbai. She asked if my aunty had a spare room for you.'

'Oh, shut up, perfect daughter,' I snapped. 'Or I'll

write and tell your parents about the lap-dancing audition at Stringfellow's.'

'I did that for a dare,' Seema protested. 'I was raising money for Rag Week.'

'Tell that to your aunty in Mumbai.'

Richard sat on the end of my bed and watched with amusement as, having decided that the t-shirt was probably a health hazard, I started flinging the entire contents of my wardrobe on to the floor, rejecting skirt after shirt after jumper until Seema came back from her room with the suit she saved for interviews.

'You can wear this,' she told me. 'If you swear you'll keep quiet about the dancing thing. But promise not to get it dirty, won't you?'

'Thanks,' I said. 'Do I look like the kind of girl who can't get a forkful of food from her plate to her mouth without dropping it?'

Richard and Seema both focused on the tea-stains that patterned the front of my pyjamas but said nothing.

Poor Richard. It was bad enough that he was going to have to meet the two extra-terrestrials that had been pretending to be my parents for the past twenty-seven years, but when we finally pulled into the street where they lived (only two hours late), I realised that even more horrors awaited him. My brother Colin's car was already in the driveway.

Colin and I are twins. But you wouldn't believe it

unless you saw our birth certificates or did a blood test. Obviously we were never going to be identical – after all, I'm a girl and he's a boy. But you'd think that we would have something in common at least. As it was, we didn't even have the same kind of hair. Somehow he managed to end up with the jaunty blond curls that should have been mine, while I got the mousy rats' tails and receding hairline. OK, so the receding hairline bit is a slight exaggeration, but what kind of cruel witch is mother nature to keep doling out the best hair and eyelashes to the boys? Tell me that the person with the best eyelashes you've ever seen wasn't a member of the un-fair sex and we'll ask that girl where she got her lash-building protein-enhanced mascara from.

So, we weren't in the least bit alike, Colin and I. He was blond. I was mousy. He had blue eyes. Mine were like shallow pools of stagnant green mud. He was athletic. I was pathetic. And on and on and on. By the time we were six he was so much more physically advanced than me that most people assumed he was at least two years my senior when in fact I predated him by a good eight minutes. But the fact that we were so different didn't stop people making fruitless comparisons once they knew that we were buns from the same oven.

All through junior school, the sadistic teachers (who ought to have been working as dominatrixes in Soho rather than moulding such tiny hearts and minds) would say to me every time I made a mistake: 'Why can't you do maths? Your brother Colin can do maths. Why can't you spell "misappropriation"? Your brother Colin can spell any word up to eight syllables long.' I wondered if anyone ever asked him why he couldn't do a decent French plait? Or name all the members of Bucks Fizz *and* remember their birthdays? I don't think so.

'Nice car,' breathed Richard when he clocked Colin's egg-shell blue Ford Focus in the driveway. It would be, wouldn't it? My Ford Fiesta (red from rust, not a paint job – it was supposed to be yellow) looked as though it had seen active service in the Crimean War. It stood to reason that Colin could only have turned up in a vehicle so spanking new it was still smarting.

'That's my brother's car,' I told him despondently.

'You never said you had a brother,' said Richard.

'Twin actually.'

Richard looked at me in a very peculiar way. 'Then I'm doubly surprised you didn't tell me about him. I thought twins were supposed to be really close. Don't you have a telepathic bond or something?'

'It got cut off when I forgot to pay the bill,' I said dryly. I turned off the juddering engine of my poor little car and pulled the handbrake up so hard it sounded as though I had done something an injury. 'Are you ready for this?' I asked Richard, giving him one last chance to escape. But Richard already had one hand on the door handle on his side of the car, a bunch of service-station flowers clutched in the other.

'I'm ready,' he said, giving me the thumbs up like

a Second World War fighter pilot about to go into action.

'Well, I just need a few more seconds,' I told him. But it was too late anyway. Mum had spotted us turning into the driveway and was already opening the front door while deftly removing her apron like some superwoman from the 1960s who could flit between kitchen and dining room boiling spuds and drinking cocktails while simultaneously holding a coherent conversation about the lunar landings.

She was upon the car before we could get out of it.

'Was the traffic terrible?' she asked as she kissed my cheeks off. 'I could only think that that was why you're so late,' she added pointedly.

'I overslept,' I told her.

'Oh, late night was it?' she tutted. 'Been out partying so hard that you forgot you were coming to see your poor old mother?'

'Mum, this is Richard,' I said, reminding her that I had brought a guest before she brought up the time that I dawdled on the way home from Brownies and she called out the entire South Midlands police force to look for me. They even dredged the local pond, apparently. I'd only been missed for ten minutes. When I walked through the garden gate to see Mum dabbing at her eyes with a tea-towel while a big policeman took notes on my distinguishing marks, she threw herself upon me and smothered me with kisses as though I had been missing for a month. As soon as the policemen had gone however, I got a stinging wallop across the back of the legs and was sent to bed early for making a show of us all. I can still see Colin's face, eyes glittering with amusement, as he watched me get a slapping from the safety of the first-floor landing. I had actually been dawdling home from Brownies because *he* had told me that there were fairies living in the hedge behind the community hall.

'Richard, I'm Lizzie's Mum,' Mum was saying.

'I think he might have guessed.' It was Colin. He stood behind Mum now in a sleeveless Fair Isle patterned jumper and stiffly ironed trousers. If he had been smoking a pipe I wouldn't have been in the least bit surprised. Twenty-seven going on fifty, my brother.

'Hey, little sis,' he said when he saw me. 'How's life in bedsit land?'

He helped me out of the car. I had been so tense on the drive up that I was finding it difficult to straighten out again. 'I am not your little sister,' I reminded him. 'I'm a good eight minutes older than you are. And I don't live in a bedsit. But other than that, life in the Metropolis is fine, thanks for asking. How's tricks in the sticks, Col? Must be about that time of year when you get to do interesting things with silage.'

Colin opened his mouth while he tried to think of a suitably witty retort, but Richard was out of the car too now and he was obviously waiting to be introduced. 'Richard, this is my brother Colin.'

'You don't look like twins,' Richard said reflexively.

'Good job,' said Colin. 'Imagine the looks I'd get down at the golf club. You play golf do you, Richard?'

I hurried him inside.

There's only one thing worse than an unexpected encounter with my brother and that's an unexpected encounter with his wife. My sister-in-law Sally was stirring gravy in the kitchen. When we came in, she didn't even leave the hob, so scared was she of letting her Bisto go lumpy. I introduced Richard, who, clearly very nervous, re-iterated his surprise that Colin and I didn't look more like twins.

'Mmmm,' Sally simpered. 'It is funny, isn't it? You know, lots of people have actually said that if they saw the three of us in a room – me, Colin and Lizzie, that is – they would probably think that I was his twin instead!' She giggled uproariously at that. She always said it when meeting someone new. I don't know why she thought it was so cute, though. I thought it was just plain weird to fall in love with someone who people often mistook for your blood relative.

'How are you getting on in your bedsit, Lizzie?' she asked me then.

'It's not a bedsit,' I reminded her too.

'Oh, I remember when I lived in shared accommodation,' she said with a far-away smile, as if she were a hundred years old. She was actually two years younger than me. 'No one ever doing the washing up.

People forgetting to buy the milk. It was like something out of a television programme sometimes.'

But less *Men Behaving Badly* than a temporary holding hostel for apprentice *Stepford Wives*, I should imagine. I had been to Sally's spinster flat once, for her hen
night – held, very sensibly, a whole month before she
was to be married to Colin so that there would be no
danger of her not having recovered from the hangover
before she took her vows. For a start, what kind of girl
has her hen night at home instead of in the seediest
nightclub in town? And secondly, what kind of hen
bakes three hundred cheesy scones for the occasion?
What kind of twenty-four-year-old girl even knows
how to bake cheesy scones, for heaven's sake? Or has
a baking tray, before she puts one on the wedding list
because she thinks she ought to?

That was a hen night to remember all right. There
were two bottles of wine. The red one got kicked
over by Sally's great aunty Gina who couldn't get
out of her chair without the aid of two sticks and a
Chippendale (though needless to say, there were to
be no male strippers that night). The white bottle was
wasted on trying to get the red stain out of the carpet.
Then we watched *Four Weddings and a Funeral* and had
an in-depth discussion on how Hugh Grant's character
really missed out by not forcing Andie MacDowell to
the altar in the end.

'Such a shame you're not getting married at the
same time as Colin,' Sally said to me at the end of
that evening, as I helped her pick sausage roll crumbs

off the previously pristine carpet. 'Colin would have loved for the pair of you to have had a joint wedding. if only I'd had a twin brother too,' she added wistfully. 'He would have been your ideal man . . .'

Now she was sizing Richard up to see if he would do instead.

'What do you do?' she asked him after they'd had a bit of a dance about while she tried to shake his hand with her oven gloves still on.

'I'm an accountant,' he told her.

'Oh, really? That must be exciting,' she smiled warmly, and not at all ironically.

'Come and sit down in here, Richard,' Colin shouted from the sitting room. 'The girls can get on with the dinner. Sally likes me to stay out of the kitchen. Don't you, Sally?'

'I do,' said Sally to me in a conspiratorial whisper. 'He's absolutely hopeless, you know. If I let him try to help with the housework, I always end up having to do everything again as soon as he's gone out of the house. I don't tell him that, of course. I mean, I don't want to belittle him for doing his best to help me.'

Colin grinned at her wolfishly from the kitchen door. If he had heard her belittling his abortive attempts to make gravy, he didn't seem to care. In fact, I had a sneaking suspicion that it was all part of his master plan. Burn the Sunday roast once and you'll never be asked to do it again. Most cunning. Though it had never worked for me. I burned whatever I touched in the kitchen. Even the washing up. And yet I was always being asked back for more.

'Come on, Richard,' Colin boomed. 'You're missing the match. You do like rugby, of course.' He physically dragged Richard away while Sally filled my empty hands with a potato masher and a packet of butter.

'You do know how to mash parsnips, don't you?' she asked me. 'It's almost exactly the same as mashing potatoes.'

'I think I've got it. How's your job?' I asked.

'Oh. So, so. They've given me a little promotion to deputy head of the entire personnel department and wanted me to go to a trade fair in Frankfurt next week but Colin had already asked me to cook for his boss on Friday night so I had to turn it down.'

'Is this the twenty-first century?' I asked no one in particular as I started to mash the parsnips as if I were mashing Sally's silly head.

Mum appeared at my shoulder and told me I was doing the mashing wrong.

'Not so roughly . . . I've left your new boyfriend with the other boys. I must say he seems very nice, but then I noticed that he has a tattoo on his knuckles.' Mum sucked in her breath.

'Tattoo? What tattoo?' I asked.

'Right there,' she said, indicating the back of her left hand.

'Mum,' I sighed. 'That's not a tattoo. It's just a note in biro, to remind him that we were coming here today. Richard wouldn't get a tattoo.'

'A note in biro? On the back of his hand? Can't he remember what he's supposed to be doing from one day to the next? Honestly, Liz. Where do you find them?'

Of course, Brian Coren had been a major hit with the family. I had taken him to visit the folks shortly before the end of the spring term of that heady year we shared, when he expressed a desire to see the countryside I had grown up around. The thought of introducing him to my parents hadn't really crossed my mind until he suggested it. Well, it had, but I didn't want the relationship to end prematurely and that's what always seemed to happen when the family got involved. Perhaps it was the way my Mum would leave *Bride and Home* magazine lying casually open on the coffee table whenever I brought someone round for dinner.

I tried to dissuade him by telling him that Solihull was hardly the countryside and in any case, it was too far from Oxford for a weekend away. But Brian wasn't having any of that. He, after all, had grown up in a country where people think nothing of having to drive for three hours to the nearest corner shop, and so he insisted that we take the trip. He thought it would be fun to have a real English Sunday lunch with a real English family. I tried to explain that I had spent a good eighteen years of my life trying to avoid such a torture.

I nearly died of shock when Mum opened the door to us both and Brian immediately kissed her 'hello' on both cheeks. Such behaviour was quite different to the way things happened in our family and Mum was so taken aback she completely forgot to ask me why I wasn't wearing the scarf she had given me for Christmas.

Brian also came bearing gifts, which is a good move if you're meeting someone's parents for the first time. Mum made a great show of getting out her best cut-glass vase for the huge pink roses tied in a raffia bow Brian had bought, not at a garage *en route*, but at the swankiest florists in Oxford (I noticed that she had stuck Richard's roadside bunch into a tupperware juice holder). And to top it all, the conversation with Brian flowed so easily. My past experiences of introducing man to *mater* had been text-book examples of great failures in communication. One sixth form crush of mine had read a book about vampirism all the time my mother tried to talk to him. But not Brian.

'Lovely weather, Mrs Jordan,' said Brian. Cue monologue on sunny day that belied the late frosts that were ruining all the daffs, running into questions about the weather in New Jersey. Does it really snow every Thanksgiving? Into weather in California. How can they stand it being so hot when they go jogging? There wasn't an awkward pause all day.

After that visit, Brian Coren became the boyfriend benchmark. Every man I brought home – and in six years, I'd managed two or three more – was compared to Brian. Did he bring flowers? Did he kiss Mum 'hello' with exuberant confidence or cower behind me at the front door as if he expected my mother to be a fire-breathing dragon in pantyhose? How were his table manners? Would he eat her roast pork even if he wasn't strictly supposed to? Brian's successors failed all of these important tests. One of them, a media analyst I had somehow flukily managed to pick up in Soho and get past the third date mark, wouldn't even eat Mum's roast potatoes because he was a vegetarian and the spuds had been cooked in animal fat. It didn't impress him that Brian had set aside his entire religion to please my mum by eating her pork and we split up on the drive back to London.

'Now, do you think Richard will eat everything?' Mum asked as she dished out the rock-hard Yorkshire puddings. 'Do you remember that American boyfriend Lizzie had?' she asked Sally. The one who was Jewish but still ate my pork? What a lovely boy he was. Probably got himself kicked out of Jewish heaven for having such lovely manners.'

'He did have lovely manners,' agreed Sally.

We processed into the dining room like three serving wenches with two plates apiece. Colin was sitting at the head of the table, knife and fork upended in a manner which would once have earned him a slap on the hands.

'Who did the gravy?' he asked as he took the first mouthful. 'Looks a bit lumpy.'

Sally suddenly went a bit lumpy herself, and I thought she might be about to cry.

'Only joking, my treacle,' Colin said to reassure her. 'It's gravy fit for a king. Made by my princess.'

I noticed that I had been seated as far away from Richard as possible. Too far even to share a look of exasperation without it being intercepted by someone else. He wasn't saying much. But then he didn't really need to. Colin was holding court. He started a long monologue about the new responsibilities he had taken on with his promotion, without seeming to stop to draw breath once and yet managing to eat everything on his plate at the same time.

'We ought to have a toast; for the twins' birthdays,' Dad dared to interrupt. 'Happy twenty-seventh birthdays Colin and Liz.'

'Twenty-seven,' Mum sighed as we all raised our glasses. 'Seems like only yesterday when my waters broke in the back of your father's new Morris Traveller. But now you're both adults.'

'Well, one of us is definitely an adult,' Colin smirked in my direction.

'What do you mean by that?' I asked.

'Well, what do you think I mean? You're nearly thirty now, Lizzie Jordan. It's about time you started to do something with your life.'

I was just about to eat the last of my mashed parsnip but I put down my fork to get on the defensive.

'Can't believe we came from the same place, you and I,' he continued blithely. 'You just don't seem to want to go anywhere with your life. And you haven't even got the excuse of being a student any more.'

'At least I've gone further than the outskirts of Birmingham,' I told him angrily, when I had recovered from the shock of his sudden attack. 'How dare you say I'm not doing anything with my life. I've been to university and I'm actually working really hard right now with a view to running my own estate agency in a couple of years' time.'

'I can't imagine you being able to sell an igloo to an eskimo,' Colin laughed.

'One day you'll eat your words,' I promised him.

'Mmm. I'll have lost a lot of weight if I have to wait until then for my next meal. Have you finished that?' he asked Sally, whisking the remains of her meal from under her nose even as he asked her. She nodded and Colin finished the best roast potato she had been saving till last, in one bite.

'You see,' he said, still chewing. 'You people have got it all wrong thinking that London is the centre of the universe and that everyone who goes there is automatically a success. Commuting on that stinking tube day after day? I wouldn't force that trip on a sheep. Liz, if you ask me . . .'

'I'm not asking you,' I told him.

'If you ask me,' he continued regardless. 'What you really want to do is cut your losses and move back to Solihull before it really grinds you down. I can tell you're not happy there. You're not made of the right stuff for the big city. You're not getting anywhere in London, little sis. I could get you a job with some estate agency here and perhaps in ten years or so you could start thinking about branching out on your own again. I'll help you if you like.'

'I don't want to come back to Solihull,' I said petulantly. 'I am never moving back to Solihull.'

'You talk some sense into her,' Colin said with a wink to Richard. Richard smiled treacherously in return. 'If you've got a couple of weeks to spare, that is. You know, you were always the dreamer, Liz. Always having your big dreams for the future and making your incredible plans. Rushing about pretending you were going to be the next unknown to play little orphan Annie or get spotted in the supermarket by Quentin Tarantino. You'd never listen when someone told you that it couldn't be done. Always had to find out something was wrong for yourself.'

He said it in such a way that someone listening might have thought he was paying me a clumsy compliment, but I knew better than that.

'Yep, you were always the dreamer but dreams can't come true until you wake up. Dreams are nothing unless you can put them into practice. And I was always the practical one. Your stories always made me laugh though, sis. Perhaps you should think about being a novelist.'

'You could come back to Birmingham then,' Sally piped up. 'I mean, you can write anywhere, can't you?

And you've got an English degree so you should be quite good at it.'

'Another waste of time that was,' Colin interrupted. 'I may not have gone to such a fancy college as you to get my qualifications in business studies but at least I've got a proper job.'

'Lizzie, could you stack the plates,' said my mother, trying to mediate in her peculiarly passive-aggressive way. I followed her into the kitchen before I gave in to the temptation to throw a punch. 'Evan, tell your son not to pick on his sister,' she called to Dad before closing the kitchen door behind us. Dad just laughed.

'Don't take too much notice of your brother,' Mum told me as I slid the plates into a bowl of soapy water. 'You know he loves you really. He just loves to pick a fight.'

'But all those things he said. They're so unfair. So what if I'm a dreamer.'

'So what indeed,' agreed Mum. 'Dreamers are the people who have the ideas that make the world a more interesting place. If they act on the dreams that they have.'

'I do,' I protested at her insinuation.

'Mmmm. I'm not so sure. What about that time you got the part in *Annie*?' she said. 'You pretended you had tonsillitis because you weren't the leading girl. I don't call that following your dreams.'

'For heaven's sake. I was only seven.'

'But you've been a bit like that ever since, sweet-heart. You know, all the time you were growing up I used to wish that Colin had a little bit more of your imagination and you had a bit more of his pig-headedness. Whatever you say about your brother, and I know as well as you do that he isn't always right, when he decides to do something he does it. He follows through and he doesn't let little things get him down. He's a trier.'

'He's certainly been trying my patience today,' I quipped.

'Well, if you're serious about starting your own estate agency, why don't you turn your annoyance on its head and do your best to prove him wrong. Use upsetting Colin as an incentive.'

'I don't want to start my own estate agency,' I admitted.

'I didn't think so,' Mum replied, sitting down on a stool and folding her arms in a way I had seen so often. How did she know? How do mothers know everything?

'So what are you hoping to do with yourself, Lizzie? Whenever I call you these days you sound like you've just had some terrible news. When you first went up to London I thought your life sounded so exciting. Now it just sounds awful. Nasty job. Nasty flat.'

'Well, perhaps it's about to pick up again,' I told her. 'Brian's coming to visit.'

'Not Brian? Lovely Jewish Brian from America?'

'That's the one.'

She clapped her hands delightedly. It seemed that everyone I told about the impending visit was almost as excited as I would have been were it not for the complications.

'You know, I always had a feeling he'd come back for you,' Mum whispered, squeezing my arm.

'He's not coming back *for* me, Mum. He's just coming to visit.'

'Yes, to visit *you*. I could tell the first time I met him that he was besotted with my only daughter.'

It was what I wanted to hear, I suppose, but it didn't make my predicament any easier. I pondered telling her about the whole e-mail fiasco, but she was already off on another unstoppable train of thought.

'You know,' she said. 'Some mothers would hold their daughters back from running off with someone who's of a different religion who lives in a different country, but your father and I, we just want you to be happy.'

'Mum, don't you think you might be jumping the gun? Brian's only stopping here for four nights. I'm not sure if that will be long enough to plan an elopement to Las Vegas.'

'But you've kept in touch all these years. I knew from the moment I saw him that he felt very deeply for you, darling. Shall I get a roast in? Chicken, of course. I know he ate pork last time but it wouldn't be respectful of me to expect him to do it again.'

'Don't get anything in,' I told her. 'I don't think we'll have time to visit.'

'Oh. Well, your father and I could come up to London and see you both while he's in the country. There's room in your house. Though, I wouldn't want to show Brian that house of yours if it's in the same kind of state as it was last time we visited.'

Which, as far as our dump went, had been spotless. I'd cleaned for three weeks before Mum's last visit.

'Perhaps you should bring him straight here from the airport. He's only coming to see you. It doesn't matter whether you're in London or Birmingham. But what about him?' Mum jerked her head towards the sitting room where I had left Richard to fend for himself. I could hear Dad laughing. Very few of my boyfriends had ever made Dad laugh.

'I've told him I'm going to be busy next weekend.'

'Good. Don't blow it, Lizzie. All I've ever wanted for you has been a life full of the excitement that mine never had. I dreamed all my teenage years of going to America, of New York and Hollywood, of standing in front of the White House in Washington. And I saved as hard as I could to make that dream happen. But then I met your dad, and three months later I was putting my America money towards a registry office wedding and a two-week honeymoon in Scarborough.'

'But you do love Dad, don't you?'

'Of course I love your dad. It's just that, sometimes, I wonder what would have happened if I hadn't got on that 137 bus that day and stood on his foot in my stilettos. I wouldn't change him for anything now. Unless Robert Redford suddenly becomes available,' she laughed. 'But if you don't do everything that you've wanted to do before you settle down, you won't ever stop wondering about those dreams. If I'd gone to America, I'm sure I would have been frightened and lonely and back home again within a week, but because I didn't go, there will forever be a part of me that thinks I would have walked down Sunset Boulevard and stepped on to Robert De Niro's foot instead of your father's.'

'Then how come, when I asked you for money to go to America straight after I graduated, you wouldn't let me have any?' I asked. 'That was my dream then too.'

'Rubbish. You just wanted to get out of having to go to work,' said Mum, getting a new tea-towel out of the drawer.

'Well, thanks a lot.'

'But now you've got your own money,' she continued. (Eh? I wondered where it was hidden.) 'You can do whatever you like now. If Brian asks you to go back to America with him, don't you hesitate, my girl. Just chuck that job in, say goodbye to that filthy house and go. Your father and I won't mind a bit as long as we get some phonecalls.'

Chuck my crappy job in? Leave my stinking flat? I couldn't believe she was encouraging me to be quite so impulsive.

'You're twenty-seven now,' she said ominously. 'You can't keep waiting for something to happen. You've got to start grabbing whatever opportunities you get by the throat. And this is one huge opportunity.'

'He's only coming to visit,' I reiterated.

'Perhaps that's what he thinks now but you could make him change his mind about going back alone. Men don't know what they want. Not really. If Sally hadn't taken the initiative with your brother, he'd have been happy to go on living here and seeing her on Wednesday nights and at weekends until I got too old to do his ironing for him.'

I was trying to imagine Sally taking the initiative. 'What on earth did she do?'

'She made him think she was the only woman worth having. She had her hair done differently and started to make out like she was having a great time without him on every night except Wednesdays. Next thing you know, Colin suddenly announced that he'd proposed. She trapped him.'

'And you're suggesting that I do something like that with Brian?' I said indignantly, as if I hadn't already been pretending that I'd been having a great time without him. 'It's not obligatory for a girl to bag a man these days, you know,' I told her contrarily, as if I hadn't spent all my days as a singleton praying for a knight in shining armour to take the responsibility out of my life.

'No, but it makes life easier,' said Mum pragmatically. 'I don't know where I went wrong to bring up a daughter who could let a millionaire slip through her fingers.'

'I don't think Brian is a millionaire.'

'Not yet perhaps. But he's a damn sight more likely to become one than the boy you've brought home with you today. That Richard's a dreamer like you, Lizzie. I can tell. And you know what you get when you put two dreamers together, don't you?' she asked me.

'Tell me,' I begged her.

'Mortgage arrears.'

Just then, Richard poked his head around the kitchen door. He was carrying the mint-sauce boat.

'That was a top roast dinner, Mrs Jordan,' he said, with his best cheeky chappy smile. 'Don't think even my mum could have done it better.'

Mum allowed herself a proud little smile.

'Is there anything I can do to help out here?' he asked.

'Oh no,' said Mum, in very strange overtones. 'I don't think there's anything you can do any more.'

When Richard had retreated again, Mum grabbed my hands. 'I think it's destiny, you know. When I was about your age, I went to see a fortune teller on the pier at Brighton who told me that one day, one of my children would leave these shores and go abroad. Brian is coming back to take you with him. I know it.'

'But what if she meant Colin?' I protested. 'He's already left these shores once.' It was true. My brother had worked in Germany for almost two years.

'Oh, that's hardly abroad, is it?' said Mum. Despite

the fact that she had cried for two weeks solid when Colin first announced that he was off, and packed him enough sandwiches to keep him going for a fortnight in case he found he couldn't eat the foreign food. For the first month he was away, I overheard several amazed conversations where my mother would sigh, 'It sounds as if you're just down the road,' marvelling that Germany had half-decent telecommunications.

'Well, I'd better get this apple crumble on the table before it goes cold,' Mum said suddenly. 'Let me know how it goes,' she added with a conspiratorial wink before returning to the dining room singing 'My bonnie lies over the ocean' as she went.

CHAPTER ELEVEN

I got Richard out of there as quickly as was humanly possible. Luckily it was Sunday, so we had the excuse of needing to get back to London to prepare for another week at work.

'What did you think of my brother?' I asked as soon as I was sure that the car was out of sight.

'Nice bloke,' said Richard non-commitally. Then he added, 'Did you two have some kind of big rivalry going on when you were kids?'

'Not really,' I lied.

'Only he seemed pretty intent on keeping you in your place today. All that stuff about going back to Solihull. And telling me to talk some sense into you!'

'Are you going to?' I asked him dryly.

'Of course not. I want you to stay in London, don't I? I've got to after all.' He squeezed my knee. 'And I'll be right behind you if you want to become a property mogul. Perhaps you can get me a decent flat while you're about it.'

'I don't really want to become a property mogul,' I

told him. 'It's just that if I told Colin that I wanted to become an actress or a journalist, he might have choked to death on his Yorkshire pudding.'

'Do you want to be either of those things?' asked Richard in surprise.

'Yeah. Well, I'd certainly like to be an actress.'

'Seriously?'

'Sort of seriously. It's always been my dream.'

'Then why are you working in an estate agency?'

'I need to pay my rent, of course. And keep you in chips,' I added, just a little cruelly considering that Richard had promised to pay me back as soon as he could, but an afternoon with Colin always left me feeling cruel.

'Well, I never would have thought it,' Richard mused. 'You've never told me that you wanted to become an actress. Was that what the *Annie* crack was about? Did you do lots of drama as a child?'

'Yep. I always wanted to be little orphan Annie. Mum and Dad took us to see the show when we were seven. But I gave up dreaming about that when I was only offered "third orphan" in a church-group play.'

'It was probably only because you had the wrong hair,' said Richard, running his fingers wistfully through my mousy bob.

'Praise the Lord for that,' I cracked.

'Have you done any acting since then?' Richard probed.

'I did a bit. At college.'

'What did you play?'

'Cleopatra, Juliet's nurse, Viola in *Twelfth Night*, one of Chekhov's sisters.'

We had stopped at the traffic lights as I counted off on my fingers the rest of the parts I had taken. When I had finished, Richard looked at me in shock.

'Wow. I had no idea,' he said. 'You've done loads.'

'I don't like to talk about my glory days now,' I smiled ruefully as I put my foot down to move forward again.

'But you must have been pretty good to get all those parts.'

'Anyone could act at college. There were certainly more drama groups than revision ones.'

'You must have enjoyed it too.'

'I did. Even thought about going to drama school when I finished my degree.'

'Then what happened?'

I shrugged. 'Real life. Student loans. Overdrafts.'

'They're easily overcome. You've got to take your ambitions a bit more seriously if you actually want to fulfil them,' said Richard rather heavily. 'You say that you want to be an actress and yet you've never talked about it to me before.'

'Seems a bit of a pipe-dream now.'

'Rubbish. If Michael Caine can make a brilliant career out of playing himself, I'm sure you can earn a living. Hollywood here we come. I bet you're really good.'

'Thanks.'

'Why haven't you joined a drama group since you've been in London?'

'I just don't seem to have had time.'

'Maybe you should make some time,' he suggested, giving my knee another squeeze. So hard this time that I nearly accidentally changed gear and the clutch made a terrible crunching sound.

'Maybe,' I said disconsolately.

Oh, Richard, I sighed to myself. He was trying to be so nice. He was a nice guy. Not exciting perhaps. But very nice. A dreamer like me? Mum's accusation ran through my head. I felt horribly mean for wondering whether she had been right and squeezed his knee back out of guilt.

'Don't let other people's expectations of you become your own expectations of yourself,' he continued. 'Because nine times out of ten, they don't know what's best for you. If you ask me, your brother only ridicules the fact that you used to be a bit of a dreamer because he doesn't understand the real power of dreams. He's a worker ant. He always will be. And he wants to drag you down to his level because he knows that you're a caterpillar waiting to turn into a butterfly and he finds that rather frightening.'

We had stopped at a set of traffic lights and I looked at Richard askance. 'Where did you come up with that?'

'I studied English literature too once,' he told me.

'But you're an accountant.'

'I didn't always want to be an accountant,' he sighed.

'No one does. But I lost sight of my own dreams and got sucked in by the status and the money instead.'

'The status?' I laughed somewhat disdainfully. I had never thought of accountants as having that much standing in the scheme of things.

'You may laugh, but my family are pretty proud of me for doing what I've done. I'm a professional, you see,' he adopted a weird squeaky nerd voice to tell me that. 'I may not be living out my dream existence but at least I'm not giving my poor mother nightmares.'

'Like I am,' I snorted. 'My mother thinks my only possible route to salvation is to marry out of my situation now. She's like something out of a Jane Austen novel sometimes.'

'I expect she wants you to find yourself a nice professional,' said Richard straightening an imaginary tie.

'I expect so,' I agreed. 'With an income of at least two thousand pounds a year,' I added, mimicking Austen's money-mad Mrs Bennet.

'I think I can manage that.'

'But it's rubbish isn't it?' I sighed then.

'What? Your impression of a Jane Austen character?'

'No. Being a grown-up. All through your childhood you can't wait for the day you hit eighteen. You tell yourself that as soon as you're officially an adult you can stay out as late as you like, with whoever you like, and go out in the morning to do whatever you want to do all day. Like eat sweets and play Nintendo. Except that it doesn't happen. You don't often find vacancies for filmstars and poets in the *Evening Standard*, so you end up getting a boring job like yours and mine to pay the rent, which means that you can't stay out late because you've got to be presentable for work in the morning. No wonder people were always telling me that schooldays are the best of your life.'

'Stop before I burst into tears,' Richard begged me. 'They don't have to be the best days, Liz. It is possible to continue having a good time well into your eighties if you work at it. You've just got to be determined not to let other people chip away at your efforts for happiness. If you want to be a professional actress, you'll have to start doing more practice and actually do some auditions. Join a bloody drama group for a start. If I want to be an artist, I'll have to spend some of my drinking money on paints.'

'Do you want to be an artist?' I asked in surprise.

'I've dabbled with the idea in the past. When I was eight, I did a really great picture of a spaceship and my teacher told me that I was good at drawing. After that, I drew on every bit of paper that came to hand until I got into trouble for drawing a horse when I should have been doing long multiplication. That was when my teacher explained to me that even though I was good at drawing, I was wasting my time, because drawing would never pay my wages. Unlike maths . . .'

'Hence accountancy?'

'Hence accountancy. I reckon there are a lot of secret artists out there,' he said, gazing out through the car window at the tall blocks of flats we were passing on the way into London, 'who abandoned all hope of ever making a living from it because some teacher with no idea told them that art wasn't a career but a hobby. If anyone said that to a child of mine, I'd tell the teacher concerned to have a look at Damien Hirst.'

'Do I need to turn down here if I'm dropping you off at your flat?' I asked, interrupting him before he could go into a rant.

'Oh, yeah. We're here already. Time really flies when I'm with you.'

'Yeah. Makes Monday come that much more quickly though,' I replied. I was on a downer to end all downers. 'Thanks for coming home with me today. I promise I'll never ever inflict such torture upon you again.'

'I had a good time,' he assured me. 'Relatively speaking. So, shall I give you a call some time this week? We could go out on Thursday night. Cinema or something?'

'Er,' I gripped the steering wheel extra hard. 'Thursday's not good. You know. I told you about Thursday. I've got a friend coming to stay.'

'Oh, yeah. I remember. So I'm not going to get to meet this friend of yours?'

I played a little drum roll with my fingernails on the steering wheel. 'I . . . er, I . . . don't really know. He's here for such a short time and he may already have made plans of his own. There are probably other people he wants to catch up with. He's got lots of old college friends for a start. People I haven't seen for years either. We'll only talk about the old days all night and you'd be bored rigid with all the in-jokes.'

'I get the message,' said Richard.

'Look, I don't . . . I don't mean any of this in a nasty way,' I tried to reassure him.

'I know,' he said, planting a dry kiss on my cheek before he let himself out of my car. 'Have a good time.' He turned to go inside, but suddenly swivelled back to look at me. I wound down the window to hear what he had to say.

'What's up?' I asked.

'I was going to ask you exactly the same question,' he countered. 'You still look really sad. Is it just because of the things that your brother was saying today?'

'No. I always get depressed when I come back to London after a day out of town,' I told him. 'It's only the thought of having to go back to that awful house again. No matter how long I stay away, it's always a complete pit when I return.'

'I know that feeling,' Richard sympathised. 'But perhaps they'll have washed up this time.'

'What? Sloppy Seema and Filthy Joe? Want to make a bet on it?'

'How about all the money I owe you?' he smiled.

I smiled back. Disdainful as I had been of Richard lately, he knew how to get a smile out of me. But then his face seemed to settle into a more serious expression and I stopped smiling too when I realised that he was about to go all soppy on me again.

'What is it?' I asked.

'My lease comes up for renewal at the end of next month,' he began. 'Stop me if you think this sounds a bit mad, but I was wondering . . .'

Oh no, I knew instantly what he was wondering. I clenched my hands into fists and dug my fingernails into my palms as I silently begged him not to say it out loud.

'Perhaps you and I could look for a place to live together? We could get somewhere nice and I promise I'd always do my share of the housework.'

'Richard,' I began.

'I know it seems like a massive step to take but we've known each other for seven months now. We get on really well. I swear I'd be asking you exactly the same question if you were just a friend, you know, instead of my girlfriend. I think of you as my best friend too.' His voice tailed off and I could see in his eyes that he wished he hadn't just said all that.

I tried to smile again but it must have been obvious by then that I wasn't going to leap into his arms and shout 'Yes, yes, yes!' As I would have done only a week before. When I was in the mood to settle for anything. Before Brian called.

I wanted to hide beneath my car seat now. I wondered if Richard could tell just by looking at me that I wasn't going to object on grounds of morality or the fact that we hadn't known each other long enough but rather the fact that Brian was about to come back into my life. Could he tell that I had spent the last few days hoping I could rekindle my old relationship and wondering whether I should chuck him before Brian came to the UK or wait to see if Brian still wanted me first?

'I'll have to think about it,' I said pathetically.

'Of course,' Richard agreed. 'I didn't expect you to give me an answer right away. It's not something to be rushed into.'

'I might not have time to think about it this week though. You know, with my friend coming.'

'Call me when he's gone. Yeah?'

'I will,' I promised him.

'I'll look forward to it,' he said, as if he didn't mean it at all.

I drove off as quickly as was safely possible. When I got to my own house I stopped the car outside and thumped my fists on the steering wheel. It wasn't fair. Richard had just made me an offer I had been waiting for for months but instead of being a source of great joy it was simply a source of further complication. Before Brian's call I might have accepted such an offer very happily. Now I felt like a swimmer who, having got just over half-way across the channel, has suddenly been offered a lift back to Dover in a dinghy. At one time I would have climbed on board happily, but now I had the smell of croissants in my nose and was determined to try for a better life. Know what I mean?

*　　*　　*

I went up to bed as soon as I got in. I was shattered. A combination of an almighty day-long hangover, an afternoon with the family and Richard's unexpected proposal of co-habitation had left me hanging in rags.

Families, I muttered to myself as I dragged on my tea-stained pyjamas. They were supposed to be the people who gave you the most support and yet I always came away from a visit to my childhood home feeling wretched and hopeless; my head spinning with all the subtle and not-so-subtle pressure that families inflict. All those questions about my future! Did I even have a future?

But I could be in the same position as Colin, I told myself. If I wanted to. I could have a house of my own on some awful estate. A nice boring husband. A flat-screen TV and a washing machine. Colin had all those things because he didn't ever take risks like I did. When futures were being dished out, he chose the box labelled 'assured but boring'. All he had to do was work at the same firm for thirty years and be content to holiday in Weston-super-Mare for two weeks every summer.

I had chosen a different path. I had chosen to follow a route that definitely seemed less comfortable at first, but might eventually lead to far greater rewards than Colin would find if he spent the rest of his life within three miles of our parents.

I had to be in London. I told myself that London was the only place for people like me who no longer quite fitted in the places they had grown up in. I mean, in Solihull, people stared if you wore a hat when it was seventy degrees below. In London, you could walk through the streets naked but for your body piercings and attract about as much attention as the numerous pigeons. In London, I told myself, everyone was accepted and everyone had an equal chance of success. There was no one around to say, for example, you weren't any good at painting as a child so you can't be an artist now. The galleries were full of exhibitions which proved that thesis wrong. There was no one to say: 'Yo-yos will never catch on again.' Or in-line roller skates. Or whatever it was that I wanted to invent. London was where the black sheep of every family went to join a massive flock where every sheep was black and proud of it.

I had left Solihull to follow a dream and I was going to follow it. That was the thought that had run through my mind as I squared up to my brother across the dining-room table. Seeing him grow red with indignation at the very suggestion that there was life outside the Midlands, I could almost convince myself that I was right.

But back in London, sitting in the middle of the reality of my dream, wondering whether that nasty patch of mould on the ceiling was bigger than it had been a week before, I didn't feel so sure that I was doing the right thing at all.

In reality, I knew that when Monday morning rolled around I wouldn't be brimming with positivity as I strode off to the office to get on with building my empire in my spanking new trainers bought on a shopping weekend in New York. Nothing about my so-called cosmopolitan life thrilled me any more. The *frisson* of excitement that used to run through me when I got off the tube at Knightsbridge had been replaced by a sinking feeling of annoyance that I would have to force my way through the tide of tourists heading for Harrods before I could get to the office. The office where I was junior to a Cavalier King Charles Spaniel. Perhaps Colin was right. Perhaps I really needed to go home and stick with the pond life I knew.

How stupid of me to think that I would be able to make myself into something special just by going to London. Far from being paved with gold, the streets were thronged with evidence of just how far apart the dream and the reality were. The dead-eyed people at the café near the station who slopped my coffee into a polystyrene cup each morning; the miserable tube workers who never even looked at their customers, let alone said 'hello'; the other commuters who studiously avoided each other's gaze in an attempt to convince themselves that they weren't crammed more tightly into a metal box than veal calves as they made the two-mile, hour-long commute to offices where the windows were sealed shut and the air conditioning circulated nothing but fag smoke and germs. Then there were the people who actually had to sleep in the tube underpass and asked me for money each day. All of them had come to London expecting something better than this. Lured happily to bed-sit land by the bright party pictures in the back of *Hello!*.

I closed my eyes and tried to sleep. I tried to block out the negative thoughts in the hope that I might wake up and find them gone. Eventually I did manage to fall asleep, but I was soon awoken by Seema, who was shaking me by the arm.

'I think the house is on fire,' she told me urgently. 'There's smoke coming from beneath the door of Fat Joe's room.'

I leapt from my bed to follow her out on to the landing. There was indeed a fine mist of smoke emerging from beneath Joe's door. 'Well, what are we waiting for?' she asked me. 'He could be dead already.'

I made to crash through the door in true fireman style. But just as I made contact with the wood, Joe swung the door open and I careered straight into his unmade bed. When I came round, he was looking at me as though I was the mad one, even though he was wearing plastic safety goggles and a poly-styrene bicycle helmet at one o'clock in the morning.

'What are you two up to?' he asked. 'Making so much noise in the middle of the night?'

'What are we up to? What are you doing, you idiot?' Seema asked. 'Why was there smoke coming out from beneath your door?'

'I'm making a radio transmitter,' Joe said, picking

up his soldering iron and brandishing it in Seema's direction. 'So that when I go out you can keep a track on my movements.'

'Why on earth would we want to do that?'

'You never know when they're going to come for me,' said Joe seriously.

'They?' I asked.

'I think my activities are being watched,' Joe told me earnestly. 'Ever since I hacked into Barclays Bank.'

'You mean ever since you found their website,' Seema sneered.

'Ah yes, but there are things in that website. Encrypted messages that only the initiated can understand.'

'You're bonkers, Joe,' said Seema. 'I'm going back to bed and you had better not burn the house down while I'm asleep.'

Seema shuffled back to her bedroom but I remained sitting on the edge of Joe's bed, rubbing at my shin. It had taken quite a bashing when my commando-style rescue went wrong.

'Do you want to see how it works?' he asked me, handing me what appeared to be one of my old plastic Alice bands with a battery glued on to it.

'OK,' I said. I couldn't sleep after all.

'You walk around the room and I'll keep my back to you but tell you exactly where you are by looking at your position on the computer screen.'

I dutifully wandered around the room with Joe's new contraption in my hand.

'You're by the bed,' he said excitedly.

'Yes,' I said in amazement, although in Joe's room, which wasn't terribly big (Seema and I had convinced him that girls *needed* more room as we bagged the bigger ones) you couldn't really be anywhere but by the bed.

'It's great,' I told him however. 'I'm sure this will be really useful.'

'Could save my life,' he said earnestly.

'Mmm, could do. Perhaps you ought to make it a bit less obvious though. Disguise it in some way.'

'I've been thinking of covering it with a ribbon,' he said.

I nodded slowly. 'Yes, that would be good. No reason why anyone should get suspicious if they see you wearing a ribbon in your hair.'

Joe nodded enthusiastically and turned back to his flickering screen.

'Joe,' I said softly. 'Are you happy with your life?'

He swivelled on his chair and fixed me with his big brown eyes.

'What's that, Lizzie?'

'I mean, do you like it here in London? Are you doing everything you've ever wanted to do?'

His gaze wandered to the far side of his room where an ancient and dubiously creased picture of Pamela Anderson fought for wall space with a number of cut-away layouts of the spaceships used in *Star Wars*. He was thinking about my question. I hoped.

'I suppose so,' he said. 'Obviously I may not be able to stay here for much longer though. When the net starts closing in – as it very well may – I will probably have to flee the country. Go to Rio, I expect.'

'God, how dreadful,' I said. 'Makes my life seem much more manageable,' I added.

Joe nodded and smiled. 'Sleep tight,' he said. 'If they come for me, I'll make sure they don't touch you at all.'

I plodded back to my room. I had hoped that Joe and I would be able to have a heart to heart about the meaning of life. I had hoped that he would say something which might make me think I wasn't doing too badly for a twenty-seven-year-old. I had hoped he would tell me that things get better when you hit twenty-eight. He was two years older than me and I had hoped he might have some insider knowledge about coping with late-twenties angst. But he didn't come up with the goods.

I couldn't even laugh at the fact that he was clearly a nutter.

CHAPTER TWELVE

Well, I didn't sleep tight that night and Monday morning dawned before I could finish counting the mould patches on the wall.

I wasn't usually in much of a hurry to get to the office on a Monday morning. Rupert certainly wouldn't be in until twelve at the earliest. He got away with this every single week by pencilling a lot of bogus house visits into his diary for Monday morning and claiming that all the people he was supposed to have visited had stood him up when Harriet wanted to know what the flats were like. Not that Harriet ever made it in on a Monday morning either. But she was the boss, so she didn't even have to pretend that she didn't have the hangover from hell when she eventually turned up on a Monday afternoon just as I was about ready to go home again.

That Monday however, I wanted to guarantee some time to myself before the others came in. I had decided that I needed to send Brian an urgent e-mail from the office. A damage limitation one. I would have to tell Brian the whole truth about my situation and offer him the option to come over and stay at Fleapit Towers in Balham or just write the whole incident and our friendship off to experience and forget that he ever even met me.

It seemed the only thing to do. The decent thing. I trudged towards the office that morning with my head down and my heart in my boots (as if I ever actually skipped there!) and was at my desk by half-past eight.

'Lizzie, darling. What on earth are you doing here so early?'

I couldn't believe it. It was Mad Harriet. On a Monday morning? She was usually recovering from a heavy night at Annabelle's. She looked terrifically flustered as she flung her lovely Maxmara coat haphazardly on to a peg and began to rake frantically through the cluttered drawers in her desk, while I racked my brain for a reason why I was in the office so early in case she suspected industrial espionage.

'Had a bit of typing to finish off,' I said. But she wasn't really even interested.

'Good. Good,' she muttered. 'Heavens! You haven't seen my car keys have you, darling? I can't seem to find them at home, though I could have sworn I drove home from the restaurant last night. But then I couldn't find the bloody car either so perhaps I actually parked it up somewhere around here and took a taxi home after all. Do you remember?'

I shook my head.

'Ah-ha!' She emerged triumphant from the wastepaper

basket. 'Found them. Great. Wonder how they got in there?'

It was a mystery.

'Now just got to find the car,' she said. 'Any clues?'

I shook my head again.

'Blast. I've got to be at the airport in less than an hour. Flying to Majorca at ten this morning. All a bit last minute, I'm afraid. Bunny's wife has taken herself for a fat-blitzing week at Champneys so he's taking me to the villa while she's safely out of the way.'

She grinned excitedly. I tried to grin back in return but my cheeks just weren't having it.

'Why don't you just get a taxi to the airport and I'll go and look for the car,' I suggested. 'I'm sure it's safe wherever you parked it.' It certainly wouldn't be moving. I thought wryly. The nice bright yellow clamps of Chelsea and Westminster's parking authorities might as well have been fitted as standard to the wheels of Harriet's neat little Mercedes coupe.

'Oh, darling. Would you really do that? I'd be ever so grateful if you could.'

I nodded.

She showed me the car keys on their solid silver Tiffany key-ring. A key-ring identical to the one Mary had bought me for my birthday, I noticed with more than a *frisson* of annoyance. Mary still hadn't called to apologise for being such a cow.

This one is for the driver's door and this one is for the ignition. No. Hang on,' Harriet hesitated. 'Perhaps this one is for the door and this one is for the ignition.

Oh, god. I just can't seem to remember. What will you do?'

'I'm sure I'll work it out.'

'Oh, you're such a clever little angel. I promise I'll make you permanent staff as soon as I get back.'

She was always promising to make me permanent staff when she got back. From Spain. From the corner shop. From the bathroom.

'Now, a cab,' she grimaced. 'How on earth can I get a cab to come and meet me here at the office?'

I lifted the telephone receiver and began to call one for her.

'Easy when you know how,' I said sarcastically.

'Splendid. You are so clever,' she added, as though I were some kind of magician. 'Now, have I got everything I need? Suitcase. Passport. Spermicidal jelly. You will be OK here in the office, won't you, darling? After all, nothing ever happens much, does it? You can get people to call me on my mobile if they're absolutely desperate. Oh, hang on. No, you can't. I think I must have left it on the roof of the car when I drove in yesterday morning. Could be anywhere between my house and Sloane Square, I reckon. If you could possibly have a look for that while you look for the car . . . Tell Rupert I'm really sorry to leave you both in the lurch like this but you do understand the need, don't you, sweetheart? Do you think he'll mind awfully?'

'I'm sure he'll understand.'

I imagined Rupert's gleeful face as he arranged a round of golf for every afternoon she was away.

'I'll be flying back into Gatwick on Wednesday week. Is that taxi coming yet? Do you think I should have had my hair done first?'

'You look wonderful,' I assured her. In a dragged through the haystack backwards sort of way. She was wearing her white Jil Sander t-shirt inside out. Doggy pawprints made a muddy pattern half-way up the shins of her expensive black jeans.

'Thank you so much. Now. Have I remembered everything? Look, there's the cab already. That was pretty speedy. Come on, Hercules. We're going for a nice long walkies. All the way to Spain.' She made for the door, with her passport, her Louis Vuitton . . . and her dog.

'Harriet!' I ran after her. 'Harriet! What about Hercules?' I pointed at the stinky little Cavalier King Charles, all wet nose and runny eyes. 'You can't take Hercules on an aeroplane.'

She looked at me uncomprehendingly.

'What's the matter, darling? Why ever not?'

'Hercules? Because he's a dog, Harriet. And dogs aren't allowed to fly. Well, they are. But they have to go in the luggage hold.'

She clasped poor Hercules so close that his eyes stuck out further than ever.

'And I don't know what the rules are about taking a dog into Majorca,' I continued. 'But you certainly won't be able to bring him straight back to England afterwards. He'll have to go into quarantine.'

'Quarantine?' breathed Harriet in horror.

The taxi driver confirmed that I was right.

'At least six months in a bare-walled cage,' he nodded.

'Then what can I do?' she asked me desperately.

'Leave him in a kennel?' said the taxi driver helpfully. 'That's what we normal people do with our pets when we go on holiday, love.'

'I couldn't possibly do that,' she snorted, looking at the driver as if he had just suggested having the dog put down. 'Are you trying to tell me that I should leave my precious baby with someone he doesn't know for a whole week? I'll have to phone Bunny and tell him that I can't go.' She started to get out of the cab again.

I pushed her back in and wrestled Hercules from her arms.

'Harriet,' I said firmly. 'You must go to Majorca. I know how much you're looking forward to it. Hercules can stay with me. He knows me. I'll look after him.'

'Oh, would you?' her face brightened. 'Oh, darling. That would be so kind. But do you know what you're doing?'

'I've met dogs before. And I'm sure my landlord won't mind. He can stay in my bedroom.'

'Oh no,' Harriet said firmly. 'Hercules can't sleep if he's not surrounded by his own bits and bobs.' She fiddled with her key-ring and handed me the front-door key to her apartment in Notting Hill Gate. 'Look, he can stay with you in the office all day, but you'll have to take him home at night and go back there to let him out again each morning. It has to be before seven or he'll widdle on the Persian carpet. It is on your way in, isn't it, darling? Oh, and when you do take him out, you'll have to carry him between the house and the park. He doesn't like the feel of tarmac on his delicate feet. He quite simply refuses to walk on it.'

'You should buy him some shoes,' said the cabbie, with a wry smile in my direction.

'What a wonderful idea,' said Harriet. 'Do you think anybody makes little shoes for dogs? Lizzie, could you possibly find that out for me as well? I'm sure they probably stock them on the internet.'

'Look, do you want to catch this plane or not?' the cabbie asked.

Harriet gave Hercules one last kiss on his wet black nose before reluctantly handing him over to me once more. 'What an impatient man,' she whispered. 'You will look after my baby for me, won't you?'

I promised that I would and at last the taxi sped away. Putting Hercules down on the pavement, I turned to go back into the office. Hercules didn't follow me. When I looked to see what had become of him, he was standing exactly where I had set him down on the paving stones, shaking like a hairy white-and-ginger leaf.

'Come on, Herky,' I called in a jovial doggy sort of voice. 'Come on. Let's go inside.'

Hercules's skinny body seemed to strain towards me but his little feet did not move at all. Harriet had not been joking. This was one pampered pup who did not like the feel of tarmacadam beneath his toes. Three whistles later, I gave up and picked him up. He licked my face in pathetic gratitude. It was like being kissed by an insole from one of Fat Joe's trainers.

'We're going to have to get you out of that little habit for a start,' I warned the pampered dog, as he happily took a turn around the shag-pile carpet before widdling against one leg of my desk.

The e-mail I had been writing to Brian was still on the screen waiting to be sent. I hadn't got very far with it. 'Dear Brian, there's something I need to tell you,' it began. Where did I go beyond that? Should I make a joke of the whole thing, or take a repentant tone from the very beginning? I guessed Brian's reaction to the affair would very much depend on the light in which I myself presented my horribly extensive catalogue of lies. Perhaps he would laugh it off too if I myself seemed to think of it as no more than a game that had got out of hand.

Perhaps I should sleep on it, I decided eventually, and I switched the computer off. Besides, there was still a vague chance that Brian would never need to know. He had warned me when calling to announce his troublesome visit, that he would not be able to confirm his plans until he'd seen how that month's end of period figures were received at some big meeting or other. If it was decided that his team had not performed well enough, he might have to cancel his holiday plans altogether. He had promised to let me know as soon as he knew himself, which would be first thing on Tuesday morning – his time. Tuesday lunch time, mine. Yes, I told myself. I should hold off sending any bombshells in his direction until then. No point making myself look an idiot unless I absolutely had to.

The phone rang. It was Rupert calling from his bedroom no doubt. 'Hello, is that Harriet?' he croaked in his 'might be laryngitis' voice.

'It's Liz,' I told him.

'Is she in yet?' he asked me, sounding altogether healthier at once.

'Been and gone. To Majorca.'

'What?' he spluttered. 'What do you mean?'

'Bunny's wife has gone to Champneys, so he's taking Harriet to the villa in Majorca while the cat's away.'

'Way-hey. Good old Bunny,' said Rupert chauvinistically. 'One day I would like to meet that guy and shake him warmly by the hand. He's a good sort.'

'He's an adulterer,' I snorted. 'And Harriet spends far too much of her time waiting for moments like this – putting her life on hold for some balding old man who'll never leave his missus for her. I don't know why she bothers.'

'Because there are far fewer eligible men about than women, my dear,' Rupert reminded me. 'Some of you will have to double up and lump it. It's inevitable.'

'Then how come you're still single?' I retorted.

'Who says I am? For all you know, I might have

spent the whole weekend in bed with a very lovely lady.'

I winced at the thought. I hated it when he referred to his lovely 'ladies' since he clearly treated them as anything but. As far as Rupert was concerned, it was a matter of honour that he collected girls' phone numbers but never actually used them.

'What time are you coming in?' I asked before he could elaborate on his lost weekend.

'Coming in? Are you mad? How long is Harriet away for?'

'Until next Wednesday.'

'Well, I'll see you then,' he said. 'You know I'd love to help you hold the fort, but I think I must be coming down with a terrible bout of that summer flu that's been going around. Wouldn't want to give it to you, would I?'

'Yeah right. Thanks a lot. I was hoping you might be able to help me look after Hercules. She's just dumped the bloody mutt in the office. Had no idea that she couldn't take him with her.'

'Lizzie, you know how much I'd love to help you with that too,' Rupert smarmed. 'But I'm allergic to dogs.'

'No you are not,' I protested. 'You sit in an office with him just about every day of the week.'

'And it makes my eyes stream. Haven't you noticed me sniffling?'

'I can't say I have.'

'Look, Lizzie. Just be a good girl and keep the old

office ticking over for me. I promise you I'll make it up to you one day, but in the meantime, why don't you just kick back and have a bit of fun on the internet like you usually do. Send some e-mails. Surf some porn sites. Download any good ones. I'll see you next Tuesday.' And that was that.

The pig.

Well, if Rupert wasn't coming in, then I sure as hell wasn't going to hang around either. Besides, I was hungry. There were no biscuits left in the office biscuit tin but I knew I had half a packet of fairly fresh garlic mushroom tortelloni in the fridge at home. It had been there that morning at least. I knew I couldn't guarantee its continued existence with Fat Joe and Seema both at home. I had once caught Fat Joe eating a bagful of frozen croissants, uncooked, for breakfast. He said they weren't up to much. A bit too hard for his tastes.

'Come on, Hercules. It's lunch time.'

It was almost half-past nine by now.

Hercules trotted happily behind me to the office door and stepped out on to the welcome mat at the top of the steps to wait for me to lock up. I locked the door behind us and headed down the steps to the pavement. Hercules stood at the top of the steps and watched.

I had already forgotten his little, but mightily incapacitating, phobia.

'You are joking?' I said to the canine swine. 'You don't really want me to carry you whenever we have to cross a pavement? It's a twenty-minute walk to the tube station and there's no grass between here and there. And I bet you don't even go on public transport anyway! Well, I'm not having it. Harriet's in Spain and I'm your mummy until she comes back. So you're going to bloody well heel and walk like a proper dog. Come here.'

Hercules whimpered. He tried to put one paw in front of the other but just couldn't do it.

'Heel!' I demanded, patting my shin with authority.

Once again, the little front paw hesitated over taking a step on to concrete. He looked at me with his big wet eyes.

'He-el!' I tried again. I wasn't going to be taken in by the lost puppy look – it had already landed me in too many hopeless human relationships. I patted both my shins this time.

But still no dog biscuit.

'He-el. Please, Hercules. Pur-leese. Look. I'll carry you when we get to Balham, I promise. But round here, the pavement is probably quite safe even for your paws. We're in Knightsbridge. Lovely. Look,' I patted the pavement. 'Knightsbridge! Lovely and clean. I'm sure they sweep the roads here every day. Posh people live here. Let's go for a lovely walk.' Hercules remained unconvinced.

'Oh, for heaven's sake.' I stomped back up the stairs and snatched him up. He licked me pathetically again and then lay in my arms like a baby on the longer than usual walk to the tube.

'Why is that lady carrying her dog?' a little boy asked his mother.

'Why indeed?' I replied.

But thankfully, Hercules didn't mind public transport. As long as I didn't try to put him down on the floor. Which was OK until we got to Charing Cross and had to change on to a packed Northern Line train. Have you ever tried to strap-hang with a wriggling King Charles Spaniel tucked under one arm? Then I almost dropped him on the escalator at Clapham South, only managing to save him from sure oblivion by grabbing his pedigree tail. A nation's worth of animal lovers tutted loudly behind me while Hercules squeaked his annoyance.

I was met by another barrage of tutting when Hercules did his business just outside the station.

'Haven't you got a pooper scooper?' asked a rather grand old man who had caught us in the act.

'No I haven't,' I told him, picking Hercules up again. I had only just managed to put the dog down in time to avoid having the mess go straight into my coat pocket. I was hot and bothered from having carried him all the way from Knightsbridge in the first place. I was in no mood to do any scooping.

'There's an automatic five-hundred-pound fine for people who let their dogs foul the pavement round here,' the gentleman boomed. 'I suggest you clear that mess up or I will report you to the council.'

'What?' I snapped.

'Scoop the poop,' he told me. 'If your dog fouls the pavement, you are legally and morally obliged to clean up after him.'

'Right,' I said sarcastically.

'Right,' said the grand old man. Only he was serious.

But what could I clear the mess up with anyway? I wasn't in the habit of carrying plastic bags around. If I had had a bag in my pocket, I told myself, I would have sorted the matter out right away, but as I didn't, I tried to walk on, eyes forward, ignoring the public-spirited chap who had stopped me. But he wasn't about to let the matter drop.

'Young lady. I want you to know that I am making a note of your description and a description of your dog to hand in at the police station. I can assure you that they will not take this matter lightly.'

I have to say, I couldn't imagine the police dropping a triple murder inquiry to investigate a case of serious dog mess but the old man seemed to think otherwise and was indeed making notes.

'Look. I haven't got anything to clean the stuff up with,' I told him. 'This isn't even my dog. I'm just looking after him for a friend.'

'Then the dog is your temporary responsibility and therefore his mess must be too. You can use this.' The man handed me a rather flimsy blue and white striped plastic bag.

'What's this?' I asked.

'It's a bag.'

I took it from him and said thanks, hoping that would be the end of it, but he still wouldn't leave me alone.

'Go on then.' He jerked his head towards the mess. He was going to watch me.

'Oh, you're joking,' I protested. 'It's all runny.'

'Dog ownership has its pleasures and its problems,' he told me.

'I've already told you, this is not my dog.'

'Tell that to the court, young lady,' the man said, actually grasping me by the top of the arm and pushing me towards Hercules's calling card.

'Take your hands off me. I could have you for assault,' I warned him.

'And who do you think they'd believe,' he asked me. 'An upstanding member of the community with an illustrious career in the army behind him and ten years' involvement in the neighbourhood watch? Or some kind of illegal refugee dog-stealer?'

'Now hang on. I'm not an illegal refugee and while this dog isn't mine, I certainly didn't steal it.'

'Then perhaps you would be so kind as to give me the name and address of the dog's real owner so that I can check up on that detail later on. Don't think the police don't know about the dog-stealing racket in these parts, young girl. They know all about it. You drugged-up teenagers stealing people's pets to be sold into animal experimentation labs so that you can get a fix of marijuana to inject.'

'What?'

'You heard me. I've got your number, missie. Don't you pretend that I haven't.'

Drug abusers stealing dogs? I pondered asking the man if he'd been at the kaolin and morphine himself.

'Look, I'll clean it up, OK,' I sighed. 'Just leave me alone. Why don't you go to the library and check up on your obscure bye-laws or something?'

'I'll just stand here to make sure you do the job properly, if you don't mind.'

'Actually, I do mind,' I told him.

'Well, I don't mind whether you mind or not. I'm staying.'

'Fine,' I snarled and set Hercules down on the grass verge while I sorted the mess out using the plastic bag like a makeshift glove. 'You're going to have to learn to be more careful,' I hissed at the mutt.

'Are you talking about me?' said the deaf brigadier.

'No, if I'd been talking about you, I would have been using more swear words. Sir,' I added, for facetious good measure. The poo was in the bag now and I waved it in front of his nose so that he could see. 'Good enough for you?'

'Hmm. Well, don't let me catch you at it again,' he snorted, before striking off in the direction of the tube station.

'Thanks so much,' I said to Hercules. 'That really made my day.'

I looked around for somewhere to dump my dainty plastic bag of doggy doings, but couldn't find one.

'Bugger.'

I was about to drop the bag behind someone's garden wall when I noticed that while he was not standing over me any more, the conscientious colonel was still watching from the end of the street.

'What?' I muttered under my breath. He was definitely waiting to see what I would do with the bag, so I had to carry Hercules under one arm, and the bag of shit in the other hand until I could be sure I was no longer being observed. But every time I looked over my shoulder, the neighbourhood watcher was still there. I could hear the metal cap on the end of his stick as he tapped along at a safe distance behind me.

Could my life get any worse? Now I was carrying a plastic bag full of shit to add to my sack-load of worries. I decided I would have to try to lose the old codger. But there were no dark alleyways between the tube station and the house. Next thing I knew, I was at the top of our street, standing outside the corner shop. The colonel was on the other side of the road, nonchalantly examining the black fly on someone's wilted roses as he pretended not to be watching me.

I didn't want him to know my address in case he really did send the council round, so I had to try some delaying tactics which I hoped would make him tire of his pursuit. I needed to go into the shop anyway. We always needed milk. (Having said that, we always seemed to have either no milk at all or three pints of the stuff.) And I also needed dog food. Harriet hadn't left any at the office and I was pretty sure we wouldn't have any at home. (Though Fat Joe probably had some somewhere. All those pies he ate straight from their polythene wrappers certainly smelled as though they were filled with the stuff and I knew that he was hoarding all manner of tins for Armageddon.) Anyway, Habib's – the twenty-four-hour corner shop – would have a varied and cheap selection. Emphasis on the cheap. I walked straight in, Hercules still tucked under my arm (poo bag dangling gracefully from my wrist like an elegant evening purse), and was surprised when Habib, who was usually so nice and friendly whether it was six in the morning or half-past eleven at night, demanded that I go straight back out in a not very friendly way at all.

'No dogs!' he said.

'Habib!' I pleaded. 'I only want some milk, some bread and some dog food. I'll be thirty seconds.'

'No dogs. That's the rule. Leave him outside.'

'OK,' I said, backing out into another pensioner. Why did people have dogs, I wondered? I'd been in charge of Hercules for less than an hour and already I felt like I had leprosy as well as a mutt. Dog owners were clearly that popular. I set Hercules down outside the shop and fastened his lead to the drainpipe. At which point, of course, he started to whimper and the colonel narrowed his eyes as if he suspected terrible cruelty. 'Can't I bring him in?' I begged Habib through the half-open door. 'He's a pedigree. He just won't stand on tarmac.'

'What is this silly nonsense about tarmac? You cannot bring him into the shop. What about hygiene?'

'What about it?' I was tempted to say as I looked at a dust-covered row of Roses chocolate boxes that hadn't been renewed in the two years I'd been living on that street. But Hercules looked at me as though he might have a heart attack if I left him standing on the pavement while I disappeared from his sight for a moment to buy him a tin of Pedigree. What could I do? I took off my coat, spread it on the floor, and Hercules climbed on. The whimpering stopped and I bought the dog food. Unfortunately there wasn't any Pedigree Chum so I bought something with a nice orange label instead, Cheapster's Own brand, illustrated with a dog that bore an uncanny resemblance to a polar bear. Perhaps polar bear was what the stuff was made of.

'Since when are you getting a dog, Lizzie Jordan?' Habib asked as he wrapped up my purchases in another one of those practically see-through plastic bags.

'Never,' I replied.

He looked at me strangely.

'Oh, you mean, when did I get the dog I brought in just now? Well, he belongs to my boss. And I'm looking after him until she comes back from her holidays next Wednesday. As if I didn't have enough to worry about as it is.'

'Worrying about what?' asked Habib. 'Do you want to talk about it?' He could never resist a good gossip.

And somehow I felt that if I told him what was going on, he might just have enough wide experience of life to come up with a decent solution. He had probably spoken to someone with a similar problem only that morning. I spilled the story out again.

'You should always be telling the truth,' he sighed when I had finished.

'I had a feeling you might say that,' I said. 'But what do you think I should do about it?'

'You could put some money in here,' he rattled the brightly coloured collecting tin for his Hare Krishna temple. 'And we will pray for you.'

'Thanks all the same, but I'd probably be better off selling my soul to my own devil. How much do I owe you for the dog food?' I asked. Outside, Hercules was keening like a spirit damned to hell.

'Just one moment,' said Habib. 'I'll just weigh this.'

I watched in horror as Habib picked up the bag of shit that I had absent-mindedly put down on the counter as we talked, and put it on to his shiny electronic scales. 'This is mince, is it?' he asked.

I snatched it back. 'Stewing steak,' I told him quickly. 'But I bought it in town.'

'This is looking very much like one of my shop bags,' he said doubtfully.

'I know. All the small shops are using them these days. Perhaps you should change the design you buy to make your shop more distinctive.'

'But blue and white are my shop's colours,' he said, looking most put out.

'I'll never buy anything from anywhere else again,' I assured him, taking my change and making for the door.

'Just one minute. Do you want to know what I really think you should do about your problem?' Habib began, but before he could even get started, I noticed that Hercules was looking all tremble-legged on my jacket and leg trembling usually meant only one thing.

'See you tomorrow, I expect,' I said, rushing out just in time to save my jacket from a soaking, but not able to get Hercules away in time to save the paper sack full of potatoes which formed an integral part of an artful display of veg outside the shop. I made a note to tell Seema to go to Safeway for her veg for the next couple of weeks.

'Done my shopping. Going home now!' I shouted across the road to the old git who was still following me. 'I expect my boyfriend's waiting for me. He's a big guy. Gets violent if he doesn't eat regular, like.'

It worked. The colonel nodded curtly and set off in the opposite direction.

I threw the poo bag straight over the next garden wall.

Trying hard not to gag on the fatty, meaty smell, I forked Hercules's dinner out on to a saucer as soon as we got into the house. I gave him a whistle to say that dinner would be served in the kitchen, but it transpired that he was as funny about the shiny tiles in the kitchen as he was about tarmac and refused to cross the threshold from the sitting room. I couldn't really blame him. Since getting a bare foot covered in spilt honey which subsequently picked up three pubic hairs and a couple of price tags, I never went into the kitchen without shoes myself. I took the saucer to the doorway and placed it just within Hercules's reach so that, while spillages would hopefully be confined to the tiles, Hercules's feet could remain safely on the shag pile.

He sniffed the bowl of dog food disdainfully, like he wasn't a spaniel but A.A. bloody Gill.

'I knew that would happen,' I told Seema, who had appeared behind Hercules *en route* to make a cup of tea.

'What?'

'I knew he wouldn't eat that bloody dog food. Honestly. They're all the same,' I told him. 'Whatever brand you get. They're all made at the same factory out of bits of the same old racehorse. Don't you try to tell me that by paying an extra quid a tin you're getting a bit of a Derby winner as opposed to the one that came in second.'

'Why is there a dog in the house?' Seema asked suddenly. She had been upstairs doing coursework for the Business Spanish module she was taking as part of her MBA and this was her first sight of the little mutt.

'It's Harriet's. She's gone to Majorca for a week and I've been left holding the dog. He's called Hercules.'

'Oh. wow. Hercules? What a nice name. Oh, isn't he sweet?' Seema said, getting down on her knees to ruffle his fur. 'Aren't you a bootiful little bwoy?' she said to him. He responded by licking her nose.

'Seema. Please. He's just a bloody dog.'

'Aaah.' She had Hercules on her lap by now and was cuddling him close. 'Don't be so mean to him. Here he is without his mummy and you're trying to feed him some awful crap that even Fat Joe wouldn't touch. It's not his fault he doesn't want to eat cows' lips – that's what it's really made of, you know, not horses. You got that wrong. I've got some chicken in the fridge. He can have that instead.' With Hercules still in her arms she made for the fridge and brought out a juicy piece of roast chicken breast.

'Hey,' I said. 'If you don't want that, I could have put it in a sandwich for myself.'

'Get your own,' she replied, putting Hercules down on the work surface next to the sink while she cut the chicken into little bite sized pieces and put them into a plastic bowl. I thought for a moment that she was going to add some kind of garnish. Or perhaps whip up a masala sauce. (Not that she could cook.) 'There you go, sweetheart,' she murmured as she set the new dish down. 'None of that nasty processed rubbish for you. You're a pedigree dog, I can tell.'

But Hercules still wasn't interested. Well, he took perhaps a slightly deeper sniff at his lunch but quickly recoiled again with one limp paw lifted in ever such a pathetic gesture.

'See. He doesn't like your chicken either,' I told her, not without a slight sense of triumph. 'He's just a spoiled mutt, Seema. Leave that saucer on the floor there and he'll eat it when he's hungry.'

'He's hungry now. I can tell. Look at his sorrowful eyes.'

'Hark at Rolf Harris.'

'His tummy is rumbling. I think he might be feeling dizzy. Perhaps he'll only eat out of his own bowl. My parents had a neighbour whose Yorkshire Terrier was incredibly particular like that. He would have starved to death before he ate anything out of a bowl that didn't have his name on it.'

I rolled my eyes heavenwards. 'I do hope you're joking.'

''Fraid not. He lost nearly half his body weight when the bowl got broken and it took two weeks to find an identical replacement. Didn't Harriet give you all Hercules's bits and bobs to make him feel at home?'

'She was in such a bloody hurry to get to the airport that she almost forgot she couldn't take him with her anyway,' I explained. 'She just gave me the keys to her flat and said I should put him to bed there every night and pick him up again on my way into work in the morning but I'm buggered if I'm going to go out of my way to do anything for this flea-bag. He's a dog. He can sleep in the kitchen and he'll eat out of anything when he's really hungry.'

Seema set her mouth in a straight, disapproving line. 'Well, if you really can't be bothered to take him home, you could at least go over there to get him his own bowl and his blanket. How would you like it if your parents had dumped you with some strange family with not even your favourite teddy bear for company?'

'They frequently did. Look, I am not schlepping all the way over to Harriet's flat to pick up a piece of stinky blanket. If he really needs a stinky blanket, he can have one of Fat Joe's. I'm going to check my national lottery numbers on Ceefax and see if I've won enough money to get me out of the mess I'm in over Brian.'

'I see. I take it Mary still won't let you borrow her flat for the weekend then? Did you call her and grovel like I suggested?'

'No, I did not. It's she who should be grovelling, anyway. She's the one who was so bloody mean. After everything I've done for her.'

'Success changes people,' Seema told me gravely.

'Is that why I'm still the same lovable person I used to be?' I muttered.

'So, who's looking after Harriet's flat while she's away?' Seema asked as she tried to handfeed Hercules some chicken. He wasn't having that either.

I shrugged. Three lottery numbers that I didn't have

later, the penny dropped. 'No one,' I said, sitting up. 'There's no one in Harriet's flat all week.'

'Are you thinking what I'm thinking?' I could almost hear the cogs in Seema's brain whirring into action.

'Hercules really does need his own blanket, doesn't he?' I said, suddenly very enthusiastic. 'Come on. Let's go to Harriet's place and fetch it.'

'Bags I carry the dog,' said Seema. I wasn't going to argue with that. She'd learn soon enough.

Though I had been at Corbett and Daughter's Estate Agency for so long that I had almost broken a chair leg by carving notches for the passing days into it like some prisoner on a life sentence, I had never been to Harriet's flat before. When Seema and I finally found the block that matched the address she had given me (Harriet's handwriting was beyond dreadful – she should have been a doctor), I looked up in disbelief. It seemed to go up for ever. An elegant red brick Victorian building with a huge front door flanked by seven brass nameplates and corresponding shiny doorbells.

'This is fantastic!' said Seema, throwing herself down on to an overstuffed leather sofa in Harriet's sitting room moments later. 'How much money must she make at that agency to be able to afford a place like this?'

'Nothing,' I assured Seema. 'I type up the accounts. But I think she may have had a thing with a Saudi prince when she was younger. And there's family money, of course. I think her family own some village on the south coast.'

I looked closely at a pencil sketch of a little girl which stood on the marble mantelpiece. I didn't know much about art, but I was pretty sure that it was a genuine Picasso. Harriet had once mentioned that her father had met the great man in Paris and swapped stock market advice for some speedy sketches.

'There's nothing in the fridge except chicken breasts for the dog and Cristal champagne,' Seema announced. She was now skulking around the kitchen. 'Oh my god, Liz, you've got to see this. She's got one of those gorgeous Dualit toasters. I've always wanted a Dualit toaster. And a cappuccino machine. Bloody hell, she's even got a juicer.' She looked inside it. 'Never used. Of course. This is a dream flat,' she sighed. 'What a lucky cow.'

We left Hercules eating his chicken from bone china and took in the rest of the flat. There were two huge bathrooms leading off from the hall. One in black marble. One in white. The white one had a massive double shower so that two people could rinse off at once. Fluffy fresh towels hung on the towel rail. Seema buried her face in their fabric-conditioner softness and laughed at the opulence of it. The towels in our house had probably been dishcloths in a house like this in a past life.

The bedrooms were vast too. All four of them. And in the master bedroom, to Seema's utter glee, we found a four-poster bed with thick red curtains. It was like something out of a costume drama on the life of Elizabeth the First. You couldn't fail to get laid if you slept in a bed like that.

'Harriet was probably born in that bed,' I told Seema. 'Her family used to own half of Scotland.'

Seema was already bouncing on it. 'Well, the mattress is a bit soft, which isn't much good for your back. But imagine having a four-poster! Liz, this is magic. Come on in.'

'Later. Later,' I told her. 'I want to finish exploring first.'

Harriet had the top-floor flat and a spiral staircase led up from the middle of the sitting room to a roof garden. I climbed slowly up the wrought iron steps and out into a little glasshouse which covered the opening. Stepping out of the glasshouse I managed to put my size six trainers straight into one of Hercules's delicate little turds but I didn't care, because, when I had finished wiping the muck off on the edge of some terracotta planter, I looked up to see the most amazing view.

Far into the distance London lay before me like a toy town. Turning to the east I could see the British Telecom tower sticking out of Bloomsbury like an upended baby's rattle. Further east still, the futuristic pyramid of Canary Wharf, the tallest building in the country, glittered in the sunlight and I could just make out the faint flash of the white light to warn passing aircraft that the tower was bigger than you might expect. That was wonderful in itself, but when I turned to the south, the view was even better. Because looking south from Harriet's roof garden I could see the tops of the tallest trees in one of the country's greatest parks. Hyde Park.

'She's got a view of Hyde Park!' I cried, almost overcome with emotion. Relief flooded through me. 'She's got a bloody view of Hyde Park!' I shouted down the staircase to Seema. 'Come up. Come quickly. It's perfect!'

'So, are you looking forward to Brian's visit now?' Seema asked me, as she emerged from the glasshouse that covered the stairs behind me.

'Looking forward to it? I can't bloody wait. Hooray for Harriet.'

'Hooray for Hercules too,' said Seema soppily, just before she too put her trainers in some of his unattended mess.

The decision was made. I would pretend that Harriet's flat was mine. We spent the whole of that afternoon scouring the place for anything that would suggest otherwise, in between bouts of sunbathing up in the roof garden which was, of course, a perfectly designed sun-trap.

Harriet's family photographs in their shining silver frames were consigned to the backs of drawers and cupboards. It would be far too tricky to try to pass off her relatives as my own since many of Harriet's relatives were faces that Brian might have recognised from the BBC's coverage of the House of Lords which he occasionally liked to watch on satellite. Bundles of unopened post (mostly bills from Harrods and Harvey Nichols) addressed to The Lady Harriet Corbett were consigned to an almost empty cornflakes box on the top of the fridge.

Seema decided that rather than change the message on Harriet's answering machine, we should just unplug the whole thing and stash it in a cupboard.

'Now all you've got to do is bring a couple of pictures of your family round and replace her clothes in the wardrobe with yours.'

'Seems a shame to have to do that,' I said, fingering a beautiful red silk tunic. But I knew that none of it would fit me. Harriet had the figure of a baby bird. A baby bird that has been dead for a couple of weeks and nibbled by maggots. Yep, the cow was too rich and too thin, can you believe it?

'Does this look like the kind of flat that I would live in?' I asked Seema seriously when we had finished making the place 'my own'.

'I certainly think so,' she nodded. 'To the manor born.'

'I can't help thinking we shouldn't really be doing this, though,' I said, having a momentary pang of conscience as I hid a photograph of Harriet as a plump-cheeked debutante face down in a drawer. 'Should we be doing this?'

'Of course we shouldn't. Not really. But they do say

that what you don't know can't hurt you and how will Harriet ever find out? If you don't do anything about the dust we can see exactly where the photos need to go when we put them back. And if she does catch you out, you can always say that Hercules refused to sleep in the flat on his own so you had to stay over to comfort him.'

'It is foolproof, isn't it?'

'Like a tetrapak,' said Seema.

It wasn't an analogy I would have chosen, considering the trouble I had opening milk cartons.

'Relax,' she added, sensing that she hadn't dispelled my nervousness. 'If you ask me, this is fate. You needed a fabulous flat and Harriet has provided you with the keys to one.'

'Yeah, you're right,' I conceded. 'Thank you Bunny for taking Harriet away for the week. And thank you Hercules for having to eat out of bone china.' I gave the dog an affectionate little pat. 'My skin has been saved.'

I looked out of the window one more time, in the direction of Mary's flat. A considerably smaller flat, as it happened. 'And up yours, Miserable Mary.'

When we got back to Balham however, I found a message from Mary on the answer machine that almost made me feel guilty for taking her name in vain like that. I called her back right away.

'Look, I'm really sorry about Saturday lunch time,'

she said, all sugary unctuousness. 'I wasn't much of a friend to you, was I, sweetheart?'

I resisted the temptation to say anything too sharp in reply.

'And I really missed having a good old gossip over lunch. I had been looking forward to it for ages.'

'Me too,' I admitted.

'We don't get to see each other often enough as it is. So I was thinking, perhaps I could make it up to you. Perhaps we could go out this evening instead. You've got to pick up your birthday present anyway and I've been invited to a party. Why don't you come? I know it's a bit short notice and it'll probably be deathly dull but at least we won't have to pay for the drink.'

'Where is it?' I asked, trying not to sound too eager. Strictly speaking it was a work night, but with Harriet out of the way, I decided it would be stupid to turn down any invitations when no one would know whether I made it to the office next day for nine or half eleven. If at all.

'It's at the Hyperion,' Mary sighed, as if she was telling me that a gang of our mates had decided to meet up at Burger King on Balham High Road.

'The Hyperion?'

'It's an after-show party for the Golden Brothers.'

'Wow.' I couldn't help myself. The Golden Brothers were fast taking over from Versace empire as purveyors of glittery Euro-tat to the rich and famous. Then it hit me. 'A fashion party?' I groaned. 'I've got nothing to wear.'

'Don't worry about that,' laughed Mary. 'Come over to my place. I'll sort you out. I just had a bundle of goodies delivered. Something is bound to fit you.'

A bundle of goodies? Sounded great. It was the kind of offer I couldn't be expected to refuse. And although I probably should have been wondering what Mary's ulterior motive was for suddenly being so nice, I agreed to be at her flat as fast as London transport would carry me.

'Oh, no,' she said. 'I can't wait that long to see you. Take a cab.' And she gave me her account number to charge it to. Mary Bagshot was number one friend again.

CHAPTER THIRTEEN

When I arrived at Mary's gorgeous flat, she buzzed me into the building from the bathroom. She was still lying in her tub, up to her neck in bubbles, looking horribly comfortable as she got all soft and fragrant. I had only had time for a quick flannel wash before I came out and felt rather grubby as I sat down on a cream velvet upholstered stool.

'I've missed you,' she purred.

'You only saw me on Saturday morning.'

'I know. But it's a long time to be angry with someone, isn't it?'

'Were you angry with me?' I asked in surprise.

'A little bit,' she admitted. 'But only because I had PMT. When I got home and took a few Feminax, I realised what a cow I'd been. You weren't asking for all that much really. So I've decided that I want to help you after all. With the flat,' she announced. I could sense that she was waiting for me to look suddenly grateful. I smiled. I should have said thank you. But although she had come up with the old PMT excuse, she hadn't actually, officially, apologised to my face as I suddenly felt she needed to.

'Actually,' I told her, wickedly relishing my sudden upper hand. 'I don't need your help on that front any more anyway.'

She raised an eyebrow. 'Really? Did you tell Brian that you'd been lying? Is he still coming over?'

'No and yes. Yes, he is still coming. And no, I don't need to tell him the full story because a friend has lent me her flat in Grantchester Square.'

Mary, who had been in the process of taking a sip from the glass of white wine on the bathrack almost choked. 'Grantchester Square? Who on earth do you know who can afford to have a flat there? That's Arab sheik land.'

'I've got lots of well-connected friends that you don't know about,' I said mysteriously.

'Obviously,' she sneered.

'And one of them is going to be out of town this weekend.'

'How very fortunate,' said Mary, unable to avoid sounding just a little bit peeved.

'But I suppose I still need your help,' I added, casting my eyes downwards. 'I mean, you won't go telling Brian the truth, will you? You won't send him an e-mail or anything that might drop me in it.'

'What kind of bitch do you think I am, Lizzie?' she asked me. 'I've just told you that I wanted to be able to help you. I've been thinking about what I could do for you all weekend,' she continued. 'It's just that, when you said you wanted me out of my own flat and assumed I could just go and stay with Mitchell, you touched on a rather sore point.'

'I did?' I was all ears.

'Yes. You know I'd love to go and stay with Mitchell. It's just that he doesn't want me to. I think I love him a lot more than he loves me.'

'Oh, Mary,' I said, leaning over the bath to put my arm around her and getting soaked in the process. 'You should have said. I would have understood.'

'I know,' she pouted out her lower lip like a baby. 'I just get so used to all the bullshitting and putting on this inscrutable face for work that I don't seem to be able to switch it off sometimes. Can you forgive me?'

'Of course I can.'

'I really want to help you make a go of things with Brian. I was going to let you have the flat and stay at the Metropolitan so that I wouldn't be in the way while you got things going again, but now that someone else has stepped in and helped you with that, is there anything else I can do?'

I bit my lower lip and allowed the thought that perhaps I shouldn't let Mary get involved at all to pass across my mind for just a second. Then I said, 'You could perhaps lend me a couple of decent outfits. I mean, I'm going to look a bit out of place sitting in my penthouse in my Top Shop specials.' I wasn't indebting myself too much with that, surely. If Mary hadn't had a wardrobe full of Armani, if all her clothes had been from Oasis, I wouldn't have thought twice about borrowing something. It was a natural thing, wasn't it? Girls swapped clothes all the time. It didn't mean that she would have anything over me.

'Help yourself to anything in my wardrobe,' she said generously.

'Anything?'

'Anything,' she said. 'You are my best friend.'

'I'm so glad we've made it up,' I told her. 'I really hate falling out with you.'

'I hate arguing with you too, Liz. It makes me so unhappy. Now help yourself to anything you need for Brian's visit from my bedroom. Except the red Armani,' she added as I raced to raid her cupboards.

Her wardrobe was like every girl's dream. Mary had made a lot of designer friends during her days in fashion PR and they were still keen to keep in touch now that she had the ear of some of the world's most beautiful men and women as a talent agent. I was green as a gherkin when she told me that she rarely bothered to go shopping any more since sooner or later someone would bike over the ideal outfit in exactly her size, gratis.

They biked over a lot of outfits that weren't exactly her size too, I noted with a grin. Mary wasn't terribly good at passing on the dresses she received for some of her skinny actress clients, preferring to keep them for herself in anticipation of 'thin days' ahead.

I pulled out a gorgeous green sequinned dress that

looked like it had been pinched from a mermaid's suitcase.

'That'd look lovely with your hair,' said Mary, who had emerged from her bath and was now wrapped in a big fluffy robe. 'But it's only a size eight.'

'Size eight?' I gasped. 'Who on earth is a size eight?'

'I might be one day soon,' she said hopefully. 'I've signed up with a personal trainer.'

'Is that good?' I asked.

'I don't know. I haven't had time to see him yet. Why don't you try the brown dress instead?'

'Brown? That's not really my colour.'

'No? I think it might be.'

She held a brown dress up in front of me. All the colour seemed to drain from my face. 'Lovely,' she said.

'I don't think so.'

'Well, at least try it on. A bit of make-up will soon stop you from looking so pallid.'

'Only a year in the sun would stop me from looking pallid now.'

'I know,' she said, opening her industrial sized box of make-up tricks. 'I keep meaning to book myself into that spa in Malta again, but I can never seem to find the time.'

'I'd make time if I had the money,' I told her, as I shrugged on the brown silk shift.

'I don't think you'd really want to go there.'

Mary cocked her head to admire me in her dress. 'I think that looks classy.'

'Mmm. I think I look like one of those sausages wrapped in bacon that you get at parties.'

'Not at any parties I've been to recently,' she said, but I could tell she was trying hard not to agree. 'Anyway, you're wearing that tonight.'

'Are you sure? I look so pasty.'

'Once you've got a bit of slap on you'll look like a star. Let me put some of this new eye-liner on you,' she said, stepping forward with a pencil. 'It's not available over here yet. That travel show girl I've been looking after brought me a couple of sticks back from a trip to the States. It's supposed to tighten your eyelids and brighten your eyes as it decorates.'

'How on earth can it do all that?' I asked sceptically.

'It contains some extract of emu oil but don't let that put you off.'

'Emu oil? Is that?' I decided not to ask her to elaborate but she had already decided she would.

'Mmm, it's rendered from emu fat. Boiled down in huge vats. It's the new miracle cosmetic ingredient. Incredibly moisturising and yet non-comodogenic,' she added, as she poked the pencil right into my eye.

'Ow.' I stumbled backwards on to the bed.

'Oh, shit, Liz,' said Mary, rushing forward with a tissue. 'I didn't mean to do that. Look, the line's gone all smudgy. Do you want me to do it again?'

'I think I'll do it myself, thanks all the same,' I told her, safely removing the pencil from her unsteady hand.

'Are you OK?'

'I think so.'

'You don't think we should rush you to the accident unit and see if you need an eyepatch like you did that time at college? What was the name of the girl who stabbed you when you were getting ready for that play?'

'Phylidda Crawley.'

'That's it. Phylidda Crawley. God, she was really jealous of you, wasn't she? Probably wanted to make you have to have a glass eye,' she added with a laugh. 'Wasn't she mad at you because she thought you were trying to steal her boyfriend?'

'Well, I wasn't,' I said, struggling to open my eye so that I could look at the damage in the mirror. 'And I'm not after Mitchell either, if that's what you were thinking.'

'I just slipped,' said Mary, rather seriously.

Fortunately, no major surgery was needed. By the look of the streak of blue liner on my lid, I had managed to close my eye before too much harm was done. But I was still squinting just a little when we got to the party an hour later. Mary handed me her sunglasses.

'I'll look a prat,' I told her.

'You'll look just like everyone else,' she said.

She was right, of course. The lobby of the hotel was full of people wearing sunglasses, though the sun had long since set; all conspicuously trying to look inconspicuous. While I waited in the long queue to hand our coats in at the cloakroom (Mary had people she simply had to talk to – and as she thought I might be bored she promised to get all business out of the way while I dealt with the coats), I watched more new arrivals, all hovering for slightly longer than necessary by the door, in case the paparazzi hadn't had time to get their best sides.

The stinging pain in my eye had somewhat taken the edge off the anticipation I had felt when Mary called to invite me to the party – the only bash she had ever taken me to before was an afternoon launch for a new brand of tights. But now that we had actually arrived, I felt the bubbles of excitement begin to rise inside me again like the bubbles in the champagne that was being handed out all around me. And, if the truth be known, I was still reeling from the fact that as I had walked through the huge double doors of the Hyperion, a paparazzo had actually focused his camera on me, even if he did stop clicking as soon as his blunt Australian colleague told him, 'That's no one, mate.'

But no one or not, that night I had an invitation to what was clearly the hottest party in town. For once I was not one of the pale-faced girls in the crush on the wrong side of the red rope, trying to ignore the rain, hoping to catch a glimpse of some children's TV presenter or a minor British film star as they raced from limo to lobby. Nor was I one of the people walking back to the tube from some awful smoky pub who would pass events such as these and try to convince themselves, even as they craned their necks to look inside, that they had been having a better time at the Slug and Lettuce. I *was* on the inside. Even if I was being largely ignored in the queue to hang up coats.

Every face I cared to focus on seemed familiar. I found myself saying 'hello' in ever such a familiar way to a friendly looking man before his blank gaze reminded me that I didn't know him from anywhere but a cough sweet commercial.

The gregarious star of a West End musical, his face still orange from that evening's greasepaint, helped a former soap actress with her jacket. I couldn't help staring at her – I was used to seeing her playing the battered wife in a tatty nylon cardigan but here she was in a strappy blue dress, her glossy hairstyle very much more London than Liverpool. And when I heard her cut-glass vowels float across the lobby towards me as she shared a joke with the hotel's manager, I felt even more strongly that I had been admitted to an inner sanctum. How many of those poor sad people outside would ever guess she spoke like that, for example?

'Hello again,' said a man behind me. He put his hand on my bare shoulder and turned me towards him for a kiss. But his face echoed mine in surprise when he saw who I was. Or rather who I wasn't.

'God, I'm sorry,' he said. 'Man-handling you like that. I thought you were Arabella Gilbert, for a minute there. God, I'm so embarrassed.'

'Don't be,' I said.

'I'm really sorry.'

'You've made my night,' I told him.

But he had already gone in search of the real McCoy.

As he scuttled away though, the words sank in. Arabella Gilbert? He thought *I* was Arabella Gilbert. Did that mean she might be here? At the same party as me? My heroine. I searched the crowd for her face but couldn't see her.

'D'you want me to take that or what?'

I had finally reached the front of the queue and the coat-check girl grudgingly took my coat without even meeting my eye. She was under no illusions. She knew I was a no-namer. And probably a no-tipper, as a result.

But the surly coat-check girl couldn't ruin my night. Moving back into the room, I searched the thickening crowd for Mary, hoping to ask her whether the social columnist would be there. Would Arabella Gilbert be there reporting on the party for her column? If I could just get myself into the background of the little picture that usually accompanied her party diary I would be happy for a million years. I felt as though I were in the presence of some kind of magic. At last I was part of *Cool Britannia*. Or whatever they were calling it now . . .

Even if I was part of it without another part to talk to. I couldn't see Mary anywhere.

'Do you have your invitation?' asked a stick-thin girl on the door that led from the lobby to the room where the party proper was being held. The girl, who was flanked by two huge security guys with headsets, was dressed from head to toe in black and her matching black hair was pulled so tightly back from her face that it made her eyes look oriental even though she was clearly pure home counties.

'No, I don't,' I said. 'I'm here with my friend. She must have gone on inside without me. I think she's got the invitations.'

'Who's your friend?' she asked disinterestedly.

'Mary Bagshot,' I said.

'I'd like to believe you,' she replied with a totally warmth-free smile. 'But I'm sure you can appreciate that quite a few people claim to be friends with Mary Bagshot. She's the hottest new agent in town.'

'Yes,' I said. 'But I really am her friend. We were at college together.'

'Which college?'

'St Judith's. Oxford.'

'Wrong,' said the door girl triumphantly, crossing her arms to underline her point and nodding me back in the direction I'd come from. 'You can find your own way out.'

'Now, hang on,' I protested. 'I should bloody know which college she was at. I was at St Judith's with her.'

'She didn't go there.'

'She did,' I insisted.

'Look, I'm not even going to argue about this with you,' said Stick-girl. 'I don't recognise you. You don't have an invitation to this party. You can't come in.'

'Are you looking for this?'

Suddenly Mary appeared behind the anorexic Cerberus on the door and handed me my gilt-edged invitation. 'She's with me, Amaryllis.'

'Oh, hi Mary,' Amaryllis blushed. 'Did you get a chance to look at my show reel yet? You know I'm really keen to do anything. Even adverts. Have you had a minute?'

I couldn't believe it. The hard-faced bitch was suddenly rolling over to have her tummy tickled by my best friend.

'Not yet,' Mary said sweetly to the aspiring star. 'Nor will I ever,' she whispered to me as she dragged me into the party proper. 'That girl's tape is going straight in the Westminster Council filing cabinet.' (Which was what Mary called the wheely bin.) 'Where did you go? I waited for you *for ever*.'

'I was trying to put our coats in the cloakroom,' I reminded her impatiently.

'Oh, yeah. Thanks for that.'

I knew I'd been waiting in the queue for the cloakroom for a long time, but in the meantime Mary appeared to have necked enough champagne to make a Gladiator tipsy. At least, that's what I assumed she'd been doing because, considering the moaning and groaning she had done in the cab about hating this kind of party but needing to see and be seen, she looked pretty relaxed and sparky now. Her eyes glittered and she laughed as if she'd just heard that one of Pamela Anderson's boobs had exploded when

I told her that the girl on the door had tried to tell me that Mary hadn't been at our college.

'It wasn't that funny,' I found myself saying when she couldn't seem to control herself. 'But while I was in the queue for the cloakroom, a man mistook me for Arabella Gilbert,' I told her then.

'That's quite possible,' said Mary. 'She does have the saggiest arse in the business.'

'Thanks a lot.'

'I was only joking,' said Mary, really stretching out her words. 'Now, do you want to meet some interesting people?'

Did I ever! Just as she said that, Jed Thunderton – the guitarist of Mental Strain, an early nineties grunge band of which I had once been a massive fan – appeared to Mary's left and reached out to tap her on the shoulder. Was she going to introduce me to him? It was almost as good as Christmas! Jed Thunderton! That hair! Those eyes! I pulled in my stomach and prepared my best smile.

But no.

Mary didn't even seem to notice the man who wanted to make himself known and before I could protest and draw him to her attention, she was dragging me by the arm in the direction of the ladies'.

'Come to the loos with me,' said Mary. Nothing unusual in that. Girls always go to the loo in pairs, on account of the fact that we always have to wait so long for a cubicle to become free that we'd miss valuable gossiping time if we didn't.

'I thought we were going to meet some interesting people,' I reminded her.

'We are,' she said. 'All the best people hang out in the loos at these parties.'

CHAPTER FOURTEEN

There were certainly enough people hanging out in the loos that night. Girls and boys. The elegant gold scrolled gender notice on the door didn't seem to have bothered anyone. The subtly lit ante-room was full of animated chatter as people reapplied their make-up and adjusted stray hair. Mary nodded 'hello' to a few familiar faces but she didn't seem to want to introduce me to them. Then, when one finally became free, she asked me to go into a cubicle with her.

'What?'

'Come in here with me. Quick.'

I'd noticed it while we were waiting. Pairs and even threesomes of girls slipping in and out of the toilet cubicles together as if it was the most natural thing in the world to watch your close friends having a pee. I hesitated but Mary dragged me inside and locked the door behind us.

'Er, I don't think I really need to go after all,' I said.

'Me neither,' she replied cheerfully. She closed the lid of the loo down and put her handbag on top of it.

'Then what are we doing in here?'

We may have been at one of London's best hotels, but still the ladies' wasn't exactly the most salubrious place to while away a week-night.

'You're so naive, Lizzie,' Mary laughed, as she opened her purse and took out a tiny little envelope of white paper. 'I don't know about you, but I was really starting to flag out there. All that social obligation. All that kissing and creeping. I need a little livener to help me carry on.'

She opened the handmade envelope to reveal a minuscule amount of dense white powder which looked like finely ground flour. She took a piece of loo paper and wiped the top of the cistern clean, then she tipped some of the powder straight out on to the enamel. 'Pass me my platinum card,' she ordered, handing me her bag. Then she set about chopping the little pile of powder into two neat and equal lines.

'What is that?' I asked in a whisper. 'Speed?'

She pulled an amused face. 'Oh, please. That's hardly my style. Any more,' she added with a chuckle. 'It's Charlie. Really good stuff too. Mitchell knows this really great little man in Highgate who can get him as much as he wants.'

'Charlie?' I whispered.

'Cocaine,' she explained.

The words swam about my head. Why wasn't she speaking more quietly? She rolled a crisp twenty-pound note into a narrow tube and held it out towards me. 'You do want some of this, don't you?'

I shook my head. 'I'm not sure.'

'Why not?'

'It's just . . .'

'You've never had any before, have you?' she asked acutely. I shook my head again. 'Seriously? Not in all the time you've been in London? Not once? I thought estate agents were at it all the time, stuffing their fat commissions up their big fat noses. One of my clients told me that one estate agent showing her round a flat actually nipped off to do a line in the middle of the viewing.'

'I'm not an estate agent,' I reminded her. 'I'm just the secretary and I don't get any commission to waste on Class A narcotics!'

'Well, you won't be wasting any of *your* money tonight,' she reminded me. 'This is on Mitchell.' She bent over the cistern and hoovered up her share of the two thin lines. 'Look, I've done it. I'm fine.'

'You've only just done the stuff,' I hissed. 'You could die any minute. What would I tell your mum?'

'This is OK. I had some of it before you came round tonight too. And I'm not dead yet, am I? Just do half a line. I'll finish the rest. But do it quickly because there are people queuing up out there. Desperate people no doubt.'

I took the rolled-up note from her hand and tried to remember which end had just been up her nostril. Apart from anything else, I remember thinking that taking cocaine was just so, well, so inelegant. Stuffing a paper tube up your hooter and snorting the stuff to your brain? Half of me wanted to hand the rolled note back and tell her I wasn't interested. But the other half of me was very interested indeed. I wasn't entirely innocent of these things after all. I'd smoked plenty of blow at college and even done an 'e' once. (Unfortunately I had a very bad trip and had diarrhoea for a week after that.) So it wasn't as though I was a life-long member of the 'just say no' brigade. And cocaine was just so glamorous compared to those little printed ecstasy tablets that made you want to make love to men you wouldn't look twice at if they were standing next to you at a bus stop.

It also seemed to be yet another perfect detail for my perfect night. Cocaine. In a top London hotel. While outside the cubicle famous faces from the worlds of TV, film and fashion adjusted their hair and body-sculpting tights in front of the brightly lit mirrors. My mother would never believe it. Not that I'd ever actually be able to tell her, of course. But the cocaine just seemed to fit the bill. And the bill fitted right up my nose.

I bent over the cistern, just as Mary had done. When I glanced up at her, she seemed to be shining. Her eyes were wide open. Her grin was a mile across.

'Go for it,' she whispered. 'It makes life so much more interesting.'

I inhaled hard and was surprised that when I looked down, all the little line had gone. Absolutely all of it. Right up my nostril.

'Like a pro,' commented Mary. 'You must have good lungs.'

I shook back my hair. Then suddenly the innocuous-looking powder hit the back of my nose like sherbet. I could taste it in my throat too. A weird metallic taste. But nothing amazing had happened yet. At best, I felt like I was choking on a sherbet fountain.

'Let's get back to the party, shall we?' Mary asked.

We squeezed out of the cubicle at the same time. Another pair of girls squeezed in after us, talking intently. Mary started to tell me a story about one of her clients. A washed-up soap actor who had been stitched up by a journalist. He had procured a minuscule amount of dope for the journo and ended up doing six months in prison for his pains.

'Got made an example of. But it will probably improve his work prospects no end when he comes out,' she assured me. 'People like a bit of "history". And it wasn't as if he was ever going to present *Blue Peter* anyway. Champagne?' I took a glass from a tray that seemed to be floating past. 'Now what are we going to do about that nuisance, Brian?'

'I'm just going to have to do some pretending.'

'Darling, you'll be perfect at it. Just look at you tonight. You fit right in.'

'Do you think so?'

'Absolutely,' she said, through a mouthful of bubbly. 'Nobody would know you're just an estate agency secretary. And I do hope it all goes well. You've had a rough time of it lately and you deserve to have a wonderful time while Brian's around. Besides, I can't wait to hear the gossip. If he asks you to fly back to New York and marry him, you have to promise that you won't ask me to be the bridesmaid.'

'I'm really glad we've patched things up between us,' I told her.

'I'm glad too,' she said.

We hugged.

'So what are you going to do about that new boy-friend of yours while Brian's in town?' Mary continued.

'I've told him I've got a friend coming to stay over the weekend.'

'Doesn't he want to meet him?'

'Yes. But I've told him that Brian and I will want to spend time with mutual friends. I told Richard he'd probably find it boring, to dissuade him from coming along.'

'Nice touch. But if I know anything about men, he'll probably tag along to check up on you anyway. Perhaps you should have chucked him to make sure he didn't get in the way.'

'That seems a bit harsh.'

'Of course it's harsh. But you do want to get things on with Brian again don't you? You don't want some sad accountant hanging about and spoiling your chances.'

'But what if Brian doesn't want to get back together with me? I'll have chucked Richard for nothing and I'll end up with no one at all.'

Mary shrugged. 'That's always been your problem,

Liz. Hedging your bets. You're never going to get the glittering prize if you don't point your arrow right at it.'

'That's very profound,' I said.

'I know. Coming to the loo again?'

It couldn't have been more than two minutes since we had last been, but I let myself be led.

This time, Mary saw someone she recognised touching up her make-up in the mirror. The woman's sharp brown bob hid most of her profile but she was still unmistakably familiar. In fact, the back of her head was almost as familiar to me as the back of my own.

'Is that?' I asked. But before she could answer, Mary was enveloping Arabella Gilbert in her arms. Arabella Gilbert. My heroine. Sort of. And Mary knew her. I was open-mouthed with awe.

'Hello, darling.' Mary and Arabella air-kissed extravagantly.

'How are you?' Mary purred. 'You look fantastic.'

'Shame I don't feel too fantastic,' she sighed. 'Do you find coke has a laxative effect, Mary?'

'Only if that's what it's been cut with, sweetheart. Any time you want some really good stuff you know who to call. Call me about anything in fact.' She handed Arabella one of her little Smythson business cards.

'Who's this?' Arabella said suddenly, jerking her head towards me. 'Do I know you from somewhere?'

she asked, addressing me directly. 'You used to write for *The Mirror*, didn't you?' Her eyes narrowed suspiciously.

Sensing her concern, Mary wrapped her arm around Arabella's shoulder and assured her that I most definitely wasn't a journalist. 'She's just an old friend of mine. Lizzie and I were at college together,' she explained. 'I've brought her out this evening to show her a bit of the glamorous world of showbiz. Lizzie works for an estate agency. This really crappy agency in one of the tattier parts of Knightsbridge. She's actually not even an estate agent, just a secretary really.'

Thanks a lot, I thought.

'She's a big fan of yours, Arabella.'

'That's nice.'

'Do you want to get Bella's autograph?' Mary asked me.

'I don't have my album with me,' I smiled.

'I'll get my secretary to send you a photo in the post,' said Arabella, totally sincere.

'Thanks,' I said flatly.

'Well, enjoy yourself this evening,' Arabella told me. 'If anyone can show you the social ropes, Mary Bagshot can. She's the A-list party queen. Gets almost as many invitations as I do. Is Mitchell coming this evening, by the way?'

'He's in the studio,' Mary told her.

'Still? I didn't think he actually had to record anything himself. You will give him my regards, won't you?'

'Of course, I will.'

'I'll expect an invitation to the launch party of course.'

'Yours is the first name on the guest list.'

'Then I take it you've forgiven me for that little debacle at the video shoot,' Arabella smiled with her eyes downcast.

'A simple misunderstanding, I'm sure.'

'Good. Er, Mary. I don't suppose you've got any powder I could borrow for my nose? I seem to have run out.'

'Of course,' Mary handed over her handbag. 'Don't use it all at once,' she told her as Arabella disappeared into a cubicle. 'It's incredibly rarefied stuff.'

'What happened at the video shoot?' I couldn't resist asking in a whisper as soon as Arabella closed the cubicle door.

'What indeed?' sniffed Mary. 'I found her in the bedroom of Mitchell's winnebago with no clothes on.'

'Was he with her?' I asked agog.

'No, he was sitting by the catering van at the time, stuffing his face with sausages.'

'But had he? You know. With her?'

'I very much doubt it. Though that didn't stop her implying the opposite in her bloody column.'

'It must be very hard going out with someone so many people want to get their hooks into,' I said.

'You can't blame Arabella for wanting to raise her profile.'

'Well, I know you're in the business of raising

profiles yourself, but I still think you seem very calm about it. I would have kicked her arse.'

'I know I can trust Mitchell not to mess around with the likes of her.'

Just then Arabella emerged from the cubicle and gave Mary her bag back. 'Great stuff,' she said, wide-eyed. 'Really great. You know what, I think I will give you a ring tomorrow morning after all.'

'You do that,' said Mary. 'We could do lunch if you want to. Enjoy the rest of the evening.'

Arabella gave her a dazzling smile. Her eyes, I noticed, were so dark you couldn't see where iris ended and pupil began.

'I can't believe I've been standing in the ladies' with all these celebs drifting in and out,' I sighed when Mary and I were alone again.

'The trick is to act like you're used to it.'

'Well, you are. Do you know Arabella Gilbert really well? Are you friends?'

'No. She's not the kind of girl I'd be friends with. Though my cousin Edward had a brief thing with her once after some Benenden/Eton disco. She was gutted when he chucked her for her brother. And I must say, her rise and rise has certainly surprised me. She's thicker than double cream but potentially worth a fortune,' Mary assured me.

'Thick? How can she be thick if she's a journalist?'

'She doesn't actually write her column, stupid. She

wouldn't have got the job at all if her parents hadn't been involved in that pot-holing accident with Prince What's-his-face of Sweden.'

'Oh.'

'But whatever the obscure reason she rose to fame she seems to be hot property all the same. She's been on the panel for every game show imaginable and now she wants to move into presenting herself. There's a lot of interest. And not all of it from Channel 5. Her current agent is about to retire to Tuscany and I want to be standing underneath the tree when that particular apple drops. Arabella Gilbert is on the up and up and I am going to be right behind her.'

'Sounds a bit mercenary.'

'Sounds business-like to me.'

'Hi, Mary.'

Another familiar face appeared. A weather girl. One who had been on the panel game scene for rather longer than Arabella. She was just the wrong side of thirty and had probably even reported on the great storm of 1987. 'Did you hear that Michael is going to retire next month? I'm devastated.'

'Janie shares an agent with Arabella Gilbert,' Mary explained for my benefit.

'I'm fishing for a new agent if you're interested.'

'Oh, Janie,' Mary sighed extravagantly. 'You know I'd be after you like a shot but my artist roster is totally full for the foreseeable. You know my theory. Stay small and personal for the very best results.'

'Surely you could squeeze me in?' Janie protested. 'I'm only very little.'

Mary winced at Janie's baby voice before telling her, 'I wouldn't want to take you on knowing that I might not be able to give you the time and attention you deserve, sweetheart.'

'Perhaps we could do lunch one day in any case?'

'I'll get my assistant to call you.'

The weather girl left without powdering her nose.

'I don't understand. You just told Arabella you were after new clients,' I said.

'I am after new clients like Arabella,' Mary explained to me. 'But dear old Janie should be thinking about having kids and presenting a daytime animal rescue show. Television presenters are a very highly strung bunch. I'm willing to take terrible tantrums from someone like Arabella because I've got a feeling that one day her fees will keep me in anti-stress massage and aromatherapy oils permanently. But I don't want someone like Janie. She's a charity case and I already have a direct debit donation going to the RSPCA.'

I couldn't help chuckling at that.

'I'm glad to see you haven't totally lost sight of the old Mary,' I told her. 'Still looking out for helpless animals, eh?'

'It's a tax break,' she said flatly.

I followed her back out into the party, marvelling at the professional businesswoman she had become. She could barely move through the room for people trying to air kiss her and ask her out to lunch. She introduced me to most of them, but I saw their eyes glaze over when she explained that I was a friend from college and that no, I wasn't in the business myself. The feel-good factor of the little line of coke Mary had given me soon wore off and I found myself wishing the fire alarm would go off, or there'd be an earthquake – anything to get me out of that ballroom – when I found myself in conversation with a television producer who never met my eye but was constantly looking over my shoulder for someone more useful to talk to.

In the end, I didn't bother to look at him either. Over his shoulder I had the most wonderful view of Arabella Gilbert. She was standing at the centre of a circle of equally glittering admirers and from the way they were laughing, it seemed she was telling them all a joke. When it came to the punchline, she had to put down her handbag. It was the very same pink leather strapless Hermes number she had written about in her column. Exquisite.

Anyway, whatever joke she was telling, Arabella had to get down in a squat to illustrate the last bit. She puffed out her alabaster cheeks and made flapping movements with her arms. Anyone else attempting such an inelegant move would have looked like an idiot but to me she still looked ridiculously glamorous. When she had finished, she straightened up and flicked her shiny hair back over her shoulder. Then, as if she had sensed my gaze upon her, she turned in my direction and smiled at me. Straight at me. I shifted to my left as subtly as I could, so that the TV producer obscured her view of me.

Oh, dear. I had been star-struck. Seeing Arabella Gilbert in the flesh had made me feel twenty times as inadequate as reading her bloody column.

Unfortunately, Mary didn't seem to want to leave the bash and end my agony any time soon. Occasionally she glanced over at me and gave me a little thumbs up sign or a smile that asked 'How are you?' but she never actually paused for long enough in her important conversations for me to say that I wanted to go home.

In fact, when the party ended, Mary was keen to follow a particularly select group of people upstairs to the suite the Golden Brothers had hired for the duration of their stay in London for Fashion Week. I tagged along because, while I hadn't been having such a great time since my celebrity moment in the loos, I felt I still ought to make the effort to join the inner sanctum while the opportunity was being offered to me. I had often tried to hint to Mary that I would love to go to a VIP party with her. Now I was being taken upstairs to the best suite at the Hyperion to raid the mini-bar with three supermodels, two top fashion designers, an up-and-coming Hollywood actor and one of my best friends.

Mary linked arms with the Hollywood supernova-in-waiting, Rad Bradbourne – he had just made a film about the Second World War in which he played a GI who single-handedly saved an entire French village from the Nazis without even messing up his hair. I can't say I had ever thought much of him as an actor, but seeing him in the flesh, I could understand why he had been the darling of the casting couches since his voice broke. Even his back view was extra special. Imagine the buttocks of Michelangelo's *David* made flesh.

Just as we reached the door to the suite, Mary turned to me and said, 'Do you think you could be a darling and pop downstairs to get a bottle of something nice? We could ring room service but they'll take for ever. Tell them to put it on the room bill.'

Then she slipped in through the half-open door and closed it behind her leaving me in the hallway outside. There was nothing I could do except do as I was told.

I had made my way to the twelfth floor with my eyes firmly on Rad Bradbourne's buttocks. Without such a good view to keep me occupied on the journey back downstairs I waited impatiently for the lift; but when it finally arrived the door opened to reveal a couple who were getting to know each other rather intimately and before I could get in – as if I would have wanted to at that point – the girl reached out one elegant foot in a very pointy heeled shoe and pressed the button that closed the lift door again.

I waited for another two minutes while the floor counter indicated that the happy couple had become stuck between the fifth and sixth floors. I doubted very much that the lift had actually broken. How selfish was that? Making love in the lift of a high-rise building? I pressed the up button one more time, hoping to dislodge them, but I couldn't.

So I had to walk down the stairs. All the long walk down I met people walking up who were clearly a lot more disgruntled by the lift failure than I. Someone had given up altogether half-way between the tenth and ninth floors and lay slumped against the wall looking like she had just had a coronary.

It was Arabella Gilbert. She didn't look quite as polished as she had done at the beginning of the party. Her pale face was red with puffing her way up so many stairs. Her slinky cat-suit was looking decidedly crumpled. She carried a bottle of champage in each hand.

'Are you OK?' I asked her as she tried to stand up but swayed backwards violently and looked in real danger of tumbling all the way back down the stairs.

'I'm fine,' she slurred. 'Weally, we-ally fine.'

'You don't look it,' I observed.

'I don't feel it,' she admitted then, sliding down the wall to find herself sitting on the stairs. She looked totally bewildered. As if she didn't have a clue where she was.

'Do I know you?' she asked. 'You're not that girl who used to write for the *Sun*, are you?'

'No,' I said. 'And I'm not the girl who used to write for the *Mirror* either. We've been through this before. My name's Lizzie Jordan. We met in the loos earlier on.'

'Oh, Lizzie. You're the one with the leaking boob job, right? That's too awful. I can see it leaking now.'

'Er, no,' I said, looking down at my chest nervously. 'You've got the wrong girl.' Though there was a wet mark on my chest where an energetically camp make-up artist had stumbled into me and spilled his drink earlier on. 'I was with Mary.'

'Oh, Mary. Mary, Mary quite contrary. Is she still sleeping with that gorgeous brother of hers? I've had a crush on him for ages, you know.'

I raised an eyebrow. 'Think you might have the wrong girl. Again. I'm talking about Mary Bagshot the agent. She gave you her card.'

'Oh, Mary the agent!' cried Arabella, as if enlightenment was thumping her between the eyes. 'Mary the agent one. What's your name again?'

'Lizzie.'

'Well, Lucy,' she wiped a string of dribble from her expensively powdered chin. 'Why don't you sit down here with me for a little while? Talk to me until I get my breath back.'

'Where were you trying to get to?'

'To the party upstairs. I know Rad Bradbourne is in there with those supermodel sluts and I've simply got to talk to him. He told me that I drink too much to be his girlfriend. I've got to tell him that's he's wrong.'

'I don't think you'll have all that much luck trying to convince him of that right now,' I warned her. 'Can I take one of those bottles for you?' She was waving her arms about and occasionally thumping me in the side. She gave up the bottle fairly easily though, then started to wrestle with the cork in the top of the other one. She tried for several minutes, resisting all my attempts to help her, before giving up with conventional methods of opening a champagne bottle and smashing the neck of the heavy green bottle against the wall. It took two whacks to break the top off, but when it did break we were both soaked with champagne and bits of broken glass.

I snatched the bottle away from her just as she was about to put the jagged neck to her mouth.

'Are you mad?' I asked.

'That's what he said to me,' she sighed.

'You could have cut half your face off, drinking out of this.'

'I don't care.'

'I'm sure you would in the morning,' I told her.

'I just want him to know I'm not mad. I'm just sad. I'm really sad.'

'What about?' I was fascinated to know.

'Don't know,' she sniffled. She leaned her head momentarily on my shoulder. 'Just very sad.'

'But you've got such a great life,' I told her. 'You seemed very happy earlier on. I heard you telling a joke. Everyone was laughing.'

'That's just it. I seemed very happy. But I'm not, you know. Rad will never love me.'

'I'm sure he does.'

She turned her face towards me. Her eyes were red.
Tears edged towards the corners of her lower lids,
ready to spill down her increasingly puffy face.

'My life is in ruins.'

She was crying properly now.

'You've just won columnist of the year,' I said.

'And I've just been told that I'm too fat to be on
TV.'

Too fat? She was like a pepperami. And hadn't she
ever heard of Vanessa Feltz?

'I've just found out that I've got to have liposuction
and a tummy tuck if I want to make it in television.
It doesn't matter when I'm writing a column but
television adds ten pounds and I know exactly where
it would be added.'

'I don't think you look fat,' I said.

'Of course you don't,' she said. 'I'm thinner than
you.'

'Thanks.'

'But compared to the other girls I'm up against in
the television world I might as well be an elephant. I've
tried everything. Amphetamines. Cocaine. I even went
to India for a week and drank water straight out of a
toilet bowl in the hope of getting amoebic dysentery
but it didn't happen and I came back weighing three
pounds more than I did before I went because I'm so
fond of tikka masala and gulab jamun.'

'Maybe you should try exercising more?' I suggested.

'What if someone snaps me looking all hot and

sweaty on the way out of an exercise class?' she replied as if that were a perfectly logical objection to working out.

'Well, at least they couldn't accuse you of doing anything other than looking after yourself,' I said. 'Which has to be better than accusing you of having had liposuction.'

'God, I wish I were you,' said Arabella. 'You really have no idea how easy your life is, do you? You get up in the morning, you look a wreck and you don't have to care about it. You don't have to worry if your hair looks awful day after day.' She picked up one limp side of my bob to illustrate her comment. 'No one cares if they can see your knickers through your dress.'

I looked for a knicker line nervously.

'Your life is perfect.'

'And yet I've been pretending to be you,' I told her.

'Yeah, well, I've been pretending to be me too,' she said, waving her arm in my face. 'I don't write that column, you know.'

'Don't you?' I said in mock surprise.

'I don't even know how to type. If my parents weren't who my parents are, I wouldn't be anybody either. I'd be just like you. Do you have any idea how scary that thought is? What do your parents do, Lucy?'

'Lizzie,' I corrected.

'I bet your dad wears a flat cap and your mother goes to the shop in her slippers.'

I opened my mouth to protest. Shop in her slippers?

My mother would have gone purple to hear such an accusation.

'I bet she has his tea on the table every night when he gets home from work. Or the dole office. I bet they drink cans of lager while they watch *Brookside*.'

'Actually—' I wanted to tell her that she was wrong. But she was on a roll.

'I bet that your dad used to take you to football matches.'

He hated football.

'And you used to eat chips every single day.'

If only.

'I hardly ever saw my parents when I was a child,' she continued. 'They packed me off to boarding school aged three and a half and I didn't see my father again until I turned sixteen.'

'That sounds awful.'

'I think that's why I'm like I am.'

'I think you're really nice,' I said comfortingly.

'Of course you do. Lots of ordinary people think I'm nice. But how can they possibly know? The girl who writes the column – that's not me. I mean, obviously it's not me. It's some secretary at the paper. I don't have the time. But the girl they think I am because they read my column, that really isn't me either. Are you following?'

'I think so.'

'I've got a horrible feeling that underneath it all, I'm ordinary too. I'm just the sum of my expensive outfits. That's the only difference between me and you.' She

poked me in the chest. 'I wear nice clothes and you
. . . don't.'

I knew the brown shift had been a mistake.

'But that's actually Calvin Klein, isn't it?' she added,
momentarily sounding as if she wasn't completely out
of her head on booze and drugs.

'It is,' I told her. And even though she had just
made one of the most offensive remarks about me
I had heard in a long while, I suddenly felt rather
elated. The only difference between me and Arabella
Gilbert, as heard from the horsey-girl's mouth itself,
was a matter of superficial appearance. It was a great
comfort to me.

'You know, you should be careful of that Mary,'
Arabella slurred. 'She seems to be your friend, but
really she just wants something you've got. When she
has got it, she'll dump you. All agents are like that.'

'Well, I'm happy to say that she's not my agent.
And I can't think what I've got that she could possibly
want. We've been friends for a hundred years. Well,
at least nine.'

'I still say you should watch your back,' said Arabella.
'Always watch your back and never trust anyone ever.'

'Thanks for the advice,' I said.

'Watch out below!'

Talk of the devil. Mary suddenly tumbled down
the stairs and came to a stop right next to me and
Arabella.

'I've got to go home,' she said to Arabella. 'It's
getting too crazy up there. One of the supermodels

produced a bottle of absinthe – it went down the wrong way and I think she may have choked to death. Hey, Arabella. You haven't seen that mousy girl I came here with tonight?'

'Hi, Mary,' I said, hoping that she had known I was there all along and that she had been having a joke.

'Oh, hi, Liz. Do you mind if we get a taxi home now?'

'I've been waiting for you to say that for about the last two hours,' I admitted.

'What's up with you, Arabella?' Mary asked the society girl who had finally abandoned the idea of sitting up under her own steam and was now slumped against the bannister like a puppet with its stuffing knocked out.

'Had a few too many, I think?' I suggested.

'Well, we'd better take her home with us,' said Mary, getting to her feet and very quickly recovering her sober self. 'The last thing I need is for one of my clients to be found drowned in a pool of her own vomit.'

'But she's not one of your clients.'

'She will be after tonight. Easy as tickling trout. Take her other arm, will you?'

I dutifully slung one of Arabella's arms around my shoulders and helped to lift her to her feet. I soon learnt what Arabella had meant when she said she was 'deceptively slim'. She weighed a ton.

CHAPTER FIFTEEN

What a night! All the way back from the West End I prayed that Seema would still be up when I got in. I was ready to burst with the news of my night with the stars and I especially wanted to tell her in blow by blow detail how *the* Arabella Gilbert had cried on my shoulder and told *me* about her impending liposuction. I wanted to tell Seema about the champagne, the canapés, the cocaine.

But Seema wasn't up – I had a vague recollection of her having said that she had an early shift at the video shop next day – and neither was Fat Joe to be found outside the confines of his bedroom-come-bunker. He would have been a passable ear to bend in Seema's absence even if he had no interest in canapés whatsoever and no idea who Arabella Gilbert was either. So I had to hold my magical stories inside me for another night.

Instead I went to my bedroom and sat down on the end of my bed to admire myself in Mary's designer dress. I still couldn't see the knicker line that Arabella had so cruelly referred to.

I stood up and sashayed across to the full length mirror on the back of my wardrobe door in a fairly close approximation of Arabella's model-style wobble. I could do the walk all right. But would Brian be impressed with what he saw when he stepped off that plane at Heathrow? That was *the* question.

I looked pretty good from the front at least, I thought. Though I had ballooned from a ridiculously skinny size eight at the age of eighteen to a size twelve now (ten at Marks and Spencer) my body still curved in all the right places. I still had a pretty narrow waist between my bigger boobs (I was happy with those) and my bigger hips (not so sure about that). I mean, I didn't need them to be quite so *childbearing* yet.

But then I turned sideways to get a profile view. Not so good. The girl in the mirror now definitely wasn't one that I wanted to recognise as me. My back was so hunched and curved with slouching over a computer keyboard at Corbett and Daughter all week long that my head jutted out from my shoulders like a tortoise's from its shell. I looked like an eighty-year-old lady. And worst of all, my belly jutted out almost as far as my chin did.

Shocked and horrified by the thought that other people had seen me standing like that, I pulled myself up straight and instantly looked as though I had lost twelve pounds. Well, that wasn't so awful. I would just have to stand up straight while Brian was around. But I had spent so long slouching that it felt weird to stand up straight again and by the time I had walked around my room picking up the clothes I had thrown off and on to the floor after getting home from work every night the previous week, and looked in the mirror again, my body had reverted to its previous shape.

If only Brian had given me more notice, I sighed. If I'd had, say, a whole month to prepare for his visit, I could have greeted him with a body like Anthea Turner's in her workout video (not the face or manic grin, of course). If I'd had six months . . . Well, I could have achieved anything in six months! It just wasn't fair that he should spring a visit on me like this.

But would extra time really have made such a difference? I leaned over to pick up a stray sock and discovered a leaflet I had picked up from a new health club in town three months earlier on one of my cyclical 'must get fit' kicks (which generally kicked in on one of those days when I couldn't get my jeans done up). I had circled in thick black felt tip all the classes I promised myself I would attend starting with water aerobics on Mondays (ideal for the elderly, pregnant women and people who have not been near a gym for a very very long time) and working up to advanced kick-boxing on Friday nights (ideal for SAS-trained PE teachers and Gladiators).

I snorted when I saw all those optimistic little circles. I had ringed six classes. Six a week!! Can you imagine it? In reality, on the evening when I was supposed to get the ball rolling with a little light water aerobics, I had arrived at the health club to discover that I had completely forgotten to pack a towel. The girl on the desk told me that I could hire one of the club's own towels for fifty pence but much as she insisted that they were boil-washed clean every evening and nice and fluffy from the tumble drier, I just couldn't bring myself to rub my body down with a towel that might have been used by someone with impetigo or body lice the night before.

Well, that was my excuse.

It would have been so easy to stay fit if I had been one of those weird people who actually enjoy exercise, I told myself. You know, the type who claim they get a natural high from jogging around the block avoiding the dog shit. Unfortunately for me, much as I wanted to get fit, I couldn't get over the psychological hurdle of seeing exercise not as pleasure but as a punishment. I blame the PE teachers I had at school. When your PE teacher lands you with the nickname 'Crash Bang Wallop' (Wallop for short) at the impressionable age of four and a half, you haven't really got much hope of growing up to be the kind of adult who regards the prospect of raising a pulse rate with anything other than trepidation.

But how much weight can you lose in four days anyway? All the diet books I had amassed over my years as a woman (i.e. all my years of being weight-obsessed and longing to be in control of my body), didn't promise anything in less than a month. Take things slowly, they all said. Sudden weight loss usually only indicates dehydration. A total fast was cheating and would only lead to dangerous binge eating later on. Did I want to be a yo-yo dieter? the gurus threatened. If the Yo-Yo diet involved eating nothing but those chocolate covered minty biscuits, then the answer was probably yes.

Seema, stick thin on three Mars Bars a day, would surely have the answer. I collared her next morning as she was shovelling in a Snickers bar for breakfast. The answer was, she suggested, three Mars Bars a day and absolutely nothing else. Put that way it wasn't quite such an appealing regime.

'You've left it a bit late to worry about losing weight anyway, haven't you?' she said.

'I would have started the moment he called but I was too depressed by the prospect of having to tell him the truth about the flat. Now that I've got the flat sorted out, I've only got to look as though I've been working out at the Harbour Club for six years to complete the illusion.'

'Did you tell him that?'

'As far as Brian's concerned, the gym is my home from home.'

'I can only see you being a regular at a gym if you have to get a job cleaning one,' said Seema. 'You could buy him a blindfold. Or you could try the cabbage soup diet,' she suggested only slightly more usefully. 'That has very quick results or so I've heard, so you could lose half a stone by the weekend. You just make a huge vat of cabbage soup at the beginning of the week and you can eat as much of that as you like but nothing else. Only problem is, it makes you a tad unsociable, if you know what I mean. It's all right now, while Brian isn't here and you're with us in Balham, because we won't be able to tell if it's you or Hercules, but when Brian turns up, you don't want to be farting like a shire horse.'

'I'll probably be farting through fear anyway,' I told her.

'Yeah, but not cabbage farts.'

That was a good point.

'Then if the cabbage diet is out, what do you suggest?'

'How about a pair of those big knickers from Marks and Spencer? The industrial-strength lycra ones that hold you in all over.'

'They're hardly very sexy,' I replied. 'And besides, all the fat that's meant to be held in is really just squashed out over the waist band or even worse through the leg holes. All this so-called amazing underwear is hopeless. And if you look good while you've got your clothes on, you've still got the problem of how to breathe without fainting or explode discreetly when you get your kit off.'

'I know,' Seema sympathised. 'I've given up on Wonderbras ever since one of my pads fell out on the dancefloor at the Ritzy leaving me with one peak and one valley at the crucial moment. I was so embarrassed. I could see the pad lying on the floor between me and the bloke I was cruising at the time but I could hardly just bend over and pick it up, could I? Then he stepped on it and picked it up himself.'

'What did you do?'

'I crossed my arms over my chest, told him it was probably someone's shoulder pad come loose and got out of the club before he came in for a grope. He could have had me under the Trades Description Act. Anyway, does all this panic mean that Brian's visit is definitely going ahead? Has he called to confirm?'

I opened my mouth to say 'not yet' but as if by telepathy, the telephone rang.

'Good news,' said Brian. 'I've just come back from a great night out with my boss.' It was four in the morning his time. 'He's had a sneak preview of the figures for this month and he was ecstatic. I'm definitely coming to see you. Who knows, I might even be able to stay for longer than I thought.'

Eeek!

'Er, that's great,' I said. 'But I've got to be in Jersey on Tuesday for a business meeting so I don't know if I can put you up for longer than four days.' Seema gave me the thumbs up for my quick thinking.

'That's OK,' said Brian. 'I'm sure four days will be plenty of time for us to get to know each other all over again.'

'I'm glad your figures looked good,' I told him.

'Not as good as your figure has always looked to me,' he flirted. 'I'll see you Friday.'

I put down the phone with a freefalling feeling that was midway between ecstatic anticipation and bottomless misery.

'He commented on my good-looking figure,' I told Seema. 'I used to have one, once.'

'Oh, for god's sake. You don't look that bad,' Seema tutted. 'Get your hair done. Get some streaks. Have a manicure. Brian won't notice that you've put on three pounds if you get your eyelashes dyed.'

Mmm. Perhaps she was right. Perhaps the body-work wouldn't look too bad if the paintwork was up to scratch.

I had to get my hair done in any case. My chic city bob was no longer quite as sharp as it had been and was instead getting to that length where it wouldn't do anything but part in the middle like it belonged on the head of a hippie unless I plastered it with enough lacquer to waterproof a yacht.

Since Harriet was away and I didn't have to go into the office, I could get an appointment with the best stylist in town in the morning. It cost so much money – my bank manager would have passed out – but once you factored in the money saved by not having to buy the glossy magazines I could read for free while I was waiting, it almost seemed reasonable. I even found a mag with a picture of Arabella Gilbert in it, snapped grinning in Armani as she attended the opening of another envelope.

'I'd like to look like that,' I told Guido the stylist, waving the picture in front of him.

'OK,' he said, flicking back his own blond Princess Di layered job. I expected him to say 'dream on' but instead he put his fingers to his chin in a pensive gesture and said, 'I think we can do that. You know what? You even look a bit like her already. Same jaw-line.'

To hear that comment alone I would have paid the price of two haircuts. *I* had the same jaw-line as Arabella Gilbert? Suddenly I was proud of my slightly soft chin.

Anyway, it was while I was reading one of those magazines that I also happened upon the miracle weight-loss cure. *Want to lose weight instantly?* the article asked. *Why not try colonic irrigation?*

Mmm. Sounded scientific. By the time I'd finished reading the article it also sounded quite horrific, but the magazine's game guinea pig claimed she lost five pounds in her first session. That was it. I decided my excess weight was in fact due entirely to the volume of compacted red meat in my colon – although apart from my Mum's Sunday lunch I hadn't actually eaten red meat in five years, not since the BSE crisis (and a final Oxford kebab that nearly landed me in hospital). But there were other benefits too. Bright eyes and clear skin. A feeling of total well-being that lasted for – ooh, I don't know – minutes!! The humiliation of a backless gown and a hose-pipe up the jacksy was a small price to pay for such side-effects, I thought.

The actual price to pay for the humiliation however, was far from small.

Guido the hairdresser recommended a clinic where he had undergone the treatment himself.

'Tell them I sent you,' he said. 'You might get a discount.'

'Guido who?' asked the receptionist before quoting a three-figure sum.

'Have you ever had colonic irrigation before?' the clinician asked moments later, as she led me into a small room which was not unlike the room where I got my legs waxed in Balham. (Which was yet another torture I needed to fit in before Brian's arrival, I reminded myself.)

'Where did you hear about the clinic?' the white-coated woman asked me in her bright, put-at-easy voice.

'In the back of *Complete Woman*,' I piped up.

'I see. So would you like me to tell you a little bit about what actually happens before we start?'

'I think I got the general idea from the article,' I assured her. As with ear-piercing, I figured that the best approach to take with a colonic was to pretend it wasn't happening and hope that the therapist took you by surprise.

'Well, feel free to ask any questions,' my therapist said, getting what looked like a pot of vaseline out of the cupboard. 'You might want to change out of your clothes now and put this on.' She handed me one of those paper gowns that are split right the way down the back and fastened with totally ineffectual ribbons. I slipped behind a curtain and changed into it. It was just like a hospital gown – exactly as I had expected. And by the time I emerged from behind the curtain and saw her greasing up her fingers, I might as well have been going in for major surgery, so nervous did I feel at the prospect.

'Can you tell me when you last had an evacuation?' she asked me.

'Excuse me?' I said. I wondered for a moment whether she wanted me to tell her about the evacuation of children living in London to the safety of the countryside during the Second World War to concentrate my mind elsewhere while she started to do the business down below. She didn't.

'A poo, dear,' she said impatiently. 'When did you last do a poo?'

'Er, this morning, I suppose.'

'And are you regular?'

'I've never really thought about it before.'

'Not a lot of people do think about their bowels,' she said, fixing me with a sad and serious look. She crossed her rubber-gloved arms across the front of her apron and started a lecture I sensed she had delivered several times before. 'Just because a part of your body is hidden away doesn't mean that it's not important,' she warned me. 'People care so much about their hearts and their lungs and their kidneys.

All the *popular* organs. Even their spleens get a look in. Everybody forgets about the good old bowel. But can you imagine what would happen if it suddenly decided to stop working?'

I shook my head like a school-girl caught smoking by the bike sheds.

'Well, how about if all the bin men in London suddenly decided to go on strike?' she asked me. 'Tomorrow? In this weather? Putrid, that's how it would be. Putrid.'

She prodded my belly accusingly. Was that going putrid too?

'As it is, you've probably been abusing your bowels for far too long,' she sighed. 'It may be too late for you already. Lie on that couch and roll over.'

As the little tube went up my bum, I asked in an anguished whisper, 'Brian Coren, are you worth it?'

'What was that?' the therapist enquired. She could hardly hear me because she was cranking up some kind of machine that made alternate whooshing and sucking sounds.

'Oh, nothing. I was just swearing.'

'Swear away,' the therapist said. 'Everybody does. And let me tell you that no man is ever worth it.'

Perhaps not. But colonic irrigation was certainly a faster method to a flat stomach than sit-ups. I hoped.

'I'm going to start introducing the warm water into your body now,' the therapist continued. 'In a short while you will be able to see all that nasty debris flowing from your body into this pipe. You can watch if you like. You might find it interesting.'

'I think I'll just close my eyes,' I said.

After the irrigation I was so worried about seepage that I spent the rest of the day wearing three pairs of pants.

Of course, I didn't look as though I'd lost an ounce – though the therapist had assured me that all sorts of stuff had come out through the tube (I didn't like to look when she invited me to). And far from being filled with a sense of well-being, I felt totally grotty. Not to mention slightly sore.

I may have had a spotless backside but I certainly wasn't in the mood for visitors, so I was slightly less than welcoming when Richard came round uninvited that evening. He must have guessed that I wasn't all that pleased to see him, because he remained on the doorstep until I invited him in, instead of bounding straight into the sitting room, stealing my place on the sofa and demanding a cup of tea as he usually did.

'You've had your hair done,' he said.

'No one else has noticed. Did Seema tip you off?' I asked.

'No,' he said indignantly. 'I noticed it immediately. You look different somehow. Radiant. What have you been doing with yourself since the weekend?'

'I didn't tell him I had been spending that month's rent money on having someone stick a tube up my bum to suck out the solidified contents of my guts.

'Oh, nothing much,' I said instead. 'Do I really look different?'

'Yeah. You look really lovely.'

'Thanks.'

'Look, I don't want to keep you long. I know we didn't arrange to see each other tonight, but I just wanted to see you again before your mate comes to stay. I'll really miss you, Lizzie.'

'It'll only be a few days,' I snorted.

'I know but I think I'll still miss you all the same.'

'Don't be so soft. Go and practise your football or something.'

'Well, it probably needs it. Look, if you change your mind about bringing your mate out to meet us lot at any time, just give me a ring. I mean, if you get fed up of him and want to pack him off to play football with the boys or something. To give you a bit of a break. I'll be happy to look after him.'

'Thanks. But I don't think I'll need a break from Brian,' I said. 'And he doesn't play football anyway.'

He hovered by the door, hand still on the handle. 'Brian. That's his name, is it?'

'Yes.'

'Funny name.'

'I suppose so.'

There was a pause. Normally I would have said something to get the conversation going again – something silly and affectionate – but that night I wanted to get back to painting my fingernails. It was Richard who broke the silence.

'Er, Lizzie, have you, er, have you thought any more about what I said on Sunday?'

'About what?'

'About getting a flat? You and me together.'

Oh, no, I sighed inwardly. I had completely forgotten. I felt my heart make a quick trip towards my feet.

'I've been sort of busy,' I blustered to Richard. 'I'm holding fort at the office on my own. Harriet's gone away for the week, but she's left the dog behind.'

As if on cue, Hercules came to investigate the visitor. Richard crouched down to pat him on the head.

'He's sweet,' he said.

'He's a complete pain in the proverbial.'

'Could we take him out for a walk perhaps? Have a bit of a chat?'

'He doesn't like going for walks very much. He's pretty highly strung.'

'OK,' Richard nodded. 'Well, look, I guess I'll see you when your friend's gone back home then. I just wanted to say "hello" tonight. And let you know that . . .'

'What?'

'Oh, just that you look really lovely and all that. You always do, of course.'

I put a hand to my hair self-consciously, then I planted a little kiss on Richard's cheek and encouraged him back towards the street. 'I've got to be in work early tomorrow morning to open up the office,' I lied.

'And just one more thing,' he started again.

'What?' I said, finding it very hard not to be snappish.

'I know I haven't got you anything for your birthday yet but I'd like you to have this in the meantime. Until we can go shopping.'

He handed me an envelope.

'You've already given me a card,' I said.

'Yeah, but I did this one myself.'

I opened the envelope and pulled out a piece of thin paper that had been folded in half to make a card. On the front was a pencil sketch. Of me. I recognised the pose at once. Richard had drawn me from a photograph taken on a trip we'd made to Brighton. Back when I was still too excited by the novelty of having a boyfriend to be churlish enough to want to change him. To make him, say, richer.

'Thanks. It's very good,' I said.

It was.

'You're easy to draw,' said Richard. 'I'd like to draw you from life one day.'

'Yeah,' I said, non-committally, putting the card back into its envelope and putting the envelope on the plant stand just inside the door, where it would stay for quite some time.

Richard was finally on the pavement outside the house. 'I'll see you then,' he said again. 'When your friend's gone.'

'Yeah. See you. Look, I'm going to close the door

now because we're letting all the heat out of the house standing here like this.'

Richard nodded. And I closed the door to save the heat, even though it was possibly the hottest day of the year so far outside. I raced up to my room and, hiding myself behind the curtains, I watched Richard walk down the street, kicking at stones and lamp-posts until I couldn't see him any more. Then I sat down in front of the mirror and gave myself a long hard staring at, again.

But I wasn't staring at myself because I was filled with disgust for the coldness with which I had treated my boyfriend – letting him wander off like some poor kicked puppy – instead I was dwelling on something he had said.

Did I look unusually lovely? I was reasonably impressed. My hair certainly looked much tidier since Guido had done his miracle work and my skin suddenly seemed much clearer too. Perhaps the colonic irrigation had done the trick. I struck poses like a fourteen-year-old whose only ambition in life is to be a supermodel. I was trying to imagine Brian's first sight of me after so long apart.

Did I have a best side that he should see first? Should I be pouting moodily like a hopeful starlet when he first caught sight of me, or grinning like a looney? Did my friendly smile make my face look fat as my cheeks bunched up beneath my eyes? I pouted again, suddenly deciding that smiling too broadly made me look like a demented hamster.

'Hello, Brian,' I murmured in my most seductive voice. 'Long time no see. Did you have a nice flight?'

More questions. Should I wear the shimmery lipstick that made my lips look bigger but my teeth slightly yellow? Or the dark red pout that made me look slightly tight-lipped but with teeth that were pearly white?

I tried on some of the outfits I had borrowed from Mary for the adventure ahead.

'I am drop-dead gorgeous,' I said, reading from the post-it note that Mary had advised I stick on the mirror to remind me of my priceless worth every time I went to inspect my blackheads. 'I am the most wonderful, unique and beautiful woman in the whole damn world.'

Well, near enough.

Upsetting Richard was suddenly as far from my mind as pension schemes. Right then I knew that what I really wanted could be mine.

'Brian Coren,' I murmured to the fox in the mirror. 'Meet your destiny.'

CHAPTER SIXTEEN

I couldn't sleep at all the night before Brian's plane arrived, even though I went to bed at eight o'clock with two slices of cucumber sellotaped to my eyes as a last-minute rescue remedy for my panda rings and my hair slathered in conditioner and wrapped in a plastic bag.

I had decided to spend the evening before Brian's arrival in Harriet's flat, with the intention of getting to know it a little better so that I might seem a more likely resident when he became my guest. But it certainly didn't help me to get any rest. When I turned the expensive-looking bedside lamp out, the flat began to creak and yawn as flats in old houses do and the unfamiliar sounds of beams expanding and water-heating systems making knocking noises as they cooled sent me racing to turn the lights back on.

I even managed to convince myself that the antique four-poster bed in which I had installed myself for the night was possessed by some ancient Corbett family ghost that would exact a terrible revenge on me as soon as I drifted off. I just couldn't seem to get comfortable and when I finally did, the sensation of cold fingers resting on my cheek awoke me just after midnight. I banged my knee on a chest of drawers as I stumbled across the room with the cucumber slices still on my eyes, only to discover when I could see again that the cold fingers had in fact been Hercules's wet black nose. He had climbed into the bed beside me and from his contented snores as he snuggled down into a pillow, I guessed he must always have slept with Harriet in that way.

I moved my pillow to the other end of the bed and lay top to tail with the pampered mongrel until dawn brightened the room. My mind raced throughout the early hours, playing out the precious nine months I had spent with Brian scene by giddy scene. I hadn't imagined how good it had been, had I? We had been incredibly well-suited, hadn't we? Considering we came from such different backgrounds. I wasn't setting myself up for the most embarrassing knock-back of my life, was I? I tried to resummon the faith in my remarkable attributes I had experienced six hours after getting my guts sluiced.

The glowering antique clock in the hallway began to strike the hour. I had lost track of the exact time and told myself that if the hour was an even one, everything would go according to my complicated plan. The clock struck five. I even got out of bed again to check that the chime hadn't become stuck in some way when it should in fact have struck six. But the clock was in perfect working order. I told myself that if

I could get back into bed without waking Hercules up, then the clock deal didn't count. As I slipped beneath the covers, Hercules opened a lazy eye and licked my pedicured toes.

I closed my eyes tightly and offered up a little prayer. If I could pull this off, if Brian would only fall for my charms once again and invite me to accompany him back to New York, I promised whoever might be listening to my pleadings that I would dedicate the rest of my life to helping other people – preferably by organising charity balls for my rich American husband's banking colleagues to attend – but I would be good whatever. I deserved this break, I told myself. I deserved to be rescued from my lowly London life and elevated to the Empire State heights of Manhattan society. I had done five years in London after all. Surely I must be up for parole by now.

And miracles did happen, didn't they? How else had Arabella Gilbert got her column in *The Daily*? And what about the time when Seema had her credit cards cut up by her bank manager one day and won three hundred pounds on the lottery the next? She wasn't even being particularly good or nice at the time, but her prayers had been answered – although she had been praying to Ganesh, the elephant-headed Hindu money god whose effigy she kept on her dressing table next to her Jolen creme bleach. I hoped I hadn't been praying to the wrong god for romantic miracles. Was there a god for romantic miracles?

Dawn was definitely with us by then. I looked out

of Harriet's bedroom window in the direction of the park. Down below, the main road into central London was already busy with commuters hurrying to beat the worst of the traffic on their way to work. The dustbin van made its halting way with them. It was an ordinary day for everybody. Everybody except me. I felt as though it was the most important day of my life. Far more important than the day I sat my finals. Infinitely more important than the day I started my first job.

Even as I scrubbed at my face in Harriet's en-suite bathroom, my destiny was winging its way towards me. He was passing over Greenland even as I brushed my teeth.

'Please let this go well,' I muttered beneath my breath. 'Please let that psychic who talked to Mum be right about me going abroad. Please let Brian Coren fall for me again. Please let Seema be right about this cream suit.'

I had booked a limousine to bring us back from the airport to Grantchester Square on Harriet's private account, hoping that when the bill arrived she would assume she had booked the car herself and forgotten all about it – she was forever booking cars that she denied all knowledge of when they turned up at the office. I travelled *to* the airport, however, on the tube, trying hard not to get any muck on the cream trouser suit that Mary had lent me for the occasion of my joyous reunion with the love of my life. It was the suit Mary had been wearing in the café that awful morning when she refused to let me borrow her flat. I had actually promised that I would get the suit dry-cleaned after wearing it, but I was hoping I would be able to get away with giving it a quick press with the iron and handing it back unwashed.

As the train sped through the tunnels to the west, I studied my reflection in the dark glass of the window opposite. A sleek-haired, smooth-cheeked face gazed back. I could hardly believe that the calm face framed by such a sophisticated hairdo belonged to me, but when I fingered the gold chain around my neck (another loan from Mary – a firm believer in the power of small but chic accessories) the reflection did the same. I couldn't take my eyes off myself between Green Park and Gloucester Road, as if I were worried my composure might disappear if I didn't keep an eye on it. But at Gloucester Road a tourist wearing a stetson sat down opposite me and blocked out my view.

All went well until we got to Hounslow, then some kind of security alert at the airport meant that the tube train was kept waiting on the tracks between stations. I tried not to panic as the extra time I had factored into my journey for emergency make-up touch-ups in the airport loos started to ebb away. Londoners are so used to security alerts that they don't worry about being blown away by terrorists, only about being late for work or last orders. After twenty minutes the train began to move again, limping towards the terminals at Heathrow. When I arrived at the airport, I raced to the arrivals lounge, only to discover that Brian's flight was expected to arrive half an hour late anyway, which gave me half an hour longer to study my reflection in a murky mirror in the ladies'.

As the moment when Brian's plane was due to touch down approached, the butterflies which had taken up residence in my stomach upon hearing his voice again in that first phonecall, went into a frenzy. At one point I was convinced I would be sick with nerves the minute he walked out through customs and so I spent five minutes attempting to chuck up manually so that if I did heave with nerves when I finally saw him, there would be nothing left to heave out all over whatever fantastic suit he was bound to be wearing. As it was, I hadn't eaten anything that day anyway. My stomach had been looking flatter since the colonic . . . *Hadn't it?*

But then the landing of Brian's flight suddenly flashed up on the arrivals board, and I raced to find my place at the barrier where the families and friends of the people who had just flown in on flight 607 were gathering in anticipation. The guard at the exit to immigration control however told me that it would take at least another twenty minutes before the first passenger came through. Twenty more minutes. Everything seemed to be conspiring to make me wait, wait, wait. I was sooo nervous. My stomach groaned. My palms were sweating. I suddenly needed to hurl.

Would he recognise me? I began to worry. Would I

recognise him? Should I have brought a piece of card with his name written on it just in case? All these things were going through my head as I stared at the empty doorway that led to immigration. Finally, after numerous baseball-capped disappointments had caught my eye and raised my spirits unnecessarily, Brian emerged into the hall pushing a trolley.

He blinked in the bright lights as if he had just spent a year underground. The room faded into a blur around me. He was the only thing in my sight. The noise of the other people milling about the arrivals lounge retreated into a distant hum as my mind was filled with a romantic fanfare more suited to this wonderful moment. Brian scanned the crowd for me, starting at the wrong end of the barrier and taking for ever to spot me while all the time I shouted, 'Brian, Brian! I'm over here!' At least two other guys looked up before Brian finally saw me and made his way across to the barrier where I stood shaking so hard that my legs felt about to give way.

I thought I would definitely pass out then. If it hadn't been for the sheer pressure of the eager people behind me – waiting for a flight of pilgrims to come back from Mecca – I probably would have fallen over. But they held me pressed up against the barrier until Brian took my hand, leaned over the flimsy rail and planted a huge smacker right on my mouth.

Instantly, it was as if he had never been away. He smelled the same. He tasted the same. He was the same. I swayed backwards dangerously.

'Brian,' I murmured.

Then he took both my hands in his and just looked at me, with the barrier still between us. He stared deep into my eyes, saying nothing but communicating everything with a look. He *was* as glad to see me as I was to see him. That much was clear from his eyes. My heart soared towards the high ceiling of the arrivals lounge then swooped down to wing about our heads in ecstasy.

'We got a bit delayed,' was the first thing he said to me. The first thing he said to my face after six whole years.

'I would have waited for ever,' I assured him.

'I hope not,' he said, passing me his suit bag before jumping over the barrier instead of going round it like he was supposed to. 'I don't like to think of you sitting here all night. Is there somewhere we can go to get a coffee before we catch the tube to your place?'

'We're not catching the tube back to my place,' I told him. 'Follow me.' I linked my arm through his and pulled him towards the exit, eager for part one of *Operation Impress Brian* to start.

'You look fantastic,' he chattered as I looked for the limo I had hired for us on Harriet's account. 'I feel so untidy compared to you in that wonderful suit.' He was wearing jeans and a faded blue sweatshirt but I thought he looked delicious. He wasn't any fatter. If anything he looked much fitter and leaner than the

Brian I had kissed goodbye. His thick black hair still fell across one eye, begging to be brushed out of the way. I reached across and did just that, hoping that he didn't notice as my hands shook.

'Still, not much point getting dressed up to cross the Atlantic,' he continued. 'I hate travelling cattle class. It's such a nightmare having to sit with your knees under your chin for six hours. You just don't appreciate business class until you have to be at the back of the plane again. Still, I don't suppose that'll ever happen to you. First class all the way from here for you, Lizzie Jordan. You high-flyer, you.'

'What?'

'With your business doing so well,' he elaborated.

'Oh, I sometimes fly cattle class too,' I said modestly.

In fact, I hadn't flown anywhere at all for almost six years. My life had been strictly National Express since college. But I was almost flying then as we waited outside Terminal Two. In a brief moment of silence, Brian squeezed my hand. The feel of his palm against mine after all that time apart sent me sky-rocketing. It was for exactly this reason that I had requested a hire car. I could have driven to and from the airport in Harriet's Mercedes – which I had rescued from the car pound (it had been towed away after she left it at a bus stop on Oxford Street) – but I didn't trust myself to be able to drive in a straight line in my excitement.

'So, are we waiting for a taxi?' Brian asked.

'Not a taxi,' I smiled, as a smooth grey car finally

slid forward into the taxi rank with my name on the
card in the window. 'A limousine.'

The limousine driver, like most professional drivers in
London who don't drive a black cab, had never been to
London before. In fact, he told me proudly, we were his
first ever pick-up since leaving Newcastle for an even
bigger smoke.

'You'll have to start directing me once we get inside
the M25,' he said as we cruised back into the city.

'Er, aren't we inside the M25 already?' I asked. 'Just
follow the signs for London.'

'And you'll give me the directions to your place once
we get a bit closer?'

I nodded irritably. I had wanted to be able to enjoy
this journey without worrying about how to get to our
destination. Brian and I were sitting at either end of
a leather back seat that was almost as big as my bed
in Balham. Brian told me it was great to be able to
stretch out after six hours with only nineteen inches
of leg room, but I hoped he would soon cuddle up.
Perhaps some booze would loosen his reserve.

'There should be champagne in here,' I told him,
flipping open a neatly upholstered stool that contained a secret fridge. But when I looked inside I
discovered that there was no champagne, just three
cans of Stella.

'Where's the champagne?' I buzzed the driver via
his intercom.

'Champagne?' he asked with a blank look on his face. 'Was there meant to be some?'

'Yes. I ordered it specially.'

'Well, no one told me,' he shrugged. 'You can have one of my cans of Stella if you like.'

I raised an eyebrow towards Brian. 'It's hardly the same. Would you like a beer?'

'I think I can manage until we get back to your place. I'm just intoxicated by you,' he smiled.

I dissolved into my own puppyish grin.

'Are we getting anywhere near your place by the way?' the driver interrupted.

'Where are we now?' I asked. I hadn't really been following our progress. I'd been too interested in looking at Brian. 'Have we passed Hyde Park?'

'About ten minutes ago. I think.'

Looking out of the darkened windows, I tried to spot a landmark I recognised but the street along which we were cruising was totally unfamiliar.

'Well, I don't think this is the right way,' I said.

'Well, what is the right way?' said the driver, mimicking my voice.

'Haven't you got an *A to Z*?' asked Brian.

Of course he hadn't. Not for London anyway. The driver pulled out a map of Manchester instead. 'Bugger,' he muttered. 'Picked the wrong one up. Don't you know the way to your own house, lady?' the driver asked me when I expressed my consternation. It was clearly my fault as far as he was concerned.

'Well, I don't usually drive around London,' I

told him. 'I usually take public transport. More eco-friendly. I only know London from the underground.'

'Seems an awful waste to have a Mercedes and not drive it all the time,' Brian commented.

'Sorry?' I was confused. I'd forgotten that as far as Brian was concerned I did actually have a Mercedes.

'Your car. The silver soft-top you bought last month.'

'Oh, right,' I laughed nervously. '*My* car. Yes, well it's a wonderful drive, but who wants to sit in this traffic in a car when they could be whizzing along in the bus lane on the top of a double decker instead?'

In fact, I did. Almost every night. When the bus lane was parked up with Mercedes Benz coupes carrying diplomatic numberplates, I wished that I owned one of them very much indeed.

'You always were such a green fiend,' Brian joked. 'It's kinda odd that you ended up in the evil world of property development given the way you always felt about the environment. I have to say, I almost choked when I read you had a Mercedes. A huge great gas guzzler like that? I thought you'd get one of those 2CV things if you ever got a car at all. Do you remember those pram-cars we used to see around Oxford from time to time? I guess it would hardly go with your image now.'

'No. In any case, those are about the only cars that can't take unleaded petrol,' I reminded him. The driver still hadn't reset our course and now we were sailing out into a no-man's land of lock-ups and railway arches.

'Er, I think we need to turn around and head back towards the City again,' I suggested. 'Then the West End.' A sign for Docklands whizzed by. 'Docklands is definitely not right,' I told the driver hurriedly. 'I'm really sorry about this, Brian.'

'That's OK,' he assured me. 'I'm enjoying the ride.'

And so was I, at last, with his warm thigh finally against mine. At one point, when I said something that made him laugh – probably something sarcastic about our driver's map-reading abilities, Brian even covered my knee with his hand and squeezed it. The rush of excitement that shot through my body then was enough to make me want to pass out. But before I had a chance to swoon, the driver pulled the car into the kerb and addressed me via the intercom again.

'Is it the Street, the Square or the Mews? Only there's all three here and I can't remember what you said.'

'Mews,' I replied confidently. But almost before I had finished the word, I changed my mind. Mews. That didn't sound right. 'I meant Street,' I said.

'Well, make your mind up. They're in two completely different places.'

'No, hang on. It's the Square. Yes, definitely the Square. Grantchester Square. I haven't lived there long,' I said by way of an excuse.

'I thought you moved into this place in January,' said Brian in surprise.

'January?' What? What had I said about moving flats in January? 'Oh no,' I stumbled. 'That was my last place. Didn't like it much at all. Put it on the market almost as soon as I moved in and I've been in this place for about, oh, two days.'

'Two days?' Brian exclaimed. 'Liz, you should have told me you were moving. I would never have imposed myself upon you if I'd known you were in the middle of moving house.'

'That's OK. You can be my first house guest. Like a house warming.'

'I'm honoured.'

I smiled with my teeth clenched. I had promised myself that I would tell the absolute minimum number of lies needed to get through Brian's visit with the minimum of embarrassment and no more. Already the untruths were spilling from my lips more easily than my two-times table. Just moved in? I cursed myself. That would have been easier to pull off if I'd taken the precaution of passing a duster over everything in Harriet's flat first.

'We're here,' said the driver, proudly. He stopped the car and got out to open the passenger doors. 'Grantchester Square.'

Well, it looked right. I climbed out on to the pavement and realised that I had remembered the square, but in my nervousness at seeing Brian again the house number had since escaped me. I knew it was on the left-hand side of the square and somewhere towards the middle, but every block looked exactly the same and I was suddenly very unsure whether Harriet lived in block seven or block five.

'Where to?' The driver had lifted Brian's lighter bag

out of the trunk, leaving Brian to carry the heavier one. 'Only I can't carry too much with my back and I've got to be in Maida Vale at two o'clock to pick up Chaka Khan. Remember her?'

Brian looked towards me expectantly. I scanned the upper windows of blocks five and seven for clues. Of which there were none, of course. I prayed that Hercules would jump up against a window pane in a desperate attempt to follow Harriet to Spain. Bloody mutt must have been asleep again.

I made my way forward as confidently as possible, considering I didn't feel very confident at all, towards block number five and tried to jam my key into the lock. It went all the way in, but refused to turn.

'Let me have a go,' said the driver, after I had twisted it pathetically for what felt like half an hour. 'You women,' he sighed. I wondered if he meant it in a kind way, but guessed he probably didn't. 'Got no upper body strength, have you?' He gave the key an almighty twist but still the door did not budge. Brian and I looked on with some amusement. 'Just gonna give it one more.' He put his boot against the door and tried again, just as a rather smart woman with a dog almost identical to Hercules appeared behind us and harumphed in an annoyed sort of way.

'Can I help you?' she asked, in that way which does not mean 'Can I help you?' at all, in the sense that friendly shopkeepers mean it. What she meant was, in any other language, 'Should I be calling the police to have you removed?'

'Hercules?' I asked the Spaniel, which was looking at me almost as intently as his boss. I was going to be in big trouble if this was some close friend of Harriet's come to check up on the dog because Harriet had called from Majorca when she remembered how canine unfriendly I really was. 'Is that you, Hercules?'

Everyone, including the dog, looked at me as if I were mad.

'This is Camelot,' said the woman archly. 'Hercules lives next door.'

'Oh, my god,' I exclaimed in as light a manner as I could muster. 'I'm awfully sorry. That's it. Next door everybody. I've got completely the wrong block of flats. Silly me.'

Three pairs of eyebrows dipped in confused amusement.

The posh woman put her key into the front door of number five and it opened effortlessly. She went inside and shut the door behind her, but I could see her peeking out through the letter box as I rallied my troops and hustled them on to the next doorstep.

'You really haven't lived here long, have you?' said the driver sarcastically.

'Who's Hercules?' asked Brian.

'My dog.'

'You've got a dog?'

'Didn't I tell you that I'd bought a dog? Well, not bought it exactly. Inherited him really. From the lady who used to own my flat.'

'I thought you hated dogs,' said Brian with a note of rising concern.

'So did I. Until I met Hercules. Top floor,' I said to the driver, who had by now let himself into the hall.

'You must be joking, love,' he replied, putting Brian's suit bag down on the front step. 'I can't go up all those stairs with my back. I'm going to have to love you and leave you, my darling.' And yet he didn't. Leave, that is. He just stood there, looking expectant. I started to climb the stairs. He coughed. Brian, realising what the man was waiting for, dug into his pocket and pulled out his wallet. 'I haven't changed much money yet. Will a twenty do you?'

He handed the driver a twenty-pound note! A twenty-pound note! That was just about my weekly food budget. 'Twenty?' I said, when the driver had gone. 'A twenty-pound tip for someone who didn't even know the way here?'

'Hey, compared to New York taxi drivers, I thought he was rather nice. And at least he spoke English. You know, a guy in New York got killed last week when he didn't realise that his taxi driver was only asking him not to smoke in the cab. The driver asked him to quit puffing in some bizarre language from Kazaksthan or something. The passenger thought the driver-guy had insulted him and threw an insult back and then all hell broke loose. Next thing you know, the passenger's lying on the pavement with his brains blown out. Witnesses saw him fall out of the back of a yellow taxi, but how many of those do you see around town?'

'I guess we'll count ourselves lucky that he was just an imbecile and not a gun-toting imbecile then.'

'Hey, you really have got snotty since you joined the working world. The old Lizzie Jordan would have been pushing tenners on to every beggar we passed, even when she didn't have one to spare.'

I hesitated to tell him that the old Liz probably had more disposable income when she was on a student loan.

'Come on,' I said, eager to get off the subject. 'Let's go on in.'

'Er, Liz,' Brian stopped me by putting his hand on my arm. 'I just have to ask you one thing before we go inside. What kind of dog is this Hercules?'

'He's a Cavalier King Charles,' I told him. 'Bloody smelly breed but he's reasonably well house-trained.' I had opened the door to the flat and stepped through with a welcoming smile. Brian waited outside.

'Come on in,' I beckoned.

'Oh no,' he said, looking rather wobbly.

'What's up with you?'

'Liz, did I ever tell you about the time I was bitten on the neck by a King Charles Spaniel when I was just two years old?'

Oh god. He had! I remembered the story very well – the creature had almost severed Brian's jugular – and yet it hadn't even crossed my mind when inviting him to stay in a flat with Hercules.

'You know, if it was any other kind of dog . . . Any other kind at all. Rottweilers, dobermans, Irish wolfhounds. I could sleep in the same bed as one of those. But King Charles Cavaliers? I can't explain it, Liz. I mean, it's been almost twenty-five years since it happened, but I still can't be in the same room as a King Charles. They give me panic attacks. Even if I just walk by one in Central Park, even if it's on a lead, it can bring me out in a sweat that lasts for hours.' He mopped his forehead with his cuff. 'See.' He was indeed already sweating.

'Well, what are we going to do?' I asked. 'You must try to come in. He's very nice. Very gentle. Ever so small. If you don't show him you're afraid I'm sure everything will be fine.'

'You might trust that dog to babysit your children, Liz, but I know I can't be in the same flat as a King Charles. I know it's ridiculous. I know I'm a grown man and I shouldn't let a little pooch stop me from going anywhere. But nobody really knows why phobias are so persistent and my therapist advised me that the best way I can deal with my fear is simply by avoiding the focus of that fear.'

'You've been seeing a therapist?' I asked disbelievingly.

'Everyone in America sees a therapist. You know I don't really think they're up to much but I decided I had to go to one when I started to date a girl who kept a King Charles in her apartment. She was a great girl. Fantastic girl. And I was really fond of her. But she had this dog so we could never go to her place and she couldn't stay over at mine because she couldn't leave the dog on its own all night.' He shrugged his shoulders. 'You look shocked, Lizzie.'

I was. But not about the strength of his dog phobia. I was reeling from the fact that he was telling me he had *dated* someone. Someone he really liked? Though I hadn't exactly been celibate since we last saw each other, I hadn't let it cross my mind that Brian might still be in the dating game. I didn't think he had the time to date from what he said in his letters and e-mails. And I had liked it that way.

Now he was telling me, 'I was so disappointed that it had to end. I tried everything to get through my fear. Therapy. Hypnosis. Got myself stuck all over with acupuncture needles. I wanted so badly to overcome my phobia so the relationship could work but I just couldn't do it. Every time I saw her dog I ended up having a panic attack. Once I even fainted.' He smiled a little wistfully. 'She took it very well considering. And we're still friends. How long does this type of dog tend to live for?'

'Hundreds of years,' I found myself telling him testily. 'She should have had it put down.' I wouldn't have let a pooch stand in the way of my future with Brian Coren.

'Well, listen, Liz. I'm really sorry about this but if the dog's in the flat I'm going to have to stay in a hotel tonight.'

'No,' I almost shouted. I wasn't going to let that mutt spoil my plans. Not now that I had come so close. 'I'll sort something out. Perhaps if I just locked Hercules in one of the spare bedrooms? You wouldn't even have to see him.'

'What if he escaped in the middle of the night?'

'He won't escape,' I sighed.

'He might. He'll smell my fear and get out to find me.'

'You really are scared, aren't you?' I groaned.

'I'm afraid so. Can you think of a good hotel?'

'No,' I told him. 'But I can think of a very good kennel.'

'I couldn't possibly ask you to put your dog in a kennel for me. It's not really fair. It's his home.'

'Brian, you're much more important to me than some bloody dog!' I nearly snapped.

'I thought you English were mad about your animals?'

'Pur-leese. Anyway, I'm not really going to send him to a kennel. I'm just going to call someone I know and see if she would like to look after Hercules for the weekend. She's a dog lover without a dog of her own so she'll probably jump at the chance. I'll get her to come over at once. In the meantime, I suppose we'll have to wait over the road.'

So, at the precise moment when I had hoped that Brian and I would be re-acquainting ourselves on Harriet's fat leather Chesterfield sofa, we were instead sitting on two rather less alluring red plastic seats in a greasy café, waiting for Seema to come and take Hercules out of the way.

She came as quickly as she could, bless her. But I was still ready to cry when almost an hour after I'd called her, Seema burst through the café door wearing a ridiculously skimpy pink sari top under her denim jacket. She was also wearing lipstick, which wasn't a good sign. She never wore lipstick unless she thought she had a chance of pulling somebody and she looked gorgeous. Every man in the café was transfixed. Including mine.

'Brian, this is Seema.'

'Liz's secretary,' she added quickly as she pumped Brian's hand to a cacophony of jangles from her real Indian gold bangles and slid on to a plastic seat beside him, eyelashes fluttering all the while.

'Her secretary? Did I speak to you the other day?'

'Yeah, that's right,' said Seema, putting on a coquettish accent that I had never heard her do before. One that made it seem utterly impossible that she was in fact studying for an MBA part-time. 'I can't believe how lucky I am working for Lizzie. She's such a good boss to have, more like a friend than a boss really. And my work is *so* varied. One minute I'm doing her typing. Next, I'm looking after her lovely little dog.'

'Sounds like she takes advantage of you,' Brian joked.

Seema laughed a tinkling laugh and patted Brian on the arm, lingering way too long as she did so. 'Oh, I hope I'm not giving you the wrong impression of her.

She doesn't work me *too* hard. Wouldn't dare to on my salary.'

I shot her a look which I hoped she would interpret as 'don't overdo it, Gwyneth Paltrow'.

'Would you care to join us for a coffee before you go to the flat and fetch the dreaded hound?' Brian asked her chivalrously. 'It's the least I can offer after putting you to so much trouble over my silly phobia.'

'Oh, that would be lovely,' Seema said, slipping off her jacket.

'Brian, wouldn't you prefer to have another coffee in the privacy of the flat?' I asked him before he could attract the waiter's attention. 'You've had a long day already, with the flight from New York. And I'm sure Seema has got plenty to be getting on with. The office doesn't close until five on a Friday, remember, Seema?'

The last thing I wanted was for her to stick around for a chat. The more Brian saw of the people from my real life, the more likely someone was to make the remark that would unleash the sorry truth. And Seema was hardly the best liar I had ever met. She was forever clapping her hand to her mouth moments after a careless remark of hers had flown across the table and slapped someone about the face. I remembered particularly vividly the time she had greeted Mary with the immortal line, 'You sound so much thinner on the phone.'

'I suppose I have got tonnes of filing to do,' she said then, rolling her eyes in my direction. 'That's the problem with working for such a high flyer, Brian.

Lizzie generates so much more work than anybody else in the office. Has she told you about the 20:20 project yet?'

The what?

'I bet she hasn't,' Seema continued as a smug grin spread across her plum-coloured, irritatingly beautiful lips. 'She's so modest about her achievements. But don't let her gloss over this particular coup, will you, Brian?'

Brian smiled at me. 'I won't. What was that again? The 20:20 project.'

'That's right.'

I glared at Seema. 'Shall we fetch the dog now?'

'If you insist,' she said.

'Oh, I insist most strongly.'

Brian stayed behind in the café. I would fetch him when the dog had gone. On the way to the flat, I linked my arm through Seema's in what I hoped would seem a friendly gesture from behind in case Brian was watching, but I was using my other hand to pinch her on the front of her arm. Hard.

'What was that for?'

'Coming out looking like that, you cow.'

'Like what?'

'Like you're about to go clubbing.'

'Perhaps I was.'

'On a Friday afternoon? You can see your bra through that top by the way.'

'Perhaps that was the intention.'

I pinched her again.

'Ow.'

'And what was all that crap about the bleeding 20:20 project?' I asked.

'Didn't you like that?' asked Seema. 'I thought it added a very authentic touch, mentioning a specific deal. I made up the name while I was sitting on the tube.'

'I asked you to come and pick up the dog, not audition for a part in *EastEnders*. You're such a bloody bitch.'

'Well, how about you? Treating me like I'm your servant. *Packing me off back to the office* indeed?'

'I had to. What if you'd blown my cover? Well, you probably already have with that 20:20 project crap,' I grumbled. 'What am I going to say when he asks me about it?'

'You'll think of something. You're always telling me you used to be an actress so improvise! Tell you what though,' she sighed. 'I can see why you're going to such ridiculous lengths to impress him. What a babe! He's amazing. Those eyes.'

'Yep,' I agreed. 'He is still truly delicious. I felt like a teeny bopper spotting the lead singer of BoyZone when Brian walked into the arrivals lounge.'

Seema and I both inclined our heads at the thought of Brian's loveliness.

'His eyes are so penetrating,' Seema sighed. 'It's as if he can see into your soul when he looks at you.'

'He was looking at you like that?' I said, suddenly snapping back out of my swoon.

Seema sensed my annoyance and muttered, 'No, of course not. I was just imagining . . . So, do you think you've got a chance with him?' she added to change the subject. 'I mean, to get it back together in the sexual sense?'

'I certainly hope so. He kept putting his hand on my knee on the way back from the airport.'

'You lucky cow. That's a pretty good sign.'

I couldn't help grinning. 'Guess you wasted your lipstick.'

'Damn. I even broke out a new pair of pants.'

'Don't even try it,' I warned.

'I won't,' she sighed.

'Thanks for agreeing to take Hercules,' I softened.

'My pleasure. It's the only male company I'm going to get this weekend. Besides, I like dogs. Especially Hercules. Did you remember to give him his tablets this morning?'

'What tablets?'

I just hoped that Hercules was still alive and hadn't made too much of a mess in his loneliness. When I opened the door to the sitting room he was chewing on a shoe. One of my favourite Pied a Terre loafers, I noted angrily, and not one of the hundreds of pairs of Manolo Blahniks belonging to Harriet that lay around the flat waiting for someone to break their neck either by wearing the damn things, or by tripping over them. As you can imagine, I had tried a few pairs on. Unfortunately, Harriet had size three feet to go with her size three frame.

I pulled my shoe from Hercules's mouth and hissed, 'I thought you only liked to eat exclusive things.' He'd also had a little go at my imitation Hermes handbag. It was covered with doggy slobber.

When he saw Seema behind me, Hercules went into ecstasies, wagging his tail so hard that his entire backside wagged with it. He wasn't bothered about letting me know exactly where his affections lay when it came to me and my flatmate. She crouched down to greet him with her baby voice and he leapt into her arms, slobbering half her make-up off with his big pink tongue.

'How can Brian not love a wonderful dog like you?' she said with a motherly cluck.

'Well, thanks for the vote of confidence,' I replied. 'But I wouldn't have called myself a dog. I'm not that bad if I get enough beauty sleep.'

'I wasn't talking to you,' she rolled her eyes in exasperation. 'Now, you'd better get Hercules's things together. He'll need his bowl and his blanket. His coat-conditioning tablets were on the windowsill when I last saw them. And you'd better bag up some of that chicken from the fridge.'

'Yes, sir. No, sir,' I whizzed around the flat collecting Hercules's stuff. I couldn't wait to get rid of him. Or Seema. 'Remember he won't walk on tarmac or paving stones,' I reminded her.

'I wasn't going to make him walk on paving stones,'

she exclaimed as if she were horrified by the very suggestion of such cruelty. 'You're going to have a lovely weekend with me, aren't you, Herc? Oh, and you owe me big time, by the way.'

'Are you talking to me or the dog this time?'

'You, stupid.'

'What is it you want?'

'I'll think of something. Something that fits the enormity of this favour.'

'Anything you want. But can we just get the dog out of the flat now? Brian has been waiting in that café for almost two hours.'

'And you want to get him into bed,' Seema smiled.

'Only to get over his jet lag,' I insisted.

'Yeah, right. Give him one for me while you're at it.'

'Seema!'

I walked back in the direction of the café with Seema and the dog. We parted ways at the café door. Seema couldn't come inside again, for obvious reasons, but she caught Brian's eye through the glass and waved at him. He waved back, trying hard not to look at Hercules.

'She's nice, your secretary. Very sharp. But why was she carrying the dog instead of walking it?' Brian asked.

'He has bad feet,' I explained. Harriet may not have been embarrassed to own a phobic dog but I was. 'Well, that's sorted out now. Shall we go back to the flat?'

'Wow.'

At last Brian was standing in the middle of Harriet's living room, taking in the view.

'Wow. This is great. Considering you've only been here for a couple of days, you've really made this place look like home. Wow, Liz. It's fantastic. Where did you get all this wonderful stuff?'

'You know,' I shrugged. 'On my travels.'

'Do you mind if I take a closer look at this?' he asked, picking up a vase that I guessed would probably cost me more than a year's salary to replace.

'Er—' My heart stopped as he turned the vase over and looked at the mark on its bottom.

'Oh. It's not what I thought it was,' he told me as he deciphered the little sign. 'Did you know it's not what it looks like it is?'

I nodded, dumbfounded. I didn't know what it looked like, other than a vase.

'Pretty though,' Brian conceded. 'Hope you didn't pay too much for it.'

'Put it down,' I ordered, unable to contain my panic.

'OK.' He put the vase down again abruptly. 'Guess that's pretty rude of me isn't it? Coming round here and appraising your antiques before I've even got my coat off. Blame it on being American. I can't get over all this old stuff. I just love antiques.'

He wandered over and threw his arms around me then, picking me up and swinging me around and around on the Persian rug, with me petrified the whole time that my feet might take out something that was real.

'Alone at last. I am so glad to see you again,' he sighed, finally placing me back on my feet and gazing tenderly into my eyes.

'I'm glad to see you too,' I told him. Our lips hovered so close for a moment, I felt sure that he was going to kiss me. Properly.

'I have a present for you in my bag,' he said instead, breaking away to hunt through his luggage for my gift. 'It's only a little something but I hope it might mean more than a little to you.'

He handed me a flat square parcel, carefully wrapped in layers of silver and gold tissue paper, tied with a metallic gold ribbon.

'I found it yesterday,' he explained. 'In an antiquarian bookshop in the Village. Bearing in mind that I was coming to see you, it seemed like an omen. I had to get it. Open it up.'

I peeled away the tissue paper. Obviously it was going to be a book, but an omen? I wondered what on earth it could be.

'It's a really old edition of *Antony and Cleopatra*. Obviously, it's not a first edition, but look inside. Look at what it says on the nameplate. I couldn't believe it.'

I opened the book up. A nameplate was pasted to the inside cover and in swirly black, somewhat faded, old-fashioned handwriting, the book's previous owner had written her name.

'Elizabeth Taylor,' I breathed reverently. 'Do you think this belonged to the real one?'

'Maybe. Maybe not. But I thought you'd like to have it anyway. Do you like it?'

'I love it,' I assured him, turning the little book over in my hands and admiring the gilt lettering on its hard red cover.

'Perhaps you'll give me a solo performance later on. You were the best one-eyed Cleopatra I ever saw.'

'I think I'm probably the only woman who ever played Cleopatra with one eye,' I reminded him.

'But you were still magical,' he told me. 'Really moving. You know, I think I fell in love with you that night. While you were playing with your asp.'

We shared a meaningful gaze for a moment before I had to look away, cheeks flushing furiously.

'Well, where do you want me to put these bags?' Brian asked me, and the moment was broken.

I took him not to Harriet's bedroom but to one of the other bedrooms. Although I hoped he wouldn't actually be sleeping in there, I didn't want to make an idiot of myself by putting his bags in the room I had been sleeping in and having him ask for them to be moved. I had however also taken the precaution of choosing the most uncomfortable bed to help him make his mind up in the way I hoped he would.

Looking at the inscription he had added to his gift to me, I had every reason to think I would be getting my way.

'To my own darling Lizzie,' he had written. 'To old times and new. All my love, Brian.' He had underlined the 'all' three times and signed off with five big kisses.

'Would you mind if I had a little nap now?' Brian asked me. 'Only I'm starting to feel real tired. Wake me for dinner?'

I assured him that I would. He disappeared into the bedroom and I returned to the sitting room where I sat reading his inscription in the front of the book again and again and again. I was in heaven. Mission almost accomplished. Brian Coren was back in my life.

CHAPTER SEVENTEEN

I insisted that we went somewhere really special for dinner that night, despite Brian's protestations that he was very jet-lagged and would be happy with Marmite on toast – a taste he had acquired during his year in Oxford. But I had it all planned out and wasn't going to let Brian waste a moment of his visit on sleep if I wasn't in the bed with him.

I had picked the Capricorn restaurant from *Tatler*'s best restaurant list for its reputation as being a wonderful place to impress and seduce. Besides, Mary had lent me the most amazing Donna Karan dress imaginable and I could hardly change into it to make toast, could I?

'Come on, Brian,' I jollied him. 'You're not here for long. I want you to make the most of your trip to London. We're going out.'

'Couldn't we go tomorrow instead?' he pleaded.

'No. You have no idea how difficult it was for me to get a reservation at this restaurant. It's only just opened. Last time I was there I found myself sitting between Michael Caine and Sly Stallone. Sly is terribly

short, you know.' At least the first part of that spiel
wasn't a lie. It had been difficult to get a reservation.
In fact, I'd had to use Mary's name simply to get a
look in.

'OK,' he said. 'Point me in the direction of the
bathroom again.'

I pointed him in the direction of the broom closet.
Absolutely accidentally, of course. But I think he
thought I was joking.

I, meanwhile, retired to Harriet's bedroom to deck
myself out in the DKNY. I had put Brian in the 'spare'
room but I had no intention that this arrangement
should actually persist when we got home from the
restaurant. I had splashed out on the most incredible
set of underwear imaginable. From Rigby and Peller
– corsetiers to the Queen, no less. I had seen the set
I wanted on a model in *Cosmopolitan* and Rupert
from the office had agreed that if anything could
persuade a man to give up a pair of Rugby World
Cup tickets it would be the prospect of an evening at
home with a girl in burgundy-coloured lacy half-cups
with a matching g-string and suspender belt. Well, if it
could persuade rotten Rupert away from the rugby, it
would definitely work on a man with no obvious need
to suspend real life whenever twenty-odd grown men
started kicking around a leather sac full of air.

My most expensive knickers yet gave me just the
confidence I needed not to trip over with surprise

when the doorman at the Capricorn actually opened the door for us.

'Have whatever you want,' I insisted just before I opened the menu and clocked the astronomical prices. Brian's menu didn't even have any prices on it. We were in that kind of place. 'Mmm. Doesn't this look wonderful,' I said, scanning the menu for anything under a tenner. Bread rolls perhaps. I could have two of those.

'Pick whatever you like,' I bumbled on. 'I'll be putting it on my expense account.' If only. 'I'm going to say that you're a potential customer so we can go as mad as we like.'

'Excellent,' said Brian. 'Shall we start with some champagne in that case?'

The wine waiter was already hovering. Meanwhile, two waiters appeared with something they termed an *amuse bouche*. I was confused and told them that they must have got the wrong table because we hadn't ordered our meals yet.

'Madame. These are complimentary,' the waiter smiled. Bloody condescendingly, I thought, for someone who cleared plates for a living. 'This is a quail's egg in caramel. This is seared tuna on sushi rice. And that,' he said, as I popped something that looked like a mushroom vol-au-vent into my mouth, 'is escargot in a garlic sauce.'

'Snails,' Brian translated obligingly.

My hand went to my mouth instinctively, but I just about managed not to hurl.

'I wonder if we might have some champagne to wash this lot down?' I asked as I choked my mouthful down.

'Certainly. And which champagne?'

'Cristal,' I said confidently.

Brian raised an eyebrow – subtly. As did the sommelier – not so subtly. And I would raise both of mine when I finally saw how much the bloody stuff had set me back.

'I was drinking Cristal by the bucketload only the other night,' I said, loudly enough for the sommelier to hear as he minced off to fetch some. 'At an after-show party for the Golden Brothers. You know the Golden Brothers?'

'The designers?' said Brian.

'Yes. The hottest duo in town.'

'Even I've heard of those guys. How did you get to meet them?'

'Oh, through Mary,' I had to admit.

'Mary?' Brian leaned forward, looking altogether more interested than he had been at the mention of the Golden Brothers. 'Not Miserable Mary? Do you still see much of her?'

'From time to time.'

'What's she doing now?'

'Oh, she runs a little business of her own,' I glossed.

'Really? What as?'

'Agent,' I said briefly. 'You know, you really should try these quail eggs.'

'What kind of agent?' Brian wasn't about to give up.

'A sort of talent agent for actors and footballers and things,' I muttered. 'Sorts out deals for lots of adverts. Voice-overs.'

'That sounds interesting.'

'I'm sure it is. Would you like half of this egg with me?' I tried again.

'Have you told her about my visit?' Brian asked. 'Because I'd really love to catch up with her if that were possible.'

'I think she's pretty busy.'

'Not all the time, surely. We could call her.'

I frowned.

'What's up? Have you two fallen out?'

'No,' I smiled. 'Nothing's up at all. I'm just wondering how Mary will be able to fit in seeing us.'

'She'll make time when she hears that I'm over in England. Mary would do anything for her old friends.'

I tried not to snort into the glass of champagne that had just been placed in my hand by the diligent sommelier. Anything for her friends. Ha! If only Brian knew. Having said that, I was actually spilling my drink down *her* dress at the time.

'Good old Mary,' Brian sighed. 'Tell you what, let's make the first toast of the evening to old friends. To Mary and Bill, in fact.'

I raised my glass. 'To Mary and Bill.'

'We must call her as soon as we get home,' said Brian.

*   *   *

For the whole of the meal, I couldn't stop worrying that Brian really would insist on calling Mary when we got back to the flat. It was the last thing I wanted, for him to see just how successful and sophisticated Miserable Mary had become. And though she had promised she would not tell my secret to anyone – except any of her glitterati friends who might find it amusing – I had decided that keeping Mary and Brian apart was the only way to guarantee that she didn't drop me in it with some careless comment about how good I looked in her dress, or her necklace, or someone else's flat.

But Brian was on a real nostalgia kick. He wanted to talk about the past, to go over the times we had shared in Oxford; and I suppose I should have been grateful that it saved me from having to elaborate on my fictional present. However, I wasn't too happy that he wanted to talk not just about the time that he and I had spent together snuggled up in our bedrooms, but the times we had spent as a foursome, Brian, Bill, Mary and I.

'Do you remember the night when Bill and Mary got off with one another?' he laughed.

Anyway, the thought that he wanted to see Mary so badly rather distracted from the calamari I had ordered. I couldn't even relax and enjoy my mousse au chocolat.

When the bill came, I didn't even look at it. I knew that looking at it would in no way diminish the horror. Instead, I threw my RSPCA-sponsoring Mastercard on top of the bill with as much nonchalance as I could muster. I had given up counting after the first course, but I had probably just agreed to write off the best part of a month's salary on less than two hours' enjoyment. Not as well enjoyed as it could have been considering the amount of time Brian spent talking about Mary. And I still felt hungry, having avoided eating any of the petit fours because I wasn't sure if they were actually supposed to be edible with all that gold leaf.

'Er, I'm afraid there seems to be some kind of problem with madame's card,' said the maître d', bending close so that he could whisper subtly in my ear. My expression must have let Brian know almost instantly that there was a problem. And I knew exactly what the problem was. I must have been up to my limit.

'What's up?' he asked.

'My card,' I said, in a very little voice.

'It often happens, madame,' said the maître d'. 'The magnetic strip gets damaged and then the card won't scan through our machine. We would have punched the number in manually, but the last digit seems to have been . . .'

Chewed off.

I took the card and looked at it in wonder. Hercules must have put a tooth through it when he got hold of my handbag.

'I'll deal with this,' said Brian, throwing his own card on to the plate.

'I'll pay you back,' I said weakly.

'No,' he said. 'This can be my treat.'

Thank god I hadn't drunk so much that I went into the 'No, I will' type of scenario that had preceded this whole debacle.

'Anyway,' said Brian, as he signed the receipt with a flourish. 'At least this way I come away with some of my male pride still intact. It's a bit disheartening for an old-fashioned guy like me to be taken out by a really successful career girl like you . . .'

I was about to ask the maître d' to call a taxi, all the better to take me quickly home for a lie down after that narrow shave with the credit card, when Brian suggested, 'Let's walk back across the park.'

'What? Hyde Park?' I asked.

'Yes. It's not too far is it?'

'No. But it's dark.'

'Are you scared? You'll be with me.'

I could hardly tell him that the thing I was most scared of right then was stepping in something unspeakable in a pair of Mary's expensive shoes. Brian took my worried smile to mean that I thought he had proposed a wonderful idea and soon we had crossed Park Lane – at a gallop through the traffic instead of taking the sensible underpass – and we were climbing over the fence into Hyde Park.

'Doesn't this feel like old times?' Brian asked. 'Do you remember that time when we climbed over that gate to get down to Christchurch meadow after dusk?'

'Of course I do. I ripped a hole in my one and only jumper.'

'I'd forgotten that. But it was romantic, wasn't it? With the moonlight glittering on the river and the mist rolling across the fields.'

'Very romantic,' I had to agree. It wasn't quite the same to be looking at the moonlight on the Serpentine, where empty plastic bottles floated like ghostly submarines, but that was where Brian chose for us to sit down and take in the night air.

'That was a great restaurant,' he said. 'But you know what, I'd have been just as happy to get a bag of fish and chips and eat them out here, with you.'

Now he tells me, I thought.

'I mean,' Brian continued, 'That restaurant was clearly very well-designed and decorated but no matter how much money we throw at things, we can never quite recreate the beauty of the things that surround us anyway. Nature's beauty. What could be better than the reflection of tall trees on water? The sound of night birds calling to one another.'

I tilted my face up towards his in case he thought it was about time he kissed me. But he hadn't finished talking.

'You know,' said Brian, 'it doesn't feel like I haven't seen you in six years at all. You're almost exactly the same, once you take into account the accoutrements of your incredible success, of course. But it's nice that you haven't let success go to your head. All the women I meet in New York are successful, sure, but they're so hardened by it. Always thinking about the money. Always listening out for the hot tip that will make them their next million. Never relaxing and being themselves. Not like you. You still let the old Lizzie Jordan come out to play. It makes me feel like we're at college again. Transported back in time.'

'It's as if we're back where we left off?' I suggested eagerly.

'Exactly.'

He turned so that he was facing me more squarely and stretched his arm along the back of the bench. Next, he started to play with the hair on the back of my neck.

'This haircut really suits you,' he told me. 'I love this bit at the back.' And he ran his fingers up the back of my neck, sending shivers running down my body in the opposite direction. 'It feels so fluffy. So soft. Like you.'

My internal organs gave a collective shudder.

'I've thought about you often,' he said, leaning a little closer. 'Sometimes I would see a girl who looked like you on the subway, or coming out of a store and then I wouldn't be able to get you out of my head for hours.'

'I know exactly how that feels,' I murmured.

'I even followed a girl for half a mile once because she looked so much like you. I thought she was you.

But when I caught her up, she was nothing like you. She didn't have your eminently kissable lips.'

Kissable lips? Were they really? I licked them to make sure.

'Kissable, missable lips,' Brian whispered as finally his own lips landed on mine.

'Let's go back to the flat,' I said urgently, once I'd come up for air.

'That's the best idea I've heard all day.'

He got up and pulled me to my feet after him. I stumbled on the grass in my borrowed high heels. Brian reached out to steady me but even when I was steady again, he didn't let me go. Instead, he wrapped his arm around my waist and held me tight all the way to the next perimeter fence. And when we got back to the flat, he still didn't let me go.

CHAPTER EIGHTEEN

O h, magical morning! When I woke up and rolled over in bed to find Brian beside me, all the disappointments of the past six years seemed to have faded away with my quickly forgotten dreams.

Even the weather was with me. Outside, London was already bathing in the early sunlight of another beautiful day. The sky above us was pure baby blue but for a handful of cotton-puff clouds. Stepping out on to the roof garden while Brian slept on below, I was wonderfully surprised to discover that it was already warm. A few of Harriet's badly neglected flowers were slowly unfurling to turn their faces to the sun. I picked a miniature pink rose, not quite open yet, from a straggling rose bush that had long since outgrown its peeling trellis. I carried the rose into the kitchen, where I placed it in an egg-cup full of water to decorate Brian's breakfast tray. A better fate had no flower, I thought poetically as I made some toast. In a proper toaster for once.

But Brian was already up before I could take the tray to him. He walked across the polished wooden floor of

Harriet's sitting room, pushing his fringe from his eyes and looking as though at any moment we might hear a voice-over artist boom out a slogan for a new brand of instant coffee. It was perfect. A snapshot from the perfect life I had always hoped for. We smiled shyly at each other across the breakfast bar as if we had just spent our very first night together.

'I was going to bring you breakfast in bed,' I told him.

'Perhaps we should go back there,' he said, taking my hand and kissing me on the palm. 'Wow, you look beautiful in the mornings.'

I took the compliment gracefully. He didn't have to know that I had spent a good half hour making repairs to my face in the bathroom before he woke up.

'Come on, let's go,' he said, taking me by the hand and leading me back to the bedroom. Our breakfast remained uneaten until lunch time.

'We must call Mary,' Brian said as we finally ate our toast. Cold and hard, it was by then. Just like the toast at college.

Brian took me by surprise. I was rather hoping he had forgotten about our other old friend.

'I can't come to London and not see Mary,' he continued. 'I'd be gutted if I found out she came to the States and didn't drop by to see me.'

He picked up the fake antique telephone on Harriet's bedside table. 'What's her number?'

I wondered whether I could get away with pretending that I didn't have it. But I knew that Brian would only look in the telephone directory and Mary was in the phone book, of course. Blast her. I trotted out the number and Brian dialled.

'Let's hope she's in,' he said to me.

'Be out,' I prayed silently. 'Be out.'

But she was in.

'Brian! Darling!'

Brian held the receiver between us so that I could hear Mary too as she shrieked her hellos.

'What do you think of Lizzie's lovely new flat?' was the first thing she asked.

'It's great. Really beautiful. And I've been having a wonderful time. But it doesn't feel right to be in England and not see you. Liz feels the same. We need to have a reunion. Get the whole old gang together.'

'What a fabulous idea!' she said. She would.

'How about tonight? If you're not too busy.'

Be busy, I prayed. She was always too busy when I called and tried to get to see her, but . . .

'I'm never too busy for you, Brian,' she flirted. 'You know I'd drop anything for my friends in any case.'

The cow. That wasn't the way it had seemed when I last asked her for a favour.

'Tell you what,' she said excitedly. 'I'll throw a party for you. Just a small one. My apartment isn't as sumptuous as Lizzie's, of course,' she smarmed. 'But I'm sure I can get four around my little kitchen table.'

'Sounds wonderful,' said Brian. Genuinely.

'Are you up for that, Liz?' Mary shouted for my benefit.

'Of course,' I said.

Brian handed the phone to me so that I could make the arrangements. A rendezvous was fixed for seven.

'You don't mind coming to my place tonight, do you, Lizzie?' Mary asked.

I grunted my assent.

'You should wear that gorgeous white dress of yours. You know the one.'

I did indeed. It was one she had lent me, naturally.

'Isn't that great of Mary to go to the trouble of having us over for dinner,' said Brian when she finally hung up.

I nodded. And it was good of her really, if I was honest with myself. I had been selfish in hoping that Brian and I would get to spend our four days together entirely alone. He hadn't seen Mary for six years either. I shouldn't begrudge her one night of his company with me to chaperone. And it wasn't as if I wouldn't benefit too from a night in with Mary. It would give my credit card a break. It was a good idea.

The dress which Mary had suggested I wear for this particular occasion was particularly gorgeous. Versace, she claimed, though the label had been cut out so I couldn't confirm whether that was really true. Whatever it was, it was beautiful. Possibly the most beautiful dress I had ever worn. A column of glittering white pleated silk encrusted with crystal and gold beads. I felt as if I was on my way to the Oscars. Not round to Mary's for spag bol and chianti. Except that Mary threw a very different kind of dinner party now.

On the way to her flat, Brian reminisced about Mary's infamous spaghetti, cooked in an old kettle in the overflowing pedal-bin extension that passed for a kitchen in our halls of residence. But when the door to her flat was opened by an unfamiliar young boy in a smart white shirt and a black bow tie, I guessed that whatever we were having, it wasn't going to be Ragu.

Though it was August, and an unusually hot British August at that, Mary had lit the fire (living flame gas – this was a smoke-free zone) to complete the ambience which she had clearly been throwing a cheque book at all afternoon. She stood by the fireplace, staring into the flames as though she were looking for omens. When we walked into the room she took an age to turn round and I cursed her for trying to create some kind of tableau. It was something she used to do while we were still at college. She would spend ages arranging herself in her room just before someone she fancied came round. She told me it was about making a grand entrance without having to be the one who was doing the entering. And that night she was doing it considerably more successfully than when she used to lounge half-naked on a bean-bag with The Doors playing *sotto voce* in the background.

If I had thought the dress she lent me was great, it now became clear that Mary had been giving me her cast-offs. The red dress she was wearing now had a scooped-out back that dipped almost to her knicker line (not that she had a VPL, of course). To emphasise the perfection of her rear view, a long string of pearls dangled from a knot between her shoulder blades to her waist.

I glanced nervously from Mary's back to Brian and back again. Brian's mouth was ever so slightly ajar. When I looked at him he smiled as if he had just been caught picking his nose.

At last Mary turned around.

'I didn't hear you come in,' she said.

'Yeah, right,' I muttered.

'Brian,' Mary purred, advancing towards him with her arms wide open. 'It's been so long.' She embraced him in a glittering bear hug and shot me a wolfish smile over his shoulder. 'I'm so glad you could make it. You look wonderful. You look nice too, Liz. Is that Armani?'

'Versace apparently,' I corrected the cow.

Mary left off the boa constrictor act for a moment and held Brian at arm's length to get a better look at him.

'I can't believe you're really here,' she almost whispered.

Brian put his hand to his tie, nervously I thought. I wondered if he was even sure who he was talking to. As far as I knew, the last time he'd seen Mary, she had been doing an impression of a hobo, a particularly dirty one at that, in a huge hairy black coat that covered her from neck to feet even though it was high summer. He had certainly never seen her with her natural hair colour.

'You . . . You've changed,' he stuttered.

'I know,' she said, smiling broadly, confident that she had changed for the better. 'But you haven't. Still so slim! Are you working out?'

'I don't really get a lot of time for that right now, but thanks. Er, are you?'

Mary ran a lazy hand down across her hip. 'I try to take care of myself.'

'I've never seen you in anything but black before. Red suits you.'

'Doesn't it? I hardly ever wear black these days. I can't believe I spent so much time looking like an undertaker's moll.'

'You were going through a phase,' Brian laughed. 'Lots of creative people make themselves deliberately ugly so that people concentrate on what they can do, rather than what they look like.'

Mary agreed. But I could tell by the way her eyebrows dipped together ever so slightly that she wasn't entirely happy with the implication that she had actually looked ugly during her gothic years.

'Well, let's get you two some champagne,' she trilled.

'Good idea,' Brian agreed.

Mary clicked her fingers and the young man who

had opened the door to us appeared with a bottle of bubbly and three glasses.

'You got staff in,' I said incredulously.

'Don't you?' she replied. 'Well, here's to us,' Mary raised her glass ever so slightly. 'Old friends.'

'Such a shame Bill isn't with us as well,' said Brian. 'Then it could have been exactly like old times.'

'Not exactly,' Mary laughed. 'Dear old Bill. Can you imagine him here? He'd have to wear gold lame cycling shorts or something. I think he's best where he is, looking for rocks in the mud somewhere hot.'

'Come on,' Brian nudged her with his elbow. 'Don't be so cruel. We all know that you love Bill really. What about that night at the Two Items of Clothing party?'

'What about that night?' said Mary with a piranha grin and a naughty wink.

'Is Mitchell going to be joining us tonight?' I asked. Somehow, during the course of their conversation, Mary had insinuated herself between Brian and me. Now, she had her long bare arm linked through his and somehow she managed to end up sitting next to him on a very small white sofa.

'Oh, I don't know. Maybe. He's very busy.'

'Is this a boyfriend?' Brian asked.

'Depends who's asking,' Mary replied with another wink.

'Got something in your eye?' I asked her.

We sipped champagne in Mary's recently feng shui-ed

sitting room for what seemed like an age. But even though I must have had at least half a bottle to myself, I simply couldn't relax. Without a fourth person to bounce conversation off, our banter was strictly limited to reminiscing about college and talking about what we were doing now. Brian was keen to hear all about Mary's business but Mary kept throwing his questions back at me.

'You don't want to hear about my boring little agency,' she smiled. 'Lizzie's the big business woman around here these days.'

'That's very generous of you,' I retorted. 'But I've been boring Brian about my work all day. Why don't you tell him about the time you met Michael Jackson.'

I had another, very momentary, reprieve while she told the tale about her meeting with the man himself and, even more interestingly, I thought, the man's pet monkey. But she wasn't about to let me off the hook.

'Didn't you once look for a little flat for Michael Jackson?' she asked me when she had finished.

I shook my head and stuck my nose into my glass.

'I'm sure you told me that,' Mary persisted. 'Honestly, Brian, she's so modest. Liz gets to meet even more celebs than I do in her business. In fact, nine out of ten celebrity house-hunters wouldn't trust anybody else.'

Brian looked at me expectantly. I shrugged.

'You know,' he said. 'Come to think of it, I'm sure you e-mailed me to say that you were flat-hunting for Michael Jackson . . .'

I felt like a drowning sailor whose life is flashing in front of his eyes. Flat-hunting for Michael Jackson? Was that to be the lie that put the puncture in my dinghy? Please, no. I looked from Mary to Brian. Both of them were smiling at me. Brian in a nice way – hoping to hear a juicy story he could take back to New York. Mary however was smiling like the cat that's got the fieldmouse running backwards into a milk bottle.

Then, inexplicably, she snatched me back to safety.

'Come into the kitchen, Liz. I want to ask your advice about the bouillabaisse.'

'But you're not cooking,' said Brian. He was right. There were two further serfs in the kitchen doing battle with Mary's unpredictable Smeg hob.

'Brian, don't be such a tease,' said Mary, waving his objection away with a flick of her red-nailed hand while simultaneously hauling me to my feet. I followed her mutely. I was so shocked by my brush with the truth that I didn't even complain that Mary had been the cause of it.

In the kitchen, Mary strolled about dipping a teaspoon into various bubbling pots like a home counties missus. The hired help addressed her as 'madam'. She complained that there wasn't enough salt in the sauce.

'It's meant to be like that. Besides, too much salt is bad for your blood pressure,' said the fresh-faced young chef.

'I think my blood pressure's about to shoot the top of my head off,' I said.

'You did look a bit stressed in there,' Mary commented. 'Everything all right?'

'Oh yeah,' I started to say. No thanks to her. But before I could add that I was all right compared to someone who's just been bitten by a scorpion or discovered that their house has been blown away by Hurricane Mitch, Mary was finding fault with the vegetables.

'Did you go anywhere good last night?' she asked, when she had finished explaining the right way to cook peas.

'Capricorn,' I told her.

'I'm surprised you got a table,' she replied.

'Not half as surprised as I was. I'm afraid I had to use your name.'

She snorted in an amused sort of way. 'Well, you might have asked me first, Liz. What if I'd decided to go to the same restaurant last night and hadn't been able to get a table because the *real* Mary Bagshot had already booked? What if I'd needed to wine and dine an important client? It might have been very embarrassing.'

'I didn't think of that.'

'Seems to me like you've given up thinking ahead altogether lately. Have you had any serious discussions with Brian about your glittering career yet?' she asked sarcastically.

'I can't say we have,' I admitted. 'For obvious reasons.'

'I suppose your biggest worry must be other people

dropping you in it,' she added, with just a glint of malice beneath her blue eyeshadow. 'Have to keep him well away from your usual haunts, eh? Just in case one of your friends asks how the place in Balham is, or something.'

'Mary, you won't, will you?'

She blinked her eyes innocently. As if the thought had never crossed her mind. 'Liz! How could you suggest such a thing! I'm throwing a dinner party for you. I even lent you my favourite dress for the occasion. I've been trying to help you pull this whole stunt off.'

'And I am so grateful,' I said warily. 'You know I am.'

'Is it exactly as it used to be or better?' Mary asked suddenly.

'It's all exactly as it was before he left to go back to the States. Which is fabulous,' I sighed.

'How wonderful. I'm very pleased for you. Seems like everything is going according to your plan.'

'Do you think Mitchell will be coming tonight?' I asked. I can't tell you how much I wanted him to be there too. I thought if Mary and I both had men to hang on to that night I might feel a little more secure about her promises.

'He might do,' she sighed. 'He's trying to put the new album to bed before he runs into another week's studio time.'

'You deserve more attention,' I told her, hoping to butter her up. 'Isn't he worried that you might run off with someone else if he leaves you on your own all the time?'

Mary shook her head. 'Who else would I run off with? All the men I know are attached or gay. Besides, why would they be interested in me? Good old Mary Bagshot?'

'Why? Because you're beautiful. Witty. Hugely successful. Why wouldn't everybody be interested in you?'

She nodded modestly. 'Some men are threatened by all that.'

'Brian isn't.'

'Mmm. Funny isn't it? And really rather ironic. Brian's absolutely mad about you and you're basically pretending to have my kind of life.'

She pulled a Chanel lipstick out from her delicate velvet pochette and smeared on a deep-red smile. When she had finished, she offered the lipstick to me.

'Put some of this on. Then I can almost pretend that I've kissed him myself. He is looking incredibly gorgeous tonight.'

I had taken the lipstick from her before the significance of her words hit home. 'Mary, you're not . . . I mean, you don't want to be with Brian, do you? Not after all these years.'

'God, no,' she laughed. 'I was joking. I haven't thought about Brian in a romantic way since the night that you first got off with him. After we had that long conversation in Tesco's about how neither of us should ever get off with him because it would break up our happy little social scene, remember?'

'I thought we made the actual pact in the chip shop.'

'Well, there you go. Perhaps we did. You see, it's all so unimportant to me that I can't even remember where we had such a supposedly pivotal conversation. So much has happened since those days, Liz. We were practically children back then. I was attracted by Brian because he seemed so glamorous and cultured compared to the likes of boring old Bill. Now that I meet cultural icons on a daily basis, I'm rather bored by all that sophistication. Perhaps if Bill were to walk through the door tonight dressed in his muddy archaeology gear I might actually be tempted to give him another go.'

'You never really did tell me what happened between the pair of you that night,' I probed.

'Well, what do you think happened? We were students, we were drunk, we got our kit off and had the worst sex imaginable. After which he sat back with a cigar, singing along to his bloody *Led Zeppelin Live* album like he had just performed for his country. I had barely felt a thing. Except the bloody hair on his back. Tell me,' she linked her arm through mine, has Brian got any hairier since your last encounter?'

'If he has, he must get them waxed.'

'That's another thing I like about American men. So fastidious. Did I ever tell you about the American guy I met who made me sit in a bath of hot water and baking soda before he would come anywhere near me?'

'Jeez! And you did what he asked?' I said, wrinkling up my nose. The hired girl who was shelling a fresh pile of peas cocked her head in our direction and wrinkled her nose too.

'I was in love,' Mary told us. 'And I actually quite liked the smell of the stuff. Sure I must have had plenty of baking soda up my hooter without knowing it since then anyway.'

She looked at the young waiter meaningfully. He pretended he hadn't been listening and carried on folding napkins.

'We should get back to Brian,' I said, heading out of the kitchen.

'No, wait,' she grabbed my arm. 'I've got a secret to tell you first.'

She pulled me close. 'You've got to promise that this won't go any further. If I want press leaks, I'll arrange them myself.'

'Why would I talk to the press? What have you done?'

'I'm sorry, Lizzie. I'm just so used to everyone I know knowing someone worth knowing. I keep forgetting that you don't really know anybody except students and penniless loonies.'

'Thanks for reminding me. So, what's the big surprise?'

She didn't seem unduly bothered that there were

three hired hands in the room so it couldn't have been that incredible, I figured.

'Mitchell and I have decided to get married,' she said in a stage whisper.

My mouth dropped open. The girl on pea duty stopped shelling.

'But I thought you said that he couldn't. I thought you said that it would ruin his career to get hitched,' I protested.

'Well, I did think that last week. But Mitchell is absolutely desperate to make us official and so I've decided to let him have his way. It might help him to work more effectively and I don't think marriage will be too much of a turn-off to his fans. Heaven knows, the fact that my father is married has never stopped women throwing themselves at him and he doesn't have Mitchell's abs or his bank balance.'

'I'm really pleased for you,' I told her sincerely. Although, oddly, she didn't look as though she was bubbling over at the prospect herself.

'I hope you won't mind if I don't ask you to be a bridesmaid,' she added matter-of-factly.

'Mind? I was dreading it,' I said, before it hit me that much as I had always complained that I would hate to don a puff-sleeved satin number for any of my friends, I was actually quite offended not to be considered. 'Are you going to ask your nieces?' I suggested. She had two gorgeous nieces, aged seven and five.

'Er, no. I'm going to ask Arabella Gilbert actually.'

Now my mouth dropped open again.

'Obviously the wedding will be covered in all the big gossip mags and Arabella could do with the exposure.'

'But . . . I mean, you hardly know her. Not really.'

'We've become very close since that party last Monday.'

'Right,' I snorted.

'Anyway, the Golden Brothers have promised to make my dress and something nice for Arabella too so that we won't look like a pair of meringues. I was thinking red. Do you think that will go with her hair?'

'The Golden Brothers are designing the dresses?' I whimpered. Not only was my best friend telling me that I wasn't to be her bridesmaid, she was also torturing me with the thought of a gorgeous designer dress that might have been made especially for me instead of for Arabella Gilbert who was a girl with plenty of amazing dresses already.

'You do understand, don't you?' Mary asked.

'I understand,' I assured her. 'You can't stop thinking about the opportunities for a front page in the *Mirror* even on your wedding day.'

'Don't say it like that,' she chided. 'You make it sound as though I'm *only* doing this for publicity. I'm talking about my wedding day. You know how seriously I take the institution of marriage. It's taken me a long time to come to the decision that I should give in to Mitchell's demands and marry him.'

'And to think you thought that he didn't love you

as much as you love him,' I commented, remembering the conversation we'd had before the party at the Hyperion.

'Did I say that?' Mary asked. 'I'm always over-reacting when Mitchell goes off into one of his creative huffs. Look, whatever I said, I wanted you to be the first to know about the wedding but you've got to promise to keep it under your hat until I make the official announcement. There are a few things I have to make absolutely certain of first. I mean, if it turns out that Arabella's agent isn't going to retire after all – and I have heard rumours – it might not be such a good idea for me to have her as my bridesmaid. I could be calling you up after all.'

'Thanks a bundle. I'll hold my breath, shall I?'

'Lizzie, don't be bitter, sweetheart. I'll be perfectly understanding if you choose someone over me when it comes to your own big day. And you will have one. Brian's clearly still crazy about you.'

'He is, isn't he?' I said, because I wanted to hear her confirm it.

'Yes,' she assured me. 'I think he is. And I swear I won't mention Michael Jackson again.'

CHAPTER NINETEEN

'You still haven't told us what happened with Michael Jackson,' said Brian when we joined him once more.

I was saved this time by a far more unexpected knight in shining armour.

The specially hired waiter didn't have time to get to the door to let the new guest in. The young man staggered into the pristine sitting room looking as though he should be instantly ejected, in a suit that, although well cut, had clearly been used as a sleeping bag for more than a couple of nights. His hair stuck up all over with god only knows what kind of sticky substance making it particularly stiff on one side. Brian got to his feet as if he thought he might be called upon to sort the intruder out. Mary's mouth turned down at the corners as she introduced us to the fourth member of our exclusive party.

It was only when he took his broken sunglasses off that I recognised the superstar.

'This is Mitchell,' she said. He stuck out his hand in my direction and gave my hand a cursory shake. Then he took Brian's hand in his and planted a wet kiss on the back of it.

'Wrong way round,' Brian joked.

Mitchell looked at him blankly before snorting with what might have been amusement, might have been a head cold.

'I'm sorry I'm late,' he said, collapsing on to the cream-covered sofa.

I could tell that Mary was already computing the dry-cleaning bill. Her smile tightened.

'Running late at the studio. Bloody drummer couldn't get anything right.'

'I thought you were using a drum machine,' said Mary.

'Yeah, right. Well, that wasn't working properly either, was it?'

'I don't know,' she said. 'You tell me.'

'Aren't you going to get me some champagne?' Mitchell asked her.

'When you've tidied yourself up a bit,' Mary told him, guiding him expertly in the direction of the shower. 'We've got guests.'

'Creative types, eh?' she laughed in a brittle way when he was out of earshot. 'Gets a bit out of it sometimes. One of the hazards of the business.'

Brian and I said nothing.

'Of course, once he's finished recording the album he'll be fine again. Doesn't touch a drop between recording sessions. It's just the studio atmosphere. Everyone gets a bit tense.'

'You don't have to explain,' Brian said kindly.

But Mary clearly felt otherwise. 'I only put up with it because I know how difficult these times are for him. If he couldn't have a couple of drinks he might, quite literally, dry up. It's a small price to pay for the end product.'

I resisted the temptation to raise my eyebrows at the thought of Mitchell's creative output to date.

'He'll be fine in a minute,' said Mary. 'Shower should sober him up.'

'Well, he's arrived just in time to eat,' said Brian cheerfully. 'That should soak up some of the alcohol.'

Mary smiled at him gratefully.

But Mitchell still hadn't emerged from the shower when we were getting to grips with the towering meringue confection that might have been made into a listed building if you left it in the centre of London for long enough. The conversation was rapidly going the way of the wine – that is to say, it was running out.

None of us could help glancing towards the hall that led to the bathroom between each mouthful. Mitchell had been in the shower for at least an hour. If he wasn't clean by now, then he had probably drowned. Finally, Mary excused herself to check. Her expression upon her return at least told us that he wasn't dead.

'He wasn't even in the shower,' she said. 'He must have fallen asleep with his head on the loo seat.'

Brian and I smiled and nodded as if that was perfectly reasonable.

'I just put a towel under his head to make him more

comfortable. Though he'll probably still have a stiff neck when he wakes up. I hope you don't mind if I leave him there for a while.'

'Not at all,' we said politely.

'Good job I've got two bathrooms, eh? Coffee, anyone?'

I would have hurled myself through her plate-glass window to get out of that room right then, but instead Brian and I agreed to coffee and continued to sit there in silence. Every so often, a peal of laughter would ring out from the kitchen and remind us that we weren't alone. Eventually, Mary asked the help she had hired to leave and promised to send their cheques after them.

When the doorbell rang again seconds after the waiters left, I assumed they must have forgotten something. Mary went to inspect the entry system, but this visitor had already got past the main entrance to the block, bypassing the snoozy porter. He was standing right outside Mary's door.

Brian and I tried to talk amongst ourselves but pretty soon it was impossible not to be drawn to the events taking place at the door. Mary hadn't let her visitor in. She stood with the door between their bodies like a shield, chain on.

Mary was whispering, but her visitor was less concerned about keeping quiet for the sake of the neighbours.

'I want to see him,' the visitor said.

'You can't see him. He's passed out in the bathroom.

I assume it's your fault he got into such a state in the
first place.'

'I want to see him,' the visitor insisted.

'I'll call the police and have you removed.'

Brian started to get out of his chair and, for the second time that evening, prepared to throw his weight
behind Mary's problem. But she glanced back into the
sitting room, saw him getting up and motioned him
to sit again.

Brian and I returned to our coffee. Conversation was
impossible. I clinked my cup against saucer loudly as
if to show that I wasn't ear-wigging.

'Well, that's fine,' said Mary, suddenly talking at full
volume again. 'If you're prepared for him to turn up on
your doorstep in Rio with his Louis Vuitton suitcase
and nothing else ever again, you can have him. I'll tell
him you called.'

At last she slammed the door in her visitor's face.
She waited a few beats before returning to the table,
grinning manically, and handed round a plate of handmade Belgian chocolates as if she had just popped
out to the kitchen to fetch them and not spent the
last five minutes rowing with someone through a
half-closed door.

I ached to ask her what was going on. And would
have done too if Brian hadn't gone into gentlemanly
overdrive and changed the subject to an excruciating
discussion about the best way to clean silver. I thought
we should leave, but when I suggested as much,
Mary looked distraught. We stayed for another hour.

Mitchell never came out of the bathroom. The other visitor wasn't discussed.

The evening had ended on such a strange note that I wasn't even sure I could talk about it safely in the cab back to Harriet's house.

'She's done really well for herself hasn't she?' I began just as we reached Grantchester Square. Brian looked at me doubtfully.

'I mean the flat and everything,' I clarified.

'Oh, yes. It's a great apartment. Really great.'

We went back to staring out of our respective windows.

'That was really tense, wasn't it?' said Brian when we got into Harriet's flat.

'Terrible,' I admitted. 'Poor Mary.'

'I was dreading having to take a shot at some massive guy for her. My shoulders are in agony from the anticipation.'

'You sound like you need a massage.'

'Naked,' he said.

I stopped thinking about Mary's mystery guest pretty soon after Brian suggested that.

CHAPTER TWENTY

I thought about calling Mary the next morning to check that she was OK. And also to check that Mitchell had come round after his night on the tiles. The bathroom tiles.

I decided I would call her after breakfast. But after breakfast I went back to bed with Brian. And then it was lunch time. The fact that I hadn't called Mary either to check up on her or to thank her ran through the front of my mind at high speed as I dipped a carrot stick into some guacamole and then into Brian's gorgeous mouth. But I decided she would have called me if anything really awful had happened. If something really *really* awful had happened to Mitchell, we would have heard about it on the news. If we had turned the TV or radio on. Which we didn't.

Fact was, I didn't want to have to think about anything but Brian and myself.

'Don't you want to call and see how your dog is getting on?' Brian asked me at one point.

'He'll be fine,' I assured him. Brian was feeling a hell of a lot more guilty about Hercules than I was.

Besides which, I didn't want to know what was going on in Balham. I hadn't told Richard that I wouldn't be at home for the duration of Brian's visit and I didn't want to call Seema about the dog only to have her tell me that Richard had been mooning about the place demanding to know where I was hiding with my mysterious visitor.

Richard. I felt only slightly more guilty when I thought of him than when I thought of Hercules, but having Brian back in my life threw even clearer light on to the things that had always bothered me about my accountant boyfriend.

For a start, there was the way Brian could throw his credit card at everything like some magical talisman that melted away all problems. Just that morning he had called the local deli and had them deliver breakfast so that I didn't even have to boil the water to make a cup of tea. By contrast Richard was always counting up pennies and trying to persuade Habib at the corner shop to change them into silver so that he could catch the bus to work.

Then there were the little things – like the way Brian would walk on the roadside edge of the pavement to protect me from drivers splashing through puddles. The way he opened doors for me and insisted on carrying anything heavier than a lipstick. There had been plenty of occasions when Richard had let me struggle back from Safeway with loaded shopping bags, let the front door swing shut in my face as he let himself into the house first, and then started bleating for a cup of tea before I had even unpacked the milk. I know it's old-fashioned, and I'm all for sexual equality and that, but I liked the way that Brian treated me as if I were ever so slightly fragile. As far as Richard was concerned, it seemed that equality of the sexes simply meant that he no longer had to offer me any help with the heavy lifting work at all.

But it wasn't all superficial money and manners. Brian was so much sexier too. And it was a self-perpetuating energy. His obvious interest in all my hitherto slightly underestimated charms filled me with self-confidence that in turn made me feel sexier as well. With Brian complimenting me at every turn, I began to feel as though I really could achieve some of the things I was pretending I had achieved already. (And he didn't go to bed with his socks on either as if the stench emanating from them might ward off any things that go bump in the night.)

I could never go back to Richard after this, I thought, as Brian massaged my feet. It would be like putting UHT milk in my coffee after getting used to drinking it with double cream. But how could I carry on affording the cream once Brian had gone back to the States and Harriet had come back for her flat? While Brian sucked my toes under the breakfast table, I plotted my escape to America. I could ask Mary to lend me the money for a flight. Brian would be happy to have me to stay with him. I would make a pretence at setting up a property business in New York but before I actually had to do anything. Brian would have asked me to marry him for fear that he would lose me when my visa ran out. Once Brian had agreed to marry me, I could give up the pretence. It would be too late for him to change his mind.

I even managed to convince myself that it wasn't entirely an evil plan because Brian would have realised that he loved me whether I was a successful businesswoman or not by then. I would be just as good at bringing up the little Brians as anyone who actually understood the financial pages.

Brian looked up from sucking my toes. 'You are so gorgeous,' he told me. 'Even your toe jam tastes good.'

I swatted him round the head with a newspaper, folded to the travel page for flight prices.

'I wish you lived in New York,' Brian said.

Oh, Brian, I thought. Your wish is my command.

CHAPTER TWENTY-ONE

W hen she called later that day, Mary didn't
seem at all bothered that her dinner party
had turned into something that resembled a made-
for-television film by Mike Leigh. When I apologised
for not having called to thank her or enquire after
Mitchell's health, she assured me that it didn't matter.
She had some exciting news that had really cheered
her up.

'I've got a new client,' she said proudly. 'Guess who?'

It had to be Arabella Gilbert.

'She called at my flat at four o'clock this morning
looking for some decent Charlie. I said I'd sort it out for
her on condition she signed on the dotted line before
she left my doorstep.'

'And she did?'

'She did. She was completely out of it. But I think
she'll find it legally binding. Anyway, it was just the
push that she needed to fall into my lap. We had lunch
on Friday and she'd near as dammit agreed to move to
my agency then anyway. And I've already got a job for
her lined up.'

'What job?' I asked.

'Do you ever watch that talk show at tea time where ordinary people pour their hearts out in front of a live studio audience? Like Jerry Springer only not quite so grubby.'

'How would I have seen it?' I asked. 'I'm at work at tea time.'

'Come on, Liz. You're forever taking sickies. But since you claim you haven't seen it, it's called *Lorinda*. At least, it was called *Lorinda* until she checked herself into the drying-out clinic last weekend. For the next three weeks it's going to be called *Arabella* and the Arabella in question just happens to be my new client. Ta-daa.'

'Well done,' I said. 'That's really good news.'

'Thank you,' said Mary. 'The competition for the spot was amazing. I am rather delighted.'

She sounded more delighted than she had done when telling me about her forthcoming wedding.

'I have never lunched so hard in my life,' she continued. 'But I think Arabella knows a professional when she meets one. Anyway, I've got you two tickets for a pilot recording tomorrow afternoon.'

'You mean you've got us tickets to see the show?'

'Uh-huh. I thought Brian might be interested. See how the English deal with the skeletons in their closets? I'm not sure what the topic will be, but I can guarantee some scandal and a punch-up. Shall I bike them over to you at your love-nest?'

'I'll just ask Brian.'

His eyes practically popped out of his head. Though his day-to-day life in Manhattan seemed incredibly glamorous to boring old me, he was still totally over-awed by everything to do with that little glowing tube in the corner of the sitting room.

'A TV show? Like, can we really do that?'

'Mary's got us some tickets. One of her clients is the presenter.'

'Wow. I'd love to. And thank her for me.'

I took my hand back off the mouthpiece. 'Brian says he would love to see the show and thanks you for sorting it out. Thanks from me, too.'

'Oh, believe me. It's my pleasure entirely,' she purred. 'Absolutely my pleasure. Now, you will wear something special, won't you? They show the whole audience in the opening credits and I don't want my best friend to show up my fave new client by appearing in her tatty jeans. Why don't you wear that suit I loaned you? The cream one? Cream always looks good on TV.'

'OK. Though I'm going to try to sit at the back if at all possible. I don't want to get caught in the cross-fire when some poor bugger finds out that his girlfriend is really a man.'

Mary laughed. 'Oh, Lizzie,' she said. 'Getting caught in the cross-fire is all part of the fun.'

Brian and I decided to spend the rest of that day doing some sight seeing. Brian put on a baseball cap for the occasion, and when I winced he told me that he had to wear it or people wouldn't know he was an American. I didn't like to tell him that his grey silk blouson jacket had already marked him out. I vowed one day I would bin that jacket and buy him something truly gorgeous to wear instead – with his credit card, of course.

We went to the Tate Gallery first. Brian had read about that year's Turner Prize nominees in the newspaper that week and was eager to see two works in particular. One was a giant sculpture of a vagina that incorporated (don't ask me how) two tonnes of melted chocolate; the other was a triptych of the crucifixion painted entirely in horseshit.

'I expect it will all be horseshit,' said Brian as we climbed the steps to the Tate's grand entrance.

The gallery lobby with its impressive vaulted ceiling was buzzing with tourists and art lovers. The shop was even busier, I noted, as we walked through into the first big hall. A row of magnificent sculptures led the eye down the cool white room to a gigantic illuminated cross. It didn't look much better than the cross they erected outside the Baptist Church in Balham each Easter, but this one, being in the Tate, was obviously art.

Brian and I drifted down the long room, pausing momentarily to look at each sculpture. Brian even ran his hand over the liquid curves of a Henry Moore, which brought one of the gallery curators scuttling out from her corner to tut.

'The moisture from your hand may damage the surface of the sculpture,' the uniformed woman explained.

'Don't think it would make much difference to some of this stuff,' Brian sneered to me when the curator was safely out of the way. 'Where are the real paintings? All this stuff is like something my nephew does in his remedial pottery class.'

We drifted into the permanent exhibition of Turner paintings. Brian liked the sea-scapes but commented that Turner couldn't draw people. He preferred the pre-Raphaelites, and I got rather jealous of poor Ophelia, lying drowned in her flower-strewn stream when Brian said that he thought she was the most beautiful woman ever painted. But even she couldn't hold his attention for very long and we soon found ourselves back in the echoing white hall where we had started our whistle-stop tour of art.

'Isn't that your secretary?' Brian asked me suddenly.

At first, I didn't know what he was talking about. It took a while before I remembered that as far as Brian was concerned I did actually have a secretary.

'Where?' I asked worriedly.

'Over there, by that painting of the two seventies types?'

The two seventies types were Ossie Clark and Celia Birtwell, immortalised with their pet cat by David Hockney as *Mr and Mrs Clark and Percy*. The secretary to whom Brian was referring was obviously my erstwhile flatmate Seema, but when I looked over towards the place where Hockney's masterpiece hung in a dimly lit alcove, I couldn't see Seema anywhere.

I could however see Richard. Richard my boyfriend. The boyfriend I'd neglected to mention. He was right in front of the Hockney, tapping his lower lip thoughtfully as he took the painting in.

I dragged Brian behind the Henry Moore he had laid his hands on earlier.

'Was that her?' he asked innocently.

'I couldn't see her,' I shrugged. 'Would you like to go to the Natural History Museum now? I hear they have a fascinating exhibition of maggots.'

'We haven't seen the Turner Prize exhibition yet,' he protested.

'Well, you said yourself that it's probably all horseshit. I don't think we should waste our time.'

'Sure,' said Brian, giving in. 'But don't you think you should say "hi" to your secretary before we leave?'

'I couldn't see her when I looked. You must have been mistaken.'

'No. I'm sure I'm not. See! There she is again.'

This time when I glanced back towards the alcove where Mr and Mrs Clark kept their cool-eyed watch, I did see Seema. She must have been obscured by the crowds taking illicit photos last time I looked. And there too was Richard. My boyfriend. And Seema was linking her arm through his!

I tried not to look in the least bit surprised as I popped back behind the Henry Moore to gather myself and come up with an escape route. Suddenly the hole in his famous reclining nude's midriff didn't seem such an enchanting feature.

'Was I right?' Brian asked me.

'Yes, you were right. It's Seema. But she's with someone. Someone I've never met before,' I added in a hurry. 'She might be on a date or something. It doesn't seem right to go barging up and interrupt. She sees enough of me at the office.'

'You're only going to say hello,' Brian protested. 'We're not going to play gooseberry.'

'I don't think she'll be too upset if she finds out that I left her in peace instead.'

'Sure. But aren't you a little concerned to find out where she's left your dog while she's out on this hot date?'

'I'm sure he's fine.' I linked my arm through Brian's in an echo of Seema's gesture with *my* man. 'Let's go.'

'We can't leave now. They're coming towards us.'

And to my absolute horror, they were. Seema and Richard had finished looking at the painting and were heading in our direction though as yet they didn't appear to have spotted Brian and me.

'Look at this,' I said, falling to my knees behind the Henry Moore and dragging Brian down with me. 'Have you ever looked at a piece of granite really closely?'

'Lizzie? What are you doing?' he asked in a voice of pure exasperation, brushing the dust from his knees and attempting to straighten up again.

'Brian, I don't want to spoil my secretary's date,' I hissed, keeping him close to the floor.

I began a close inspection of a strand of lucite flecks in the base of the reclining nude. I would be OK as long as Richard didn't stop to look at the sculpture too. Through the hole in its midriff I saw him pass by without pausing, clearly intent on an exhibit on the other side of the hall. But they passed by so closely that Brian and I could clearly hear their conversation, or rather, we could hear Seema simpering like some brainless eighteenth-century socialite as Richard explained some of the finer points of art.

'The composition of Mr and Mrs Clark is particularly interesting,' he told her. 'Normally, the woman would be in the sitting position, but in Hockney's painting, it is the man who takes the chair. And his direct, challenging gaze is all the more pertinent when you realise that he probably knew at the time that the artist was screwing his wife.'

'Really?' Seema gushed.

'Yes. Celia Birtwell was about the only woman who ever slept with Hockney. It broke poor Ossie Clark's heart.'

'Infidelity's a terrible thing, isn't it?' observed Seema and although I couldn't see from behind the Henry Moore, I could well imagine her batting her eyelashes to devastating effect.

'Sounds like her man knows a bit about art,' said Brian as we straightened up in time to see Seema and Richard disappearing into the Turner Prize exhibition. Still arm in arm.

It certainly did. So how come Richard had never

taken me to an art gallery to benefit from his superior knowledge of all things cultural?

'You know about art though too, don't you, Brian?' I asked, suddenly needing to be reassured that anything Richard could do, Brian could do better.

'Never really seen the point of it. Not this modern stuff. Except perhaps as an investment. A friend of mine bought an unsigned sketch in Paris once. Turned out to be a Monet. Doubled his money like that.' He clicked his fingers.

'What was it a picture of?'

'I don't know. Hell, it hardly matters if it was a Monet.' He pronounced it 'Moan-ey'. 'But when he found out what it was he sure wished that he'd bought the matching pair. Monet equals Money. That's all I need to know about art.'

'That's a terrible story,' I said. 'Let's get some lunch.'

'We could eat in the café here?' Brian suggested.

No. No, we couldn't. I needed to get Brian at least three tube stops away from the Tate before Richard and Seema came out of the Turner Prize exhibition again.

I chose an Italian place in Soho. We were the only customers. The whole of Soho is pretty much deserted on a Sunday afternoon while the type of people who normally frequent the noisy bars on Old Compton Street are at home sleeping off a good twenty-four hours' clubbing before the working week starts again.

Away from Oxford Street none of the shops were open either. I can't say it was a particularly great time to be in Soho. It felt like the morning after a bomb has been dropped, but I felt secure that it was one of the few places where I could guarantee that we wouldn't bump into Richard and Seema.

'Are you sure you want to have lunch here?' asked Brian as we stepped out of the balmy afternoon sunshine into the chilly shadows of a restaurant that was far better suited to the night. The languid French waiter seemed equally unimpressed with my choice of lunch-time venue since it meant that he had to abandon the Sunday papers to attend to us. He practically threw a basket of ciabatta towards us when we sat down at the table nearest the kitchen.

'You've gone all quiet,' Brian observed.

'I have not,' I almost snapped at him.

'You have. You've been all quiet ever since I told you I'd seen your secretary in the gallery. And now you've brought us to this dark and gloomy place. Is there something wrong?'

'Nothing at all. Do you want to go somewhere else?'

'I'm not bothered about where we eat, Lizzie. I only want to know what's eating you?'

'It's just . . . it's just that sometimes art overwhelms me,' I burbled. 'Don't you ever feel that way?'

'Can't say I do,' he said, biting down on a chunk of bread. 'You shouldn't let yourself get worked up about a few old pictures. Heaven knows the artists didn't.'

'How can you say that?'

'Do you think Picasso's heart bled when he painted those weeping women? No way! He was laughing all the way to the bank. Don't let it bother you. Let the latest market crash in Asia bother you. Let earthquakes in California bother you. Something really serious. Buck up, Lizzie. I've only got a couple more days.'

'I'll try,' I said, forcing a smile, as the waiter slapped a menu into my hand.

Of course the irony of my situation had struck me. Here I was, being eaten from the inside out by with jealousy at the fact that Richard was out at a gallery with my flatmate Seema while I was having lunch with Brian, having made mad passionate love to him, and not to Richard, my official boyfriend, for the past two nights. Richard hadn't technically done anything wrong. He was merely enjoying a Sunday trip to an art gallery with a friend. It was probably utterly platonic. Definitely, in fact, since I could be absolutely sure that Seema wouldn't even consider dating a lowly accountant. On the other hand, I knew I had been doing wrong. I had definitely been unfaithful. For heaven's sake, the only reason I hadn't chucked Richard the very second that Brian announced his impending visit was that I was too much of a slimeball to risk losing out on a birthday present unnecessarily. I was the emotional pond scum. Not him.

And hadn't I decided that it was all over between me and Richard now anyway? I would have to tell him it was over in order to go to America with Brian. I should have been pleased that Seema was prepared to help him lick his wounds in my absence. Nope, I could find no justification whatsoever for the unreasonable feelings of having been betrayed that were currently keeping me from eating my olive ciabatta and instead making me tear the bread into a pile of little chunks.

'You going for a Turner Prize nomination?' asked Brian, cocking his head towards the heap of crumbs. 'Something is wrong, isn't it? Don't you think you'd better tell me what's going through your mind before the waiter brings you a bib?'

Brian took my sideplate away from me, depriving me of more bread on which to vent my anger.

'Tell me,' he demanded, while simultaneously rubbing my thigh beneath the table to help coax out an answer.

'OK,' I said, thinking quickly. 'There is something wrong. I was having a wonderful day out but now I can't stop thinking about work and the 20:20 project. I know I should be able to trust Seema in my absence but seeing her at the gallery today has made me wonder if I was right to trust her with so much. Perhaps she's too young for all the responsibility I've been giving her lately. I think I've been relying on her good nature just a little too much.'

At least the last part of what I had said was true. I was certainly beginning to wonder if Seema had decided to take her reward for looking after Hercules already. And she had decided that the reward in question was to be *my* boyfriend.

Brian reached across the table to take my hand. 'Lizzie, it's a Sunday. Even if Seema is ruining your business while you're looking after me, there isn't a great deal you can do about it now. But since we're on the subject, just what is this 20:20 project I keep hearing about? You promised to tell me all about it.'

Great. I hadn't bothered to make anything up, hoping that I might be able to get away with never mentioning Seema's damn invention again.

'You don't want to hear about it,' I tried. 'It's boring. Seema's just excited because it's the first real project she's had responsibility on.'

'But why 20:20? That's a great title,' Brian continued. 'Like 20:20 vision.'

'That's it,' I said; a lightbulb had suddenly been switched on between my ears. 'It's a project for a national chain of opticians.'

'Oh.'

'See? I told you you'd find it boring.'

He nodded.

Phew.

We ate our lunch quickly, with the waiter standing over us to snatch away our plates as soon as we had scraped up a last mouthful. Brian wanted to go to another museum. The British Museum this time, to see the Egyptian mummies and to marvel at the stolen marbles.

I followed him through the room stuffed with

Egyptian antiquities, making suitably impressed noises when we saw a carved hand big enough to make a pretty comfortable armchair. But I still couldn't block the sight of Seema linking her arm through Richard's out of my mind. I tried to tell myself that I should be glad for them both. I liked Richard, and Seema was one of the best women I knew. But though I had made the decision to throw my hand in with Brian, I couldn't help feeling just a faint twinge of regret at the thought of the other budding relationship which now had to end.

To make matters worse, Brian was now standing in front of a statue that Richard had admired when he and I had bunked off work to spend an afternoon trawling the museum in the heady early days of our acquaintance. When Brian reached out to take my hand, I was reminded of Richard making exactly the same gesture seven months ago. I felt happier with Brian's hand in mine, though. Didn't I?

Of course I was happier with Brian, I told myself firmly as we gazed at each other over another spectacular dinner that night.

I had spent the early evening making a mental list. Brian versus Richard. Pros and cons for both.

In Richard's favour: he was a nice bloke, he made me laugh and he knew a bit about art. On the other hand, he was an accountant, which is international shorthand for boring, and yet he never had any money. He would make a nice friend. But he was hardly husband material, was he? Not if I was intending to be a lady who did nothing but lunch from the moment I had that gold band on my finger.

The list in Brian's favour was clearly very much longer. He was a nice bloke too, he made me laugh and he knew enough about art to make money from it, money that he could use to buy me presents. He was also handsome. And he made me do things in bed that I had hitherto only imagined in a very abstract way.

The only disadvantage to being with Brian was that he lived in New York. New York. An advantage and a disadvantage. I wanted desperately to get out of London. I wanted to go somewhere even more exciting. But I also wondered whether I would miss my family and friends.

'Did you miss your family and friends when you came to spend a year at Oxford?' I asked him now.

Brian shrugged. 'I made new friends. And hey, there was always the telephone. I've missed you though since I went back to NYC.'

That was what I needed to hear. I decided to take the plunge. 'I'd like to come and stay with you in New York.'

'I'd like that too,' he said.

'I mean, stay for a long time, Brian.'

There. I had said it. And Brian didn't say no.

CHAPTER TWENTY-TWO

W e stayed up late discussing the possibilities. Brian suggested that I entrust my business to Seema's capable hands while I checked out the situation in America. I would need a working visa and other paperwork, but Brian would be more than happy to have me stay with him for as long as I needed to.

As long as I *needed* to? I wasn't sure I liked the sound of that since it seemed to imply that at some stage I would be moving into a place on my own, but I told myself that Brian was just being polite. Perhaps he thought I might be put off if he offered me a home for life right away.

We decided that I would follow Brian out to the States about a week or so after he returned. That would give me a chance to hand the business over to Seema properly, I told him. In reality, it would give me enough time to earn one more week's wages at Corbett and Daughter to pay for my air fare.

'Of course, you'll have to find somewhere for Hercules to stay while you're away,' Brian said. 'Are you sure you can bear to leave your dog behind?'

If Harriet didn't come back to collect her pooch that week, he would be straight off to Battersea Dogs Home. I didn't tell Brian that, naturally.

'I can't believe this is really happening,' I said. 'Crazy isn't it?'

'Crazy, but wonderful too,' he replied.

I couldn't wait to get to the TV recording the next day. Mary would be shocked to hear that I had pulled off my grand plan, but I hoped she would be pleased as well. When we got to the studio, however, Mary was nowhere to be seen. I guessed she would be backstage with her new client but thought better of interrupting pre-recording preparations even if I did have the most incredible piece of gossip to impart in the entire world.

Brian and I chose to sit somewhere near the middle. He wanted to sit right at the front but to my immense relief, we discovered that all the seats down there had been allocated prior to our arrival. Next to us was a man with the name 'Melinda' tattooed on his forearm. His wife introduced herself. She was called Anita.

Despite Mary's warning that we ought to dress up, I have to say I felt distinctly over-dressed as the rest of the crowd took their seats wearing tracksuit bottoms and tattered denims. I slipped off my jacket and went to hang it casually over the back of my seat but the man behind me was eating a packet of Maltesers rather messily and the thought of sticky chocolate fingers on Mary's silk soon had me putting the jacket back on again.

To get things warmed up, one of the production team came on to the stage and sparked off a little debate in the first couple of rows by asking one woman what she would do if she discovered that her husband habitually dressed up in her underwear while she was out on the town with the girls. She said she'd be disgusted and that it meant he was probably gay – which went down very well with the six-foot-tall plumber beside her who was dressed as Joan Collins's big sister.

'This is fun,' Brian whispered to me, as we watched the row unfold. 'I had no idea that English people could get so passionate.' I punched him in the arm. But before the rest of the audience could come to fisticuffs, another member of the production team, wearing headphones and one of those funny-looking mikes, emerged to announce that Arabella was on her way up to the studio from her dressing room.

An awed silence fell over the room as we waited for the woman herself to arrive. It seemed like aeons before the production assistant who had started the transvestite row stepped out briefly in front of the cameras and raised her arms to signal that it was time for everyone to cheer and clap as Arabella finally appeared from behind a curtain at the top of the auditorium and made her way down to the stage, shaking hands as she went like every other talk-show host you've ever seen.

'Arabella! Arabella!' the crowd chanted in time with the theme tune. Well, nearly in time. There were too many syllables. I wondered if Mary would make them change the theme tune.

Arabella shook seven people by the hand then headed straight for a cross which was painted on the studio floor, ignoring anyone else who pleaded to press her flesh. She flicked back her glossy brown hair and fixed the nearest camera with a glitteringly expensive smile. She looked fantastic, although I couldn't help wondering idly how much better she might look when the liposuction was done.

'Thank you for coming, everybody,' she said straight to the camera, including the audience at home. 'It means so much to me.'

'At least she's got better legs than Jerry Springer,' Brian commented. Anita glared at him to be quiet. She'd come a long way to have her fifteen minutes that day and she was taking proceedings very seriously.

'On today's programme we're going to be talking about secrets,' Arabella continued. 'Secrets or lies. What's the difference? When does a secret become a lie? Are we right to keep secrets from people who love us or are we only storing up trouble for the future when what we thought was just a teensy little thing we wanted to keep to ourselves becomes a huge explosive problem that tears families apart?' She looked deeply serious for a moment. Frighteningly so, in fact. The audience was gripped.

'My guests today all have a secret that they finally want to tell. They need to unburden themselves, admit to their dishonesty and get things off their chests. But how will that feel to the people they have to admit something to? By unburdening themselves, will my guests be doing the right thing or will they simply be passing their problems on for someone else to handle? My first guest is Jane from Worcestershire. She's been keeping her secret for almost five years. Let's have a big hand for Jane.'

The audience erupted dutifully and Jane crept out on to the stage, looking as if she had already changed her mind. The crowd whooped its approval as she found her way to a pink velvet upholstered chair and sat down blinking like a deer caught in head-lights.

'You're looking lovely today, Jane,' Arabella told the girl in a red dress that was way too small and left nothing to the imagination. Especially the control top on her tights. Jane blinked her thank you.

'Now, Jane. You've taken a very long time to come to the decision to tell your secret, haven't you?'

'That's right,' said Jane, inaudibly. She cleared her throat and said, 'That's right,' again. This time she angled her chin down so that her words boomed from her mike.

'Just talk naturally,' Arabella coached. 'Just imagine that there's no one here in the studio today except you and me. Imagine you're having a one-to-one chat with your closest friend.'

'I bet she'd feel more comfortable having a one-to-one chat with General Pinochet,' I whispered to Brian. 'She looks terrified.'

And little wonder. For Jane from Worcestershire had chosen that day's episode of *Arabella* to make the announcement to her husband, in front of heaven knows how many millions of people (about three – Mary had estimated), that the boy he thought was his son, was in fact his nephew. Brian peeped through his fingers when Jane delivered the blow. It was like road-kill. I didn't want to look myself, but my eyes were forever being drawn back to that poor girl's face as she spilled her beans on national TV.

'Do you think you'll be able to work this out?' Arabella asked sincerely. Jane and her dazed husband nodded, but despite the promises of counsellors behind the scenes, I couldn't imagine that any fate awaited poor Jane back in Worcestershire but a pair of suitcases dumped on the front step.

'Why do they do it?' Brian asked me. 'Why do they let themselves get so set up?'

'Everyone wants their fifteen minutes,' I said wisely.

'Fifteen of fame and a lifetime of pain,' agreed Brian.

After Jane's revelation, the next guest up was practically light relief. Norman wanted to admit to his great aunt that it was he who had broken her favourite vase fifteen years before. The old woman was so profoundly deaf, I was certain that she left the show none the wiser, but she seemed happy to have had her fifteen minutes too. As was Deirdra, who discovered that the secret her boyfriend Mark had been keeping from her was a whopping great diamond engagement ring.

'That's sweet,' said Brian, squeezing my hand in a way which seemed loaded with meaning to me. Deirdra's boyfriend got down on his knees to make the proposal and had to be helped to his feet afterwards as the emotion of the moment overcame him.

'Jesus,' said Brian. 'What happened to the good old British Stiff Upper Lip?'

'It's not good to suppress your emotions,' said Anita. 'The death of Diana the Queen of all our Hearts showed us how important it is to feel and show what we're feeling without embarrassment.'

'Is that so?' Brian asked her.

'Holding everything in has been proven to cause cancer,' she nodded.

'Are we in California?' Brian asked me.

Three guests down. I was sure we must be coming to the end of the show when Arabella stepped in front of the row of seats where Jane and her husband sat staring into space like strangers while Deirdra and Mark canoodled.

'I hope she's not going to do one of those cheesy summing-ups,' Brian muttered.

If only she had been. Arabella gazed deeply into the camera on her left. 'We've got one more person here today,' she began. 'Someone who's been keeping quite a big secret from her friend. Several big secrets in fact. Or perhaps you might prefer to call them lies. Let's see what you think when we ask Lizzie Jordan to come clean on *Arabella*.'

I looked around expectantly as the spotlight turned on to the audience. Which poor sucker had been caught out this time? It was only when I saw Brian's amused expression that I realised it was me.

'Lizzie Jordan?' Arabella smiled. She was suddenly standing right beside me. A spotlight cast a circle around my head.

'Yes,' I squeaked. 'Er, yes,' I said a little more deeply into Arabella's microphone.

'Have you got any idea what secrets we might be referring to here?' she asked me.

What could she be talking about? That my friend Amy Weskey and I had cheated in the maths GCSE exam twelve years before? That I saw the family dog lick a jam tart but didn't tell my brother before he bit into it? I didn't have any other secrets that I could think of right then.

'Nope,' I said, grinning nervously. 'I'm afraid I really don't have a clue.'

'Oh, come on now,' tutted Arabella. 'Don't play the innocent with us. Try one more time. Have a really good think. What big secret have you been keeping from your handsome friend here?'

She looked at Brian. Brian looked at me expectantly. And then the penny dropped.

'No,' I breathed. 'Noooo.'

'Perhaps you'd like to tell your friend Brian, who's come all the way from America to visit you, who it is who actually owns the flat in Grantchester Square and that flash sports car you've been driving around in? What you really do when you say you're going out in the morning to broker some high-powered property deal? Who owns the designer suit you're wearing today on my show? Who owns those shoes you're wearing? Don't you think that Brian deserves to know?'

'Know what?' asked Brian, looking faintly bemused.

'The truth,' boomed Arabella.

'Are you going to tell him, Lizzie? Or shall I tell him what I heard in the ladies' room at the Dorchester less than a week ago? That you had actually been typing up tales lifted straight from *my* social column and sending them to your former lover in e-mails on the pretence that *you* were in fact living *my* exciting life?'

Suddenly, Arabella's face seemed to grow clown-like, looming in and out of my vision as the room started to blur. I got to my feet and pushed past the painted presenter as I headed for a door – any door. I got as far as the stage. Production hands leapt out from behind the backdrop to restrain me. Jane and her downtrodden husband looked momentarily distracted from their own pain as mine began.

'You see, Brian, Lizzie Jordan isn't quite the high-flying executive she led you to believe she was during the course of your torrid internet affair. In fact she is a lowly secretary at an unsuccessful estate agency. The flat that you've been staying in belongs to her kindly boss. That suit she's wearing belongs to her friend Mary. Lizzie's been lying to you, Brian, in an attempt to persuade you to fall in love with her again and rescue her from her dire situation. And by the look of the pair of you sitting so closely together before you heard this revelation, I would have said she was succeeding. But how do you feel about her now, Brian? Can you ever feel the same again now that you know she's been lying to you?'

Without saying anything, Brian got to his feet and walked from the studio. He had the sense to choose the back entrance however and made it away from the camera's gaze before anyone could stop him. I remained rooted to the middle of the studio floor as Arabella summed the programme up and then disappeared to her changing room without so much as a backward glance at the people who had humiliated themselves so spectacularly for her career advancement.

Not knowing whether to laugh or cry, I stood on the stage until everybody had gone but the production staff.

'I have to see Arabella,' I told someone.

'Arabella won't see anybody. You'll have to leave now,' the stage manager told me. 'Unless you're also in the audience for *Kilroy*.'

'But she knows me. And so she must know how much she's humiliated me.'

'Arabella meets a lot of people,' the stage manager said to humour me. 'She doesn't remember them all. You'll have to go now.'

I followed the stragglers down the corridor to the car park. I felt in my pockets for Harriet's car keys but I was still shaking so hard, I wasn't sure I would be able to drive anyway. And where had Brian gone? I couldn't see him anywhere.

He wasn't in the car park. He wasn't leaning on the car with a grin on his face, waiting for me to explain the joke. He must have left the studio complex altogether and got a taxi somewhere. But did he know anyone in London other than me who he could stay with until his plane left the next day? Would I get a chance to explain to him why I had been such an almighty fool?

I let myself into the borrowed Mercedes and collapsed into a sob with my head on the steering wheel. I couldn't believe what had happened. Another twenty-four hours and everything would have been perfect. Mission accomplished. But Mary Bagshot had clearly set me up. Set me up and ruined my life.

CHAPTER TWENTY-THREE

Afer briefly going back to the flat and discovering that he hadn't made his own way back there either, I headed straight for Mary's. Mary was the only other person Brian knew in London so perhaps he was at her place, getting the whole story from her. And even if he wasn't, I was after her blood anyway.

I parked Harriet's car at a forty-five degree angle to the kerb outside Mary's plush portered block and stormed up to the door. I jabbed at the doorbell and kept my finger on it until she answered. She sounded pretty groggy on the entryphone, and came to the door wearing her dressing-gown, which was odd, since it was only six in the evening. She looked a little red around the eyes but I put that down to some kind of herbal facial treatment. She spent more on the surface of her skin than NASA spent getting to the surface of the moon.

'I hope I haven't interrupted anything,' I said sarcastically. 'Having your moustache bleached?'

'Actually, I think I'm coming down with the flu,' she told me flatly.

'Well, don't expect me to feel sorry for you. What did you think you were playing at, Mary, sending me to that studio to be humiliated?'

'What?' she asked.

'Don't play the innocent. You know what happened to me this afternoon.'

'No. I don't.'

'Right.' I squared up against her on the doorstep. 'Are you telling me that your precious new client decided off her own pretty, empty head to spew out all the lies I've been telling Brian for the benefit of a live studio audience? You set me up. I could knock your bloody head right off.'

'Lizzie, what are you talking about?' Mary sighed.

'Arabella told Brian that I'd been lying to him! More precisely, she tried to force me to own up on national TV.'

'Don't panic. It was only a pilot.'

'Do you think that makes it better?'

A woman with a King Charles walked past and gave us a very disapproving stare. In fact, I think it was the exact same woman with a King Charles who had caught me trying to break into her mansion block with Harriet's key three days before.

'Liz, I think you'd better come inside.' Mary grabbed me by the collar and yanked me in off the step. 'I promise I don't know what you're talking about.'

'Don't even try to pretend,' I shouted as Mary dragged me up the stairs to her apartment. 'Your client told Brian I had been lying to him in front of an entire studio audience. The only way she could have known is because you told her.'

Mary twisted her Cartier watch around her wrist. 'I wouldn't do that.'

'God, you're such a liar. I thought you were my friend.'

'I am your friend.'

'You *were*.'

'Where's Brian now?' she asked.

'I don't bloody know. He walked out of the studio in front of everybody. I thought he might have come here. Just admit it, Mary. Admit you set me up.'

I'm ashamed to say that I grabbed her by the arms and shook her. She cracked instantly.

'Oh, all right. I did set you up,' she squeaked. I let her go. 'But it's not as though you didn't deserve it.'

'What?' I grabbed her again. 'Why? What have I ever done to you, Mary Bagshot? You've got everything,' I spat. 'You've got everything and you had to go and spoil the best thing that's ever happened to me.'

'I haven't got everything,' Mary sneered. 'You don't know what you're talking about.'

'You have,' I insisted, counting off the reasons on my fingers. 'You've got a great job, a nice place to live, a fast car and a bloody pop star for a fiancé. What more could you possibly want, Mary? All I wanted was one great weekend with the love of my life. One single weekend. Why did you have to have the satisfaction of seeing me trip up as well?'

'Because you were getting the one thing I wasn't.

Brian loves you. It's obvious. Mitchell doesn't love me.'

'Of course he does. You're getting married.'

'He doesn't.'

'Stop feeling sorry for yourself.'

'Look, he really doesn't. Mitchell's gay.'

'What?'

'You heard me, Liz. Mitchell's gay. Our whole relationship is bollocks. I don't love him and he certainly doesn't love me. Mitchell loves a male model from Rio with a 44-inch chest and a handlebar moustache he can swing off. He wanted to marry me so that the journalist who's been speaking to his boyfriend would be put off the scent until the new album hit the shelves. I was just Mitchell's beard.'

'But why would you do that?'

'What did I have to lose? It wasn't as if I was ever likely to have a real relationship, was it? I've never managed to have a decent one so far. No one has ever fallen in love with me,' she cried dramatically. 'You've always attracted the decent blokes, Liz. The ones I attract are either married or mad or both. All I want, all I've ever wanted, is someone to love me the way Brian loves you. Preferably Brian. He wasn't just the love of your life, Liz, he was the love of my life too.'

'What?'

'He was the love of my life,' she repeated haltingly. 'I was in love with him too. Brian. All the time you were together.'

'No, you weren't. What about that post-grad?'

'What about him? He was just a distraction.'

'Why didn't you say something?'

'I did. I said it all those years ago in the chip shop, remember? I told you that I fancied Brian. But he chose you. And you chose him over me, too. After that, there didn't seem to be much point protesting about it. You wanted each other. Not me. I had a miserable year while you two swanned around like love's young dream, kissing and cuddling and making me sick to the very pit of my stomach every time I had to stop and be civil to you while you were holding hands. When Brian went back to America, I cried almost as much as you did. I watched him walk out of the quad from my bedroom window and then I threw myself down on my pillow and cried until I thought I would die. After that, I felt a bit better. I was almost relieved not to have him around any more because at least I wouldn't have to watch him getting all loved up with you.'

'I didn't know,' I promised her. 'You didn't make it clear enough.'

'Would it have made a difference? Anyway, you might have guessed, if you hadn't been so wrapped up in yourself. If you'd given a damn about me you'd have known that I was unhappy.'

'But that was so long ago, Mary. Six years.'

'Yes. And I thought I'd got over it. I thought I'd put that whole stupid crush out of my mind. I thought I'd see him with you again, see that he'd got fat and old like the rest of us, and put all the feelings I once had for him behind me. But it didn't happen like that. He was just the same as ever and just as mad about you. I saw you standing there looking like a goddess in a dress that I had hoped would make you look like a sack of potatoes tied up with string, and Brian couldn't take his eyes off you. I knew that it didn't matter how much *I* had changed since he went away. I still couldn't compete with you in the one area of my life that I'll never be a success in. Men fall in love with you all the time. No one loves me. No one.'

She looked at me with a strangely smug look, as if she had just delivered a foolproof excuse. I was dumbfounded. 'So that's why you dropped me in it. Because you're jealous. You are really, really sick.'

'I know.' She clutched my sleeve desperately. 'And getting Arabella to do what she did to you this afternoon must have been a cry for help. Yes, that's exactly what it was. Can't you see? A cry for help.'

'Then keep on crying,' I snarled. I shook my arm free of her grasp. 'Because you needn't ever expect me to help you again. You were supposed to be my best friend, Mary. But best friends would never do what you did to me, no matter how big a crush they once had on someone about a million years ago. As far as I'm concerned, I don't even know you any more. You tried to ruin my life just because yours isn't exactly how you want it to be. Even though your life is exactly the way I'd like mine to be. You're a spoilt, selfish brat. You've had every advantage in life with your private schools and your loaded parents. They even bought you your company. You've never had to work for anything. Perhaps that's why you're such a hopeless case. Perhaps that's why nobody loves you.'

Her jaw quivered and I knew she was about to cry, but I walked towards the door with my head held high. I wasn't going to take anything back right then. No mercy.

'Well, if that's how you feel,' she shouted after me, momentarily regaining her legendary poise. 'You can take off that bloody suit you borrowed and go home in your underwear.'

'OK then. I will.' And I did. I took the suit off, stepping all over it with my dirty shoes as I did so.

'And that necklace,' she shrieked at me. 'Don't forget that necklace belongs to me too!'

'Have it,' I spat. 'I never liked it anyway.'

I dropped the simple gold chain on top of the crumpled suit. 'You're pathetic.'

'You're the one who's pathetic round here,' Mary muttered as she picked up the chain.

'No, you are,' I retorted. 'You're the one who can't face the world without your drugs. Snort, snort, snort. You can't even put your knickers on in the morning these days without having a quick line first.'

'I can,' she protested. 'My drug use is purely recreational.'

'Right. And so the line you had before I came up here today was just because you thought we were going to have some fun together?'

She glanced back at the coffee table where one of

her many credit cards lay beside a little white paper package. 'It's none of your business. Anyway, you know you'd be doing it too. If you weren't such a loser. If you could afford it.'

'And how do you afford it?'

'I, in case you've forgotten, run my own successful artiste management business.'

'Bought for you by your Daddy,' I sneered.

'I did it all on my own,' she told me indignantly.

'You never did anything on your own, Mary. You've always had someone to give you a leg up in life. If I came from your background I'd be running the bloody country by now not some stupid poncey agency.'

'Oh yeah,' she spat back. 'Cos you've never had any advantages in life, have you? You haven't had the stable family background I would have killed for. If I had your background, perhaps I wouldn't need these drugs.'

'You're so sad,' I mocked, as I put on my coat and wrapped it tightly around me.

'No, you are. I'm not the one who doesn't even own the clothes I stand up in.'

'I don't need to hide a fat arse behind designer trousers,' I said with extra spite.

'Well, I'm not the one who's going to be walking back across Notting Hill naked,' she sobbed, as she buried her face in the jacket of the borrowed suit and finally let the floodgates go.

'I am not naked,' was my parting shot. But I did leave Mary's flat wearing nothing but my underwear and the coat I had borrowed from Harriet. I might as well have been completely naked though, since the coat was more a novelty silk kimono than a sensible mac and I was bloody freezing despite the fact that it was supposed to be August (a very British August). But at least I left that flat with my pride.

'Yeah!' I shook my fist up at Mary's panoramic window. 'I've still got my pride.'

What I didn't realise at that point was that I also had the small problem of retrieving Harriet's car which, having been parked so badly in my hurry to get to Mary before Brian did, was even now being loaded on to the back of a council tow-truck.

'What are you doing?' I squeaked at the balding man who was watching Harriet's Mercedes being lifted into the air with no regard for its expensive paintwork at the mercy of the rusty towing chains.

'Is this your car, darling?' the man asked me, clearly amused by my outfit. I wrapped the coat tightly around me.

'No. I mean, yes. Yes, it is my car. Put it down at once.'

'Can't do that, love. We've already started to lift it, see. Once we've started to lift the car we can't put it down again until we get it to the pound. If you'd got down here just a couple of minutes ago you could have sat in it and stopped us. We couldn't have touched it. Not with you in it, see. In case you had an accident and sued us. But you're just a bit too slow today, ain't ya?'

'But you haven't even clamped it! How can you be towing it away if you haven't even clamped it? I was only upstairs for ten minutes. Why didn't you give me a ticket first? You didn't give me any warning.'

'We don't have to give a warning if we find a car this badly parked. Two foot out from a double yellow line. Not to mention the fact that it's right across a bus lane. You passed your test yet have you, love? You're lucky we don't have the power to arrest you for dangerous driving.'

'Great. Thanks for that,' I said sarcastically. 'Look, can't you put it down again? Please? It's hardly off the ground yet. It's easier to put it down than pull it up. Put it down. Just this once. Just for me. I won't tell anyone you did it.'

He let his eyes run lazily down the length of my body which only made me pull the coat about me more tightly.

'Now, what possible reason could I have for wanting to put your car back down for you? What would make it worth my while?' He licked his lips. I crossed my arms. 'I could get into trouble for helping you. Why should I want to risk that?'

'It'll give you a feel-good feeling?' I tried. 'Look, I've got to get to the hospital,' I said, thinking quickly. 'My aunt has just been admitted to the Chelsea and Westminster with chronic appendicitis and I'm the only relative she has in town.'

'Yeah. Like I haven't heard that one before,' said the traffic warden, crossing his arms to match mine.

'Please. She really has. What if she dies or something while I'm standing here arguing with you? I could never forgive myself,' I sobbed. My eyes were starting to fill with tears, which must have helped my story because the speccy chap who had been working the hydraulics from inside the van popped his head out of the driver's window and said, 'We could do it, Bob. I could call the control room and say that the car had been moved before we got here. I haven't told them that we've started to shift it yet.'

'And then you'd owe me a favour,' said Bob, pressing his fat finger hard into my breast bone. 'So I'd have to take your phone number so that I could collect it.'

'Yeah. Of course,' I replied blithely, figuring that I would give him Mary's number just as soon as the wheels of Harriet's Mercedes hit tarmac again. That'd teach her to be such a good friend. Not.

'But we'll need to see your driver's documents first,' said the speccy one. 'I need proof that this car belongs to you before we can release it.'

I bit my lip. 'I haven't got anything like that with me. But I've got the keys so obviously it's my car, isn't it? Can't I send that other stuff on?'

'I'm afraid not. No proof. No car. Go back into your flat and get the papers and we'll put the car down while you run upstairs.' He clearly thought I had just come out of my own flat.

'But I don't live here. I was visiting a friend.'

'Call you out of your bath to visit him, did he?' snorted the fatter guy.

'She, actually. Look, can't you just put the bloody car down and pick on someone else!' I shouted, unable to wait any longer.

Bob's face hardened. 'You posh girls,' he said, poking me in the breast bone again. 'Seem to think that all you have to do is shout loud enough and everyone will step to it. Well, I'm here today to teach you a lesson in working class manners. You shout. You don't get. You don't got no papers for this car, you don't get. Now why don't you just call yourself a taxi to see your imaginary Auntie and get Daddy to drop by the car pound with his cheque book later on. Finish lifting her up, Phil. The girl ain't got no documents.'

'Please!' I begged. I even tried loosening the front of my coat a little to entice him into mercy. But to no avail. The creaking hydraulics steamed into action again and moments later Harriet's Mercedes settled on to the back of the van with an ominous clunk.

'See you at the car pound,' said the fat guy Bob as he clambered back into the tow-truck cab.

'You! You! You fat, ugly bastard,' I yelled. 'You mean, fat ugly bastard. You must be descended from Hitler. Your mother must have been Stalin. Do you get a kick out of picking on helpless women, is that it? You must be bloody gay!'

Bob the fat warden merely raised his eyebrows in an absurdly genteel gesture and wound up his window. I went to kick the tyre of the tow-truck and they nearly ran over my foot.

'I'll sue you. You bastards!' I screamed after their fast disappearing tail-lights.

'You damn right, they bastards,' said a rasta guy who was walking past. 'You should have got in the car. They can't take the car with you in it.'

'I know that now,' I snarled at him. You've never seen a six-foot-four man walk away from a five-foot-two girl so fast.

'Bastards,' I said once more, kicking a stone on the pavement and getting it wedged in the open toe of my stupid silver shoe. 'Bastards,' I muttered as I hopped on one foot while pulling the sharp-ended stone back out. My big toe was bleeding. As if it wasn't going to be hard enough to walk home as it was in my stupid too-small Manolo Blahniks. Call a taxi? I had, of course, no money on me at all. I had left my handbag in the glove compartment of the car. The only minute chink of silver lining was that I still had the keys to Harriet's flat in my hand. But only because I had been clutching them with the intention of gouging Mary's eyes out.

I looked up at the window of her flat now and was sure that I saw the tartily swagged curtains twitch. I imagined her watching with glee as I tried in vain to stop the car being towed away. Bitch. I flicked a finger at her empty window just in case she could still see me. Double bitch.

I took off my ridiculous sandals and began the long walk back to Harriet's flat. It wasn't too long before I started to see Hercules's point about pavements and bare feet, I can tell you. Never had less than half a mile seemed so bloody far.

And all the time I was having the worst possible inner dialogue with myself about Brian. Where had he gone? If he hadn't gone to Mary's flat, then I was really left without a clue as to his possible whereabouts. Perhaps he had got the next plane back home. Perhaps even as I felt I was doing serious penance on the streets of London, he was sitting in a coffee shop at Heathrow waiting to board a flight back to JFK.

I had blown things so badly.

CHAPTER TWENTY-FOUR

Brian was sitting on the doorstep of Harriet's flat when I finally limped into the square.

'Oh, Brian!' I cried, flinging my arms around his neck. 'Oh, Brian. You've come back to me. I was so worried.'

'Don't get excited,' he warned me. 'I'm only back here because when I went to check into a hotel I discovered that I left my wallet in my other jacket which is up there in your . . . or whoever's it is, flat. Otherwise, I was just going to get you to send my luggage over, believe me.'

'But you're here now. You will stay won't you? You'll give me a chance to explain.'

'I don't know if I want you to explain, Lizzie.'

'Oh, but you'll laugh so much when I do,' I said, as playfully as possible. 'It was all a set-up. Hilarious really.'

'I certainly feel as though I've been set up,' he snorted.

'You know that the girl presenting that show was one of Mary's clients?'

'Yes,' he said cautiously.

'Well, she's new to the business and she's got so much competition that Mary wanted to make sure that her first show really went with a bang. She needed some scandal, you see. But you know what English people are like. Even when an English girl is telling her fiancé that she's pregnant by his brother, everyone keeps their cool and no one throws any punches. It's not like Jerry Springer, where you can get punched for saying that you dislike your neighbour's choice of net curtains. Mary was afraid that the show wouldn't be very interesting, which is why she called me yesterday morning.'

Brian looked doubtful.

'I said I'd be a stooge for her, you see. I said I'd pretend to have done something awful to get the show going a bit. All that stuff about me not owning the flat is rubbish. Mary and I came up with the idea while we were in the kitchen at her dinner party. I do really own this flat. I was just pretending not to for the cameras.'

'You did a very realistic impression of someone who had just been rumbled,' Brian commented.

'I was petrified of being on TV. I think that helped my performance.'

'And if it was a set-up, why didn't you tell me?'

Good question. But the long walk across Hyde Park had given me time to come up with an answer.

'I felt really awful about having to do that to you. But if you'd known what was coming, you wouldn't have reacted half as spectacularly as you did. You've never been much of an actor, have you? If you'd known, it would have been so obvious that the scene was set up. Mary would have killed me. But as it was, she's already seen the edited version of the show and she's absolutely ecstatic with the results. Sends her love,' I added for authenticity.

'Does she?' said Brian. 'Well, in future you can tell her that I don't appreciate being made to look a fool for someone else's career enhancement. That show won't be going out in the States, will it?'

'I don't think so,' I assured him.

'Good.' His frown relaxed a little. Had he gone for it?

'But what I don't understand,' he continued. 'Is why you didn't try to stop me when I stormed out of the studio? Or why none of the production staff stopped me and took me aside to explain the real situation?'

'That was a major oversight,' I told him. 'And I'm sure heads will roll. Do you want a drink?' I certainly needed one. All this rubbish about having been acting was the most difficult role I had played for a long while.

'Do you think we were really convincing on the small screen?' Brian asked, as he accepted a large whisky with ice from Harriet's cabinet.

'Absolutely. I'm expecting contracts to pour in,' I added with a forced laugh. 'Now, what do you want to do on your last night in London?'

'Find out what happened to your suit,' he said

'Oh, that old thing? I took it to the cleaners.'

'You're bizarre, he said affectionately.

'And after that?'

'Perhaps we should catch up with Mary,' he suggested. 'After this afternoon's performance I think she owes the pair of us dinner. Shall we call her?'

'Er, I don't think so,' I said hurriedly. 'When I popped by after the recording to see if you'd gone there, she was up to her eyes in paperwork. One of her clients is just about to sign a new recording deal with a record company in America so she's got to stay in and call people in Los Angeles all evening. Time difference, you know.'

'I know about the time difference,' said Brian. 'So why don't we pick up a take-away and keep her company while she makes her calls?'

'She wouldn't like that. These calls are confidential.'

'We could promise not to listen.'

'Look,' I said, my tension coming out in a little snap. 'She said that she really needs to work tonight. She's sorry to have to miss you on your last night in the UK but she's sure she'll see you in America very very soon. OK?'

'OK,' said Brian apologetically.

'So we'll go out on our own, shall we? And get an early night so that you're ready for your flight home,' I added coquettishly, as I twisted a curl of his thick black hair around my forefinger.

'I'm not flying until the afternoon, so we can stay out as late as you like.'

'I don't want to stay out late,' I told him, planting a kiss on his mouth.

When I pulled away, he was smiling like a baby. I muttered a silent thank you to whoever it was who was watching over me. Lizzie Jordan, the Teflon girl, gets out of a sticky situation yet again.

We didn't make it to the restaurant. We were lying top to tail on Harriet's leather sofa having watched the sky turn red with the sunset before London was plunged into inky black night as I told Brian how unhappy I had been on the last occasion when we spent a 'last night' together.

'But you won't have to wait six years to see me again this time,' he told me.

Then the doorbell rang. I had never heard the doorbell to Harriet's flat before so it didn't immediately register that someone was trying to attract my attention.

'Isn't that the doorbell?' Brian asked as I continued to reminisce while apparently taking no notice of the visitor.

'It can't have been,' I said, looking towards the ringer as if it had just sounded the bell for Armageddon.

'I could have sworn it was,' said Brian, as the bell sounded again.

'I don't know who it could be. It's very late.'

'Maybe it's the pizza guy,' said Brian.

'I haven't ordered a pizza.'

'I was trying to be funny.'

But he wasn't making me laugh.

The doorbell requested my attention again. Urgently, this time. But what would I do if it was one of Harriet's busy-body friends? What if it was Harriet herself, having forgotten her keys?

'Aren't you going to answer it?'

'I don't know. I mean, I'm not expecting anyone. What if it's an armed robber?' I said, hoping I didn't sound too ridiculous. 'There've been quite a few incidents lately. A lot of single women live in these flats. The robbers come round in the middle of the night posing as people from the gas board in search of a leak.'

'Then why don't you have a look through this,' Brian said, pointing out the little screen that would show me who was waiting in the lobby. 'We'll see if it's a robber who won't let off ringing the bell.' His voice rose very slightly in exasperation because the bell was now ringing without ceasing, as if the caller was leaning upon it and had forgotten that somewhere the bell would be making a terrible noise. Brian pressed the button that would show the caller's face.

'I don't know him,' I said automatically.

But Brian said, 'It's Bill.'

CHAPTER TWENTY-FIVE

'**B**ill? It can't be.'

But indeed it was. Now that he turned towards the camera I could see him clearly. He was a little thinner perhaps. He definitely had less hair than when I last saw him. But it was unmistakably Bill. He put the flea-bitten fedora he had been carrying back on his head and made as if to leave.

'Wait, wait,' said Brian excitedly, pressing on the button that would allow Bill into the hall. 'Wait. Bill!'

But Bill was already back on the street. Brian flew to the window, threw it open and let out an ear-splitting whistle. 'Bill! Hang on. We're up here!'

Like Clint Eastwood taking one last look at a town where he has just left all the menfolk dead or dying, Bill turned slowly and looked up towards the flat, tipping back the brim of his hat with one finger in lieu of a smoking gun.

'Hey, Brian-man!' he shouted back. 'I'm coming on up.'

*   *   *

What a disaster! My last night with Brian and Bill had turned up to play gooseberry. Who had given him the address? Well, that was easily answered. Mary had obviously sent him round, knowing that any plans I had would be ruined while Brian spent the rest of the night slumped on the leather sofa with his other old buddy, smoking gigantic doobs as Bill regaled us with long and rambling stories about hill-tribes in the Andes or rampant diarrhoea in south-east Asia. A night with Bill was the most effective contraceptive money couldn't buy.

'This is so lucky,' said Brian. Unlike me, he was very excited. Totally thrilled in fact. 'This is fantastic. I'm going to get to see the whole gang after all. I haven't seen Bill for six years. This is incredible.'

I nodded in half-hearted agreement. It was incredible. I hadn't seen Bill for six years either, but I wouldn't have minded too much if I'd had to wait just one more day for the pleasure.

Brian opened the door to Harriet's flat and shouted encouragement to Bill as he climbed the four flights of stairs to the penthouse. For someone who could be found jogging up Kilimanjaro at least twice a year, he was taking an awfully long time to cover a climb that even I had become quite used to over the past few days. Finally, his fedora came into view. He was walking terribly slowly, with his head bent low.

'Must be stoned,' I commented in annoyance.

'He's not the Messiah! He's a very naughty boy!'

Brian shrieked à la Monty Python's Terry Jones when Bill lifted his face and tried to smile at us. But the old in-joke didn't help him to crack into his familiar grin. Instead of punching Brian on the arm as he might once have done, Bill shook Brian's hand in a very formal way.

'Hello, Brian. Hello, Lizzie,' he said, turning his big black eyes towards me. When he took off his hat, I saw at once that he had been crying.

'I'm really sorry to disturb you guys in the middle of the night, but I didn't know who else to go to. I found your new address scribbled on a pad by Mary's phone, Liz. She's been taken into hospital. They think she's taken an overdose.'

I felt as though someone had taken one of those big rubberised hammers to the back of my knees and taken my feet out from under me. I backed into the flat and collapsed on to the leather sofa.

'Which hospital?' Brian was asking. 'What did she take? Why?'

As Bill told his story, I could hear only snatches of what he said. The conversation racing through my mind was the showdown Mary and I had after the television recording. It *had* been a terrible argument. She had told me that she wasn't happy. But Mary had never been really happy, not in all the years I had known her. It was part of her personality, wasn't it? If she won a million pounds, she would complain that her purse wasn't big enough to carry it in. Miserable was her natural state. There had been no reason at all for me to suspect that this time she really did feel suicidal.

'Why would she try to kill herself?' Brian asked again. 'We saw her just the other night. She was on top of the world.'

'She was always good at hiding her true feelings,' Bill said solemnly.

'No, she wasn't,' I protested. 'She never pretended that she was happy. Miserable was her middle name. But she never wanted to kill herself.'

'Perhaps she didn't tonight. She didn't leave a note.'

Bill had found her. He had been passing through London *en route* to Nepal and called in at her flat to wash some shorts and eat her food. When she didn't answer the door, he got someone else in the building to let him in, intending to sit on the landing outside Mary's flat until she came home. But the door to her flat was open.

'I found her face down on the coffee table,' he said. 'The door to her flat wasn't locked. I just walked in and there she was, lying on the coffee table with a rolled up tenner in her nose.'

'God, how awful,' Brian breathed. 'You mean she overdosed on *that* sort of drug?'

Bill nodded. 'Last time I saw her she promised me she was going to get cleaned up. She even went to some secret clinic in Malta.'

'I thought she was having anti-cellulite treatment in Malta,' I interrupted, and was immediately aware how stupid that must sound. Bill snorted, though not too unkindly considering. 'I didn't know she was using so much,' I added quietly. 'I thought she just took coke when she went out. She told me it was purely for recreational purposes.'

'I'm sure it was. At first. That's how every addict starts. Will you come to the hospital with me? Her family are on their way but I don't know when they'll arrive. I'd hate for Mary to wake up and find herself all alone.' Brian had already fetched my coat.

'So, she will wake up?' I said hopefully. 'She is going to be OK isn't she?'

'I think it will be a while before we find out just how many internal organs she's fried this time.'

In the cab to the hospital (I hadn't even considered how I was going to afford to get Harriet's car out of the pound again) both Bill and Brian were silent. I sat between them, holding hands with both. Every so often, Bill or Brian would squeeze my hand as if to remind me that we were all still together. United and reunited.

But I couldn't help being sure that they knew Mary's overdose was my fault. The television show fiasco had been a cry for help. She wanted to stop me on my road to happiness before I waltzed out of sight and left her alone in her despair. She had wanted to stop me and ask me to help her. But I hadn't been able to see beyond my own embarrassment and anger. My refusal to help her had pushed her to a suicide attempt.

I couldn't stop going over all the conversations Mary and I had had over the past week. Were there clues before she broke down when confronted about Arabella's stupid TV show? She had definitely been snappish at my birthday lunch but she had explained that away as PMT. She hadn't seemed on the edge of a nervous breakdown when she had told me in such a matter-of-fact manner that Arabella would be her bridesmaid at her wedding to Mitchell.

'She was supposed to be getting married,' I squeaked, as the taxi pulled up under the brightly lit canopy where ambulances discharged their limping passengers.

Bill and Brian looked at me as if I had told them that Mary was a victim of extra-terrestrial abduction.

'She was. She told me on Saturday night. She's supposed to be getting married to Mitchell.'

'What? The gay one?' asked Bill.

'Yes. The gay one,' said Brian.

The gay one. Was I the only person who hadn't noticed that?

Bill led us straight to the ward where Mary had been taken. The nurse, recognising him, stopped us and said, 'She's woken up. But her parents are with her now.'

I breathed a secret sigh of relief. It seemed as though now that her parents had arrived, the responsibility had been taken from us.

Two people emerged from the room where Mary was being kept under observation. The man, tanned from a holiday someplace warm, kept trying to put his arm around the woman's shoulders but she refused all his advances. She was crying openly. He was red around the eyes.

'She did it because of you,' the woman sobbed as they passed by. 'Because you keep going off and having stupid affairs the whole time.'

'You've had your affairs too.'

'Only in retaliation. God, Bunny, you're so selfish.'

'Me, selfish? You're her mother. Where were you when she needed someone to talk to?'

'She had my mobile number. She knew she could have called me at any time of the day or night.'

I could see that Bill was wondering whether he ought to interrupt the fight to ask Mr and Mrs Bagshot how their daughter was, but he thought better of it and instead made his way to the door of Mary's room.

'Are you coming?' he asked me. 'Two of us can go in at a time.'

'Take Brian with you. I'd quite like to see her on my own.'

Brian followed Bill, leaving me alone to read the poster advertising the Samaritans which was starting to peel away from the wall. Bit late if they're reading it in here, I thought.

Why had Mary tried to top herself? When I took off her borrowed suit and left it on the floor of her apartment, she had been giving at least as good as she got from me in terms of blind fury. She didn't seem like someone who would be attempting to commit suicide just eight hours later. What she said about my having it all while she was emotionally bereft was just another one of her set pieces intended to make me feel guilty enough to forgive her for having humiliated me so utterly on national TV, wasn't it?

I mean, ever since I first met Mary she seemed to be determined to see the dark side to everything; no silver linings for her, but there had never been any hint that she would try to take her own life. There was always some new skinny goth to lust after or a Bauhaus reunion concert around the corner to look forward to. And she was so squeamish. She couldn't take a single aspirin without gagging, let alone enough to kill her. And then there was the time she had fainted when I trapped my fingers in a door and had to have a fingernail cut off. That was hardly the kind of attitude that was going to help her top herself. No, Mary had always seemed more likely to be one of those people who would bore the rest of the planet to death with her problems before she took any action about them, positive or otherwise.

Now Brian and Bill were coming out of her hospital bedroom, joking nervously like two small boys who have just got off a ghost train. They've spent the whole ride holding on to each other tightly through fear and now they have to pretend that they weren't really that afraid.

'Is she OK?'

'She's fine. Physically. They think she'll be going home tomorrow. But she's got to see a shrink first.'

'Did she say why she did it?'

'I don't think she really knows,' said Brian. 'Look. She's waiting for you. You'd better go on in.'

The walk to her room seemed interminable.

She was like a tiny china doll propped up against the big white pillows in a ridiculously frilled nightdress that her mother had supplied. Her wrists, from which opaque plastic tubes led to bags of saline, were crossed neatly on her lap in front of her. Her face was white, but for the big black rings around her eyes where fatigue and old mascara had joined forces to make her into a passable panda.

'Hello, Lizzie,' she said. Her voice seemed incredibly small and far away.

I sat down on the chair next to her bed. For a moment, we just looked at each other. It was unreal, seeing the girl I had been rowing with so violently that afternoon suddenly looking so breakable. So broken.

'I'm sorry to do this to you all,' she began. 'I know you wanted to have a special last evening with Brian.' She sniffed away a tear.

'Why did you do it?' I asked her in a whisper. 'Why did you try to kill yourself?'

'I wasn't trying to kill myself,' she protested. 'I just felt so lonely. I was trying to make myself feel better with a couple of lines.'

'A couple? Bill said you had a novel's worth of lines chopped out on the coffee table.'

'I only managed three. But I'd been drinking as well. I think that's what did it. They had to pump out my stomach with some horrible charcoal stuff. I feel terrible. Imagine your worst ever hangover times twenty.'

I nodded sympathetically.

'Twenty million that is.'

'You'll soon start to feel better,' I promised her banally.

'I've got a feeling that the nightmare has only just begun. This is bound to get into the papers.'

'Why should it?'

'Because Mitchell is going to come out of the closet tomorrow. Coupled with my suicide attempt, it's a perfect story for the silly season.'

'You once told me there's no such thing as bad publicity.'

'That's what I say to my clients. I'm not sure it's actually true.'

'Look, I'm sorry for what happened earlier on. For the argument. I've spent the whole night thinking that this is my fault. Is it?' My voice came out whiny and I hated myself for having to ask. But I needed to know all the same.

Mary shook her head. 'No. Not really.'

'Is that the truth?'

'You know it is. In fact, I had a good laugh when the car got towed away.'

'You saw that?'

'I called the tow-truck. But it wasn't your fault, Lizzie. You've been the best friend ever. It's me who should be apologising to you.'

I grabbed her hands gratefully, nearly yanking out one of her drips.

'Careful,' she winced but she squeezed my hands back.

'You're my best friend too,' I told her. 'I want to do anything I can to help you get better.'

'I think I'm starting to realise that there are some things I'm going to have to work on by myself,' she half-smiled.

'We can work on them together.'

She squeezed my hands again, then let me go. 'Look, you don't have to stay here all night. I know that Brian is going home tomorrow. I swear I didn't do this deliberately to keep you from getting your oats.'

'Thank you for not telling him.'

'I think I can keep my mouth shut for another twenty-four hours. Come and see me when he's gone. You can give me all the gory details then.'

I promised I would. Then I left. I wondered if I should stay for longer, but Mary told me that she felt exhausted and wanted to be alone.

Brian and Bill were still sitting in the waiting room, swapping reminiscences. They looked up at me expectantly.

'She says we should go. She wants to get some sleep.'

Bill had to go anyway to catch his flight to Nepal, leaving me and Brian alone to watch the sun come up over the hospital car park as we had a coffee in the visitors' cafeteria. He was quiet. As you can probably imagine. He had just seen one of his oldest friends looking like a barely animated corpse.

'Liz, what is going on?' he asked.

I shuddered. Before I realised that it was a rhetorical question.

Back at Harriet's flat, Brian took my hand and led me into the bedroom. He had been stroking my hair in the taxi back from the hospital and now he continued in the dark gloom beneath the canopies of Harriet's four-poster bed. I curled my body against his, breathing in the warm smell of him. He tilted my face towards his and kissed me tenderly.

Slowly, he unbuttoned my shirt and slid it from my shoulders. He kissed a path down across my neck to my breastbone. He cupped my breasts and murmured loving words into my burning ears.

The years we had spent apart had done nothing to diminish the heat between us when we found ourselves together again. We made love as gracefully and easily as old dancing partners, responding to each other's moves as though they had been choreographed. Brian knew exactly what to do to make me melt in his arms. When we came that early morning, we came together of course.

Afterwards, we resolved to get a couple of hours' sleep before Brian had to get ready to catch his flight, but

I was actually awake when I heard the sound of a key turning in the front door of Harriet's flat. I had been lying on my side, looking at Brian's profile as though I was trying to burn the image of him into my memory for the lonely Balham nights ahead. Except I was planning that there wouldn't be too many of those. As soon as I had paid off the damage Brian's visit had done to my credit card, I would buy a one-way ticket to New York and my brilliant future. I really thought I had just about pulled the scam off.

Even as the front door was creaking open, I planted a kiss on Brian's sleeping forehead.

'Herky? Herky?'

The landing light clicked on. Though it was morning, some parts of Harriet's flat were still terribly dark and shady. 'Herky? Where are you, darling? Mummy's home.'

I sat bolt upright in bed. The clock on the bedside table told me in big luminous numbers that it was quarter past ten in the morning. Harriet was not due back for another twenty-four hours at least.

'Herky? Are you hiding from me? Where are you hiding from your mummy, sweetheart? Are you having a little sulk because I've been away for so long?'

I didn't know what to do. What should I do? Should I race out into the hallway and intercept her before she got as far as the bedroom? I didn't have time to decide. Before I could pull on anything to cover my modesty, Harriet had opened the bedroom door and turned on the light.

'I bet you're in he-re!' she sang.

Brian woke up instantly.

'Hey!' he shouted. 'Who the fuck are you?'

Harriet went white.

'Well, who the . . . who the blinking heck are you?' she replied.

Brian jumped out of bed with a pillow across his privates and before I could stop him, he was striding menacingly towards Harriet with the nearest thing to hand he thought he might be able to clock her one with. Her, undoubtedly priceless, rose vase.

'Brian,' I shouted. 'No.'

'Lizzie,' Harriet shouted.

And the world went into slow motion as pieces fell into place all round.

CHAPTER TWENTY-SIX

'I am Lady Harriet Corbett and this is my flat.'
'You're mistaken, old lady,' said Brian.
'I'm afraid she's not,' I had to admit.

Harriet looked as if she had swallowed a goldfish. I wasn't sure whether it was the shock of catching us in her bed or the indignity of being called 'old'.

But that was how it finally caught up with me. To cut a long story short, I told Brian simply to take everything I had told him and know that the opposite was true. There was no point in trying to give my admissions and apologies in any further detail now. My best friend was in hospital and my boss was back in her flat.

So what did Brian do? Well, at first he had a weird, weary sort of smile on his face as he waited for me to say that this was just another of my crazy, hilarious set-ups, all designed to make his holiday in London more interesting. When it became clear that wasn't going to happen this time, that finally he had heard the truth, the weather over Brian's expression turned first cloudy and then thunderous.

'You really have been lying to me all the time,' he said slowly.

I couldn't do anything but nod.

'Do you take me for some kind of fool?'

He spoke very quietly and somehow that was even more frightening than hearing him shout.

'I can't believe this.'

He reached to pick up his boxer shorts from the floor and tugged them on.

'I think we ought to get up, don't you?'

He threw me my dressing-gown. Well, it was actually Harriet's dressing-gown, as he would soon find out.

Harriet remained in the doorway, not knowing where to look and yet seeming unable to leave us alone. It was like something out of a seventies farce. I toyed with the idea of jumping through the window to make my escape. Four floors up. It wasn't such a great idea. Instead, I pulled the dressing-gown tightly around me and followed Brian and Harriet into the sitting room where they stood on either side of the fireplace while I, in the hot seat that was the sofa, wilted beneath their hostile glares.

Impossible to believe that only hours before Harriet had turned up early, Brian and I had been making plans for a future together. If I had been an employee he would have sacked me. If I had been his child, he would have had me adopted. As his girlfriend, I was definitely finished.

'Why?' he asked.

Good question.

'Because I love you,' I began hopefully. 'Because I wanted things to be just like they used to be. Because I didn't think you'd want to know the real me. The girl with the dead-end job . . .'

'In my company,' Harriet added helpfully.

'With a horrible flat.'

'In Balham,' said Harriet. 'Not here in Notting Hill. This is mine.'

'And the Mercedes?' Brian asked.

'That's mine too. Where is it, incidentally?'

'In the pound where it was when you left for Spain,' I snapped. Brian shot me a look. I was lying again. 'OK. So I borrowed that too and I parked it illegally,' I had to admit. 'It got towed away yesterday but I'll pay to get it back.'

'I don't want to hear any more of this,' said Brian. 'I'm going to get my stuff together and go straight to the airport. I might be able to get an earlier flight.'

'Brian. No.' I reached out to touch his arm as he passed but he brushed me off quite brutally.

'I'm very sorry about all this, Lady Corbett,' he said. 'You have my word that had I known we were trespassing on your property, I would not have come here at all.'

'Apology accepted,' Harriet nodded graciously and Brian left the room to pack. I strained to follow him but Harriet, who was surprisingly strong for someone so dizzy, held me back in the sitting room.

'I think you had better tell me,' she began in a voice trembling with anticipation of the awful, 'just what you have done with my dog.'

As I opened my mouth to tell her, I heard the front door to the flat slam shut. I raced to the window just in time to see Brian emerge from the building into the sunlight. He must have thrown his clothes into his bag any old how. He wanted to be gone. He wanted to be gone right away. And he didn't want to say goodbye.

A hot tear inched its way on to my cheek. My lover, my true love, my future, was driving away from me in a London cab.

'Brian!!!'

But Harriet wouldn't let me follow him. She told me that if I didn't take her to see Hercules right away she would call the police and have me arrested for squatting in her flat and stealing her car. She was like a lioness in defence of her cubs when it came to Hercules.

'Brian!!!' I yelled one more time in vain. He didn't look up.

'No use shouting after him,' Harriet told me. 'I think you've really cooked your goose with that one.'

In the cab to Balham she softened up a little when she realised just how inconsolable I was.

'Lover's tantrum,' she told me then. 'He'll be back when he's had a chance to calm down.'

I sniffed and nodded but I knew that Harriet wasn't right.

By the time we were within a mile of her beloved dog. Harriet was actually apologising for having blown my gaff.

'I'm sorry I had to come back early,' she told me. 'Bunny and I were having an absolutely wonderful time. He even told me that he would leave his wife and set up home with me. I know he's said that before, but this time, I think I believed him. Anyway, all that's gone out of the window now.'

'What happened?' I asked. Though I really didn't care.

'He got a phone call from his wife, who was at the Chelsea and Westminster hospital with their daughter. Apparently, she'd tried to commit suicide, the little fool. And of course Bunny's wife expected him to rush back right away. I told him that when I was a girl I tried to kill myself at least once a fortnight. She's just seeking attention, I told him. But he wouldn't listen to a word of it. And before I knew what was happening, he was on the next flight home. I had to wait seven hours for the next available flight home.'

'Poor Harriet,' I said sympathetically. 'Still, I'm sure he'll call you as soon as he knows his daughter is OK.'

'I wouldn't count on it. He'll have to play happy families for at least a month now. The selfish girl. It's not even as though she's a child any more. She was twenty-seven last birthday. You'd think she'd have got over the histrionics by now.'

Which was very funny coming from Harriet, who could throw a tantrum over a difficult-to-dislodge staple.

'Bunny was forever telling me what a success his little girl is. Runs some kind of agency for footballers and pop stars. MB PR. Ever heard of it?'

Mary Bagshot Public Relations. You bet. Bunny was Mary's father. How on earth was it possible that of all the married men in London, Harriet had picked Mary's father?

'I think I know the firm,' I groaned.

'Well, she's ruined my life,' said Harriet.

Ditto, I thought.

'I don't suppose I'll ever find a man like Bunny again. I don't know what I'd do if I didn't have Hercules. Are you sure he's safe in Balham?'

'What could possibly have happened to him in Balham?' I said.

'Hercules has gone.'

Seema's eyes were ringed with worry.

'Gone potties?' said Harriet hopefully.

'Gone walkies,' said Seema. 'On his own.'

The smile on Harriet's face hardened as she waited for an explanation. A good one.

'It's not my fault,' Seema began. 'I didn't let him

out. Fat Joe did it. I told him not to. He attached that bloody chip thing to Hercules's collar and left him in the middle of Clapham Common to see if he could find his way home.'

The chip thing. The tracking device that Joe had been making in the middle of the night. He had attached it to Hercules's collar with the intention of seeing whether he could plot the dog's route home. Except that home to Hercules was not a stinking terraced house in Balham. As soon as he was off the lead, the daft pooch set his internal compass in the direction of Harriet's flat overlooking Hyde Park. Within half an hour – despite the pavements he would have to cross – Hercules and the tracking device were out of Fat Joe's range. When Seema got back from her visit to the Tate with Richard, Joe told her what had happened right away. They'd searched the Common all evening. Seema, Joe and Richard. They gave up when it got really dark but began again as soon as dawn broke.

Harriet exploded into tears.

'My baby. My poor baby!' she wailed, punctuated by Seema's chorus of 'It's not my fault.' It was like all the worst parts of a Gilbert and Sullivan operetta made flesh.

I dragged Seema into the kitchen, leaving Harriet sobbing on the only patch of the sofa that was remotely sanitary, and closed the door that had never quite fitted behind us.

'I trusted you,' I snarled at her as soon as we were out of sight.

'I told Fat Joe not to let him out,' she whined.

'Is Fat Joe out there looking for Hercules now?' I asked.

'I think Fat Joe's under his bed at the moment.'

'You had better sort this out, Seema. Because I hold you totally responsible. This wouldn't have happened if you hadn't been out with my boyfriend!'

'What?' she stopped whining and stared at me. 'What did you just say?'

'Don't pretend you don't know what I'm talking about. I saw you, on Sunday. At the Tate. With Richard. And you were all over him.'

'Well, I won't deny that I was in the Tate with your boyfriend,' she said defensively. 'But I was certainly not all over him.'

'You were. You had your arm through his arm and you were batting your eyelashes so hard you could have turned back the tide.'

'I was not.'

'You were wearing your leather trousers,' I said, which was the ultimate accusation. Seema's leather trousers were her official first-date garb, especially when she had a first date with someone she wanted more than a free dinner out of. 'What do you have to say about that?'

I thought I had her bang to rights. But instead of admitting her guilt she squared up to me.

'I have to say that just about everything else I own was covered in dog hairs. From the dog that *you* were supposed to be looking after, remember? Except that you couldn't do what you had been asked to do because your ex-boyfriend, who you wanted to get back together with, is allergic to King Charles Spaniels. Ring any bells?'

'Phobic. Not allergic,' I quibbled.

'Whatever. *I* was doing *you* a favour. And I was doing you another favour by trying to keep *your* boyfriend occupied while you had a dirty weekend with someone else. I wasn't flirting with him. Far from it. He spent the whole day talking about nothing but you.'

'He wasn't talking about me when I saw you in the Tate,' I persisted.

'God, Lizzie, what did you want him to be doing, pulling out clumps of his hair while he wails your name from the top of the British Telecom tower? Trust me, he was really pissed off that you refused to let him meet your American friend. I think he guessed what was going on. He said that he was having second thoughts about how you felt about him. He said he was thinking about telling you that he didn't want to carry on with your relationship. It was me who persuaded him that he was being ridiculously suspicious. I persuaded him that he should just wait until Brian went home and everything would be great again. I was trying to help you out. Keeping all your bets hedged. That's what I was doing in the Tate on Sunday afternoon. Though god only knows why I bothered. Richard's too nice a bloke to be messed around.'

I snorted.

'I didn't know it until I spent the afternoon with him.

I always thought he was just another bog-standard bloke with no interests except Denise Van Outen and lager. But he's not like that at all. He's really knowledgeable. He's interested in art and music and architecture. Do you know that he knows the names of all the people who designed the most famous buildings in London? He's amazingly well-read. And he's very funny too.'

'I know,' I groaned.

'And he's not so bad-looking either. When we'd finished at the Tate I dragged him to Harvey Nicks and made him try on some decent clothes. I've made him promise that he's going to buy some next time he gets paid.'

'He could do with a haircut too.'

'Yeah. But what's most important, Liz, is that he really loves you. He says he's never met anyone to compare with you. He'd do anything to make you happy. Including take a day off work to search for that bloody dog.'

'What?'

'When Hercules didn't turn up last night, I called Richard at work. He booked himself out of the office and promised to start searching right away. He should be here soon. Are you going to make yourself scarce before he arrives? Only I don't think it's fair that he should have to find out the truth about Brian now, not when he's gone to such efforts to help you out. You are going to chuck Richard now that everything's back on with Brian, I assume?'

'It's not. Brian's gone. When Harriet came home early I had to tell him the truth and he's gone.'

Seema sighed. 'It was inevitable, I suppose.'

'No, it wasn't. I nearly did it. If Harriet hadn't come back early. If bloody Mary hadn't overdosed on coke and booze so that Harriet's lover had to fly back from Spain to be with her, I would have got away with it. Why did Mary's dad have to be Harriet's bit on the side? They've ruined things for me.'

'For heaven's sake, I don't think you can blame them,' said Seema.

'Well, who should I blame?' I asked her.

'I can't believe you're asking me that. You set up a ridiculous number of lies and you're blaming everybody else for getting on with their lives around you. Aren't you in the least bit concerned that your friend nearly died last night?'

'She wouldn't have died.'

'Well, if she had, at least you wouldn't have had to worry about her telling Brian the truth about you, would you? That seems to be all you care about. You've used everybody. You used Harriet's flat, Mary's clothes, even me as your dog-sitter. You've lied to everybody. Not just Brian. You lied to Harriet and to Richard.'

'I didn't lie to Harriet.'

'You would have done if she hadn't come home to find you in her bed,' Seema pointed out.

'I just wanted to be happy,' I shouted. 'Why shouldn't I get what I want for once?'

'Because you didn't deserve it this time?'

'Why not? What's deserving got to do with anything? Does Mary deserve to be so bloody rich? Does Harriet? Why should they have such great lives for doing absolutely nothing?'

'Great lives? Mary's so lonely she tries to kill herself and Harriet has to make do with another woman's man. Lizzie, you don't know when you're on to a good thing. You've got a family who loves you. You had a boyfriend who worshipped you. The real you.'

She put her arm around my shoulders, sure that she had made a point I would understand. It was like the night when she had tried to convince me that our flat was all right really. She wanted me to be happy with what I had. Look, she was telling me, count your blessings. But right then, I still wasn't ready to.

'I'm sick of this existence,' I snarled. 'I'm better than this fucking flat. I deserve a better life.'

Seema pulled her arm away from me again. 'What you deserve, Lizzie Jordan,' she hissed, is a bloody hard slap.'

'Why don't you just shut up?' I said inadvisedly.

And she gave me the slap I deserved.

'Ow!' I balled up my fist and thumped her in return.

But while I had scrapped with my brother Colin throughout my childhood, Seema had had sisters to fight with. Before I could get another thump in, she had grabbed hold of my hair and twisted it hard.

'Don't even think about it,' she roared.

'Are you going to help me find my dog?' Harriet interrupted. When she saw Seema holding me in a headlock she got an instant migraine.

'Put each other down!' she shouted. 'How can you girls fight like children when nobody knows where poor Hercules has gone?!'

Seema let go of my hair and shoved me away.

'Well, now are you going to help me find my dog?' asked Harriet again. The look on her face told me that if I didn't, she would have my skin flayed off my back and made into a collar for her winter coat.

'I don't know where to start,' I admitted.

Suddenly the house was filled with a whirring and crackling noise.

'I've done it!' Fat Joe yelled at the top of his voice. 'Come in number seven, your time is up.'

Harriet clutched her throat in horror again as Fat Joe came thundering towards us in his sky-cam gear, cap pulled down over his eyes, a pair of swimming goggles that he liked to think gave him night-vision over the top of the cap.

'Operation Hercules is back on line,' he told us. His face was deeply, deadly serious and yet more animated than I had seen it in a long time. 'I stayed up all night to increase the range of my signal receiver,' he chattered. 'They said it couldn't be done, but I took the . . .'

There followed something which sounded like 'I took the doo-berry out of the what-sit and stuck it in the eugynon' but the upshot of this nonsense was that Joe had picked up a signal from Hercules's tracker collar again. And what's more, it wasn't moving.

Was that a good sign or a bad one? Perhaps the collar had just fallen off. But perhaps the dog was dead. Whatever, with Fat Joe's portable tracking system to guide us, we set out to follow the signal and to find out whether there was still a live pedigree dog attached to it.

We crossed the Common and raced down streets that I had never been down before, quickening our step as the bleeps got closer together. As the streets became less salubrious as we neared Clapham Junction, Seema clutched her tail-ended comb like a dagger in case we had to attempt a daring rescue from a mean dog-smuggling gang.

Harriet clipped along in her high heels beside Joe, saying nothing, her mouth set in a determined line. She had only one thing on her mind.

As did I. Every time a plane passed overhead I wondered if Brian was on it. I wanted to tell Harriet to stuff this stupid dog hunt and race to the airport. I might still have time to see Brian before he left. I might have time to explain. But Harriet had threatened to make me explain all to the police already.

And it was outside the police station that we found ourselves now.

'It's the police station,' said Seema. She was very quick.

'The signal's coming from inside,' Fat Joe insisted.

'You think Hercules is in here?' Harriet asked him.

A helmet-less bobby was already peering through the station window at our unlikely gathering. A looney in combat gear, two girls dressed for a night at Stringfellows and a faintly shabby aristocrat in high-heeled toe-less sandals. None of us were dressed for a Tuesday afternoon on Lavender Hill.

'Can I help you?' the bobby asked.

'My dog has been kidnapped!' Harriet told him.

'Oh, so it's *your* dog.'

CHAPTER TWENTY-SEVEN

H arriet pushed past the policeman and raced into the station like a mother who has just discovered that the son she thought she had lost at sea may still in fact be alive.

'Where is he?' she begged the woman behind the desk, who was trying to take down details of a car theft at the time. 'Where is he? I've lost my baby,' Harriet explained to the man she had pushed in front of.

'Well, in that case,' he said, stepping out of her way. He was rather less sympathetic when the duty sergeant brought Harriet's 'baby' round from the back.

The sergeant put Hercules down on the tiled floor, where the little dog stood with shaking legs. Hercules looked at Harriet and blinked, as if he too couldn't believe that they were really about to be reunited.

'Is that him?' the sergeant asked.

'Oh, yes. It's him.' Cue that movie moment. Hercules suddenly leapt into Harriet's arms and smothered her face with sloppy pink-tongued kisses. 'I'm sorry I

left you with that nasty lady,' she told him, referring, I guessed, to me. 'I'll never ever ever leave
you again.'

'Where did you find him?' asked Seema.

'This gentleman here brought him in.'

As if that day couldn't get any worse. In the corner
of the waiting room sat the man who had tried to
nick me for not pooper scooping when I first brought
Hercules home.

'And the man who was trying to kidnap him,' the
sergeant continued.

Someone was really trying to kidnap Harriet's
dog?

'That's her!' shouted the colonel when he caught
me staring at him. 'She's the ring-leader. You should
be taking her into custody too.'

'What?'

'Perhaps you might be of some use to our inquiries,'
the sergeant nodded. 'What do you know about a
drug addict called Richard Adams? He's the man that
the colonel here caught trying to kidnap this dog.'

Drug addict Richard Adams? Not my Richard Adams?

'Richard Adams is my boyfriend,' I squeaked. 'Sort
of.'

'I told you,' said the colonel. 'There's a whole ring
of them stealing pedigree dogs for animal experimentation.'

'I was looking after him for Harriet.'

'You were trying to sell my dog into animal experimentation?' Harriet breathed in horror.

'No, I wasn't. And neither was Richard. Probably.'

'I think you'd better come in here,' said the sergeant opening the door to interview room number one.

We were led into an interview room where Harriet finally confirmed that I had indeed been *in loco parentis* as far as Hercules was concerned. I hadn't been living up to my responsibilities very well, but Harriet had entrusted her dog to me. That much was true.

It turned out that the interfering colonel had made a citizen's arrest on Richard when he saw him trying to coax Hercules into his rucksack with a piece of Belgian sausage (which would never have worked, confirmed Harriet, since Hercules wouldn't touch anything processed). Anyway, when Richard made a grab for Hercules, the colonel made a grab for Richard. He brought Richard down with a flying rugby tackle to the legs and sat on him bodily until the park warden happened by.

Now Richard was being held in custody on suspicion of dog-napping.

'You can drop the charge now,' said Harriet.

But the sergeant couldn't drop the fact that Richard had been found to have a half-smoked spliff in his pocket when he was searched. Hence the drug addict bit.

I dropped my head in despair.

'This is all your fault,' hissed Seema.

As if I didn't know.

No one needed to remind me that if I hadn't wanted to be with Brian so badly, Seema wouldn't have been put in charge of Hercules. Neither would Seema have found herself having to spend a Sunday afternoon consoling my boyfriend while I went ahead with my dirty weekend, giving Fat Joe the time and opportunity to incorporate Hercules in one of his experiments, which resulted in Hercules being lost, which resulted in Richard going out to look for him, which resulted in Richard suddenly finding himself drawn to the attention of the police by the strong arm of the local neighbourhood watch.

Richard didn't even smoke dope. At least, I hadn't known about it, if he did.

'He bought a spliff off his flatmate because he thought it would help him forget about you,' Seema told me later. 'He smoked half of it round here, had a coughing fit and gave up. He was never even going to finish the damn thing. He was going to throw it away.'

But now it seemed that little ill-timed spliff was going to be with him for the rest of his life. And it was all my fault.

I felt like holding my hands out to the sergeant and telling him to cuff me there and then. I was the villain. Because of me, my boyfriend was in the cells, my best friend was in hospital and the love of my life was spending the last day of his vacation at Heathrow Terminal Two.

It's little wonder that no one was talking to me on the walk back from the station.

CHAPTER TWENTY-EIGHT

I left several messages for Richard to call me when they finally let him go home. But he didn't. I called Mary at her flat. The phone there was picked up by her mother who informed me curtly that Mary's office was dealing with any enquiries that day. There hardly seemed to be any point in calling Brian on his mobile. But I did.

'Hello.'

I don't know why I was surprised that Brian answered his own phone. I think I believed that everyone was screening their calls in case they heard from me that day.

'Who is this?' he said.

I hadn't yet breathed a word.

'OK,' he sighed. 'Lizzie, is that you?'

He should have been half-way over the Atlantic Ocean, but Brian was still sitting outside Burger King in Terminal Two. His plane had been delayed by some technical hitch he didn't particularly want to think about – he'd always been a nervous flyer. He'd read all that day's papers, including the classified ads. And yes, he could use some company. Even if it was mine.

I was there in an hour, looking rather less polished than I had done for our last airport assignation but grateful for the chance to see him all the same.

'I hate saying goodbye to people at airports,' I reminded him.

'Isn't it better than not saying goodbye at all?'

Considering the terrible fallout from my lies, I know I didn't deserve a chance to explain why I had told them. But Brian listened. It was getting on for ten in the evening and his plane still wasn't fit to depart. He'd been at Heathrow for a whole day, which I suppose can leave you rather desperate for quality entertainment.

In the corner of the airport lounge I told him about my real life since college. I told him the truth about the crappy degree, the dead-end jobs I'd found myself as a result and the squats that I had lived in. I told him about the nights Seema and I had spent sneakily finishing the dregs of other people's expensive cocktails in bars we couldn't really afford to drink in. I told him about customising clothes from Oxfam and telling Mary that I had picked them up at Voyage. I even told him about the *night of the fleas* – though I stressed that I had seen no evidence of the infestation myself.

I told him that nothing had worked out as I planned it after university and as soon as I started to waver, I couldn't seem to steer a path back towards those plans. At first I'd sent off job applications by the post-box full. But with every rejection my confidence slipped a little further away until there came a point when I was almost grateful for my temp job at Harriet's firm. That feeling didn't last long though and soon I was looking for an escape route. At first it had been lottery tickets, but then it had been Brian.

'I don't understand how this happened to you,' Brian said. 'You were one of the most talented people I ever met.'

'I guess I must have had my moment of greatness when I played my one-eyed Cleopatra. I couldn't really have hoped to repeat that kind of success in the real world.'

'Sounds like you've given up trying.'

'Wouldn't you? With all the rejections I've had . . .' I began.

Brian grabbed my hands and started passionately, 'But the rejections you had were for jobs in accountancy, for fuck's sake. Jobs punching figures into a spreadsheet. What about the auditions you should have been going for? You didn't get any of those office jobs because anyone with half a brain could tell within seconds of meeting you that it's not what you were designed for. You'd be bored within days.'

He kissed my fingers and rubbed them as if he was trying to keep them warm. 'When I met you,' he continued, 'I knew at once that there was something different and special about you. I knew that you could never be mediocre. But with that blessing comes the curse that you could end up at one of two extremes. In the stars or in the gutter.'

'I can see the stars from where I'm lying in the gutter now,' I joked.

'I know. It looks bad. But what I'm trying to say is, you can be either rubbish or brilliant, Lizzie Jordan. It's up to you which one. And you won't have to put all that much effort in to be brilliant.'

'How?' I asked in a tiny voice.

'Channel some of the energy you've put into making such a pantomime of your real life into showing someone that you'd be just as convincing on stage. Hell, you could even use this whole debacle as an interview piece if you like. I'll vouch that I was utterly taken in. But join a drama group. Do some auditions. Do it properly. If you let your dreams go, you can't expect anyone else to catch them for you.'

Déjà-vu. I could hear Richard on the drive back from my parents' house saying almost exactly the same words.

'I'll try,' I promised. 'But I'm really sorry, Brian. I made a fool of you.'

'It doesn't matter now. Especially as I haven't been exactly straight with you either,' said Brian.

I waited for him to tell me that he was really a post-boy rather than a rising star at his bank. But he didn't.

'See, the thing is, Lizzie, I've sort of been using you too.'

'Using me?'

'I don't know how else to put it. I've been using you to help me sort out a few things in my life. You know I told you about that girl, the one I was going out with, with the King Charles Spaniel?'

I had an awful feeling that I wasn't about to be relieved by what I would hear.

'Well, she and I haven't split up. Not altogether. In fact, I want to ask her to marry me.'

'Marry you?' I squeaked, like an unhappy echo.

'Yes. But before I came over here I wasn't sure. And it wasn't just the issue of the dog. I wasn't sure that I had finished being on my own. Worse than that, I wasn't sure that I was completely over you. You probably won't believe this – I mean, I'm sure you've met loads of guys since I went back to the States and some of them must have given you a good time, but it hasn't been like that for me. Since I waved you goodbye, I haven't met anyone who could live up to the memory of you. Except perhaps Angelica.'

'That's her name?'

'Angelica Pironi. You know, I think you'd like her. She's a lot like you.'

'What? A failure? A loser? An incurable liar?'

'No,' he hugged me. 'She's funny, generous, lovable. In fact, she's so much like you that she brought back all the memories of the time we had together. I found myself running every minute we had together over and over. I used to wait all day for your e-mails to arrive. I started to think that I could never love anyone the way I loved you.'

'You loved me?'

He was saying all the right things, but in absolutely the wrong context.

'That's why I had to come to London. I didn't really suddenly get time off. In fact, when I go back, the bank will probably have gone belly up in my absence. But it was getting ridiculous. I was trying to pluck up the courage to ask Angelica to be my wife, but all I could think about was you. I needed to know the reality behind the dream. I needed to see you again and find out if we had a future. I figured that if I came to England I'd know for sure. I was going crazy; hesitating over the biggest thing in my life so far in case you still wanted me. I didn't really think I had a chance but I needed to be certain. You never spoke about your love life in your e-mails.

'So I got on that plane. And I spent the whole flight wishing you'd got fat or dyed your hair some awful colour. Anything to make me find you less attractive and help me make my mind up.'

'I was wishing pretty much the same thing of you,' I half laughed.

'But you looked better than ever.'

'And so did you.'

'And it seemed like the friendship between us hadn't altered much either.'

'I felt the same.'

'By the time we found ourselves sitting by the Serpentine on that first night together I felt sure that I would be telling Angelica that it was over between us as soon as I got back home.'

'But I cocked up. You found out about all my lies and decided that it wouldn't work.'

'No. No, it wasn't exactly like that. I made my mind up that we weren't going anywhere last night, Lizzie. When we were sitting in the hospital. I was playing one of those silly mind games where I was thinking about what I would do if it were you instead of Mary in that bed. Then I got to thinking about what I would do if it was Angelica, and my heart almost exploded. I realised that I loved her after all. I've never had a fear of her dog. I've just had a fear of commitment.'

'When were you going to tell me?' I asked.

'I was going to send you an e-mail as soon as I got home.'

I tried to feel indignant, but I couldn't.

'Cheers,' I said.

'But it wasn't only that, Liz. I sensed that your heart wasn't in it either. That afternoon at the Tate, and later at the British Museum. When you were preoccupied. I guessed that it wasn't just about the office.'

'But . . .' I started.

'You called me Richard when we made love last night.'

I coloured from the toenails up. 'You're joking?'

Brian shook his head. 'You definitely called me Richard. Is he someone special?'

I looked down at the floor and though I couldn't bring myself to admit them, my feelings must have been obvious.

'If this Angelica girl says yes to your proposal, will you invite me to the wedding?' I asked.

'You're top of my guest list. But you've got to promise to do the same in return.'

'Who am I going to end up with now?' I snorted.

'There's already someone special for you.'

The loud-speaker system announced the imminent departure of Brian's flight back to New York.

'I had the best holiday,' Brian said, squeezing my hand. 'Despite everything. Really good fun.'

'And things are still the same between us, aren't they?' I said, hopefully.

'No,' he said. 'They're better. I think we've reached a new stage in our relationship, don't you? I hope you think you can trust me now when I tell you that you're doing fine. Though you're going to work hard at doing better, aren't you?'

'I am.'

'Good.'

The silky-voiced airport announcer announced once more that Brian's flight was boarding. My heart contracted in anguish.

'Thanks for coming to say goodbye,' he said. 'I know how much you hate goodbyes. But it won't be for so long this time. You will visit, won't you?'

'Try and keep me away.'

'I've got to go. I've got to be back in the office tomorrow morning, can you believe?'

'You work too hard.'

'I've had a wonderful holiday.' He leaned forward and kissed me. On the cheek. I didn't know whether I felt disappointed. But then he wrapped his arms around me and pulled me in for a long hard hug. When he pulled away, I wondered whether I saw the glitter of tears in his chocolate eyes.

'I'll see you soon.' He picked up his carry-on bag and made for the gateway to passport control.

I stood where he left me and waved until I couldn't see him any more. When he had disappeared through the gate, I went upstairs to the café from where you can see the planes taking off through big picture-windows. I watched three American Airlines flights take off. I didn't have a clue which one he was on, but I wanted to feel as though I had seen him safely out of British skies. Then I turned and joined the rest of the heavy-hearted people who had just said goodbye to someone they loved and made my way to the tube.

I was sad for about three stops, but by the time I changed from the Piccadilly to the Northern Line, I was feeling altogether better. Perhaps it was because I was mentally writing my letter of resignation to Harriet and filling out forms for a course that would change the direction of my life. I could do it. I knew that now. In the end, Brian's visit had been a strange success.

I realised that I had never really wanted Brian after

all. I had merely wanted what he represented. Escape. Escape from the life I had found myself in five years after leaving university. The boring job. The awful flat. The social life that revolved around pub quizzes and promising each other that the very next week we would all sign up to do a line-dancing class.

I had wanted Brian to take me away from all that. To fly into the UK on a white charger of a 747 and return to New York with me riding beside him, to find my rightful place in Manhattan's glittering social whirl. Never mind whether Brian wanted to take me there or not. Never mind whether it would actually be so much better than my life in London anyway. It was simply easy to imagine that there was a magic bullet that would solve all my problems and Brian was it.

I finally realised that I had done exactly the same thing during my finals, mooning about over that fat-headed rugby player, spending too much time thinking that things were going wrong because I wasn't the centre of his universe, when I would have been better off doing a bit of revision instead. I had projected everything, my future, the apex of my ambitions, on to him. A mere man. I had effectively tried to make him responsible for my happiness because it was easier to be unhappy when I thought it was someone else's fault that things were not going as well as they should have been.

Well, all that was going to change. At long last I realised that the fact that my life was not the life I had always wanted for myself was something only I could remedy. I could change my life. Me, alone. But I had to clear up Harriet's flat first . . . And get her car back from the pound . . . And start making a lot of apologies.

EPILOGUE

It's almost a year since Brian's visit and at last I've got a life I'm happy to e-mail him about. I took his advice and started to make an effort to change things rather than cover the bad parts up. I even sent an article about my experiences on that painful television programme to a magazine who published it and paid me. I sent off a few more about various dilemmas I had known and before I knew it, people were actually calling me and asking me to write about this or that.

Harriet was sorry to see me leave Corbett and Daughter to devote myself to becoming a freelance writer while I wait to take up a place at drama school, but soon after I quit she decided that she wasn't all that bothered with keeping the estate agency going anyway and has set up a high class dog-sitting company instead. She has also started seeing a real bona fide bachelor since Bunny resolved to make one last attempt to rebuild his shambolic marriage to Mary's mum.

I kept my head down when the colonel who had been so ruthless about Hercules's dog mess came to take Harriet to dinner on my last day as chief paper pusher at Corbett & Co. Harriet had made the rather kindly gentleman's acquaintance properly when she thanked him for his part in rescuing her dog. The colonel was instantly smitten. Good old Hercules acting Cupid. I knew he'd come in useful for something.

Unable to see himself as a highly paid dog-walker, Randy Rupert has moved to an estate agency where he is actually expected to do some work. He says he is very unhappy. Now that he has to work weekends, there's less time left to woo 'lovely ladies' and improve his skills at golf. I wish that I could feel sorry for him, but I told him to his face that the women of the United Kingdom should be relieved that he was no longer free to pursue them so rabidly. I think he may have taken that as a compliment.

Mary and I are on better terms again. After her cocaine crisis, she spent a month detoxing in Malta and came back with a clear head and five new celebrity clients from her exclusive therapy group. Her talent agency goes from strength to strength, specialising in launching the media careers of ex-wives and fiancées of the rich and famous. Mitchell, however, has disappeared. Last seen dancing to 'Copacabana' in some seedy Rio nightclub. Mary isn't terribly bothered about that though. Mitchell's records are actually selling in larger quantities than ever, thanks to a whole tribe of misguided teenage girls who think his sudden disappearance rather romantic. Mary still has her percentage points on his royalties, of course.

She also has Bill. For the time being, he's taking a break from his mission to see the four corners of the earth by bicycle and has moved himself and his dirty lycra into her hitherto pristine flat. He was always in love with her. We all knew that. And she just needed to be woken up to the fact that it is possible to love someone who isn't intent on running away. Her days of lusting after the unreliable and unavailable are over now. She's realised that she actually deserves better.

'But you have to have had a few pigs in your life to help you recognise the truffles,' she told me last time we had lunch. That made sense to me.

She also said that she even adores the hair on Bill's back these days. That didn't quite make so much sense but I didn't press her for more details.

Ace tracker Fat Joe bought an exercise bike with a view to getting slim and getting himself a relationship. He spent two weeks fiddling with the heart-monitor cum speedometer cum microwave oven thing that came attached to the handlebars but then he met 'Venus' in a chat room on the internet and now he comes out of his room even less frequently than before. He says that he's definitely in love with her. Assuming that Venus is a 'her'. One day they're going to meet up in real time, he told me. He's been talking about mailing her a marriage proposal. Needless to say I have warned him about the dangers of losing perspective in cyberspace.

As for Seema. She finished her business studies course and left sunny Balham for sophisticated Harvard to do a

PhD in something terribly complicated in an attempt to stave off marriage to a rich second cousin from Madras. She's been given until she's twenty-nine to find herself a husband now. Doesn't even have to be a Hindu boy any more as long as he's prepared to eat curry.

Shortly after she arrived in the States, Seema took a trip to New York to spend a weekend with Brian and his fiancée, Angelica. She had a wonderful time in their company and sent me a postcard of the Statue of Liberty confirming that Brian does indeed have a gorgeous apartment in one of the best parts of Manhattan. But guess what? She said that he doesn't have a view of Central Park after all! I had to smile when I read that.

The fiancée, Angelica Pironi, wrote to me herself to thank me for helping Brian to overcome the debilitating 'phobia' that had kept them apart. Apparently Brian's even been taking her dog for walkies. She told me I should visit too, but I think I'll give it another six years. Hopefully by that time Brian and I really will be able to laugh about the web of lies that surrounded his visit to England.

Looking at how things have turned out, I can't imagine the frame of mind I must have been in back then. What low self-esteem I must have had. Not only that, my actions also implied that I had a very low opinion of Brian to think that he wouldn't have wanted to know me if I didn't put on that high-flying act. The implication was such an insult to his broadmindedness and generosity. Sometimes I think back and shudder with the realisation that I'm very lucky I still have my American friend.

Which leaves only Richard. Of all the people I treated so badly, he took the longest to come round to even thinking about forgiving me. After the ridiculous dog-napping incident, he was cautioned for his possession of a minuscule amount of the evil weed and that caution was enough to lose him his job as an accountant. Drug conviction equals the sack. His bosses weren't interested in any mitigating circumstances, and it was a long time before Richard would start to see his enforced resignation as a positive thing. Naturally, he felt that I was in some small way responsible for his having to disappoint his mother and sign on the dole. He sent me a stinging letter to that effect, enclosing the Blur CD I had bought him for Valentine's Day and asking for the return of his *Fawlty Towers* video collection forthwith. That was the end of us, of course. And there was no way I could pretend that I didn't deserve his utter contempt.

But one day, while I was mooning over the fact that he wasn't ever likely to phone me again, I showed Mary the picture that Richard had drawn for me as my birthday present. I had been beating myself about the head with the memory of how disdain-fully I had discarded the drawing back then, anxious to get rid of Richard so that I could prepare for Brian's arrival and even slightly irritated that he hadn't given me a 'proper' present, that is, something I could wear.

Mary held the picture up and compared likeness against reality.

'It's really very good,' she told me.

'I know it's good,' I half-sobbed back at her. 'He's an incredibly talented man. And I lost him!!!'

'Yeah, well,' said Mary brusquely. 'I think you've learned your lesson. Can I take this?' she asked.

'What for? It's the last piece I have of him.'

'I'll give it back,' she promised. And she did. But not until she had shown it to Arabella Gilbert and Arabella, who had begun to fancy herself as a bit of a Renaissance-style patron of the arts since a guest appearance on the *South Bank Show*, gave Richard his first commission as a society portrait artist. The result – a stunning painting of Arabella Gilbert as Diana the Huntress – made the cover of the *Sunday Times* Style supplement. Richard was hailed as a rare new talent, lauded by art critics who felt that it was about time young artists started using proper paint instead of elephant dung. He was the talk of the country. And my mother couldn't believe that I'd let him slip from my grasp.

'I knew he'd make something of himself,' she said, with a stunning display of selective memory. 'You could have been going to all those society parties with him.'

'I know. But I blew it.'

'Why don't you give it one more try?'

I'd done more stupid things in my life.

I got Mary to stand over me when I picked up the phone, ready to cut me off if the conversation started to get ridiculous.

'Take a deep breath and smile before you start talking,' she advised me, as though I was one of her clients. 'Let him hear the smile in your voice. Talk to him as though you were talking to any other friend.'

I pulled a rictus grin and dialled Richard's number. 'Act as though I'm talking to any other friend.' But I wasn't. I was calling the love of my life. The real love of my life. The one I'd lost. Even before he picked up at the other end, I had almost started blubbing.

'Richard, I really miss you. And I don't think that feeling's ever going to change.'

There was silence at the other end of the line.

After that, he agreed to see me for one cup of coffee as a thank you for the roundabout way in which Arabella Gilbert had made contact with him and kick-started his glittering career. Three bottles of wine later, I agreed to pose nude for his re-working of *The Birth of Venus*. I'm sure I don't need to tell you what happened then but when we woke up on the pile of cushions on the floor of his studio next morning, covered only by a paint-splattered dust-sheet, our grand romance was back on.

Two months later, Richard's looking for a new flat. A flat with lots of light and room for *two* struggling creative types. And I'll never tell even the littlest white lie again. I won't have to.

CHRIS MANBY

DEEP HEAT

Ali Harris emerges from hospital minus two useless
organs: her appendix and her fiance. Winning a dream
holiday for two in Antigua should cheer her up – but
the holiday is first prize in Complete Woman magazine's
Most Romantic Couple of the Year Competition. And
there's no way Ali can claim to be one half of Britain's
Most Romantic Couple on her own.

With a holiday in the offing, Ali's fiance is keen to kiss
and make up – but he's not prepared to give up his new
girlfriend. So Ali takes matters into her own hands and
discovers that revenge is sweet. It's also a whole lot of
trouble . . .

HODDER AND STOUGHTON PAPERBACKS